To Ragine,

Dare to dream the impossible for someday the impossible will become the new reality.

Charles C. Graham

SURVIVE!

Marooned on Planet Tau Ceti g

CHARLES P. GRAHAM

iUniverse LLC
Bloomington

SURVIVE!
MAROONED ON PLANET TAU CETI G

iUniverse books may be ordered through booksellers or by contacting:

iUniverse LLC
1663 Liberty Drive
Bloomington, IN 47403
www.iuniverse.com
1-800-Authors (1-800-288-4677)

ISBN: 978-1-4917-3276-2 (sc)
ISBN: 978-1-4917-3277-9 (hc)
ISBN: 978-1-4917-3278-6 (e)

Library of Congress Control Number: 2014907104

Printed in the United States of America.

iUniverse rev. date: 04/28/2014

Prologue

Wearing a bloodied long-sleeve khaki shirt with T-shirt and bloodied khaki trousers, rugged boots, and a light water-repellant jacket, Chris Elliott stepped out of the escape capsule and donned his backpack. The bumps and bruises he'd received while making his escape were already beginning to take their toll, dragging him down with nagging pain. He squinted from the bright light of the sun and attempted to survey his surroundings, but his dazed mind refused to fully cooperate. Somewhat lightheaded from the frantic pace of his efforts to stay alive, he walked a few meters from the escape pod, parted the tall grass, and sat on the ground to rest and collect his thoughts. He had to lean forward to balance the backpack he was wearing. The pack was heavy on Earth but felt somewhat lighter here. Looking over this green and lush foreign landscape, he wondered how he could survive long enough to be rescued or whether rescue was even a possibility. Chris considered the irony of it all. His ship could jump, traveling faster than the speed of light, but the distress signal-burst sent from the bridge just after the disaster could travel only at the speed of light, meaning it would be a very long time—just over twelve years, in fact—before the message would reach Earth.

His escape pod was sitting mostly upright after landing on a grassy plain. About one hundred meters off to his left was a small copse of what looked similar to Earth trees. The trees had tall trunks, smooth grayish bark, and leaflike greenery on the ends of the branches and branchlets. Everywhere else was flat, grass-covered land as far as the eye could see. The sun was not quite overhead in a cloudless, bright blue sky. A light wind rustled leaves in the treetops and created gentle rhythmic waves in the grass. The breeze carried with it the light, fresh scent of plant life. If a person ever wanted solitude, this would be the place. It was like being in an ocean of grass, horizon to horizon of tall grass, with a rare outcropping of trees and bushes. Once out of sight of the trees, a wayward traveler would have no other landmarks to guide him.

Chris wanted to stay outside in the open air. He couldn't remain cooped up in the capsule waiting for someone to call on the communications system. Even looking at the capsule reminded him of the friends he'd left behind, and those thoughts weighed heavily on his conscience. He had survived, and they hadn't—survivor's guilt. Thoughts of how horribly they had died—and of his own imminent encounter with death only a hairsbreadth away—ran rampant through his mind. He needed to calm down. He closed his eyes and took a couple of deep breaths, letting the air out slowly. It helped … some. He opened his eyes. Looking at the escape capsule, he decided he would use it as a place of refuge, but only when necessary for safety and sleep. He still had the two-week standard issue of rations and some survival gear that came with the escape pod, but there just wasn't enough room in his pack for any of it. If he couldn't find readily available food nearby, he could always come back to restock before heading out to new territory. Right now, he preferred to remain mobile for others, if any successfully made their escape from the ship. The *Copernicus* had been destroyed so quickly, Chris doubted that many, if any, crew members had made it safely off. Fighting pain and despair and trying to take his mind off the loss of his friends on the ship, Chris removed his backpack and closely examined the contents. He'd known in advance that in case of an emergency, he didn't want to have to depend solely on standard-issue emergency gear, so he had packed his own backpack with what he thought was necessary.

The usual food and fire-making stuff, paracord, folding shovel, comm gear, yada yada yada. Great! Why didn't I bring something more lethal than this old-fashioned .22-caliber pistol? Well, at least I have a decent water filter.

The water filtration unit was one of the better ones available, with a four-liter-per-minute filtration rate and the ability to supply 5,200 liters of good drinking water before cleaning or replacement of the filter was necessary. He had bought the filter from a popular outfitter supply warehouse on Earth while attending the United Earth Space Force Academy for Scientists. Any scientist selected to be part of a ship's scientific team shared certain classes with the military cadets. When his classmates found out the capacity of the filter, Chris had taken a lot of razzing. The military cadets were the worst, especially the upperclassmen. They had been unmerciful, riding him every chance they got. Right now, he didn't care. He was grateful that he had the filter. What he really wanted was company, someone to talk to, someone with whom to share his fear. Never before in his life had he felt so isolated, so alone. Solitude was definitely not what he wanted.

Looking skyward, Chris fervently hoped that he was not going to be marooned on this planet by himself. He desperately wanted to see more emergency capsules falling from the sky with as many survivors as possible. He knew the chances of survival here could increase from near zero to possible, but only if there were enough people to share the workload. More people also meant a more secure living environment on this potentially hostile planet. He also needed someone to talk with to keep from going crazy, to soften the pain he would experience from memories of what his life had been like, and to mitigate the depression he would suffer from knowing what his life could have been in the future. His life's plans and ambitions were now impossible. Trying not to think of the dangers and difficulties he was about to face, Chris sat in despair, watching the sky, knowing that the dead ship containing the bodies of his dead friends and shipmates continued to orbit above the planet as his racing mind relived the day's events.

1

Chris Elliott, at 180 centimeters, carried eighty-two kilograms of lean muscle on an athletic frame. With regulation-cut dirty blonde hair, hazel-green eyes, and a chiseled chin, he was an exceptionally handsome thirty-six-year-old xenobiologist from St. Clair Shores, Michigan. He had obtained his PhD from Michigan State University in East Lansing after receiving his master's degree in microbiology from Eastern Michigan University in Ypsilanti. Chris had been asked to participate as a civilian researcher at the Tarpon Springs scientific colony based near the North Pole on Mars because of his extensive training and expertise as a xenobiologist and full professorship at the University of Michigan in Ann Arbor. The name, Tarpon Springs, was a tongue-in-cheek joke at the base—the name came from an Earth city in the state of Florida where it's warm all year round, but the scientific base had been constructed in one of the coldest spots on Mars, where there was an abundance of frozen water, at and just below the surface. Having that much water available was a boon for the scientific researchers. Water in any form on Mars was scarce, so finding a source large enough that it could be used for consumption and as a source of hydrogen for power and breathable oxygen was essential. Finding enough water to run a large scientific base on Mars was like finding an artesian well in a desert on Earth, and this gave extra significance to the last part of the name, "Springs."

Chris spent four years on Mars as a scientist studying microbial fossils found deep below the surface, within and under the ice layers. There was not much in the way of entertainment at the Mars research center except watching movies, or "vids," and playing 3-D and holographic video games. Instead, in his free time, Chris took advantage of the excellent educational facility and obtained a bachelor's degree in starship engineering; he had completed a little over a year toward a master's degree in the same subject before he completed his Mars tour. When his Mars research was finished and his findings published, he submitted an application to the United Earth Space Force and accepted an officer position as a scientific researcher. Soon after accepting his commission, he was assigned to serve aboard the deep-space science exploration ship *Copernicus.*

The *Copernicus,* NSG 002, started its life as the second in its class in the year 2249 in the United Earth Space Force Expedition Fleet. The ship was named after mathematician and astronomer Nicolaus Copernicus (1473–1543), who was the first person to suggest that the sun, not Earth, was at the center of the solar system and who was considered the initiator of the scientific revolution.

The United Earth Space Force had been formed in 2225, not as a military force, since worldwide peace had been the norm for over a century, but as an international space exploration force. The first galaxy-class ship, *Galileo* (NSG 001), named after Galileo Gailei, the first astronomer to use a telescope, was then launched in 2246. *Galileo* and *Copernicus* were the first true exploration spaceships to use faster-than-light, or FTL, technology to explore beyond Earth's solar system. Another FTL spacecraft, the *Josephine A. Brookfield* (NSGL 003), was nearing the end phase of construction when the *Copernicus* left on its five-year exploratory journey, the former having been named for an astronomer in a group of top astronomers who studied Cepheid variables as a tool to establish galactic distances, a very useful tool when using FTL travel.

Though discovered in 2211, FTL technology had a long way to go before the drives were stable. Many unmanned drones were lost in space. Another drone exploded while on the ground, killing forty-three technicians and scientists and destroying two buildings. Before the engines became reliable, two manned prototype ships with volunteer crews of fifty-two each were lost and never recovered. The only tribute to the dead volunteers' contribution was an engraved plaque mounted near an elevator on the ground floor of the research building where scientists had first discovered the secrets of FTL travel.

FTL technology changed humankind's relationship with the universe. Short jaunts, such as those within the solar system, would take from minutes to a few hours as ships traveled to the outer reaches at just over light speed, and the navigational mathematics were relatively simple. Soon the technology advanced to where humankind could exceed multiples of the speed of light. From *C*, the speed of light, *C* times nine became possible.

The job of the United Earth Space Force Expedition Fleet ships *Galileo* and *Copernicus* was to continue exploration of specific galactic sectors, map gravitational variances, calculate present and future positions for all stellar masses in their assigned area, and explore habitable planets for alien life and possible human colonization. Tau Ceti g, a planet newly discovered during exploration of the Tau Ceti star system, was to be the last planet explored by the *Copernicus* before the ship returned to Earth.

With the captain's permission, Chris relished the chance to stand in for an occasional engineering watch. He was fascinated with the technology and enjoyed the camaraderie that the engineering crew shared. Giving the crew a break was also good for morale, both his and the crew's. In addition, it broke up the boredom he had to put up with between star systems. Being a xenobiologist was exciting only when you had strange new biology to study. On this occasion,

Chris had just joined the engineering officer of the watch, Lieutenant Theodore "Ted" Stevens, in the engine room.

"Hey, Ted!" Chris had to raise his voice to be heard over the moderate equipment noise.

Ted looked up from his tablet computer to see Chris approaching before he resumed making an entry. "Hi, Chris. What brings you back here? You're not due to stand a watch right now, are you?"

"No, not until tomorrow. The captain only lets me fill in once or twice a week. He says he doesn't want me to miss any opportunities to add to the libraries in my chosen profession. Right now, there's not much to do since I finished entering the data from my last survey, so I thought I'd drop by to chat a bit if you had the time."

"Sure. I just have to finish my hourly log entries," said Ted.

"You know, there's animal life down there, and some of it looks *very* large. My first impression is that this planet developed very much as ours did after the Cretaceous-Paleogene event on Earth."

"The what event?" Ted asked with a puzzled expression, still looking at his tablet computer as he entered his log reports.

"The Cretaceous-Paleogene event. It happened about sixty-five million years ago, when approximately 70 to 75 percent of all life on Earth died. There are several scientific hypotheses as to why the event happened. According to the Alvarez hypothesis, a huge asteroid struck the Yucatán Peninsula in the Caribbean Basin about sixty-five million years ago. The impact ring, called Cenotes, can still be seen from orbit with ground-penetrating radar. That radar puts the crater and impact ring in rock strata that's sixty-five million years old and … and by that glazed look I see in your eyes, I've lost you," Chris said with a smile.

"Yeah, you lost me after the asteroid struck and all that life died," Ted admitted while he continued making his hourly status entries on his tablet, which was linked to the ship's main computer.

"I understand. It can be a bit boring if biology or geology isn't your thing. Anyway, the life I've cataloged isn't anywhere near as diverse as on Earth, but then I can only detail so much from up here. What I need to do is to go down there. When do you think the shuttle will be ready to fly again so we can go down and do a close-up study? I heard it got banged up after the last flight."

Ted replied, "Yes, it did. The last time the shuttle was used, the braking and rotational thrusters failed just as the pilot was about to land in the shuttle bay. The pilot told me that he quickly declared an emergency, and the shuttle recovery crew got the emergency barrier nets up just in time. Apparently, though, the pilot hadn't yet synchronized the shuttle attitude with the ship, and it was still rotating on its long axis when the attitude thrusters quit. It hit at an angle and struck the deck with the starboard wing tip first and then landed hard on the starboard main landing skid before slamming level with the landing deck when it came under the influence of the shipboard artificial gravity field. The damage was quite extensive, and it probably won't be ready unt—"

Ted never got the chance to finish. Both men felt the ship shudder just before utter chaos broke loose in engineering.

"What in—" Chris started to say as a fist-size piece of what looked like a stone meteor struck an overhead beam a half-meter above Ted's head and exploded almost straight down and diagonally into the port-side FTL engine control panel. A fragment of meteor shrapnel the size of a thumb tip struck Ted just under his left ear and behind his jaw, carving into his neck a four-centimeter-deep, two-centimeter-wide gash that extended through his collarbone. The speeding fragment broke the collarbone, leaving a portion of the bone sticking outside his torn one-piece uniform, and continued into his chest cavity. Blood from a ruptured vein and carotid artery on the left side of Ted's neck instantly spurted in a tall, pulsing fountain onto Chris and the nearby equipment. Chris watched the gory scene in shock and horror as Ted, wide-eyed and terrified, dropped to his knees, desperately grasping at the gash in an attempt to stem the flow of blood, before he fell over and died in an expanding pool of the thick red fluid. Then the *Copernicus*'s main lighting failed. Chris could smell the burning electrical circuitry, and smoke was already billowing in the air when the lighting went out. Meteors and meteor shrapnel continued to crash through the engineering compartment, creating intense sparks, like flint striking steel, as the ship's orbit carried it through the meteor storm. Bright lightning-like flashes of light from the wiring and circuit boards shorting out in the FTL engine electrical panels created an eerie scene and caused Chris to shut his eyes in pain. He choked on the smoke and retched when, through the strobing light, he saw Ted's body lying on the deck. He tried to wipe Ted's blood from his shirt and trousers, but succeeded only in smearing it into grotesque shapes. Chris stood there a few moments longer and stared at Ted lying in the enlarging pool of blood that was spreading beside the dead engineer's head and shoulder.

Hearing the roar of escaping air, Chris snapped out of his shocked trance and looked to his left. In the intermittent, strobe-like flashes of light, he watched helplessly as two engineering technicians, who were standing near where one of the larger meteor pieces had just exited the ship, were quickly propelled into empty space because of the differential pressure from inside to outside the ship. The first technician didn't have time to scream. Grotesquely folded in half and seemingly sucked through the newly created thirty-five-centimeter, irregularly shaped hole in the hull, belly first, he slowed the evacuation of air from the compartment for only a moment. Still frozen in place with fear and from the suddenness of the assault on the ship, Chris watched as the second technician tried to hang on to a vertical column while yelling for help. The column proved too slippery for firm grip, and the woman was tugged violently toward the same hull breach once the first technician's body had cleared it. She too was pulled into the near vacuum of space, buttocks first. Chris watched as six engineering technicians were killed outright when shrapnel from destroyed equipment and meteor fragments cut them down. He heard the loud buzzing and snapping of electrical arcing and then screams off to his right and turned to see two others die from electrocution; the backup power conduit and cabling to the

FTL control panel had been severed before the circuit breakers cut the power. The conduit power lines now dangled lifelessly from the overhead and between the bodies of the dead technicians as they lay on the deck.

The warning sirens wailed in the dying ship, although the sound was beginning to attenuate because of lack of air pressure. Air continued to roar loudly, however, as it escaped through the multiple hull penetrations and into space; Chris's ears began to pop as pressure continued dropping in the compartment. Loose papers, clipboards, and tablet computers that had been lying on workstations added to the nightmarish confusion as the debris flew toward the punctures in the hull. Vainly, replacement air pumped loudly and automatically from on-board air tanks into compartments that were depressurizing, but the tanks couldn't keep up with the outflow. Chris instinctively knew the ship was critically injured.

After what felt like several minutes but was actually only a few seconds of darkness, punctuated by light from the shorting circuitry, Chris felt momentarily relieved when the light of the independent battery-operated emergency lanterns automatically turned on. Trying the intercom to the bridge, he reached no one. Fear quickly replaced disbelief when he saw all the chaos and death that surrounded him in the surreal lighting. Chris was spurred into motion by the warning sirens blasting loudly into the thinning air as the fight-or-flight hormone, adrenaline, dumped into his system, adding urgency to his actions. Every second counted. With only a few minutes left before death by asphyxiation would occur for anyone alive who remained behind, Chris started making his way toward the hatch that exited the engineering compartment.

The "abandon ship" alarm, in addition to the equipment-failure sirens, screamed loudly, adding even more disorientation to the smoke, death, and flying debris. The main computer panels that controlled electrical power were severely damaged, so there was no computer-generated female voice calmly announcing for all hands to abandon ship. The emergency lighting thankfully stayed on but cast odd shadows on the blood-soaked deck and spattered bulkheads as Chris attempted to make his way out of the engineering space. Dust, loose papers, lightweight diagnostic tools, and lightweight manuals were rapidly making their way toward the hull breaches. Chris batted away the flying debris as he made his way forward to the hatch exiting engineering, but he still took several blows to his head and body from notebooks, coffee cups, and someone's pocket recorder. Low visibility from the dim light, flying debris, and smoke made seeing ahead more than a few meters difficult. His head started to buzz from lack of oxygen and low air pressure. Chris twice stumbled over dead bodies, his clothing soaking up more of his shipmates' blood. One dead woman wore an oxygen mask. He recognized her as medical technician, second class, Amanda Steward even though part of her forehead was missing at the hairline, exposing an area of missing brain. With tunnel vision, ears buzzing, and a feeling of faintness coming over him, he took the bloodied mask from the corpse and put it on as air pressure in the compartment continued to drop. The mask helped his eyes stop watering from the acrid smoke, and after a couple of deep breaths, the oxygen helped clear his mind. Stooping low and guarding his head with his arms to avoid being struck by the flying debris, Chris Elliott crawled and clawed his way to the exit, fighting the pull of air escaping from the ship. Small stools that weren't tumbling with the escaping air were sliding on the slippery floor, attempting to keep Chris with his dead shipmates.

Finally, reaching the hatch, he thanked his lucky stars that the automatic emergency hatch-closing motors had failed when the ship lost power. He never would have been able to open the hatch against the flow of escaping air. Chris exited the engineering compartment, turned, and released the catch that held the hatch in the open position. The door slammed shut, and he spun the locking wheel to secure the dogs around the hatch. With the hatch now secured, the depressurization of the ship slowed somewhat. Debris making its way along with the escaping air clogged punctures in the hull and the bulkheads between compartments, slowing the depressurization further but not stopping it. Any air entering engineering through the punctures in the shared compartment bulkheads escaped just as quickly through the holes that the meteors and fragments had created upon exiting the hull. Moments later, the engineering compartment was all but depressurized. Fortunately, the artificial gravity unit remained online with its backup batteries still functioning, so up was still up, and down was still down, and for that, even though he was not a particularly religious man, Chris said a simple, silent *Thank you, God.* Making his way through the passageway that led to his personal escape pod, he paused just long enough at an emergency cabinet to grab a clean oxygen mask to replace the bloodied one he was wearing. He also quickly retrieved a jacket off the back of an overturned chair in the doorway of an open cabin. He had no idea to whom the jacket belonged and at the time didn't care.

There was no one else in EDC, the Emergency Departure Compartment, when Chris arrived. Of the 110 crew and science team members of the research vessel, Chris Elliott was the only person and, as far as he could tell, first person there. He entered his personal escape pod, shut the hatch, and strapped in. Each scientist had his or her own custom-equipped escape capsule. The entire dataset the scientists collected and stored on the ship's computers, plus any information that concerned navigation, cartography, and the emergency, was automatically downloaded to all the scientists' and crews' escape pods as the information was received, so that if any of their pods survived an emergency, all the scientific and other collected data would be saved. The rest of the crew members were assigned to four-person escape capsules. Basic navigational information as to the spaceship's location and reason for demise, the pod's intended landing location, and other survival information, including any data about the planet that would aid the surviving crew members, was also stored in the scientists' and crews' capsule computers. Chris grabbed the emergency departure checklist from its place on the bulkhead where it was attached with hook-and-loop power tape and began the escape pod launching procedures.

He began reading the checklist aloud to slow his racing mind so that he wouldn't miss anything. "Main power on … check. Main battery power level in the green … check. Backup battery power is in the green … check. Air banks and oxygen tanks full with bleed rate set … check. Gyroscopes on and stabilizing … come on, come on, hurry up! Stabilize! Carbon dioxide scrubbers online … check. Thrusters on standby … check. Capsule air pressure holding steady." The *Copernicus* shuddered with several rapid, small explosions and then rocked hard with a large detonation and started a roll to port.

"To blazes with this. I'm out of here!" Chris yelled. He hit the emergency manual launch button. As Chris's windowless pod ejected from the ship, he could only imagine the meteors and fragmented pieces that were still smashing into and then exiting the ship and entering the planet's atmosphere, leaving brilliant trails as they fell toward the surface. He prayed that none would strike and puncture his escape pod on the way down. Any punctures in the escape capsule would mean certain death because he wasn't wearing a spacesuit.

Miranda Stevens, Ted's wife of twenty-three years and the ship's xenobotanist, was in her cabin in the crew's quarters on the aft starboard side. At 158 centimeters and fifty-six kilograms, she was buxom and slender-waisted. The US-born daughter of a hotel-maid mother and construction-worker father, both legal immigrants from Mexico City, Miranda was a strikingly attractive woman, with high cheekbones, dark brown hair, and eyes to match.

Miranda had just set her personal log recorder on the desk after finishing the dictation of her chromatography studies of plant life on the planet, Tau Ceti g, when the meteors struck. Panic and darkness enveloped her as the ship shuddered and the main lighting failed. She knocked her recorder onto the deck of the suddenly darkened cabin in her panic to grasp the desk for balance. Her ears popped as depressurization of the ship began. The abandon-ship siren wailed loudly, causing instant confusion and increasing her panic. Not wanting to lose the recorded data, Miranda forgot the emergency depressurization procedures and groped in the dark on her hands and knees for her recorder instead of reaching for the oxygen mask first. Unable to locate the recorder in the dark, she reached for the desk chair to pull herself up so that she could open the door to her cabin and let in more light. The ship rocked hard from another explosion. She screamed in fear as she fell, striking her forehead on the desk and spraining her right wrist as she tried to break her fall to the deck. Being on the short side saved her from striking her mouth and losing teeth when she fell forward against the edge of the desk. Crew's quarters didn't have battery-operated emergency lanterns like the passageways and main compartment spaces, but they did have small LED lighting on the deck, showing the way to exit the space. However, the LEDS didn't offer much light in the cabins. Still dazed from striking her head, Miranda crawled to the door. Using the handle to stand, she then opened the door to let in light from the passageway, still determined to find her recorder. Instead of light, pungent dark smoke from the passageway billowed into her room, filling her nostrils and lungs. Stepping back into her personal space, she slammed the door shut. Choking on the thick black air that was also stinging her eyes, she remembered and donned the emergency oxygen mask hanging on the bulkhead while she coughed, trying to clear the smoke from her lungs. Still worried about her data, she dropped to the deck on her knees, feeling around until she found her log recorder. Standing again and guarding her injured wrist, a stunned and confused Miranda Stevens opened her cabin door to the passageway and made slow headway to the EDC.

Holly Rhodes, MD, an attractive thirty-eight-year-old, 165-centimeter, sixty-kilogram, brunette woman with dark blue eyes, was in the medical examination room. She had just finished applying bandages to chief engineer Ron Layman. Ron was still lying on a portable exam table after being treated for a serious burn on his right arm and shoulder that he'd received when Gary Lindermann, engineering specialist, third class, didn't properly bleed off the pressure in the wastewater distiller steam line that Ron was to work on, leaving a portion of the piping pressurized. "Waste not, want not" was Ron Layman's motto when it came to wastewater recovery, so keeping the distillers in good operating shape required constant maintenance.

Ron had placed a wrench on the fitting and strained to loosen the ten-centimeter pipe connection with his large muscular arms. When the fitting didn't budge, he'd had to add his eighty-six-kilogram mass to loosen it. The connection to the distiller's heat exchanger had then finally broken free, but a sudden jet of high-pressure steam from the fitting blasted through his coverall sleeve, giving him a nasty second-degree burn to most of the front side of his right upper arm and shoulder. Luckily, the temperature of the steam had cooled to a "mere" 82 degrees Celsius from the original 315 degrees of high-pressure steam that would have melted the flesh off his arm instead of giving him the superficial blistering injury that he received.

The doctor had just finished applying a topical antiseptic ointment and bandaging Ron's arm when the ship shook and the lights went out. A moment later, an explosion rocked the ship. With scissors still in her hand from cutting the tape that bound Ron's bandages, Holly Rhodes was knocked partially onto the exam table. Holding her arms above her head so as not to injure Ron with the scissors, she fell forward and ended up planting her elbows squarely onto the chief engineer's abdomen. The exam table slid and slammed into the nearby bulkhead, and she continued her fall to the floor. Dr. Rhodes was physically stunned. She tried to stand in the dark, but startled and disoriented, she lost her balance and fell against an educational anatomy chart, which then came off the bulkhead and struck her face and upper body. Unable to see in the darkened room, she stumbled over an overturned chair and struck her head on the bulkhead. She hit her head yet again when she fell to the floor.

The dust that had remained hidden behind cabinets and equipment since the building of the spaceship came out in force and stung her face, eyes, and exposed skin as it followed the flow of air out to the near vacuum of outer space. Papers and small instruments flew through the air and funneled down the passageway. Thick, acrid smoke started to fill the exam room from the ship's ventilation system.

Ron Layman had rolled off the table after it slammed into the bulkhead and landed face down but had been able to avoid further injury. The emergency lighting came on. Ron struggled to catch his breath after having the wind knocked out of him from Dr. Rhodes landing on his abdomen. He spotted the doctor on the floor nearby and went to her. "Doc, are … are you all right?" he asked, gasping for air and words as smoke filled the room. "Can you stand?"

A little blood was oozing from a small cut on the left side of her forehead where an egg-size lump was starting to form.

Holding pressure on the cut with her left hand, she weakly replied, "I … I think so. I'm just dazed." Dr. Rhodes attempted to stand on her own but wobbled badly. The chief engineer caught her before she fell again. She said, "Thanks, I … I think I may need help to walk, though. I'm a little dizzy too."

Main lighting was out, and the air pressure continued to drop throughout the ship as the chief engineer donned an oxygen mask and then helped Dr. Rhodes into hers. He quickly slipped the upper half of his one-piece jumpsuit back on, his right arm and shoulder still screaming from the burn, which was made worse by all the movement. The abandon-ship sirens began to blare. As they left the medical treatment room by the light of emergency lanterns, Dr. Rhodes was mentally together enough to grab a large emergency medical kit before exiting the medical area down a passageway that was filling with smoke, litter, and flying debris. Dr. Rhodes depended heavily on the assistance of the chief engineer as they walked and stumbled through the accumulating passageway rubble and made their way to the escape capsules and off the ship.

Sandy Brooks, supply officer and food specialist, was in the galley with communications specialist Jay Johnson when the disruption from the meteor strike began. Sandy was an attractive, 167-centimeter, sixty-three-kilogram, thirty-six-year-old woman with an average build, dark blue eyes, and full lips that said, "Kiss me … and often." Gazing into her deep-blue eyes with long eyelashes set many men's hearts to racing. The one-piece uniforms issued to crew members in the fleet did nothing to enhance her womanly attributes but didn't completely hide them either. An athletic build and a slender waist, accented by her narrow hips, could still be detected. She was a woman who didn't need makeup to look feminine. Sandy could have been bald and still attractive. Fortunately, she wasn't bald, and she wore her dark blonde hair just above the shoulders, which was regulation length.

Sandy Brooks was attracted to men. She liked the attention that Jay gave her a great deal but was cautious. She had been married previously and had gone through an especially rough marriage and divorce. The physical attraction she felt to her first husband had its limits, and she left him after less than a year of marriage. Because the couple had no children, the divorce was final soon after. She had then finished her chemistry degree and left UCLA and California for a different life. Sandy wanted to do something completely different and looked into cooking, something she had enjoyed doing with her mother when she lived at home. She enrolled in a small, prodigious culinary school but dropped out after two years. She enjoyed cooking but lacked the artistic talent that made the dishes look like those in the digital magazines. She began to long for more excitement in her life. With a degree in chemistry and her cooking experience, she applied and was accepted as an officer in the United Earth Space Force.

In the present, Sandy was standing to the left of Jay with a three-kilo bag of flour in her right hand when they heard a loud bang. Startled, they both turned toward the noise. As Sandy turned, a shard from the meteor passed through the bag in her hand. Flour exploded everywhere in the galley, covering both Sandy and Jay in a white powdery dust just before the lights went out. The abandon-ship sirens suddenly started to blare as the emergency lights came on.

Still shocked by the suddenness of what was happening, Sandy almost didn't hear Jay shout, "Let's go!" She felt him grab her by the hand. Wide-eyed and stunned, she didn't resist as he led her from the galley through the crew's mess hall. Two pieces of the meteor had apparently slammed into the two vertical support columns in the mess hall, creating a fragmentation grenade–like effect, killing everyone there. Bodies were lying on the floor and across tables. Blood and entrails were splattered on the walls, tables, and cabinets. Blood pooling on the floor made it slippery and difficult to maintain footing. Sandy considered what the similar meteor fragment that had barely missed her and Jay, hitting the bag of flour instead, could have done.

Covered in flour and looking like ghosts from some horror video, Sandy and Jay stepped over the bodies lying on the floor, taking care not to slip on the blood and gore. Sandy gagged at the sight and smell. They didn't have oxygen masks yet, so the odor was free to assail their senses. Jay opened the nearest emergency-supply cabinet in the passageway and handed an oxygen mask to Sandy while he donned his. Sandy fumbled but finally tightened hers to her face. The mask helped keep the odor from overpowering her senses. She was finally coming to grips with what was transpiring, and her thinking cleared—they had to hurry.

They made good time getting to the Emergency Departure Compartment. Stepping into the EDC, Sandy noticed that the air-lock hatches to three escape pods were already shut. She peered through each of the small glass viewing ports in the inner airlock hatches and through one of them saw nothing but stars.

She shouted to Jay through her mask and over the wailing sirens, "Someone's already left the ship, and those two over there are occupied and ready to depart!"

As he inspected their four-man crew escape pods, Jay complained above the noise, "Great! Both our assigned pods are damaged."

Sandy's assigned escape capsule had a two-centimeter hole just left of the entry handle, ensuring the capsule was no longer airtight. Jay's was worse, with a long crease that penetrated the hull just outside the top hinge that connected the hatch to the capsule. Jay reached into Sandy's pod and grabbed the backpacks that held the emergency supplies for that capsule. He then grabbed the backpacks from his crew capsule, including his personalized, special communication equipment, and set everything in the passageway. Sandy looked over to the open four-person crew escape pods down the line of capsules and picked one. She figured that those who were already dead wouldn't mind.

"Let's take this one," she shouted through her mask above the din.

Entering the capsule, Sandy had Jay toss her the extra backpacks, which she stored in a locker for the trip to the planet's surface. After Jay entered the four-person escape pod, she helped him with the escape pod departure procedures, and in less than a minute, they were on their way to the planet below, safely through the meteor storm.

When the meteors passed through the ship, they killed all but twenty of the on-duty crew members. The rest of the ship's complement was in crew's mess eating just before the shift change or sleeping in their racks. The crew members who were left alive on the *Copernicus*, fearing what they may have to face on the planet below, stayed behind and tried valiantly but vainly to save the ship. They soon realized it was hopeless. Too late to save themselves, they joined the rest of their shipmates in that final peace that eventually claims all life. It was over in less than four minutes.

Chris sat on the ground contemplating his future. *How am I going to survive this? How did I even get into this mess to begin with? What was I thinking when I joined the UESF? Oh, yeah …*

Between classes at the Tarpon Springs Academy, early in his studies of starship engineering and before he joined the United Earth Space Force, Chris Elliott asked one of the professors how FTL travel was possible. When the professor asked Chris whether he was familiar with the uncertainty principle of quantum mechanics and how far along he was in his studies, Chris answered that he had a PhD in xenobiology and had to admit that he was only a second-term engineering freshman, but yes, he was familiar with that principle. The professor said that he would try to help him understand by keeping the physics relatively simple.

"Let's talk on the way to my office," Dr. Charles Karl said.

Chris took to the professor's right side as they walked down the long hallway.

The professor continued, "As you know, matter is made of atoms, and all atoms have matter waves, meaning that on a subatomic level everything has both wavelike and physical matter properties. Using the uncertainty principle of quantum mechanics as a basis, scientists were finally able to predict, with relative certainty, how physical matter could be completely converted to matter waves and be controlled. By using a specified amount of power and specific frequencies on a subatomic level, all matter can be dematerialized into matter waves and transmitted in an exact direction and distance. The matter waves are then rematerialized at a specified distant point in space-time. With this new technology, humankind was able to unequivocally defeat the universal speed limit of the speed of light by utilizing a completely different method."

Reaching his office, Dr. Karl glanced at the retina reader on the wall, and the door unlocked. The lights automatically came on as he stepped into his office and invited Chris over to an oversize computer monitor. The professor spoke a few words to the computer, which brought up a simple diagram of the principles of matter transfer that he used to teach his graduate students.

Using the schematics and pointing to the FTL engine drawing, Dr. Karl followed the diagram with his finger toward the matter wave conversion generators and then to the rematerialization area. The professor said, "Simply put, the object would be dematerialized by being reduced to matter waves, then rematerialized to physical matter at a point in our space-time continuum that was precisely calculated to be some distance away. If the calculations were incorrect for the frequency or power output, the matter waves would attempt to rematerialize, but in an unknown location, or they would be partially rematerialized as a mix of atoms and subatomic particles scattered in an unrecoverable manner somewhere in the physical universe."

Chris initially tried to memorize the diagram and listen at the same time, but he didn't recognize most of the symbols used for the conversion process, so now he just listened instead.

Continuing, the professor clarified that the term "faster-than-light travel" was actually a misnomer. "We are not actually traveling at faster-than-light speeds, but since the terminology has been around for so many centuries in science fiction, and since the end result is the same, we kept the term. Controlled by powerful computers, FTL engines provide the power and the frequencies necessary to shift all matter within a shaped subatomic field, such as all the atoms within and including a spaceship, to matter waves. Then they rematerialize the entire macro object at great distances without affecting or interacting with matter in the macro world as we see it. The matter waves are not traveling through space. They are, in effect, disappearing from the physical universe as we know it from one point in space-time and reappearing in another place, but in the same universe and time continuum. This winking in and out of existence transcends the physical universe limitations of Einstein's general theory of relativity of an object not being able to exceed the speed of light, because for the instant that you are in that matter-wave quantum state between points on a map, you are not in the physical universe."

Chris looked away from the monitor and at the professor with a quizzical expression. "Then where are you if you're not in the physical universe?"

The professor broke eye contact with Chris for a moment and spoke to the computer. The power to the monitor turned off. Turning his attention back to Chris, he said, "That information is still theoretical and double PhD material. Think of it as interdimensional or hyperspace travel. Some people like to call the process a 'jump,' since we're not actually traveling in a linear fashion. It would take me three semesters just to scratch the surface of the first few theories about hyperspace interdimensional travel. We have a good working knowledge of how to use hyperspace, but not all the specifics as to why it works. For example, the common person may know how to operate a computer, but not the details as to how or why the processors and other chips make everything happen."

Pulling up one of the chairs in front of his desk where guests normally sat, the professor sat and offered the other to Chris. Chris turned the chair to face the professor and asked, "Okay, then why the limitations at *C* times nine if we can rematerialize anywhere we want?"

The professor raised his right index finger toward the ceiling with a slight forward tap. His eyes lit up and with eyebrows raised, he answered, "Good question!" He dropped his arm and quickly poked his finger toward Chris before placing his hand on the arm of his chair. "That one I can answer for you!"

The professor shifted his weight and leaned forward in his chair. Chris could hear the excitement in Dr. Karl's voice.

"Mainly, it's because there is still a certain amount of uncertainty in the formulas. That's why we lost so many probes and good people during the testing. We tried to go too far on the jumps. Using shorter waypoint jumps and putting several of those waypoint jumps one after the other in succession still gives the effect of faster-than-light travel. Limitations of computer processor and system speeds limit how fast the necessary computations can be made to make the rematerializing object actually materialize where we predict next. The calculations are incredibly complicated. The fastest our present equipment can process the consecutive waypoints and get us there is the equivalent of nine times the speed of light."

Seeing that Dr. Karl was on a roll and knowing how much every professor he had ever had liked to talk, Chris shifted in his chair to make himself more comfortable. He was captivated.

The professor sat a little straighter and leaned a little more forward in his chair, toward Chris. The professor was in his element talking about his life's work, and he continued with a youthful enthusiasm. "Quantum matter waves are not like radio waves that are limited to the constraints of Einstein's theory of relativity and the speed of light. Before our discoveries, the uncertainty principle said we couldn't predict when or where in the universe a quantum particle would be or when it would disappear or where it would reappear and that even the observation of the process changes the outcome in very unpredictable ways. It took centuries of experiments and the lifetime dedication of thousands of scientists to finally crack the code that let us predict the unpredictable, but we did it!

"Someday, coming in the near future, we will figure out how to apply the same quantum effect principles that we use to propel spacecraft across those vast distances in the blink of an eye to electronic devices, such as computers and communication equipment, making them infinitely faster and more efficient. With better computations and equipment, theoretically, we will be able to dematerialize and then rematerialize an individual or object without the use of a container that has the FTL engines. We could, for example, transport the victim of an accident on Mars to an emergency room at a hospital on Earth or transport a spacecraft anywhere in the universe almost instantaneously. In the twentieth century, a popular science fiction television show called the device a transporter, which could *beam* people to the surface of a planet from a spaceship in orbit and back again. The outcome of our process is the same except on a much grander scale. Communications anywhere in the universe will be as I am talking to you right now, with no delay." Noting that Chris had looked at the clock on the wall several times during his monologue, the professor said, "I'm sorry. I tend to get a bit carried away when I talk about this subject. Let me wrap it so you can get on your way."

Chris, not wanting to upset the professor said, "Thank you, Dr. Karl. This is fascinating, but I do have to get to my next class in twenty minutes. I'd like to stop by another time to hear more."

"I'll tell you what," said Dr. Karl. "I have the rest of the day off, and I don't want to leave you with only part of the story. I'll walk with you toward your class."

Personally understanding how passionate a PhD could be when talking about his specialty, and with his own natural curiosity getting the upper hand on him, Chris eagerly agreed.

As they walked, Dr. Karl quickly finished explaining that the basic problems with the "jump" style of FTL travel concerned the possibility of rematerializing inside a solid object, such as an asteroid, planet, or star, so keeping a current map of the universe was critical for safe travel. He further explained that when the computations for FTL travel were perfected, humankind would be able to traverse the galaxy or even travel between galaxies—in his and Chris's own lifetime. A celestial bonus was that time dilation wouldn't be a factor with this method of travel. People on Earth would experience almost exactly the same space-time passage that a traveler would experience while gone. Another huge bonus was that it wouldn't take as much energy to cross the galaxy as it would to lift off from Earth and travel to Mars by conventional means.

Dr. Karl continued to explain that at the current time, because of the limitations of computing power, space travelers had to take short hops to a waypoint within a container that could hold the FTL engines. Navigational computers calculated the first waypoint and allowed the jump. They then did a position check upon rematerializing, accounted for nearby and destination gravity wells, calculated the next waypoint, and allowed the next jump. And they had to repeat this process again and again, daisy-chaining the waypoints, so to speak, until the destination was reached.

A bright light from above caught Chris's attention and pulled him away from his memories. He looked up into the cloudless sky and saw a meteor brightly streaking across the sky as it entered the upper atmosphere. The meteor, plainly visible even in broad daylight, left a long smoking trail behind it. *That must be a huge one to be that bright. With rocks like that out there, it's no wonder the ship was destroyed so quickly.*

The meteor was crossing from his right to his left when his eye caught a couple of dark objects behind it, falling slower than the stone from the sky. As the objects neared the surface, parachutes opened for landing. Watching them drift toward the surface, Chris estimated the capsules would land about twenty-five kilometers away.

"Yes!" he shouted to the sky as he raised a balled fist and punched at the sky. Excited to know that others had made it out of the doomed spacecraft, Chris quickly recovered from his fit of despair. He stuffed all the gear back into his pack, sprinted to his escape capsule, made sure the emergency locator beacon was working properly, and with the locator beacon microphone, recorded a message giving a brief description of his plans and the direction he was to travel in search of other survivors. He then headed out in the direction of the two falling escape pods.

2

The landing was harder than expected. Then, still reeling from the rough reentry through the atmosphere and her head injury, Dr. Rhodes had a difficult time managing the handles that opened the hatch of her personal emergency escape pod. When she finally did open the hatch after freeing the last of the dogs, she was greeted by a beautiful, clear, sunny day. The bright light hurt her head. She screened her eyes from the bright sun with her left hand while looking out the hatch. A light breeze in the twenty-degree-Celsius air blew a few strands of shoulder-length brunette hair across her face. She carefully stepped outside the still smoking capsule, being mindful not to touch it because it was still very hot from friction generated by the high-speed reentry. She walked slowly and carefully through the knee-high, wide-blade grass to the nearest object that could be used for a backrest and collapsed against it. The medium-size boulder felt cool against her back.

With the adrenaline rush subsiding, Holly Rhodes, MD, said a short thankful prayer and tried to concentrate through the headache to remember what her analysis of this planet's atmospheric report had revealed. While orbiting the planet on board *Copernicus*, she had completed an atmospheric and weather analysis with probes sent to the surface, so she knew the air was breathable and comparable to Earth. The CO_2 was slightly higher than on Earth at 612 ppm, but nowhere near the toxic level of 50,000 ppm, or 5 percent. Nitrogen levels were also comparable at 77 percent, and oxygen slightly higher at 22 percent. Further analysis had shown that there were small amounts of argon, helium, hydrogen, methane, and neon. Trace amounts of other gases were also present. Dr. Rhodes knew that anytime *Copernicus* orbited a planet, as topography, atmospheric, and weather data became available, the ship's computers automatically updated the programming on all the escape capsules with navigation instructions for landing at the most temperate and solid-surface part of the planet where there might be access to food and water, to increase survivability of the crew. Tau Ceti g was similar to Earth in terms of planet size, temperature, rainfall, and overall climate, but it was mostly deficient in heavy metals, and having a core with fewer heavy metals meant that Tau Ceti g had less mass, resulting in a gravity only 85 percent that of Earth, so everything was 15 percent lighter.

Dr. Rhodes felt exhausted. No sooner had she closed her eyes than she fell asleep.

After completing a rapid preflight checklist in the escape pod for Dr. Rhodes and instructing her on how to seal the hatch, Ron Layman set the automatic firing countdown sequence for her capsule to forty-five seconds after the hatch was sealed. The chief engineer then rushed through his own checklist while strapping in and manually launched just after the doctor's capsule left the ship.

Ron screamed in pain when the G forces generated during the initial firing of the departure rocket engines caused the straps to dig into his burned flesh. The pain subsided some when the launch engines quit. His right shoulder was still extremely painful and throbbing where blisters had broken and burned skin had peeled away, but there was nothing he could do about it. Prior to the firing of the retro rockets in preparation for an atmospheric reentry, he was able, despite his excruciating pain, to concentrate enough to use the onboard computers to calculate the approximate path and landing sites for both his and Dr. Rhodes's capsules. The capsules had maneuvering thrusters, and he used them to get his own capsule as close as he dared to the other escape pod just before they both entered the atmosphere. His calculations were very close. Upon landing and opening his hatch, he could see her capsule down the slight incline from his landing site. The incline itself didn't amount to much, less than two meters.

It felt like the fires of hell were licking at the skin on his arm and shoulder from the recent steam burn and all the movement during the rush to escape. The jostling, bumping, and pulling on the straps during the reentry had pushed Ron to the edge of unconsciousness from pain. In the sickbay of *Copernicus*, Dr. Rhodes was going to give him something for his pain, but the meteor had struck first, interrupting the treatment.

Standing outside the capsule, Ron was unable to don his survival backpack because of the searing pain in his shoulder. After trying to reposition the straps of the twenty-seven-kilogram backpack, he finally gave up and alternated carrying it in his left hand and carrying it over his left shoulder. Breathing in short quick breaths and doing his best to fight the pain, he headed toward the doctor's position.

It would take the chief engineer more than two hours to cover the ground between him and the doctor. He had gone only about two hundred meters when he saw something moving in the thigh-high grass off to his right, heading in his direction. Wincing with pain, he let the backpack swing to the ground and quickly removed the .22-caliber survival rifle. The rifle had a folding stock, so it fit very neatly in the pack. Unfolding the stock, inserting the magazine, and chambering a round, he continued his trek by sidestepping to keep a sharp lookout for the animal, or whatever it was, that was following him.

Easy does it, Ron. UESF training teaches not to kill animals or insects unless absolutely necessary when on foreign worlds, so go slow. Being judicious and not riling up the local populations of whatever beasts they might encounter had saved lives already. Some colonies of creatures had a social structure dictating that when any member of the colony was attacked, they all retaliated in kind together. The UESF handbook used the example of bees on Earth: when a hive is attacked, the responding bees leave pheromones on the attacker as a marker for other bees to target. "Until you know what the response will be of the confronting creature(s), it is better to leave it or them alone," advised the handbook.

However, not knowing what was on his trail was still worrisome and unnerving. The creature continued to move when he moved, to stop when he stopped.

"Come on out. Let me get a look at you," he whispered to himself. When he did see something in the grass, he wasn't sure whether what he saw was the thing itself or its shadow. Whatever it was, it was camouflaged very well.

Soon, a small swarm of large flying insect-like creatures found Ron and buzzed all around, some in a hover, others flying in circles, but not landing directly on him.

Still watching for movement in the grass as one of the bugs, as he'd decided to categorize them, landed on the tip of his rifle barrel, he said, "Hello there, little one. What brings you to visit me? I'm sure I don't taste as good as what you're used to eating, so no sampling the foreign cuisine today, okay?"

The movement in the grass had stopped when he stopped, giving Ron a chance to look the bug over. The insect seemed to be studying him as much as Ron was studying it. The bug was less than five centimeters long with a slender triple-segmented body. In appearance, it was a cross between a dragonfly, mosquito, beetle, and hornet. It didn't have the proboscis of a mosquito but had a heavy set of pincers outside of what appeared to be mouthparts, similar to those found on a beetle. The center segment humped upward, and the head hung low, like that of a mosquito or a dragonfly, giving the bug a distinctive "tough guy" look. The rear segment was long and shaped like the business end of a hornet. Ron did *not* want to find out if it could sting. The coloring of the bug was unusually beautiful, with deep blue and purplish iridescent coloring on the back, a shiny black underside, and four translucent red wings that folded neatly on its back. The wings were longer than the body by a quarter of its length. The creature had eight black legs that looked like typical legs on any flying Earth insect, except that these legs had hairy fur like that found on a tarantula spider on Earth. Four of the legs were on the front body segment. The front two appeared to be able to feed the mouthparts with an extra joint that acted like wrists and hands without fingers. The middle and back body segments had two legs each. Each leg had three segments and small hooks on the last segment of the leg that could latch onto whatever it landed on or caught. The bug's four eyes were stacked above each other, two to a side. The top two were able to work independently and kept watch of the surrounding area. The eyes were small red blisters with a black spot that moved around to whatever object the insect was observing. The other two spots aimed directly at Ron Layman. Ron lost the staring contest. After watching Ron for about five minutes with its unblinking eyes, the bug became bored or figured out that Ron wasn't a meal after all and flew off to join the others of its kind, landing on the tops of the tall blades of grass nearby.

As Ron continued, the creature moving in the grass never revealed itself, although it did get close enough on occasion that Ron could hear soft grunting and growling. It tried to get in front of him—probably, Ron thought, to get downwind to catch his scent—but Ron would zig or zag to cut off the advance of the animal, and it would stop. The wind out of the west carried the scent of the creature to Ron, however, causing him to turn his head away and wrinkle his nose at the unpleasant odor. He thought it smelled like a warm, wet dog with urine on its fur. The animal kept pace and followed him for more than two kilometers, but as the grass shortened to knee-high, the creature, apparently not wanting to expose itself, eventually went back the way it had come.

"Hey, Doc, are you all right?"

Dr. Rhodes startled when she felt a touch on her shoulder and heard someone call her name. Trying to concentrate through her mental fog, she blinked her eyes several times to clear her vision. A blurry human form slowly took the recognizable shape of Ron Layman. Always the consummate doctor, even while suffering in pain herself, Dr. Rhodes replied, "I'll be okay. How's your arm and shoulder?" Although she continued to be a bit foggy-headed, she was still concerned about her patient.

"Very painful. I couldn't wear my backpack because the strap pressed directly on my shoulder burn. I think I lost some skin from the safety harness during the launch and landing. I half-carried, half-dragged the pack with my left arm, but I made it here. The muscles in that arm are gonna be sore by tomorrow, but I'll get by." Ron sighed and motioned with his head and eyes in the direction from which he had come. "I had something in the grass following me most of the way here, so I had to carry the .22 in my right hand and manage the backpack the best I could with my left. I'm sure glad I didn't have to shoulder the weapon. Just thinking about that makes me hurt. If you need a nap or something, you might consider resting in the capsule from now on; that creature could be dangerous."

Listening, but ignoring his warning, she said groggily, "If you'll go into my escape capsule and bring me my med kit, I can give you something for the pain."

"No thanks, Doc. After *not* seeing what was following me, I want to be fully alert if the creature turns out to be something dangerous and challenges us. If the pain gets really bad, I'll let you know."

"Okay," she said, "help me up then. Let's go back to my capsule and see if the emergency beacon is working. Anyway, I want to take a look at your bandages, and *I* could use something myself for this dizziness and splitting headache."

3

High above the horizon and much farther to the west, Chris saw another capsule floating on a parachute to the surface. Even though the capsule looked small at this distance, by the shape of the silhouette, he knew it to be a crew capsule. Four-place crew capsules had a greater width-to-length ratio, giving them a stockier look. Knowing that the capsule programming would land the pods in approximately the same latitude on the planet, all he needed to do was walk a straight line between his capsule and the two that he had seen fall earlier, and he should be able to find the fourth one by continuing the straight path. The problem was he didn't have a compass—and didn't know whether a compass would even work on this planet. He didn't have one of the sophisticated hand navigation aids that used celestial markers to find any location on any world either. All he had were land markings that he could see with his old fashion Mark 1, Mod 0 eyeballs, which in this case included just grassland as far as he could see.

The land was relatively flat, so being 180 centimeters tall, he guessed he should be able to see at least four kilometers in any direction. If the pods didn't land in forest trees, land in a hole, or sink in a body of water, he should be able to see them. He stopped and removed the handheld radio from his backpack. Thinking he might need to defend himself against an unknown predator, he also removed and loaded his .22 pistol, setting the safety on and pulling the hammer back to half-cock for extra safety before sticking it under the belt of his bloodied khaki trousers. Having had training with firearms, he knew that when the hammer was at half-cock, the hammer was not in contact with the firing pin, and this would prevent an accidental discharge if the gun were to fall on the hammer.

Wondering if he could reach the falling escape capsule, he turned his radio on and depressed the push-to-talk button. "This is *Copernicus* XB1 to anyone that can hear me. Over. This is *Copernicus* XB1 to anyone that can hear me. Do you read? Over."

Nothing, not even static. The emergency radio he had was a traditional VHF, or very high frequency, radio that was a proven reliable unit, good for line-of-sight communication and talking over short distances.

They probably don't have their radio on. In the rush to get off the spaceship, I didn't turn mine on either. So much for checklists, he mused to himself as he exhaled a deep, disappointed, but still hopeful sigh.

For the others who were already on the ground, he was still too far away. They were well over the horizon. Chris decided to turn off the radio to save the battery and try again every two or three kilometers. All escape capsules had portable VHF radios that automatically activated upon landing if they weren't turned on before launching. The onboard emergency beacon and antenna, which automatically deployed after landing, could also receive and transmit in the VHF frequencies. He hoped the survivors remembered how to use them and didn't tune them to a different frequency intentionally or by accident. The UESF used VHF radios because of their dependability, durability, and lesser susceptibility to atmospheric interference. All the VHF radios were originally set to the default military emergency frequency of 243.0 megahertz but were tunable from 30 to 300 MHz. Packed up and ready to go, Chris headed out.

The capsule that Jay Johnson and Sandy Brooks rode safely to the ground landed perfectly upright in the center of a low area of a large grass field. The depression was about four meters lower than the surrounding land and approximately the size of two side-by-side football fields, with a gentle upward slope in all directions. The antenna that had automatically deployed from the capsule upon landing was still a meter below the rim of the depression. Had this been a wetter world, they would have landed in a large pond.

Sandy was still trembling from their ordeal.

"We made it!" Jay exclaimed. Turning to Sandy, he asked, "How are you doing?"

"I … I guess I'm okay. Frightened … but glad we're on the ground," she stammered.

After assuring a shaken and frightened Sandy that everything would be all right if they exited the capsule, Jay opened the hatch and climbed out to assess their situation and the possibility of communication with anyone else who had made it safely down. Hiking up to the rim of the depression, he looked around. Sandy stayed back in the capsule's open hatch and watched.

Jay wasn't sure his voice would carry back to Sandy, but he pointed and shouted back to her anyway. "With the exception of some trees over there, there's nothing here but grass as far as I can see."

He looked around at the square kilometers of grass fields all around him. The small groupings of tall, odd-looking trees were about two kilometers away, to what he thought was the northeast. Some were straight, others gnarly and twisted like a fig tree. Not being a botanist, he likened most of the straight ones to mangrove trees with exceptionally large, heavy, waxy leaves and long, tall roots sprouting all around the trunks as if searching for water that was hard to find. Vines growing from the ground near the trees and seeking anything vertical wrapped themselves around the trees, snaking through the branches; Jay could see them extending above the treetops searching for yet another branch to cling. There was no water at ground level that he could see.

Sandy, not having heard him clearly when he shouted to her, gathered her courage, left the safety of the capsule, and joined him at the edge of the rim. "Why did we land in a low spot?" she asked when she saw the expanse of grass and how low the capsule was in comparison to the surrounding area.

Jay responded, "Once we enter the atmosphere, the ship's computer controls where we land. We don't get to pick our spot." Looking off in the distance, Jay pointed and asked Sandy, "See those trees way over there?"

"Sure," she said.

"I'm going to walk over there and see if I can cut a thin tree tall enough to make an antenna mast. I have to get the capsule antenna as high above ground level as I can, so we can communicate with anyone else who made it to the surface. The higher the antenna, the longer the range will be that we can communicate. See"—he pointed back down toward the capsule—"the antenna is below ground level now. We can't communicate with anyone with it like that, so I have to get it up higher."

"Okay, but I'm not going anywhere. I'm staying put in the capsule with the hatch shut. Bang on it when you get back. But …" She hesitated and took his hand. "Please be careful out there. You have to be careful not to touch the leaves on the vines or get any tree sap on your skin either. Any of it could be poisonous and kill you, or you could get a poison ivy–like reaction from touching any of the plants, a reaction that could last for weeks or months if you don't die of infection first. You could get bitten by a poisonous spider or other insect too. We just don't know anything about the plant or wildlife here yet." Sandy had a frightened look on her face.

Jay took her other hand in his and smiled. "If I didn't know any better, I'd think you might even like me."

"Later," she said as a tear began to form in her right eye. "Be careful, and hurry back."

Seeing how frightened Sandy was, he said seriously, "I'll be careful, I promise."

She gave his hands a light squeeze as her eyes relaxed a bit, the hint of a frightened smile remaining. Turning around, Jay left for the wooded area as Sandy walked back and entered the capsule, shutting the hatch behind her.

With the survival knife in its belt holster, Jay walked through the wide-blade, high grass toward the trees, humming to himself. He was almost to the tree line when he saw movement in the grass ahead. Placing his hand on the hilt of his knife, he froze in place. He couldn't make out exactly what was there, but it was something unmistakably short and bulky.

Under his breath, Jay murmured, "This is a great time to remember the survival rifle back in the capsule."

As the creature moved, the grass parted, making a path about a half-meter wide. Jay guessed the animal to be under one and a half meters in length, from the way the grass tried to close around behind the moving creature.

"What *is* that?" he whispered to himself. He tried to swallow, but his mouth was dry; his heart raced in nervous anticipation. His eyes were open wide, darting left and right, taking in all he could see without turning his head. All his senses were on high alert for any sudden change that would indicate trouble, especially from behind.

The light wind at Jay's back was blowing toward the part in the grass. The movement ahead suddenly stopped. Jay didn't dare to move. Not wanting to provoke an attack with his own movement, he was breathing high, fast, and shallow, from his chest. He could hear and feel his heart pounding, as if it was trying to burst through his ample frame. He was sure the animal could hear it too. His pulse throbbed in his temples, hands, and feet. *If my heart were beating any harder, you could pick up the vibration with a seismograph!*

The standoff lasted for several minutes. Then without a sound, whatever it was that had caused the grass to part began to move away from him and in the direction of the same trees toward which Jay was headed. Jay relaxed enough to take a few deep breaths but watched for several minutes with his hand still on the hilt of his knife before deciding to move on. Still on high alert, he headed toward the opposite end of the grove of trees.

Keeping a watchful lookout for danger, Jay cautiously entered the tree line. He inspected the nearby trees for one that he could make into a post for a radio antenna mast and found exactly what he was looking for right away. The tree was about fifteen meters tall and ten centimeters thick at the base, thinning near the top. This tree, tall and thin with smooth bark, wasn't yet tangled with vines. There were several roots up to three centimeters thick growing from the first three meters of the tree. The difficulty of cutting the tree was like that of cutting soft pine, and the wood was surprisingly lightweight. He figured that the woody plant must be dry. He had the tree down quickly, which was exactly what he wanted. He wasn't looking forward to meeting up with his mystery creature anytime soon, so he headed back to the capsule without delay.

"How did it go? Did you get what you needed?" Sandy asked when she opened the hatch to Jay's rapid knocking.

Standing on the ground at the entrance to the capsule, Jay said, "I got the antenna mast, yes." Somewhat out of breath, he continued to nervously scan the area for any movement in the grass.

"What's the matter? You look worried, and that frightens me," she said.

Trying to calm himself with a couple of deep breaths, Jay said, "It's probably nothing, but I ran into something in the grass, that's all." Jay *was* nervous and couldn't hide it.

Already on edge from their escape ordeal, Sandy noticed right away. "Okay, tell me. I want to know—I *need* to know. What was it you saw? Did it look dangerous? Was it big? Was it like a snake? I *hate* snakes! Tell me! Please *tell* me!"

Attempting to evade a direct answer, he said, "I didn't see anything."

"Wait a minute! You said you saw something in the grass, but now you're saying you didn't see anything in the grass. I told you to be careful, Jay! You're scaring me! I can tell that something is bothering you. Tell me, please. I have to know! I have to know *now*! I don't want to die here!" On the verge of hysteria, stomping her feet as if marching in place, and with tears beginning to fill her eyes, she pleaded with him.

Seeing how upset she was becoming, Jay reluctantly responded, "Okay, Okay! It's not as bad as it seems. Yeah, I saw the grass moving, and whatever it was, it was large, probably like a big pig or something. I couldn't see it 'cause it stayed low in the grass. It came straight at me and then stopped about ten meters away. I froze 'cause I didn't want to spook it or provoke it into attacking me. After a few minutes it turned around and went back the way it came. Maybe it was just curious about me, maybe it didn't appreciate the way I smelled— I don't know. The good news is that it doesn't matter what it was; it didn't seem to be aggressive, and it didn't attack me."

His answer didn't calm Sandy much. She whipped around, walked to the opposite side of the capsule, and sat on the side of one of the launch chairs with her back to the open hatch, wringing her hands and wiping at her eyes. Jay entered the capsule, shut the hatch behind him, and walked over and stood behind her, placing his hands on her shoulders.

Once the hatch was closed, Sandy relaxed a little. She stood up with her back to Jay for a couple of moments and then turned around and hugged him, hard. Tears flowed down her cheeks and onto his in large rivulets. She was trembling in his arms.

"I'm scared, Jay. I've never been so scared in all my life," she said, sobbing.

"It's okay. It's going to be all right," he said softly.

Jay held her close and let her cry. Her sobs were deep and heavy. After a few minutes, her sobbing became shallower, and her breathing slowed. Finally, still holding him, she pulled away from the embrace.

With bloodshot eyes and tear-soaked cheeks, Sandy looked deeply into Jay's eyes and said, "I love you, and I don't want to lose you. This place is so foreign and frightening! We don't have a map showing where we are, or where we can get water, or what's safe to eat or … or … I … I'm so scared, Jay. I don't want to be alone here. I don't know what to do or how to stay alive in a place like this … I need you." The deep sobbing started all over again.

Jay pulled her close and just held her. He intended it to be a secure but gentle, comforting embrace that said without words, *I have you; you're safe. Nothing can harm you now*—like the kind you give to a child who has had a particularly frightening nightmare. Jay loved Sandy, and he finally acknowledged that to himself. He knew it wasn't like the plot of a novel where a man and a woman fall in love while stranded on a deserted island because there's no one else around. It wasn't only a sexual attraction either. It was love, true love. He'd known it on *Copernicus*; he just hadn't been ready to admit it to himself. Thinking back, he realized that almost every free moment he had, he spent with Sandy, and when they couldn't be together much because of her duty schedule or his, he couldn't stop thinking about her. When his duties gave him a few moments' break, he would plan how he could spend more time with her and what they could do together in their free time. Even though there were other women on board who were prettier, more willing, and smarter than Sandy, it was to Sandy he was attracted. He finally knew. He knew he'd loved her then and loved her even more now. Here, on this unexplored alien world, he would be her guardian. He would protect her with his life if that's what it would take.

Still holding her in his arms, he vocally made his commitment. "I love you too."

Sandy's sobbing slowed, and she pulled gently away from his embrace. She sat down on her seat and wiped the tears away with one hand while holding Jay's with the other. "I want you to know that I didn't just say I love you because I need your help to survive here or because I'm scared. I've loved you for quite a while. I just didn't …" She stopped to wipe away more tears that were welling up. "I … I just didn't want to have another relationship like my first marriage. Everything was grand at first but went south pretty quick once I committed. I needed to be sure you felt the same way about me. Being on board the ship with limited access to other women—"

Jay's eyes softened. He cupped her chin in his hand and guided her gaze to meet his. "You are exactly what I've been looking for all my life. I love you with my whole heart and soul. I've been in love with you for a very long time. We *will* make it. With the extra supplies, we have enough food and water in here for about twelve weeks. If we had to make it stretch, we could make it last for an additional three or four weeks. That should give us plenty of time to get acquainted with the area and what's available and safe to eat and drink. This capsule will last longer than our lifetime, so we'll always have a secure shelter to fall back to if necessary. There are others who made it to the surface from the ship too. Once we all get together, it'll be easier on everyone. We'll find local sources of food and water. We can build a better, roomier shelter. We're not destitute. I don't mean to say that it will be easy, but we *will* survive. I promise."

Sandy stood up and hugged Jay for a long time. Jay was only three centimeters taller than Sandy, so they fit together like a hand in a glove. Exhaustion from the adrenaline-fueled escape and landing finally began to overwhelm them. Sandy felt so good in Jay's arms that he didn't want to let go. There wasn't much room in the capsule to lie down, but they did the best they could. Jay held Sandy closely as they fell asleep together on the naked deck of the escape pod.

4

Chris had traveled about twelve kilometers toward the two closest escape capsules that had fallen to the west. At least he called it west. The sun was moving in that direction, so he thought it must be west; surely this planet rotated on its axis in the same direction as Earth. If he hadn't been so anxious to get to the survivors, he would have studied more of the planet's details on his capsule's computer or at least downloaded the information to his tablet computer before setting out. He was trying to remember what Kazumi Atatsuka, the ship's planetary geologist, had told him at dinner in the crew's mess the night before. He was going to miss the conversations they'd had about geology and the wildlife that could inhabit the planets they surveyed. She had been sleeping in the crew's quarters and so had probably died in her rack when the *Copernicus* was fatally struck.

The sun was already two-thirds of the way across the sky. He couldn't remember how long the day was, what seasons this planet had, or what season it was. *I must be tired. I can't remember squat right now. How long have I been awake? How long have I been planet-side? I need a break.*

He slipped off his backpack and retrieved a bottle of water and a protein bar. After he finished eating, he drank about a quarter of the water in the bottle. *Time to get moving. I don't want to spend the night out here in the open and end up being a midnight snack for some critter.* After replacing the cap on the bottle and stowing it away, he hoisted the backpack and started out again.

It was more than two hours later when Chris slipped off his backpack and tried calling on the radio. "This is *Copernicus* XB1 to anyone that can hear me. Over. Any station, any station, this is *Copernicus* XB1; do you read? Over."

He waited about ten seconds and tried calling again. No answer. Chris was about to put his radio away when it came to life. "XB1, this is CE1. I read you loud and clear! Over!"

Chris wanted to jump for joy. *Yes! Now we have a fighting chance!* Recognizing the call sign and the voice, he blurted, "Ron! Am I glad to hear from you!"

In his excitement Chris forgot to use proper radio protocol, not that his failure to say "over" really mattered out here. There was a hesitation before Ron came back on.

"Chris, where are you? Are you okay? If you were in that first capsule that left the ship, and if the computers landed the capsules on the target latitude, we should be somewhat west of you. Over."

"I'm fine. Yes, that was me in the first capsule off the ship. I was afraid that I would be the only survivor. There was no one else in the EDC when I got there, so I followed the emergency escape plan and launched my capsule. I estimate I'm about four or five kilometers east of your position right now. I can be there in about an hour or so. It's a little slow going through this tall grass. Over."

"Roger that, Chris. Be careful. I had a standoff with something in the grass that I couldn't ID because it stayed low. It was a little more than a meter in length. I have Dr. Rhodes with me here. She's shook up pretty bad and has a good-size lump on her head, but otherwise we're okay; we're alive. I'll tell you more later. Watch your six; see you when you get here. Over."

"Thanks. I'll keep a lookout for your critter. Chris out."

Inside Chris was quivering with excitement and relief. He rechecked his firearm, making sure that there was a round in the chamber and that the safety was on. His magazine held fifteen rounds of hyper-velocity, long-rifle, hollow-point .22 ammunition. He knew it was not something you'd use for large dangerous game, but for a thin-skinned, deer-size creature, it packed a good enough punch to take the animal down if you hit a vital organ, especially if you hit it fifteen times! Once again, as an added safety procedure, he set the hammer to half-cock before tucking it back under his belt. He checked that he had quick access to his survival knife too, just in case his small handgun failed to stop an attack that he hoped would never come. He re-shouldered his backpack, clipped the radio to the left shoulder strap, and headed west with renewed energy and excitement.

Ron had been looking over the grassy plain for animal trails, about twenty meters from the capsule where Holly was resting, when Chris made the initial radio call. The chief engineer made it a point to carry his portable VHF radio everywhere, not so much so that he could receive calls, but more so because he might need to call for help himself. In his excitement to answer the call, he had fumbled and dropped the radio from his left hand and had to wait for the second call to finish before he replied.

After the call, Layman didn't want to disturb the doctor with the good news right away because he knew she needed the rest. He walked over to her capsule and peered in the open hatch. He confirmed his suspicion that she was still resting comfortably, stretched out in her launch chair, and apparently hadn't heard the conversation on the capsule's radio. The volume must have been set low or turned off. He would talk to her about that later.

The launch chairs had been custom-made for the scientists and could slide into a reclining position once you released the locking mechanism. The capsules were designed to support a person with food and water for at least two weeks with the supplies on board. Most of the ship's company customized their personal and crew pods with extras as well because they knew there was no possible way for anyone to be rescued within two weeks when you were light-years away from help. Mostly, the extra items consisted of water purification units, small survival-type weapons, extra ammunition, reading material, extra food, and other survival tools that could help them create a reasonably comfortable, long-term survival camp as long as the environment could provide additional food and water and as long as they landed on a planet instead of being stranded in space.

Ron saw Chris approaching when he was still two kilometers away. With nothing but the thigh-high grass all around him, it would have been hard to miss Chris's tall lean figure. Chris's dead reckoning was about a kilometer off to the south, but otherwise on the mark. Chris started to jog the last two kilometers after spotting Ron, who walked to meet him when he was about fifty meters away.

"I could see your smile a kilometer away," Ron said, returning a smile in kind.

Chris was beside himself. "Man, you don't know how glad I am to see you too! I didn't know if anyone else had made it off the ship until I saw your capsules' reentry parachutes. Anyone else that you know of make it out besides us?"

Ron replied, "No, there was only one capsule missing when Doc and I got to the EDC and punched out. That, apparently, was you."

"Well, there's at least one four-man crew capsule that got off that I know of, but that one's a lot farther to the west, maybe another twenty to thirty kilometers or so. It was still high in the sky when it went over the horizon from where I landed, and the parachute had yet to deploy," Chris explained.

"How far did you have to travel to get here?" Ron asked.

"My guess, about twenty-five kilometers," Chris responded.

"You must be beat. Did you have any trouble getting here? How long did it take you?"

"Almost nine hours. The walking was steady and smooth for the most part. The hardest part was walking in a straight line. With no compass or navigational handheld, I had to walk backward some of the time, making sure my trail was straight. Walking around here with so little landmarks, a guy could walk circles for days and not see anything but grass," Chris answered.

"Well, look over there. See the small boulder?" Ron said, raising his left arm to point. "Don't stub your toes. It's the only natural thing I've seen that stands above ground around here. There are some short, woody, bush-like plants near my capsule, though."

Chris noticed that despite being right-handed, Ron was keeping his right hand in his trousers pocket, and his right upper arm and shoulder looked thicker than the left under his one-piece suit.

Nodding toward Ron's arm, Chris asked, "What happened?"

"The short version is that I got a steam burn when I cracked open a pipe that wasn't quite depressurized. Got my shoulder too."

"How bad is it?"

"Pretty bad. Second-degree burns from just above the elbow to the top of my shoulder. I lost a lot of skin from the capsule harness digging into the blisters during the launch and reentry."

"Ouch! That must have hurt!" Chris said, cringing from the thought of it.

"It wasn't pleasant. Still burns pretty bad, so I'm trying not to move it too much."

Chris knitted his brow in concern. "Has Doc taken a look at it?" he asked, leaning his head in the direction of the doctor's capsule.

"Yeah, she'd just finished putting my bandages on when the meteor hit. I still had my jumper suit half-off. It was chaos in spades, but we made it. Doc took a couple of pretty bad bangs to her head, so she's sleeping off some medication she took earlier. I haven't had her look at it since before the launch, and I can tell you, I'm not looking forward to it either. She wanted to look at it right after I got here, but sitting down for a few minutes to rest, she fell asleep. I'm taking advantage of the reprieve. I'm not going to bother her."

The doctor's injuries now added to his concern. Chris said, "I hope she's going to be all right."

Ron replied, "She seemed to think so. She said she just needed to get some rest."

"I hope that's all she needs. If I have to be stranded on a planet twelve light-years from Earth, Doc is one person I'd like to have on my team," Chris said.

"Say, you must be tired. You'll have to spend the night in my pod," offered Ron. "There's not much floor space, but you can't sleep out here tonight. Heaven only knows what lurks out here after dark." Pointing in the direction of his escape pod, he said, "I'm parked about three kilometers over there. You can almost make out the capsule from here if you squint a little."

Her sleep disturbed by Ron and Chris's conversation, Dr. Rhodes slowly awoke, her thoughts confused. She had been dreaming about a motor vehicle accident she'd been in when she was nineteen years old and initially thought she was feeling pain from that crash.

How long ago was that? Why do I still hurt? she thought as she opened her eyes and slowly returned to normal consciousness. Once she was fully awake and her thoughts were better organized in the present, she put her right hand to her head and closed her eyes again. *Oh, dear Lord, how long are we going to have to be here? My head still hurts, Ron's arm may become infected, and I don't know how long the drugs in the med kit will last. Well, I can't worry about that now. Time to put on my doctor face and see who made it off the ship that may need my help and then tend to Ron's burns.*

With that, Dr. Rhodes carefully raised her chair from the reclining position, stood up, and exited the capsule.

Chris saw Dr. Rhodes step out from the capsule and said, "Hi, Doc! It's really good to see you!" Chris walked over to her and gave her a family-style squeeze around the shoulders. She winced as she lightly hugged him back. Pulling back from the hug, Chris saw the pained expression on her face. "I didn't hurt you, did I? I'm so sorry! How's your head? Ron tells me that you took quite a whack."

"It feels like the morning after my twenty-first birthday, only I didn't get to have as much fun," she quipped, trying to smile, but not doing a good job of it.

"Are you going to be okay?" Chris asked, his tone now serious.

"Yes, eventually. I'm quite certain I received a mild concussion. It's possible I may have a blood clot on my brain, but other than a low-dose class III drug for pain, I'm treating myself with good old-fashioned acetylsalicylic acid, commonly known as aspirin to you. I'm taking it prophylactically—just in case. It'll help dissolve the clot if there is one, and it helps to reduce pain and inflammation too."

"How long before you know for sure?"

"I haven't lost any motor function, and my thinking is clearly improving, so if it is a clot, it would most likely be a subdural hematoma. It could take weeks to months to dissolve depending on how large it is," Holly answered.

"What's a subdural hematoma?" asked Ron.

"It's coagulated blood that forms on the brain, usually from trauma, and sits under the brain's protective covering called the dura mater. I had most of the symptoms, but they're slowly improving, so I don't think there was any permanent damage. I should be back to normal in a week or so." She then pointed to Ron and said, "Let's take a look at that arm now."

"Now?" he meekly asked.

"Now."

Ron turned to Chris with a look of dread on his face before following Dr. Rhodes back to her capsule.

After removing as much of the bandages as she could without causing serious pain, Dr. Rhodes unintentionally let her face register a look of shock and disbelief for the briefest instant before she resumed her professional demeanor. "This looks very bad. I'm going to have to do a procedure called debridement to the wound."

"Debridement? What's that? It doesn't sound pleasant," Ron said.

"It means I'm going to remove the dead and dying skin over

the wound. It'll help prevent infection. It looks like the straps from your capsule did most of the damage, breaking blisters and scraping and gouging the burned area, but all the moving around you've been doing certainly hasn't helped either. I'm going to insist that you let me give you a sedative and pain meds so I can do my work. I guarantee that you'll thank me for it later."

"But …"

As Dr. Rhodes rooted around in her med kit for the syringe, needle, and anesthesia, she said, "No buts about it, mister; you're going down and out for the count. Just close those baby-blue eyes, and you'll wake up feeling better."

"My eyes are light brown, just like my hair, Doc," Ron complained, clearly stalling for time.

"I don't care if your hair is purple and your eyes are lavender. Doctor's orders, Mr. Layman. Now lie down," she said sternly.

A few moments later, Chris stuck his head just inside the capsule. "Need some help?" he asked.

Ron had just fallen asleep following the injection. Glancing up at Chris only briefly before returning her attention to the arm, Dr. Rhodes responded, "If you think you can hold down your lunch while I remove all this dead tissue. Working on a live human being is not the same as dissecting a pig fetus or a dead cat. A monkey comes close, though."

Chris looked at Ron's arm, swallowed hard, and said, "Oh … uh … mmm … I think I'll pass on this one, Doc … Sorry." Chris backed out of the capsule, obviously feeling a little queasy.

Holly just smiled as she trimmed away at a strip of skin ten centimeters long and three centimeters wide dangling from the length of a bandage that had dried to the wound at the top of Ron's shoulder. Ron was lying back in Holly's chair, oblivious to the world and not feeling a thing.

The arm looked pretty awful. The wound had been oozing a clear fluid mixed with blood, which had dried to the bandages, so uneven strips of dead skin ripped from Ron's arm and shoulder when Dr. Rhodes tried to gently remove the bandages. There were deep gouges where the escape capsule's seat restraints had dug into the raw exposed flesh. She didn't know how he could stand the pain without medication. Dr. Rhodes carefully removed all the dead and dying tissue. The burned area covered roughly a two-hundred-square-centimeter portion of his arm and shoulder. She was intensely worried about infection. The doctor smeared half a tube of antiseptic ointment on the burn and re-bandaged the area.

I hope to God this works, she thought. *I'm not looking forward to an amputation.* Not knowing what microbes might find human flesh tasty on this new world, or whether the antibiotics in her medical kit would successfully treat an infection made by any alien microorganisms, Dr. Rhodes felt inadequately prepared to handle medical emergencies. In addition, her medical supplies were finite, with no chance of replenishment. Once they were used, there would be no more. Even if they weren't used right away, they still had a shelf life. She was worried.

What am I going to do when the drugs run out or expire? I'll have to go back to folk-style medicine with herbs and such, trying to cure the infirm with untested concoctions of ground-up weeds and seeds.

5

Still spooned by Jay's embrace, Sandy snuggled a little closer. The movement stirred Jay to consciousness.

"Hi," he said, pulling her in a little closer as a sleepy smile formed on his face. "How do you feel?"

She yawned and snuggled closer yet before replying. "Better. Just hold me for a while."

He gave her a gentle, reassuring hug.

"What do you think is going to happen to us? Will anyone find us?" she asked.

Now fully awake, he answered softly, "I don't know. But we're actually in really good shape right now, except that we're parked in this hole. That limits our communications to just what can fly over us 'cause the antenna is below the rim of the depression. That's why it's important for me to get the antenna mast up. We know that others made it off the ship. We just need to find out where they are. Together we'll have a much better chance of surviving this place. I kinda hate to leave our pod, though. There's not much out there for building materials to make us a new shelter, and right now our whole world revolves around what we have in here."

"What are our chances?" she asked.

Avoiding a direct answer, he replied, "My first priority is to get the antenna mounted up as high as possible. Then we need to find a source of food and water. The other survivors may have already done that. I haven't a clue as to what the climate is like here throughout the year. I don't even know how long a year is on this planet or what season it is either. I can find out, though. The pod's computers should have all that info stored in the database."

Jay gently peeled himself from Sandy's back, stood, and stretched. His forty years were beginning to show. Sleeping on the floor was not his thing anymore. He was sore and stiff but didn't let on to Sandy. He was just grateful they had made it safely off the ship and were together. He sat in one of the launch chairs and stretched to work out the kinks in his back and neck, listening to the pops and cracks from his spine as he arched his back side to side. Sandy sat cross-legged on the floor near him with soft eyes and a slight smile on her face, gazing at Jay. Even in the capsule's dim lighting, she looked radiant.

As she continued to watch him, he finally noticed and asked, "What?" Jay was holding back a smile and trying not to look directly in her eyes.

"Nothing," she responded musically, the smile widening on her face.

Unable to completely hold back his smile, Jay turned to the onboard computer and pushed the power button. It took more than six minutes for the computer to boot up. Nothing had changed in the hundreds of years since computers were first invented. They still had to go through a sequence of loading software into memory. The faster the computers were, the more sophisticated the operating system software became, negating the increased processing speed. In the time it takes to boot up, a person might as well go get a cup of coffee. Once loaded though, the computers processed data at speeds never before thought possible.

The boot sequence finished, Jay looked up the climate information that *Copernicus*'s science crew had accumulated. "It says here that a standard day is 28.7 Earth hours long, and a standard year should be about 284 Earth days. Great. I always wished there were more hours in the day so I could get more stuff done. I guess

I shouldn't have wished so hard," he mused. "We're an average distance of 124 million kilometers from this planets' sun, Tau Ceti. That's almost like splitting the distance difference between Earth and Venus from our sun back home. We're closer to this sun than Earth is to Sol, but then this sun is smaller with less energy output, so the climate is about the same. Most likely, whatever seasons we have here should be shorter than back home on Earth. The planet orbits the sun in an elliptical path, and there's a planetary axis tilt of about twelve degrees, or about half of what Earth's tilt is to our sun. That means that there will be seasonal changes between summer, fall, winter, and spring, but maybe not as severe as back home. Just how much of a change there will be, I don't know. I can't tell for sure from the data that was collected. No one else has studied it. We were the first ones here and only made a few orbits before—" He stopped short, not wanting to upset Sandy any more than she already was. "I could get the computer to extrapolate it, but there really isn't enough information collected for an accurate assessment. I think we're in the early fall season from what I can gather here. That probably explains the somewhat cool days and cooler nights at this latitude."

Sandy just sat there listening, with a loving look and a warm smile on her face.

Ron awoke in Holly's pod. His arm felt … better. It still hurt, but it was better. Holly was outside talking with Chris. He overheard part of their conversation, something about the limitations of modern medicine on other worlds.

"As much as medicine has advanced, there are still no instantaneous healing rays as the science fiction field contends in its make-believe medical centers," Doc said to Chris.

Ron walked outside to join them.

Seeing Ron approach, Dr. Rhodes asked, "How do you feel?"

"Actually, a lot better. Thank you. How long have I been out?" he asked.

"Just a couple of hours. I didn't want you sleeping all night on my bed, so I limited the dose that put you out," she said with a wink in Chris's direction. It was still daylight, but the sun was approaching the horizon.

Feeling more energetic, and with a lot less pain, Ron said, "We'd better get going if we want to be at my capsule before dark. Do we know how long the days and nights are yet?"

"Not yet," responded Chris, "but it seems to be a very long day cycle so far. We can look it up on the computer tonight or tomorrow."

"Right now, you two should be heading out. We don't know what creatures come out at night, and frankly, I don't want you fellows to find out firsthand," said Dr. Rhodes.

"Are you sure you're up to it, Ron?" Chris asked.

"Yep. Let's go."

They headed out for Ron's capsule. The evening sky was beautiful and clear. While walking back, Chris asked Ron to explain the animal encounter that he'd experienced on the way to Dr. Rhodes's capsule earlier that day. He also asked about the animal's behavior and made detailed notes on his tablet computer during the narration.

Darkness was approaching now. The sun had set below the horizon, leaving only a few wispy orange clouds on the horizon by the time Chris and Ron reached the capsule. Using his left hand, Ron opened the hatch. Inside, the capsule was dark except for the few lights indicating that the emergency beacon was operational and transmitting, that the solar panels were functioning well, and that the batteries were fully charged. Stepping back outside, Ron saw that Chris was fishing around in his backpack.

"Chicken or turkey?" Chris asked Ron.

"Chicken or turkey what?"

"Chicken nuggets with potato buds, corn, a brownie—"

Ron cut him off. "I'll have the turkey."

Chris set both bags of food to cooking by adding water to the pouch. He didn't realize how hungry he was until the aroma of Ron's food wafted through the air ten minutes later when he opened the hot bag. He set up the small portable table and foldout seat that came with the capsule and set the food before Ron. Ron attacked the food with his left hand as if he'd been left-handed all his life. Dr. Rhodes had placed a sling on Ron's right arm with specific instruction to leave it on and not move the arm more than necessary, except when doing the stretches she had shown him at the specified intervals. The stretches would keep scar tissue from shortening his reach as the skin healed. Dr. Rhodes didn't expect any complications other than the possibility of infection, and right now, his arm felt quite good, so he was all for complying with the doctor's orders. Chris sat on the ground cross-legged and opened his bagged meal. They ate in silence and watched the few thin clouds turn purple above the horizon.

After cleaning up the leftover debris from the meal, Chris returned to his seat on the ground, leaned his back against the capsule, and said, "You know, apparently it doesn't matter what planet you're on; as long as it has an atmosphere and weather, the sunsets can be beautiful."

"Almost as beautiful as back home," Ron said melancholily.

"Where's home?" asked Chris. "I don't think you've ever mentioned home before."

"Cedar Key, Florida, just south of the panhandle on the Gulf side of the state," Ron answered.

"Did you move there as an adult? You don't have a Floridian accent."

"My family moved there from Davenport, Iowa, when I was fourteen. I did develop an accent when I attended high school so the kids wouldn't make fun of me and so I'd fit in better," Ron said.

"When did you get rid of it?"

"In college. I did well in high school and accepted an academic scholarship for engineering at the University of Illinois. I didn't want to sound out of place there either, even though there were some pretty strong Southern accents on campus. My old Midwestern speech patterns came back without me realizing it. You know, it's funny. I didn't realize I'd lost my accent until I went back to my parents' place in Cedar Keys on my first spring break. My friends were the first to notice. I had to confess to them that my Midwestern roots were now exposed. Everyone got a good laugh from that." Ron smiled as he thought of home.

The stars in the eastern sky began to shine brighter as darkness slowly crept westward. They sat in silence for a while, watching the sky darken.

Gazing up at the stars, Chris said, "They're beautiful, aren't they?" It was more a statement than a question.

Pausing for a moment, as if contemplating some deep philosophical answer, Ron said, "Yes, but in different patterns than I'm used to."

Chris didn't know how to respond. He didn't want to admit to Ron or to himself that by the time they were rescued—if they ever were rescued—they might have these constellations all fitted with new names and committed to memory. The men sat in silence for a while longer, watching the stars make their debut appearance. As they silently relived the day's events, fatigue and exhaustion finally overcame the two men. Entering the capsule, they turned in for the night.

The night was long, and Chris and Ron slept like rocks. Chris was the first up as he roused from his deep slumber on the uncomfortable deck of the escape capsule. He opened the hatch and stepped outside to stretch and work out the kinks in his back and neck. The day was bright and beautiful with no wind, and the sun appeared just above the horizon as a blazing yellow-orange disc.

When his eyes turned to the grass around him, he leaned back into the capsule and shouted, "Ron, Ron! Get up. You need to see this!"

Ron hit the button that raised his chair from a reclining position to upright. He tossed the simple synthetic wool blanket to the side and stepped outside. “Holy cow!” he exclaimed. Ron didn’t use vulgarity. He thought people who used it needed to expand their vocabulary with better adjectives, adverbs, and nouns. In fact, most of the UESF fleet personnel didn’t swear. They were all highly intelligent and could express themselves well without the use of expletives.

All around the capsule were trails in the tall grass, trails that neither of the men had made. The area around their makeshift meal area next to the capsule was especially trampled down.

“I’d be willing to wager those trails were made by the creature that I *almost* saw yesterday,” Ron marveled.

“And all his buddies!” Chris added.

Three main trails led to the capsule from the north. The trails then split up, crisscrossing every which way and making it impossible to determine how many animals there were.

“Looks like they were interested in our leftovers,” Chris said.

Chris had dug a hole in the ground to bury the biodegradable trash left over after their dinner, and now the contents of that hole were strewn about in a nine-square-meter area.

Picking up one of the cooking bags, Ron said, “Look at the chew marks on the plastic bags.”

Chris bent over to examine the bag. “These are carnivore tooth patterns. See how the plastic has punctured holes behind some of the rips? No crush marks from multicuspid teeth. Definitely carnivore. Look at the length and width of this bite mark. From the size of the holes and pattern of teeth, I’d say we’re dealing with something bigger than a very large wolf or hyena, closer to a good-size bear. If the animal is not armor-plated, our weapons should be effective against it if we’re forced to defend ourselves. If it’s bear-size, we may have to use a lot of bullets to kill it or hopefully turn it around.”

Ron bent down to examine the ground for tracks. “Look at these claw marks.” Six sets of four deep marks each were almost evenly spaced around the excavated trash pit. Most of the other claw marks were filled in with the dirt from digging but were still visible. The animal was definitely not bear-size; the tracks were too close together. Whatever it was, though, it had one very large mouth. "I'm not a biologist," Ron said, "but it looks like there were at least three of them digging for the scraps. What do you think?"

Chris said, "I agree, but look over here … smaller tracks. The claw marks are smaller and closer together and not as deep. We may have a family with young ones."

"Too bad these capsules don't come with surveillance optics," Ron replied. "I'd love to see what they look like from a safe vantage point."

"As would I," Chris agreed.

They reclaimed their trash by stuffing it into another biodegradable bag, but this time they placed the bag in the capsule for later disposal. They gathered their traveling gear and headed out to visit Dr. Rhodes.

An hour later, they arrived at Dr. Rhodes's capsule. She was already outside, trampling the grass around the capsule.

"What are you doing, Doc?" Ron asked.

"I'm making a clear view area so nothing can sneak up on us while we're out here. How was your night, Chris? Ron, how's the arm doing?"

Ron said, "The arm still burns pretty bad, but it's a lot more tolerable since you did that de-whatever treatment on me."

Ignoring her question, Chris asked in return, "Did you have visitors last night?"

"No, I don't think so. Why? Did you?" she asked.

"Yes, and more than one," he replied. Chris explained the nocturnal visitation and his guess on the type of creature they were dealing with. "We still don't know if they pose a threat," he said, pausing upon noticing movement out to the west, "but it appears that we're about to find out."

Dr. Rhodes and Ron turned to look in the direction Chris was facing. Three trails were forming in the grass, coming from the direction of Ron's escape pod.

"Doc, I highly recommend you get into your capsule and close the hatch. Ron, you go with her," Chris said softly as he reached for his pistol.

Ron objected. "No, you may need my help. I can shoot just as well left-handed as right-handed if you switch weapons with me."

Chris swapped his handgun for Ron's .22 rifle, silently glad for the help. Dr. Rhodes entered her capsule and shut the hatch.

The men slowly backed up until their backs were against the capsule. The movement in the grass slowed, as if those causing it were approaching cautiously. One of the trails split into two smaller trails.

"They must travel in pairs," Chris noted to Ron.

Another trail split into two. The movement in the grass slowed again but continued to approach from the front and flanks of the men. Five trails were now converging on the two men, with who-knew-for-sure how many animals on them.

Chris's heart was racing. *What are they after? Might they attack? Can we shoot fast enough to stop them all? Would the .22s be effective? What if they have hides so thick, the bullets can't penetrate deep enough to kill? Will we die quickly, or slowly and painfully? What will happen to Doc if we die?*

Layman stood on the left of the capsule, so he had a clear field of fire with his left hand, while Chris maintained his position on the right. Chris looked over at Ron. He was certain that Ron was as nervous as he was; he could see the muscles in Ron's jaw tense and stand out. Chris brought his attention back to the forming trails. As the men stood there, waiting and watching, the animals in the grass approached closer.

Dr. Rhodes cracked the hatch, peered out curiously, and whispered, "Is everything all right?"

"Don't know yet," Chris said, sotto voce. "Maybe you should keep the hatch cracked for us just in case."

Holly backed away from the opening, leaving a small gap. The trails in the grass stopped advancing about five meters from the edge of the clear area that Dr. Rhodes had tamped down. One of the trails began to slowly approach the clearing from the men's leeward side.

Chris whispered to Ron, "It's trying to get downwind and get a whiff of our scent."

The other trails closed in, nearer to the edge of the trampled area. The movement stopped one meter from the clearing. The animal creating the downwind trail from the capsule crept to the edge. The xenobiologist caught sight of a twitching snout sticking out between the blades of grass. The men stayed as still as statues, their eyes the only things that moved. They heard muffled grunts and soft low growls with occasional huffing from the closest creature. Then, in less then a minute and without fanfare, the creature's vocalization stopped, and the snout disappeared. Movement in the grass suggested that the creatures had satisfied their curiosity and were quickly vacating the area. The men watched as the many trails blended back into three, moving off to the northwest.

After several minutes, when he felt sure the threat was over, Chris called, "Hey, Doc, it's okay to come out now."

"Did you see them? What did they look like?" Dr. Rhodes asked, emerging from the capsule. Her nervous curiosity was obvious and getting the best of her.

Chris took a deep breath and exhaled his relief before answering. "All I saw was a nose, and not much of that. I can tell you that the nose had two tall, narrow slits for nostrils and that it was covered with an uneven patchwork of brown, beige, and black coloring. The snout was wide and protruded through the grass at just under a half-meter high. The animal's camouflage must be perfect for this place because I couldn't see the head, and it had to be right there." Elliott shook his head. "What I can tell you is that whatever they are, they're social and travel in packs. It's uncertain whether their young travel with them during a hunt, but the tracks back at Ron's suggested that the young may indeed travel with the adults. They most likely have an either patriarchal or matriarchal hierarchy since only one approached us, and it seemed to give vocal calls while the rest responded. It also appears that they have an acute sense of smell, just as most Earth animals do. Humankind and many birds are among the few land animals that don't use the sense of smell as a primary means of locating food and identifying each other."

His adrenaline subsiding, and with relief clearly washing over him after another close encounter, Ron smiled and said, "I'm so glad. I wouldn't want you sniffing around me like a dog does to ID me every time we greeted each other."

Chris chuckled as he imagined the scenario.

But Dr. Rhodes apparently didn't appreciate the joke because she shook her head and rolled her eyes as she turned to go inside the capsule. To no one in particular, she said, "Men and their eighth-grade humor! Even at a time like this! It doesn't matter how educated they are—their humor never advances past the eighth grade!"

6

Looking up at Jay, high above the capsule, clinging to the post that was to be become the base for his antenna, Sandy shouted, "What are you doing up there?"

"I'm trying to make a platform for the transceiver," Jay shouted back.

"Why?" she asked.

"Because the antenna cabling has to be shielded coax, and there is no extra available," he explained.

"I still don't understand."

"Do you really want to know?" he asked.

"Well, let's see. The cooking, cleaning, laundry, dusting, ironing, vacuuming, and sewing are all caught up, and I also made the bed … sure, why not?"

Jay Johnson was a communications specialist with a bachelor's in electrical engineering and a master's degree in advanced communications. He climbed down from his perch atop the capsule. "It's simple really. Radio frequency energy, or RF energy for short, has to match the length of the antenna to the wavelength of the frequency that's being used. If the mismatch is too far off, you can damage the transmitter. We have a very simple whip antenna and a tuner. A tuner will make fine adjustments electronically to the antenna so the RF signal sees the antenna as being a certain length. Are you following?"

"How does the tuner know how to adjust the signal?" Sandy asked.

"It has to do with how much power is going through the antenna and how much is reflected back because of the mismatch in length." Jay enjoyed explaining something that he was very good at, and she was enjoying his company. For most of the day, he had been working hard making a platform to mount the transceiver and to get the mast secured to the capsule strongly enough to support the weight of the antenna with the platform and transceiver at the top. He'd taken only one break for food and water, so this diversion gave him a chance for some rest.

Continuing, he said, "There are complications with ground planes, ground wires, and a bunch of other technical stuff and terms that I'm not going to try to explain right now 'cause I'm trying to keep it simple."

"I appreciate that," she said, smiling and staring lovingly into his eyes, doing her best to distract him, just for the fun of it.

Holding back a smile after almost losing himself in the pools of her deep-blue eyes, the electronics expert said, "Come on. Don't do that to me now. It's not fair … I still have a lot of work to do."

Having succeeded in distracting him, Sandy smiled wider. She turned her head slightly, looking at nothing in particular, so that her eyes didn't meet his, but only for a moment.

"Anyway, I'll be cannibalizing wiring from the reentry rocket engine compartment to extend power lines to the transceiver from inside the capsule. The transceiver has to be placed close to the antenna that will be on top of this mast so that I'll have enough coax cable to reach between the transceiver and the antenna. Got it?"

"Mm-hmm," she musically hummed, smiling and gazing into his eyes again, only partially understanding, but not really caring.

"I really have to get back to work, or this will never get done," he said, smiling. Jay appreciated that his being around to distract Sandy took her mind off their dire circumstances. When he hugged her, she rewarded him with a warm loving kiss. He wanted to drop everything he was presently doing but somehow found the will to resist, for at least a little while longer. Jay gave her a light, playful pat on her back to move her along. Smiling, Sandy went inside the capsule, and Jay returned to work on the mast.

Looking at his project while standing on the rim of the depression, Jay decided the antenna needed to be higher. He had a ballpark idea of how high the antenna had to be for the line-of-sight range he wanted, but he'd check his figures on the computer to be sure. He decided to make certain that he could reach out at least twenty-five kilometers with his VHF signal to increase his chances of contact with other survivors.

"I need at least eighteen meters of height above the rim of this depression," he mumbled to himself.

Sandy came back outside and walked to where Jay was standing.

"I have to get more wood for the antenna mast," Jay announced.

"Why?"

"The mast isn't tall enough. I thought I'd be able to mount it to the top of the capsule, but there wasn't anything to attach it to up there. As it is right now, it's only about five meters above ground level because I had to run the mast from the bottom of the depression, and I need at least eighteen meters above level ground to do the job. I lost even more of the length of the antenna mast from having to dig the hole for the mast foundation."

"Is it okay if I stay here?" asked Sandy.

"Of course," he replied.

"Be careful," she appealed, giving him a worried smile.

"Always," Jay said. He gave Sandy a reassuring hug and smile before he turned and headed toward the tree line and she walked back to the capsule.

As Jay moved through the grass, he planned the design of the antenna mast in his head, paying little attention to his surroundings until an unusually large flattened spot in the grass ahead caught his attention.

He approached it cautiously. There he observed an animal that at first resembled a large muscular dog lying on its side, unmoving. Upon closer inspection, the creature looked like a cross between a dog and a wild boar. The unusually large head in proportion to the body resembled that of a large hunting dog, but this animal had a wider face. The mouth and nose were also like that of a hunting canine, except that the end of the snout was more piglike, round and flat on the end with tall slits for nostrils. The body was thicker than a dog's but thinner than a boar's. The body was very muscular, with thick and rather short legs for an animal of its size. Jay was reminded of the legs of a rhinoceros, thick and very powerful. All four toes of each foot had a six-centimeter-long heavy claw. The tail was about half the animal's body length, with a broad, vertical, almost paddle-like blade at the end. The mouth was frozen in a snarling position, as if the animal was in great pain when it died, exposing long canine teeth that looked very sharp. Unlike a wild hog or boar, this animal did not have tusks. Jay thought he could confirm that the animal was a male because of the way it was lying, but he really didn't want to touch it to find out for sure.

Glancing around to see whether it was safe to approach the creature, Jay slowly inched closer. He noticed that the eyes were partially open and glazed. He continued his cautious approach until he reached the animal. He tapped the upturned hindquarter with his foot and stepped back quickly. No response. He sidestepped around to the head of the animal to get a closer look. The head appeared unusually large.

I don't see any wounds, at least on this side, he thought. *I wonder how it died.* The animal was a little over a meter and a half long, with patchwork coloring of light and dark brown, beige, and black. The patches of color were irregular in shape and size. *So this is what was probably following me yesterday, or at least one like it,* he surmised.

There was no wind at the moment, but Jay caught a rustling sound as the dry grass shifted a few meters off to his left. Startled, he instinctively looked toward the source of the sound while placing his hand on the hilt of the knife in his belt. He saw an animal that looked just like the one at his feet, but with a different arrangement of patchwork coloring. This animal was slightly smaller and making intense, direct eye-to-eye contact with him, its large golden-brown eyes unmoving and unblinking.

"Oh, crap!" he whispered as fear began to gnaw at his core. His heart was racing and felt as if it might burst from his chest. Jay couldn't tell whether the creature was ready to spring or was assuming a defensive posture. The animal was slightly crouched but otherwise not making threatening movements or sounds. The animal broke its gaze with Jay for a moment to blink and glance at its dead companion and then quickly shifted attention back to Jay. Seemingly watching for a reaction from Jay, the doglike creature slowly lowered itself to the ground and put its head between its front legs, alternating between watching Jay and taking the occasional glance at the dead animal lying at Jay's feet.

Never having been around animals much, Jay was slow to realize that the dead animal was probably this creature's mate and that it had been mourning this loss until Jay had unwittingly disturbed the final respects. His fear and heart rate having subsided somewhat, he considered that this encounter might be the only opportunity to interact closely with the wildlife on this planet, so he decided to take a chance. He took a deep breath and exhaled to calm himself and then started talking softly and gently to the crouched animal, consoling it as if it was a young child. He knew there was no way the creature could understand what he was saying, but he hoped that the calming tone of his voice offered comfort. He watched to see what it would do, not giving a thought to the fact that staring into the eyes of an animal was usually a sign of aggression. Like an Earth animal showing submission to an aggressor, it lay there unmoving. Slowly, Jay backed up. He stopped after retreating about three meters to give the animal the opportunity to approach the dead creature, if that was what she wanted, and intently watched her actions. The female pricked her ears and raised her head as she watched Jay move away from her mate. Apparently sensing that Jay was no real threat, she shifted her focus to her dead mate. She slowly stood and approached the dead animal. She then lay by its side, muzzle to muzzle, with body-to-body contact. Many minutes went by. The female did not stir. Continuing to talk using soft tones, Jay slowly reapproached the female and her dead companion. He stopped roughly a meter from the dead male's head, directly opposite that of the female. Only her eyes moved to watch as Jay approached. He continued to talk softly to the creature as he lowered himself to a cross-legged sitting position on the ground. Emboldened by his actions, Jay relaxed somewhat but was afraid to press his luck any further. Having lost many friends on *Copernicus* himself, he empathized with this animal.

Watching the female grieve over the death of her mate, Jay continued to speak softly, offering her words of kindness and sympathy. He wondered to himself, *Man, what am I doing? This is really stupid. Why am I talking to her as if she were human? Am I crazy for doing this? Maybe, maybe not.*

He just felt it was the right thing to do at the time. He sat there for many minutes, softly talking and watching her. When she started to get up, Jay stopped talking. She slowly rose to a sitting position. She met his gaze with sad eyes, looked down at her mate, and then looked back at Jay. She was acknowledging Jay and accepting his presence as a witness. Paying no further heed to Jay, she lightly placed her right paw on the head of the dead male. She looked down at her mate and made a soft, low-pitched grumbling, a moaning sound with distinctive sound patterns at regular intervals. She then lifted her chin toward the sky and gave a grief-stricken howl. She paused for about ten seconds and then repeated the exact same sound sequence and howl. It wasn't until she repeated that sequence once more that Jay realized that the sound pattern was exactly the same. He was astonished.

Language? Chanting? Singing? Whatever it is, it's phenomenal! His attention was totally riveted on her. The female removed her foot from her mate and stood. Once she was standing on all four legs, she closed her eyes and lowered her head until her nose touched the tip of her mate's nose. Keeping her nose close to the male's nose, and with her eyes closed, she stepped back with only her rear legs and stopped.

Bowing? She's bowing to him! Jay was incredulous. Her actions were difficult for him to believe, but there they were. It was a true bow, not a stretch like a dog yawning after an afternoon nap. It appeared to be a bow of respect. She pushed back with her front legs to rise to a standing position and didn't open her eyes until she was fully upright. She made the same exact soft low-pitched moaning sounds one more time, except she added a bit more to the end. Then she let out the sad wail of a distraught being. Jay realized that her actions must be some sort of grieving ritual. It was as if she was performing a well-rehearsed ceremony. He had heard of animals on Earth that showed grief for the loss of mates, but this behavior was far beyond that. The understanding that her mate was dead was readable on her face. She not only behaved as if she was grieving; she also looked like it and took action on it, both vocally and physically. Jay also felt that she didn't just accept his presence there but actually wanted him to be there to witness the act and to share in her grief. Unreasonable as his own interpretations seemed to him, that was how he perceived the situation. He couldn't help thinking that she held much more intelligence than one would expect for a wild animal.

Jay felt true sympathy for her. She remained standing for a moment and then sat back on her haunches, staring at Jay with sad, unblinking eyes. Getting the hint, he stood and slowly backed away. Still astonished at what he had seen, Jay found himself breaking eye contact with her and dropping his open hands near his hips, palms facing the female, as he bowed his head, acknowledging respect for the dead. With his face still pointed toward the ground and his eyes cautiously looking up, he continued moving backward for twenty-five meters, holding his hand near, but not on, the handle of the knife on his belt as a "just in case" preparation if she were to follow and attack him. When she didn't, he turned around and headed to the tree line to harvest the supplies he needed without further incident. Several hours later, as he was dragging the cut wood on the way back to the pod, Jay noticed that the female had departed. Ground insect–like creatures were already devouring the corpse; indeed, most of the creature's body had already been eaten. He was truly saddened for the other animal's loss, yet excited at the potential prospects yet to come.

Unable to contain his excitement as he approached the capsule, Jay shouted, "Sandy! Sandy!"

Fearing the worst, Sandy poked her head outside the open hatch. She expected to see a bloodied Jay missing an arm or leg or something even worse. "What's wrong?" she shouted back.

"Nothing! I've had the most incredible experience!"

Dropping the wood he'd harvested near the capsule, he climbed inside. Wide-eyed but grateful that nothing seemed to be wrong with Jay, Sandy greeted her man with a full-body hug. Overwhelmed with excitement, Jay broke the embrace.

Still holding her by the waist, he said, "I had another encounter with the animals out there, but this time it was okay!"

As he told her about the encounter, he calmed down, reexperiencing the sorrow he had felt for the female at her loss. Sandy listened quietly. Now more seriously Jay said, "I think these are highly intelligent creatures … I have to think of a name for them. I can't keep calling them animals or creatures. They look like a cross between a dog and a pig or hog, but with rhinoceros-type legs and heavy claws. Hmm … doghog … no, doboarhino … but no horn on the nose. Dogoar, hogodog … no. Rhinoog … pidogg … yes, yes! That's it! Pidogg! How about pidogg, like 'pig' without the letter g and then 'dog,' with the accent on the first syllable?" he asked.

"I like that better," Sandy said, "but—"

"Pidogg it is then!" he said before she could finish her sentence.

Sandy raised her knitted eyebrows and looked at Jay with one of those "you have to be kidding" expressions. "Really? You think that's a name?"

Mocking sincerity, Jay replied, "Hey, even I know that the person who discovers a new species of some kind gets to name it. Since I haven't a clue how to name it in that dead Latin language, I'm naming it so *I* can remember it."

Sandy laughed, and Jay joined her. It was good to hear her laugh. There hadn't been any real heartfelt laughter since before they'd had to evacuate the *Copernicus*. They hugged and held each other for a long moment. Even though their situation was dismal, Jay, for the first time in his life, felt complete.

7

After spending the day resting and looking after Dr. Rhodes, Chris and Ron arrived back at their capsule as the last of the daylight was fading.

"I'm going to harvest some of that grass to make a mat. Sleeping on the floor last night wasn't the most comfortable way I've ever slept," Chris said.

"Are you sure you want to go out after dark?" asked Ron. "We still don't know if those animals are dangerous."

"I'm not going more that a few meters from the hatch. If it will make you feel better, why don't you stand watch at the hatch with my pistol?" Chris replied.

"Sure," Ron said, "but what about bugs? Aren't you afraid the grass might contain something like bedbugs, or fleas or ticks? You'd be bringing them in here to cohabit with us, and we might not be able to get rid of them."

"Uh … you're right. I must be *really* tired. You'd think I'd know that. Okay, thanks. I'll do it in the morning when I can see the creepy little buggers. Let's flatten the grass around the capsule, though. Maybe that will keep the animals from getting too close like they did last night."

Ron agreed.

Once finished and back inside the capsule, Chris spread his sleeping bag on the floor, did his best to minimize his discomfort, and promptly went to sleep.

In the morning, Chris ate a hasty breakfast. Ron was still asleep. He needed rest so that his arm would heal. Quietly opening and closing the hatch, Chris stepped outside and surveyed the area.

He knelt down and inspected the grass blades closely for insect-type life. Instead of insects, he saw a small animal resembling a vole scamper away. *Interesting. Higher life forms must evolve in similar ways on similar planets. I still don't understand why we haven't seen more insect life here. There should be an abundance of them.* He remembered the bug that Ron had described to him and that he had yet to see. *Maybe they're the reason, but I haven't seen any of them yet either, let alone enough of them to eat all the bugs that should be here.*

Not seeing any insect life on the grass, Chris harvested more than he thought he would need to make a bed mat. After making several trips to carry the grass back to escape pod, Chris sat cross-legged on the ground and began to weave the wide blades of grass together. The tough, fibrous lower two-thirds made a great base for the mattress. The upper one-third of the grass was more flexible and springy yet soft, and it made a very comfortable upper part of the mattress when he tried the small section that he had completed.

Chris had been weaving for several hours when Ron appeared in the hatch. "Morning," he said, yawning and stretching as he stepped out of the capsule.

"Sleep well?" Chris asked, somewhat sarcastically.

"Like a baby. The pills Doc gave me kept the pain down pretty good," Ron responded.

"Good. At least someone around here got a good night's sleep," Chris grumbled as he continued to weave his mat.

Ron just smiled, turned, and stepped back into the capsule to make his breakfast.

Chris, still moody, set his partially made mattress aside and said, "I'll finish this mat later. I'm going to take a radio and start walking west a few kilometers to see if I can raise anyone. I know there are other survivors out there. What I don't know is how far away they are. While I'm gone, I'll keep a lookout for something to supplement our food supply. I'll be back in a few hours."

Undoubtedly noticing the irritation in Chris's voice, Ron said, "Be careful out there. I'll listen in on the capsule radio. Check in every so often to let me know you're still alive, would you?"

"Sure thing."

Chris grabbed his backpack and the rifle and set out west. He walked for several kilometers and made several radio calls, all of which went unanswered, except those to Ron. He had a hard time concentrating on walking a straight line. For that matter, he had a hard time concentrating at all. His thoughts kept returning to his narrow escape from the *Copernicus* and the friends he'd lost. He realized this was going to be more difficult than he'd thought, and after several hours he gave up and returned to the campsite.

As Chris approached, Ron stepped out of the capsule. "Anything?" he asked.

"Nothing. No answers from my calls, and I didn't see any game animals or edible plants either." Feeling weary from the trip, Chris said, "I have to get some better rest at night. I'm feeling foggy-brained and irritable, and not enough sleep is physically wearing me out. I couldn't even walk a straight line. Following my trail through the grass back to here was very revealing. It weaved all over. I must have added a kilometer or more to the trip from all the meandering."

Ron replied, "Well, right now we have plenty of provisions, so why don't we take a few days to rest up before we try something like that again? We can't afford to have anyone get lost out there."

"Agreed."

Jay had to make two more trips to the tree lot to gather more vines and material to complete the mast. Needing the antenna mast to be tall, he had to customize the ends of the poles to fit tightly together and then lash them securely in place. He carved the narrow end of the log into a meter-long rectangular shape as the male end to insert into the female end of next log that would sit on top. In order to make the female end, Jay carved slits into the wider bottom of the log that would sit on top of the male end. Through the slits, he carved a square opening that matched the square end of the male post. That took a while longer than he anticipated because he ruined two logs by carving the hole too large to receive the male end. Once the posts were all connected, he secured them tightly with nylon seat restraints from the escape pod; those were no longer needed.

As he worked, the female pidogg he had met earlier would come by to watch him, stay for a while, and then wander off. After her first visit, Jay took some leftover scraps and placed them where she could smell them if she decided to visit again. His plan was to get to know her better. It worked. She found the food at once. She sniffed each scrap for several seconds before tasting it—foreign food. She didn't care much for the reconstituted asparagus spears, but Jay could see that she loved the dried meat and reconstituted dried fruit. He started to place the food scraps nearer to the capsule. She started coming in closer, becoming bolder during her visits, and then began visiting more than once per day. The female pidogg was also a very vocal animal. If she thought Jay shortchanged her on a treat, she would make a grumbling, growling sound with an unhappy look to match to let him know she wasn't pleased before she wandered off. Jay made sure he had an extra morsel or two saved for her after that.

Once he had the mast to the length he needed, Jay dug a hole one and a half meters deep, inserted the mast into the hole, and then secured the mast to the capsule. The hard part was shimmying up the pole to attach the vines, to be used as guywires for added support. As an afterthought, he realized that he should have attached the vines while the post was still on the ground. Once that was done, he shimmied up the mast again and mounted the transceiver and antenna to the top where he had built a small platform. Jay left the switch of the transceiver in the on position and covered the unit with one of the silver-sided emergency blankets found in the capsule, to weatherproof his project in case it rained. Having wound the power, microphone, and speaker wires down and around the new antenna mast, he attached the power leads to an on/off switch and the microphone and speaker wires inside the capsule to the appropriate devices.

It had taken four days and a couple of hours in the morning of the fifth, but Jay had finally finished. "What a job!" he said aloud to himself.

Stepping outside and climbing to the edge of the rim overlooking the capsule with Jay, Sandy admired the new antenna. "Wow! That even looks good!" she exclaimed, impressed with his handiwork.

Jay replied, "I will admit, it was a lot of work, but if we can make contact with any of the others, it will have been well worth it. Let's go inside and see if it works."

Jay hit the power switch. The reliable FM VHF transceivers, with auto squelch, received radio signals with very little static, so at first he was uncertain that the transceiver had actually turned on.

He turned the auto squelch off at the switch on the microphone, verified the transceiver was on, and reset the squelch to minimum. He hesitated and then brought the microphone to his mouth and said to Sandy, "Here goes. Cross your fingers!" Jay pressed the transmit button and using proper military radio protocol said, "Any station, any station, this is *Copernicus* CS1. Over." He released the transmit button to wait for a reply. A few seconds later, he pressed the button again and repeated, "Any station, any station, this is *Copernicus* CS1. How do you read? Over."

Chris and Ron were outside the capsule when the transmission came over the radio inside the escape pod. Hearing the radio crackle to life, both Ron and Chris turned and looked at the open hatch. Jumping up from his sitting position, Chris almost knocked Ron over running to the radio. Ron scrambled in behind him. Chris recognized the voice. Snatching the microphone from its holder on the bulkhead and forgetting proper protocol again, Chris exclaimed, "Jay! Are you all right? This is Chris Elliott. Did anyone else make it out with you?"

There was a moment of silence before Jay replied. "It's great to hear your voice, Chris. I'm fine. Sandy Brooks made it out with me. She's okay too. Over."

Chris said, "That's great to hear! Have you any idea how far away you are from us? Over."

"Well, it's complicated, but I estimate based on the height of my antenna that we have to be within twenty-five kilometers of each other. Over."

"Roger. That's about eight to nine hours' travel time from here. I'm here with Ron Johnson, and Doc Rhodes is about three kilometers from our position. Break. Doc, are you listening in? Over."

"Yes, I've been listening. It's great to hear your voice, Jay. Tell Sandy I said hello. *Copernicus* CP1 out."

"It's great to hear you too, Doc. I'm glad you made it off the ship. Break. Still there, Chris? Over," Jay called.

"That's affirmative. How are your supplies holding out?" Chris asked. "Over."

"Okay for now. There are only two of us in a four-man pod, and I grabbed extra backpacks from some damaged pods, so we have plenty," replied Jay, "but eventually we'll run out. We haven't found a local source of food or water yet. Over."

"Roger that, understood," Chris acknowledged.

Jay continued, "We have to devise a plan to get together and pool our resources to increase our odds of survival until rescue."

Chris replied, "My thoughts exactly. Ron, Doc Rhodes, and I will put our heads together to see what we can come up with. We'll give you a call back in about a day. Chris out."

Before Jay could acknowledge Chris, a different voice piped in on his radio, this one female. "This is *Copernicus* XO. CS1, do you read? Over."

At first, Jay just looked at his speakers, not believing his luck at reaching another survivor. Excited, he answered, "*Copernicus* XO, this is *Copernicus* CS1. I read you five by five! Over!"

"CS1, is there any chance of including us in your rescue plans? I have Miranda Stevens with me. Over."

"XO! Yes! Yes! Break. Chris, the XO and Miranda Stevens are safe also. Can you read their transmissions? Over!"

Chris could hear Jay responding to another radio call and knew it was the XO, the *Copernicus*'s executive officer, because Jay had used her call sign, but he could not hear what she was saying because the XO was too far from his position.

"No, she's too far away," Chris answered. "Tell her I said welcome to Tau Ceti g and that we're all grateful that they were able to make it off the ship too. Also, ask her what their current situation is. Over."

Jay relayed Chris's comments and question.

The XO replied, "We have the standard supplies for a four-man pod, so right now we're doing okay, but our water supply is running low. We have enough for only one more day. Three out of the four water containers had holes in them, probably from the meteor storm. How they got punctured without this pod being damaged is a mystery, but we do have one good container. We have access to water nearby, but the local fauna is abundant, and we're not sure it's safe to venture out. They've been by to investigate us, and some of them are massively large. We watched some of the biggest ones fight. They resemble an elephant-like water buffalo, only bigger … much bigger. There are many that seem harmless too. They look a lot like deer or antelope, and others resemble sheep and goats but bigger; we've seen these grazing on the grass. But some of the others looked very dangerous. We witnessed one pack of animals killing and eating one of the smaller of the water-buffalo animals, so we know they are carnivorous and dangerous. Over."

"What did the carnivorous ones look like?" Jay asked.

The XO answered, "Like a very muscular dog with short heavy legs, patchwork-colored fur, and a large, wide head. Over."

"Did the end of the snout look like a pig's? Over."

"That's affirmative. Over," she responded.

"It's a pidogg," he stated with authority. "I had a sad but successful encounter with one last week. A female's mate died, and I got to witness some kind of a grieving ceremony. They're extremely intelligent. They may even have a rudimentary language from what I was able to tell. It was a friendly encounter. She's been making daily visits near my camp since. Break. Chris, the XO has water and animal life near her landing site. Over."

"That's great!" Chris exclaimed. "Glad to hear they're friendly too. Ron and I also had a visit from a small pack of them, if your description of the nose is accurate, but they didn't show themselves. Once they got a good whiff of us, their curiosity was apparently satisfied, and they left. We haven't seen them since. Pidoggs, huh? Over."

Jay picked up on Chris's amused tone. "Yeah, pidoggs," he said in a mockingly smug voice. "As the first one to see them and describe them, I get to name them, isn't that right, Doctor Know-It-All Xenobiologist?"

Chris held back a chuckle and said, "Yes, in the strictest sense of protocol, but the description normally includes the species, genus, family, and class of the critter. We can talk about that later, but for now, pidogg it is. Over." The chuckle escaped Chris before he let up on the transmit button.

After a few moments of silence, Jay came back on the radio, feigning indignity. "Okay, Dr. Big Shot, I bow to your superior knowledge. Speaking of knowledge, when you're planning your foray to my campsite, figure out how we can rescue the women also. They have to be within the same twenty-five-kilometer radius from me, only further west. Over."

Still smiling, Chris replied, "Wilco. We should have something in place by tomorrow evening. We'll let you know. Are your solar panels active and keeping your batteries charged? Over."

Jay replied, "That's affirmative. Break. XO, how are your solar panels? Are they holding up and generating power? Over."

"That's affirmative," the XO replied. "Everything's working as expected so far. Over."

"Great! Break." Jay relayed to Chris the information from the XO.

Chris radioed back, "Ron, Doc Rhodes, and I will formulate a plan to get to you and then on to the XO and Miranda. Let's hope that we don't run into trouble on our way. We have small-arms weapons only, nothing that would stop anything larger than a deer-size animal. Keep your radios on, and I'll contact you as soon as we have something firm. Chris out."

Relaying the conversation with Chris, Jay informed the XO to expect them within a few days and urged caution when replacing their water supply.

Excitement overwhelming his usually calm demeanor, Chris said, "Yes! This is better than I expected. When I abandoned *Copernicus*, hell's fury was upon us, and I didn't expect anyone to survive long enough to get to the escape pods, let alone seven of us. Ron, you're the left-brained logical thinker around here—what are your ideas?"

"Well, for starters, staying here isn't an option. We only have enough food and water to last about another week unless we go on partial rations. We have to find a source to replenish what we're consuming, or we die. The only real problems that I foresee are the unknown dangers that we face going cross-country. It's not the distance that I'm concerned about. We can make it in less than a day to Jay's, and then at most it will be another day to get to the XO's landing site. It's what we might meet between here and there. The weapons we have will be inferior if we confront something as large and dangerous as the XO described." Holding his elbow, Ron closed his eyes and paused for a moment before continuing. "Somehow, we have to beef up our arsenal to ensure our safety. All we really have available, metaphorically speaking, are sticks and stones that are just somewhat better than what the caveman had against the mammoth and saber-toothed tiger. Why don't they stock the pods with better weapons?"

Chris said, "The .22 caliber has mostly been considered the best survival rifle because the ammunition is light and plentiful, and it's more than enough to take down small game. And if you can hit the chest and pierce both lungs, you can take down a deer-size animal. My guess is that if plenty of ammunition, weight, and storage space were a consideration when the UESF stocked the capsules, the .22 was at the top of the list for weapons. Laser pistols and rifles require specialized power sources that can't be charged from solar panels, and you can't eat flesh that's been shot with a disrupter weapon."

"I guess the powers that be didn't think we'd have to defend ourselves. A terajoule disrupter would be a great addition right now. What do we do if we need to kill something big and dangerous?" Ron asked.

Chris thought for a moment while rubbing his whiskered chin. "If there are any trees or other woody plants around, we may be able to make bows, arrows, and spears if the wood is suitable. We can attach our survival knives to the spears if we can't find proper stones for weapon tips. We'd just have to hope not to lose them in an animal, if the knife were to come off in an animal that then got away. Otherwise, we're down to sharpened sticks. It's not the lack of weapons that I'm concerned about; I'm more concerned with what's available for food. We don't know what's edible or what's poisonous. If it's edible, is it digestible? If it's digestible, is it absorbable and nutritious? Water is water as long as it hasn't been poisoned with some unknown contaminant. The water filters that we have should work, and we have a small supply of water-purification tablets for microorganisms as a backup. Then again, I don't know if the chemical treatment will be effective on the local biology here either. We're in unknown territory in so many ways. Let's take a walk over to Doc's place and have a talk with her." Chris grabbed his backpack, and the two men were on their way.

As Chris and Ron walked to Dr. Rhodes's capsule, Ron asked, "When you mentioned that some foods may not be absorbable and nutritious, what did you mean?"

"I was referring mostly to carbohydrates and whether they're right- or left-handed sugars, but proteins have a molecular rotation, also called handedness. You've heard of dextrose, a sugar, haven't you?"

Scratching and then tapping his head while smiling, Ron said, "Yes, there's a vague memory somewhere in here. It's been a long time since I've had any biology courses."

"Dextrose—or the preferred name, 'd glucose,' for dextrorotatory glucose—is a sugar. Sugar molecules are wound either to the right or to the left and are mirror images of each other. Just as our hands are mirror images of each other, sugars are too. Our bodies can use only the sugar molecules that are wound to the right. If we ingest left-handed sugars, they just pass through without being utilized for energy. The same principle applies to proteins and the direction the amino acids are wound. Proteins are made of amino acids. For whatever reason, all proteins from all living organisms on Earth, and from other worlds that we have studied, have left-handed amino acids. Our bodies can only use left-handed proteins. Science has not been able to determine why all life on Earth and the planets that we've investigated evolved using left-handed amino acids. There's no scientific explanation for why there are no right-handed proteins found elsewhere in nature either. Random chance tells us there should be roughly a fifty-fifty chance for the development of right- or left-handed proteins, but that's not been the case. There are *no* right-handed proteins found in nature, on Earth or the few worlds we've studied so far. It would be like flipping a coin a trillion times and having it always come up heads. Regardless of the reason for the existence of either right- or left-handed sugars and proteins, our bodies can only use right-handed sugars and left-handed proteins. If they are different on this planet, then no matter how much we eat, our bodies will starve."

Ron chuckled and said, "Now that's food for thought."

Chris smiled. "Of course, no pun intended, I presume."

Arriving at Dr. Rhodes's capsule, Ron approached and knocked on the hull next to the open hatch while Chris continued his lookout for wild animals.

"Good morning, gentlemen," she said. "I wasn't expecting you so early."

"We thought we'd get your input on bringing what's needed for the trip to get us all together," said Ron.

Dr. Rhodes stepped out of her capsule and said, "Well, we need to carry as much of our supplies as we can, and I need to bring my medical kit. There are also a few special medical instruments that I need to take that are in the capsule, but I can't carry everything." Turning her head to look at Chris, Dr. Rhodes said, "With Ron able to use only one arm, our carrying capacity is severely limited."

"I guess that means I get to be the packhorse," Chris replied.

"If we can re-rig my backpack shoulder harnesses so that the right shoulder strap comes under my arm and stretches across my chest to attach high on the left strap at the shoulder, I should be able to carry my own pack and maybe a little more," said Ron.

"How much extra bulk and weight are you talking about, Doc?" Chris asked.

"Some of the equipment is a little bulky and a bit heavy. A microscope, a lightweight and very portable mass spectrometer, slides, stain, bottles of antiseptic, antibiotics, blades for scalpels, and a small portable autoclave for small instruments … you know, medical stuff," she said with a smile. "We can store some of those items in the autoclave to save room in the backpacks while traveling. The mass spectrometer is light but a bit bulky. With it, however, I can determine if a food is safe to eat. If we have a medical emergency, having those tools can save a life."

"How about hospital gowns? Got any of those too?" Chris joked.

Dr. Rhodes frowned.

Seeing that Dr. Rhodes didn't appreciate his humor, Chris changed the subject, turned to Ron, and asked, "Do you think you can carry two or three extra kilograms in your pack?"

"Sure. I have a good idea how I want to arrange my straps so I can carry the load without hurting my bad shoulder. Yes, I should be able to do it."

"Good. Doc, do you have extra carrying cases or backpacks that all that stuff can fit into?"

"Yes, I have a carrying case for the autoclave, and I can overstuff some supplies into my backpack. That will free up another of the extra backpacks for the rest. Everything should fit. I'll do what I can to carry extra supplies in my pack, but we may have to stop and rest often. I'm not as young as I used to be, and space travel sure hasn't done much for me staying in shape."

Dr. Rhodes sat on the steps of her capsule, and the men sat cross-legged on the ground on either side of her so that they could keep a watch for predators while they finished their discussion of what they needed for travel, what they could carry, and who would carry what.

Earlier in the week, Chris had devised a way of capturing dew from the grass for making potable water to stretch their supply. It was a simple device that consisted of a plastic sheet, a container to capture water, and a small tool to be used as a weight.

Ron said, "Chris, explain to me again how that water-gathering device works."

"It's quite simple," Chris answered. "You dig a hole in the ground and place the water-capture container in it. Then you clip the grass short to the ground, chop it into small pieces, and leave it lying on the ground around the hole. Make sure the container doesn't have any debris in it and is clean. Spread the sheet over the grass clippings and make sure the middle of the sheet is over the container. Prop up the edges of the plastic sheet over the grass clippings at about twenty-five to thirty centimeters high, allowing a wall to form around the perimeter, with the edge of the plastic sheet touching the ground. We can use the tall grass for the wall support. This traps air and, more importantly, the moisture in the air under the sheet. Pull the sheet somewhat tightly across the walls and secure the edges to the ground with weights. Place a tool or rock, or whatever weight you can find, in the center of the sheet and over the container so there is a slope toward the container. As the sun warms the ground first thing in the morning, the moisture from the ground and grass clippings will condense on the plastic sheet, eventually forming rivulets of water that drain into the container. It's not much, and it tastes like grass, but it's enough to keep someone alive if their water supply ran completely out."

They decided to use this method to capture as much water as they could in the mornings until they could find a potable water supply.

Chris shifted over to sit between Dr. Rhodes and Ron and said, "Okay. To make things a little easier in finding north on this planet, I've modified an old trick hikers use when they don't have a compass, and it should work on this world. I wish I'd thought of it before I trekked all the way here. With all the confusion and excitement, I just plain forgot about it. I was extremely lucky to find Ron's capsule because with no navigational aids and no visual landmarks, it was very difficult to walk a straight line. To make our modified compass, we need an analog watch that keeps a day of 28.7 Earth hours. That's what the capsule computer had for planetary rotation here. Since we don't have an analog watch, let alone one that keeps the length of day we need, I wrote a program on my tablet computer that shows a twelve-hour analog watch face, but calibrated to match this planet's rotation." Chris retrieved his tablet computer from his backpack and started the clock program. "Look at this. To find north, you hold the watch face level to the ground and point the hour hand at the sun. Half the distance between the hour hand and the twelve o'clock position will point south since we're in the northern hemisphere. One hundred eighty degrees on the watch dial from the position that points south will be north. I'm not a math whiz like our engineering friend Ron here, but I was able to stretch out the timing so that the twelve hours shown on the watch face equals half of the 28.7-hour day on this planet. Besides, I'd rather be looking at something that's familiar, and I can read a twelve-hour analog clock. Each planet-side hour now represents 1.19583 Earth hours. So if you ever wanted to have more hours in the day to get more work done, now you have it."

Knowing exactly what Chris meant, both Ron and Dr. Rhodes

gave a little chuckle. Ron asked, "Are you sure the compass trick will work here?"

Chris responded, "I'm pretty sure it will work, but as a backup, since this method hasn't been tested here yet, we'll do a leapfrog departure that will verify our makeshift compass. I'll start out first, walking west for about a hundred meters. Doc will then follow in my trail and continue an additional hundred meters, either walking backward or checking backward every few steps to ensure that the trail she is creating is in line with me and the trail behind me. Then it's your turn, Ron, and then my turn, Doc's turn, et cetera, until we get within radio-contact range of Jay and Sandy's capsule." Chris turned the tablet computer off and put it back into his backpack. He continued, "Another trick that I have up my other sleeve is using our handheld radio as a DF unit … sorry, directional finding unit. That will fine-tune our track when we get within communication range. It's really quite simple too. It's called body blocking. We ask Jay to transmit something for, say, twenty seconds. Then while holding our radio to our chest, we turn in place until the signal is blocked. We'll then know that his signal is coming from the opposite direction we're facing. If we need to, we can do this every kilometer or so to make sure that we do stay on track. Once we can get within four kilometers of their capsule, we should be able to see it, so if we're off by a kilometer or so, or if the capsule didn't land exactly on this latitude, we should still be okay. Most likely, we'll be able to see his antenna much sooner. I'm estimating it will take between seven and eight planet-side hours to get there, provided we don't run into any trouble. Any questions?"

Standing up to stretch, Dr. Rhodes asked, "Where'd you learn all this?"

Chris and Ron stood also. "A friend of mine that I grew up with had escape and evade training plus search and rescue training in the military, and he showed me a few things. I still can't believe I didn't think of this earlier," Chris replied, shaking his head.

Ron said, "We were all under a lot of stress. It's understandable. What do we do if we run into our little beastie friends out there?"

"If what Jay told us holds true for the pidoggs here, we'll cross that bridge when we come to it. Let's just hope that the big creatures aren't aggressive. Better yet, let's hope we don't see them at all. Just keep my pistol handy, and I'll hang on to your rifle," said Chris. "Any more questions, comments, suggestions?" Chris waited a few seconds and, when no one spoke up, said, "Good. If we're all in agreement, I'll call Jay after we're done here and let him know our plans."

Chris helped Dr. Rhodes pack her backpacks for the next two hours. They couldn't fit all the regular supplies in the backpacks, so they pared down to the items that would keep them alive the longest.

Once they were done, Chris said, "Ron, let's get everything prepared back at your capsule and get a good night's sleep. We leave first thing in the morning."

Throwing one of Dr. Rhodes's backpacks across his shoulders, Chris said to her, "I'll take this one back with us now since we'll be setting off from our capsule. We'll be back for you and the rest of the packs in the morning. Ready, Ron?"

"Yep, let's go," he replied.

The next morning, Chris and Ron were outside the capsule making the final preparations with their gear for the trip. After several minutes spent bent over rearranging the gear in his backpack, Chris stood up and stretched, a big series of stretches, one at a time, arms up and out, to help his upper and lower back muscles. While at the peak of his stretch to the right, he caught movement out of the corner of his eye. There was Dr. Rhodes about a kilometer away, struggling with a bag in each hand and wearing her backpack.

Nodding his head in the doctor's direction, Chris said, "Holy cow, will you look at that? I got it."

Ron looked up as Chris trotted out to meet Dr. Rhodes.

"What the heck do you think you're doing, Doc?"

Breathing hard and looking exhausted, she said between gasps for breath, "I didn't want you to … have to walk … to my camp …

just to carry … all this gear back … this way … I guess … I'm in worse … shape … than I thought."

Chris took the two bags she was carrying in her hands, set them down, and assisted her in taking her backpack off. "That's a lot of weight for you to carry. As a doctor you should know better," he chided.

"I'll be okay. I just need a few minutes' rest," she said, catching her breath as she sat cross-legged on the ground, leaning hard on her backpack.

"What would you have done if you were attacked by a wild animal? You wouldn't have been able to get to your firearm in time to protect yourself." Chris paused for a moment to look at her waist. "And you're not even wearing your knife!" Dr. Rhodes's survival gear also included a .22-caliber folding-stock rifle with a brick of ammunition and a survival knife.

"You're right. I've never been able to take an active part in any practice survival situation. I was always back at the base camp treating minor injuries and never got a chance to do this for real. Thanks for looking after me. I'll be more careful in the future."

With that, Dr. Rhodes sat up and pulled her backpack around in front of her. She dug through the backpack, retrieved her survival knife, and put it on her belt. "If it comes to shooting, I'll leave that to you and Ron until you can give me some lessons on how to safely load it, point it, and hit the target without shooting myself in the foot—or anyone else—due to my ignorance. Deal?"

Feeling a bit ashamed about having gone after Dr. Rhodes as he had, Chris calmed down, smiled, and nodded his head. "It's a deal," he said softly.

After a few more minutes of rest, Chris helped Dr. Rhodes stand and assisted with her backpack by slipping the straps over her shoulders. He adjusted the shoulder straps correctly and made sure the waist belt was snug so that the weight rode high on her back, to minimize the chance of lower back pain or injury and to reduce fatigue.

She smiled and said, "I feel much better now. Thanks, Chris. I really do appreciate your help." Chris acknowledged her with a nod of his head while scooping up the other two bags and throwing one over each shoulder. They walked in silence back to Ron's camp with Dr. Rhodes trailing Chris through the tall grass.

He's right, Holly Rhodes thought as they continued to the capsule. *I should know better, especially after the head injury. My heart was pounding back there, and with every beat of my heart, my head throbs. I need to take it easy on myself, but I don't want to let these guys down or make them work harder than necessary. I have to be able to carry my own weight; they're already carrying more than their share.*

Ron watched from the capsule as the two approached and said, "Everything seems to be in order here. I talked to Jay on the radio to let him know that we would be on our way soon. He said that we'd probably be out of radio contact for a while because our handheld radio antennas aren't as high off the ground as the antenna on the capsule. I gave him a rundown of our plans and told him to expect us sometime later today."

"Ron, how are your arm and shoulder feeling?" Dr. Rhodes asked.

Not looking directly at her, Ron replied, "It still burns, but I'm managing."

"You should let me take a look at your arm and shoulder before putting on your backpack."

"That's okay, Doc. You can look at it later today. We really should get going now. What do you say, Chris?"

"I say it's Doc's call," Chris replied.

Doc answered, "I'll tell you what. Let me just check the bandage. If it's still in place, I'll postpone replacing it until after we reach Jay and Sandy's place, okay?"

Ron agreed. Dr. Rhodes gave his arm a quick look, and seeing that the bandages hadn't shifted since the day before, she gave the okay to wait to change them until after they arrived at Jay and Sandy's capsule.

Chris assisted Ron with his backpack and checked the modified shoulder strap to be sure it wasn't going to cause a problem. "Nice job, Ron. How does it feel?" Chris asked.

"A little tight across the chest, but I'll manage. I hope I won't have to run—it'll be hard to take a deep breath," he said, smiling but with serious intent.

Before putting anything on his own back, Chris tied one of Dr. Rhodes's bags to the top of his own backpack and the other underneath. "Can you guys give me a hand with this?" he asked.

Ron one-armed Chris's backpack up high enough that Chris could slip his arms through the shoulder straps and close the quick release buckles across his chest and abdomen. Dr. Rhodes helped Chris adjust the strapping to prevent chafing anywhere. Chris then asked Dr. Rhodes to tie his sleeping bag to the top bag on his main backpack so that the sleeping bag hung directly behind the extra bag.

Even though his arm hurt, Ron was in a good mood and was looking forward to getting together with the rest of the survivors. He shut the hatch on the capsule. "What do you think? Should I lock it? I heard this could be a pretty rough neighborhood," he joked.

Chuckling at Ron's humor, Chris looked around to make sure the camp was secure and they had all their gear. "Looks like we're ready. I've downloaded as much information about the planet as was available from the capsule's computer, and I have the analog clock-compass all set to go. Ron, Doc, I need your help in watching for danger. We've been lucky so far. Watch for movement in the grass. An animal doesn't need to be large to do us in. If you see anything at all, holler out."

Dr. Rhodes looked over at Ron with a fearful look of apprehension and then back at Chris. Ron and Dr. Rhodes nodded their heads in agreement.

"Then let's do it!" said Chris.

8

Caitlyn Clayton Carver, the XO, opened the locker where the water was stored and reached in to remove the container. She shook it. Turning around with the container still in her hand, she said, "We're almost out of water. We have to get more. It's going to be days, or maybe a week, before the rest of the survivors arrive."

Miranda gave her a frightened look. "I can do without washing for a few days."

Caitlyn responded, "We don't have enough for drinking, let alone washing. We have to replenish our supply, or we risk dehydration and death. Look." Caitlyn shook the can and poured out less than half a liter into a clear cup and set it on the table. She set the container on the deck near the locker and looked at Miranda.

Realizing their dilemma, Miranda shouted, "I can't go out there! You saw those animals—they're huge and dangerous!" Looking down at the deck and the empty water container, she was on the verge of tears.

Caitlyn walked over and put her hands on Miranda's shoulders. "We have to have water, and I can't do this by myself. I need you to watch my back while I'm collecting and filtering the water into the container. It wouldn't do you any good to have me attacked and dead now, would it? It won't take long to get the water once we reach the lake."

Miranda bit her lower lip to keep her chin from trembling. She turned and walked to the opposite side of the capsule and faced the bulkhead, hiding her frightened expression.

Caitlyn said in a softer voice, "I'm as frightened of what's out there as you are. I need you to be strong and vigilant. I need your eyes and ears watching and listening for danger while I'm stooped over getting the water. Have you ever watched those nature shows back home? Predators hang out near the water holes and attack their victims when their backs are turned toward them. I'll have my back to the land while filling the container. I'll be totally vulnerable at that point. I *need* you."

Miranda slowly turned toward Caitlyn. She wiped the tears that were streaking down her face.

Caitlyn's heart went out to Miranda, but she held firm. She knew they had to take the chance to get the water they needed, and it was much more dangerous to do it alone.

Lowering her eyes to the deck and avoiding Caitlyn's eyes, Miranda murmured, "I'll do my best."

Caitlyn retrieved the .22 rifle and made sure it was loaded. She had Miranda retrieve the water container and filter, and they exited the capsule.

The day was warm, the sun was high, and there was a light breeze coming from the lake. There were only a few wisps of clouds very high in the bright blue sky. The strong odor from the animals drinking at the lake carried on the wind to assault the women's olfactory senses.

"Keep a 360-degree lookout and watch for any movement in the grass that may be approaching us," Caitlyn warned.

The women walked as fast as they could through the tall grass toward the lake. They were both nervous but watchful of everything that moved. The breeze was coming from over the lake, so the animals that were there didn't know about the women's approach until they were within visual range. The animals looked like herbivores to the women. Most of them were small deer- or goatlike animals. A few were large and heavily armored like rhinoceroses, but without the horns on their nose. When they did see the women, the animals stood stock-still, but for only a moment. Not sure whether the women were dangerous, but seemingly not taking any chances, the animals bolted away en masse. A few seconds later, the women heard loud snarling, followed by a bleating noise that was cut short. They looked in the direction of the noise and watched as two pidoggs took down one of the larger deerlike creatures.

Miranda, wide-eyed, froze at the sight. Then she found her voice and shouted, her fear evident, "Did you see that?"

"Hush!" Caitlyn said in a loud whisper. "Yes, I did. If we keep quiet and don't attract their attention, they shouldn't bother us now that they have their meal. Besides, they're going to be a couple hundred meters from where we will be. With the other game scattered, it's less likely there will be any other predators nearby—or so I hope! Let's keep going."

Reaching the lake, Caitlyn handed the rifle to Miranda and took out the water container and filter. All UESF personnel had weapons training, so Caitlyn wasn't worried about Miranda's marksmanship, but she was worried that Miranda might panic and not shoot when she needed to. She filled the container and back-flushed the filter. The full water container was heavy and awkward to carry.

"Give me a hand with this, would you?" Caitlyn asked Miranda. "Here, hand me the rifle and let's both grab the handle."

Miranda gave the rifle to Caitlyn, and they began walking back, side by side, with the heavy load between them. They were about one hundred meters from the escape capsule when they heard the pidoggs barking loudly, growling, and snapping their teeth, sounds that were mixed with an even louder, more ominous roaring. Looking back toward the lake, about three hundred meters away, the women spotted two gigantic bearlike creatures, one larger than the other, approaching the pidoggs at a loping run.

"Oh my God!" Miranda exclaimed. Panic overtook her. She dropped her side of the water container and ran toward the capsule. The larger of the bearlike animals saw the movement and came to a stop, but for only a moment.

Caitlyn looked toward the fleeing Miranda and then back at the giant creature. She was directly between them. The creature was already moving at a full run toward her. With no time to waste, she dropped the water container and ran as fast as she could toward the capsule. She still had the rifle in her right hand and knew the creature was gaining on her. She could hear the grunts getting louder and louder behind her, but she didn't dare take the time to turn and look; she knew that the .22 was no match for the giant beast. Miranda had made it to the capsule and now waited at the open hatch.

"Hurry!" Miranda shouted.

Fifty meters more! Can I make it? Caitlyn was running for her life. Her shoulder-length medium-brown hair was trailing behind her. Breathing was getting harder, and her legs felt like they were running through molasses as they tried to move her trim sixty-two-kilogram mass to safety. With twenty meters to go, Caitlyn could hear the heavy breathing and the rush of grass being pushed aside as the animal gained on her. Ahead, Miranda stood with her hand on the handle, ready to close the hatch, tears running down her cheeks as she screamed for Caitlyn to hurry. Everything seemed to be moving in slow motion. Miranda turned her face away.

Ten meters. I'm not going to make it. Please let this be over with quickly.

The hatch closed.

Travel was a little slow. Dr. Rhodes's backpack was wearing her down bit by bit. She was thankful for the leapfrog technique, which gave her a little rest each time she stopped. She wished she had a small portable seat to sit on during the stops, but then that would have been even more weight to carry. She settled for sitting on the ground and leaning on her backpack. She noticed the pleased look on Chris's face when he looked back on the trail, apparently satisfied that it was relatively straight. There had been a few slight deviations, but those had been easily corrected. So far, his makeshift analog clock compass seemed to be working well.

They had been traveling for about two hours, keeping their leapfrog formation, when Dr. Rhodes stumbled and fell forward while trying to keep up the pace. She shouted out as she fell, and hearing her cry for help, Chris and Ron ran toward her. She was trailing the men, and Chris reached her first since he was the closest. He helped her to a sitting position and removed her backpack so that she could use it as a backrest.

"Can we take a short break?" she asked.

Chris nodded. "Sure, let's take a twenty-minute break, drink some water, and eat a protein bar. Are you sure you're going to be okay?"

Dr. Rhodes nodded and then watched as Chris walked away, busying himself with his tablet computer and studying the surrounding countryside. She was in no position to argue. After Chris helped her slip out of her backpack, she had collapsed against it. Ron offered her some water. Too tired to retrieve her own from her backpack, she gladly accepted and drank deeply.

"Are you feeling okay, Doc?" he asked.

"To be honest, I'm bushed," she said.

Dr. Rhodes watched as Ron walked over to talk with Chris and then closed her eyes. She couldn't quite make out what they were discussing, but she was almost certain it was about her. Her head was pounding, her back was sore and cramping, and her legs felt like rubber. Her breathing was labored too, and with every beat of her heart, she could feel the pulse in her hands, arms, and legs. She figured this trip would either kill her or toughen her up, and presently she was leaning more toward the "kill her" possibility. She felt awful, but she didn't want to let her shipmates down.

She finished the water that Ron had given her but didn't touch her protein bar. She was starting to catch her breath, but even though the temperature was cool, she was still sweating heavily.

Not quite out of earshot, but low enough that Dr. Rhodes probably couldn't hear clearly, Ron softly said to Chris, "Doc doesn't look good at all. My first aid's a bit rusty, but I'm afraid she may be approaching heat exhaustion. Look at her. She's breathing heavily and sweating profusely, and her face and neck are as red as an apple."

"You're right. I've been so focused on navigating, I've not been paying attention to how you and Doc are holding up."

"Other than my arm and shoulder, I'm managing okay; it's Doc that concerns me," replied Ron.

Chris and Ron approached Dr. Rhodes. "Doc, let's see how much we can lighten your load," Chris said as he knelt down behind her and opened her backpack.

"You don't have to do that. I can carry my own," she insisted.

It was clear to Chris that she felt bad physically, but it was also clear that the idea of the men carrying her supplies was distressing to her too. Chris shook his head. "I don't think so. You're in denial. How does your head feel? I bet it's pounding. Your face is beet-red, and you're still sweating buckets. If this were happening to me, what would you prescribe, *doctor*?" Chris said sternly.

Too exhausted to argue, she said in a resigned voice, "Okay, okay, you're right again. I surrender to your better judgment."

Chris pulled most of the items from Holly Rhodes's backpack. He was amazed at the number of items and weight she had in there, and he let it show in his face.

"All field medics have to carry a full complement of medical supplies in addition to the regular pack supplies for a total of sixty kilograms," Dr. Rhodes explained.

Chris exclaimed, "You don't even weigh that much, Doc!"

Ron knitted his eyebrows and whistled upon seeing how much was lying on the ground. The men decided to lighten her load by at least a third, more if they could fit it in their backpacks. Chris added fourteen kilograms to the packs he was carrying while Ron overstuffed his and was able to add nine. They extended their rest period to thirty planet-side minutes, ate another energy bar, and drank more water. Rehydrated and with a light breeze blowing to help cool her down, Dr. Rhodes was looking and feeling much better after eating the protein bar and taking the short rest. Ron and Dr. Rhodes hefted their backpacks after assisting Chris with his. They continued their journey.

Another two hours passed before Chris called a halt for a brief rest. His legs were feeling rubbery now. Chris asked Dr. Rhodes how she was holding up, and she told him she was doing much better, tired but not exhausted. They drank some water and munched on protein bars for energy. The makeshift compass was working so well that Chris decided to abandon the leapfrog technique to save time and limit their exposure to potential predators, but he slowed the pace to conserve energy.

"I'm so glad you figured out a way to make a compass. I don't know how you made it across all this grass to find us without one," said the doctor.

"It was certainly a challenge and one that I'd rather not have to repeat," Chris admitted. Looking off in the distance to the southwest, Chris saw the grass begin to undulate in large, deep waves, the grass flattening out more with each successive wave. A few gusts of wind hit his face, and his shirt fluttered in the breeze. The distant grass suddenly flattened right to the ground, and then he heard it—a great howl from the wind that grew louder and louder with each passing second. Particles of dust and pieces of dead vegetation that had been picked up by the wind stung his face. He rapidly looked around, but there was no shelter anywhere.

Chris shouted to be heard above the wind that was now at a constant roar, "Get on the ground and hang on to each other!"

The wind struck them just then, almost knocking Chris and Ron to the ground. There wasn't time to put Dr. Rhodes, the lightest of the three, between the two men. The wind was already doing its best to carry her away to parts unknown. Chris and Ron stumbled after her, struggling to stay upright, with Ron reaching her first. As Ron grabbed her backpack, Chris caught up, and they all fell heavily to the ground. They lay on the ground with Chris holding on to Ron and his backpack and with Ron doing his best to hang on to Dr. Rhodes with his good arm. The howling increased to deafening levels.

Ron lost his hold on Dr. Rhodes, and she started tumbling along with the wind. Ron shouted to tell Chris, but the wind carried his voice away. Ron tried to break Chris's grip, but Chris hung on tightly, perhaps thinking that the wind was trying to separate them. Then as suddenly as it had started, the wind died. Ron finally broke free.

"It's Doc! We gotta find her! I couldn't hang on to her!" Ron shouted as the noise level dropped.

Chris stood up and helped Ron to his feet. The grass, completely flattened just a moment before, was beginning to recover. Chris was already in motion, jogging in the direction the grass was pointing. "Ron, follow me ten meters to my right! We can search more ground that way." Chris had covered a hundred meters when he spotted some medical equipment that must have spilled from Dr. Rhodes's backpack. "Ron, over here!" he shouted. Ron ran to his position. Chris said, "Leave this stuff on the ground. If we need to pick up the trail again, it will be easier if we leave it here. Let's trample the grass the best we can so we will know where we have already searched."

The men followed the trail of medical items for four hundred meters, and twenty minutes later, they found Dr. Rhodes. She was semiconscious, with bruises on her arms and face. Chris removed her half-empty backpack and handed it to Ron as she started to come around.

Chris looked up at Ron. "Leave your backpack here and follow our trail back to retrieve the medical items that fell out."

Feeling awful and clearly blaming himself for losing his grip on Dr. Rhodes, Ron just nodded his head and headed back to pick up what he could find.

Sitting up and holding her head, Dr. Rhodes asked, "What happened?"

"Ron lost his grip, and you went for the ride of your life," he replied.

Chris did a quick check over the doctor's body but found nothing more than a few bruises and elbow scrapes. "Can you stand?"

"I think so. My head hurts, though," she complained.

Dr. Rhodes stood but held onto Chris's arm for balance. "I'll be okay. I just need to rest for a bit." Chris helped her to sit, using Ron's backpack for a backrest.

Ron returned within a half hour and said to Chris, "I think I got it all." He looked down at the doctor and then turned back to Chris. "Is she going to be all right?"

Chris quietly responded, "Nothing seems to be broken. I think she has a bad headache, but other than a few scrapes and bruises, she seems to be okay."

Visibly upset, Ron exclaimed, "Thank God! Chris, I just couldn't hang on to her. The wind rolled me over just enough to put pressure on my burn, and I—"

Chris cut him off with a reassuring tone. "Ron, it's okay. She's going to be fine. We'll just take it slow from here."

Ron could only nod in acknowledgment.

They walked on in silence, still shaken from the windstorm. All were lost in their own thoughts as they contemplated the dangers they had already faced and wondered what new threats they had yet to encounter. The surrounding scenery all looked the same—grass and more grass as far as they could see. No hills, streams, rivers, or lakes. Just grass. Occasionally they would pass small patches of low bushy plants that disappeared after only a few hundred meters. There was nothing else to break the monotony of the grassy plain and the visions of imagined dangers except conversation.

Ron was still feeling guilty about Dr. Rhodes's injuries and wanted to talk to her, just to hear her voice. "Doc, how did you come about studying medicine?"

Her headache now minimal, and feeling just minor discomfort from the scrapes and bruises, she replied, "I guess it started when I was a young girl about eight years old. I was carrying a doll when I tripped and fell on her, separating the joint of her left elbow from her upper arm." Letting some of her professional guard down and remembering the sympathy and heartbreak she had experienced, Dr. Rhodes continued, "I felt so bad! I cried mournfully, knowing that I'd broken her arm. I showed the broken doll to my mother, and she told me that I could be the doctor to fix it. She showed me how to hook the parts back together and how to put a sling around her neck and on her arm. My mother said that I had to wait ten minutes before taking the sling off to give her arm enough time to heal. It was the longest ten minutes of my childhood life. She was my favorite doll. When the sling came off, the arm was still together at the elbow, and I thought I had cured her." Smiling at the pleasant memory, she said, "I was hooked for life. I got so much satisfaction from fixing that doll's arm that I wanted to do it for people too. I downloaded textbooks about anatomy instead of playing online holographic video games with my friends. I didn't understand all the anatomy at first, but it gave me the foundation I needed for a career that has so much satisfaction."

She glowed as she spoke. "Growing up on a dairy farm in Wisconsin, I developed a good work ethic from my hardworking parents and understood that if I worked hard, I could accomplish almost anything I truly wanted. I continued my studies at home and took courses in high school that would benefit my chosen career. I went to Penn State for my premed program and the University of Pittsburgh for my MD. I've taken a variety of postgraduate courses, including emergency medicine and surgery, to round out my education. I helped to heal people from all over Earth during my 'Tour the World' internship. I can't begin to describe the feeling you get when you have helped heal people who can't help themselves—like when you fix a cleft palate on a little girl, and she gives you a meaningful hug and kiss on the cheek for making her feel and look better, or you help a young boy who had a club foot since birth, and you get to see him walk without crutches." Her smile was wide. Dr. Rhodes continued to tell tales of her worldly adventures for the next two hours. The time went by much faster for them.

By Chris's reckoning, they were well past the halfway point, so he decided to give Jay a call on the radio.

"Jay, this is Chris, do you read? Over."

Jay answered the radio on the first call. "Chris, this is Jay. I read you loud and clear. How's the trip coming along? Over."

"Tiring, but we're making progress. We had to slow our pace more than I anticipated because of all the gear we're carrying, and we also had to contend with a whopper of a windstorm. Over."

"Is everyone okay? Over."

"Yes, Doc went for a short joyride and got banged up a bit, but she's a real tough trooper and is going to be fine. Give me a long count so I can DF your position with body blocking. Over."

"If anybody can do body blocking, it's you, big guy."

Chris heard Jay chuckling before he started his count. "Wise guy," Chris mumbled to no one in particular while gradually turning his back toward the west.

Jay counted aloud slowly from one to ten and then back to one.

Verifying the direction with his makeshift compass, Chris called, "Jay, this is Chris again. We're not too far off-track, just a couple of degrees, so we should be there within a couple of hours or so. We'll keep you posted on our progress. Over."

"Roger. I understand that you will be here within a couple of hours and keep me posted. Jay out."

It wasn't long before the group could see the antenna Jay had rigged with the silver blanket near the top. They headed directly for it and gave Jay a call.

"Chris, give me a minute to get my handheld and step outside to see if I can get your signal for a DF and meet you partway. Over."

"Roger. Standing by."

The traveling group took advantage of the moment to stop and rest, especially Chris with his rubbery legs.

A couple of minutes later, Jay called back. "Chris, this is Jay. How do you read? Over."

"Jay, this is Chris. I read you loud and clear. Over."

"I had to climb on top of the capsule to get your signal with this handheld. Give me a long count. Over."

Chris gave him the requested long count.

"Chris, this is Jay. Got your position. Sandy and I are on our way. Over."

"Roger. Understood. Chris out."

"They're on the way to meet us halfway," Chris said with tired excitement in his voice. Urging his rubbery legs to proceed, Chris led the group westward.

Ron smiled, but the expression on his face said that his arm and shoulder were bothering him. Dr. Rhodes nodded, gave a weak but determined smile, and continued to trudge on.

Thirty minutes later, Chris spotted Jay in the distance waving his arms. Ten minutes more, and the groups were embracing each other in greeting.

"Wow! Are we glad to see you! This is great!" said Jay excitedly. "See, honey, I told you things were going to be all right!"

The term of endearment raised some eyebrows. Almost everyone aboard the ship knew that Jay was sweet on Sandy, but they didn't think Sandy was that interested in him; they assumed she just put up with his attention.

"We're glad to be here too," Chris said. "Let's get to your capsule. We're pretty tired."

Dr. Rhodes relinquished her backpack to Sandy after losing the brief argument over it and was visibly grateful for the reprieve. Jay had taken the heaviest of the extra packs that Chris had been carrying and the extra nine kilograms from Dr. Rhodes's pack that Ron had been carrying.

The group was within one kilometer of the capsule when both Chris and Jay spotted a trail in the grass moving toward their position on an intercept course. Chris raised his hand in a clenched fist, elbow bent as a silent signal to stop. The trail continued to lengthen. The grass was a little shorter here, at just above the knees. The trail lengthening stopped for a few moments. The group could hear low growling and teeth snapping, and they held their weapons at the ready. There was a sudden motion from the trail, but on a slight angle away from them. Sandy started to cry softly, and Dr. Rhodes hooked her arm around Sandy's elbow and held her hand in an effort to calm her. All the men readied for action, standing between whatever was in the grass and the women.

Slowly, the trail began to lengthen toward them again. When it was within ten meters of the group, a paddle-shaped tail appeared above the grass, slowly wagging. This confused Chris. A dog wagged its tail when it was happy. Dogs hot on the trail of game animals also wagged their tails.

"What does tail wagging mean for these creatures?" Chris softly wondered aloud.

The tail continued to wag as the trail lengthened toward the group. At five meters away, the trail-making stopped. A moment later, a head popped up above the grass. As suspected, it was a pidogg. The pidogg had something in its mouth, a rodent by the look of it, about the size of a large rabbit. The pidogg looked directly at Jay and headed in his direction.

Jay smiled in apparent recognition. "Wait here," he said. "I recognize that patchwork coloring. This is the pidogg I was telling you about. She's okay. She's friendly."

Chris stopped and watched as Jay and the pidogg approached each other. At about one meter apart, they stopped and looked at each other. The female pidogg lowered her head and dropped the rodent-kill offering at Jay's feet. She made mumbling, groaning sounds reminiscent of the happy sound a dog might make upon having its belly scratched. The pidogg crouched down and put her head between her front legs. Chris shifted to the side to get a better view to watch Jay as he slowly approached and touched the creature on her head. She didn't move other than to close her eyes. Jay began to lightly scratch her head and behind her ears. More mumbling and happy groaning came from the female pidogg.

Jay continued carefully scratching from the head down to the left cheek and onto her neck and under the chin. She didn't object. Softly, with his other hand, Jay began to stroke the animal's head. Her eyes remained closed, and the light mumble-groaning continued. Jay thought this must be the pidogg equivalent of a cat's purring.

He wondered what would happen if the pidogg were to meet the others in his group. *There's only one way to find out*, he decided. In a soft voice, he asked Chris to approach. Cautiously, Chris complied with the request. Jay continued to stroke the pidogg. The pidogg's purring never stopped, even as Chris arrived. She opened her eyes sleepily, looked at Chris, and closed them again. Jay handed Chris the dead rodent.

"I think Sandy has some competition," Chris said half-seriously.

Jay just smiled.

The pidogg let Jay pet and scratch her for a minute more and then opened her eyes wide. Jay stopped and pulled back his hand. She sat up on her haunches, looked at Jay, and then started walking back the way she'd come. She mumbled a noise that seemed directed at Jay. She took a couple more steps, stopped and looked back at Jay, and then took another step and another look back at Jay.

Chris said, "I bet she wants you to follow her."

Chris followed Jay as they walked on the trail created by the pidogg. After following her for about fifty meters, they began to hear whimpering. "Do you hear that?" Jay asked Chris.

Jay asked Chris to stop about five meters short as he continued forward.

After walking slowly to the source of the noise, Jay excitedly shouted, "She has pups!" The proud mom wanted to show off her brood. "Chris! Come here! You have to see this!"

Chris was flabbergasted as he watched the whole event. The rest of the group, not too far behind, observed in awe. Dr. Rhodes smiled. Wide-eyed and bewildered, Sandy quit crying when she saw that Jay was okay. Chris looked back at Ron and the women, who had followed about ten meters behind the two men, and shrugged. Chris slowly approached the mother and her pups. The pidogg mother didn't seem to mind. Jay went to pick one up.

Chris warned, "Be careful. She may be extremely protective and turn aggressive. My own dog has bitten me when I've tried to pick up a new puppy. With the size of her mouth, she could easily take off your hand and half your arm."

Chris watched as Jay hesitated and then continued, just slower. Jay started by petting the mother, and then with his other hand, he began petting one of the pups. There were eight pups total, and they all started to go for his hand. Chris smiled. He thought it was quite comical to watch these sausage-bodied, short- and thick-legged, large-headed miniatures of the mama pidogg climbing over each other to get to Jay's hand. They were licking and clawing and biting just as any terrestrial puppy would. The mother apparently approved of their behavior and seemed to accept Jay as part of an extended family.

Chris was unsure of his role in this, so he just smiled an approving, closed-mouth smile at the mother pidogg when she looked at him. He didn't know whether showing his teeth to her while smiling would be considered an act of aggression, and he didn't want to provoke her.

"It appears that she's adopted you as their surrogate father," Chris said amusingly.

"All kidding aside, we need all the help we can get here. If she has friends, they may befriend us too," Jay replied. "I wonder if they're trainable," he said, almost to himself.

"If so, get used to the idea of fried rodent, roasted rodent, rodent stew, fricasseed rodent, rodent-on-a-stick, and rodent-in-a-grass-basket," said Chris, chuckling.

"Ha, ha, ha," Jay said sarcastically. "If it did come to that, at least we wouldn't starve … You know something? These pups have really sharp teeth. Look at the scratches on my hand already. It's not like they're trying to bite me either."

"Better have Doc clean and put some antiseptic lotion on that when we get back to your place. We have no idea if the microbiology here is harmless or deadly to us," Chris said seriously. "We should get going."

Thirty minutes later, everyone was back at Jay and Sandy's campsite. Dr. Rhodes had perked up considerably. Ron, however, was looking a little worse for wear, but he didn't complain. Dr. Rhodes had reapplied an antiseptic ointment and changed the bandages on his arm. She had then cleaned up Jay's scratches, and it was decided to leave them open to the air since they weren't deep.

9

Once the excitement settled down, Jay radioed the other survivors to bring them up to speed on the events of the day. Miranda answered the radio call and started describing what had happened earlier.

Jay gasped. "Is she …"

"She's going to be okay, I guess. That creature almost got her. She's resting right now. I still can't believe what happened! Another second or so, and it would have gotten her. I could see that she wasn't going to make it and had my hand on the handle, ready to close the hatch …" Emotion got the best of Miranda, and she started sobbing. She let up on the transmit button.

"It's okay, it's okay. We can catch up on what happened later," Jay responded.

Miranda came back. "I … I'm all right."

Miranda went on to explain that their escape pod was less than a kilometer from a large body of water, a freshwater lake, and that there was almost always animal traffic in close proximity to both the capsule and the water. A shallow, narrow stream occupied the center of a wide, otherwise dry riverbed that fed into the lake. Just to the south of the capsule was a large wooded area that seemed to be a refuge for some of the animals. Miranda reiterated that the two women were very uncomfortable leaving the safety of their capsule after witnessing the brutality of a kill that the carnivores had made a few days ago on some of the smaller animals near the lake and after the close call that the XO had experienced.

Jay said, "I understand. Doc told me that she'll need to rest up for a few days before she'll be fit for travel, and Chris and Ron want to take some time to discuss what we may need to travel safely to your location. Did you ever go back for your water container? Over."

"Yes," said Miranda. "It wasn't very far from the capsule. I don't know how the XO had the nerve to go back out and get it after what happened, but she did. She's a lot braver than I am. Thanks for asking, Jay. We should be fine until you get here. Over."

"Roger, understood. See you in a few days. Jay out."

Evening came with another cloudless sky and a chill in the air. As darkness fell, the men built a warm campfire from the scrap wood left over from Jay's handiwork with the antenna mast. The fire felt good in the cooler evening air. Earlier, Dr. Rhodes had proclaimed the rodent safe to eat, and it was slowly roasting on a stick that was stuck in the ground beside the fire.

When standing outside the influence of the fire's light, the group could see the stars were brilliant. "Too bad none of the constellations look familiar from this planet," Jay said when he and Chris left the campfire for a needed nature call.

Chris pointed up. "That one could substitute for the North Star, Polaris. It would make nighttime navigation very easy. Too bad, though," he mused.

"What do you mean?" asked Jay.

"We can't travel at night. It's too dangerous. Many predators on Earth hunt at night. I would imagine the same applies here."

After cleaning up, Chris and Jay rejoined the group sitting around the campfire and volunteered to try the fresh meat. Everyone else ate emergency rations. Chris and Jay proclaimed the roasted rodent tasty, but in need of salt. Chris and Jay moved on to discussion of why a wild animal would befriend an unknown and possibly dangerous creature, offer him food, and then take him to see her pups. Why did this animal trust Jay? It didn't make any sense to Chris.

Chris stirred the campfire and threw on a couple of logs. He shook his head and said, "That is *not* the way of the wild. She should have either attacked you and us or run away as fast as possible to protect her young."

"Doesn't your degree, xenobiology, mean the study of strange life forms?" Jay asked.

"Yes, and today's encounter certainly fits the bill of 'strange.'"

The two men discontinued their discussion about the wildlife on the planet and began planning how they would be able to safely make the trip to rescue the XO and Miranda Stevens with the weapons they had available, in addition to what they would need for the trip.

"Would the wood from the trees here good for making a bow?" Chris asked Jay.

"There appeared to be some hardwood that may, and I emphasize *may*, be suitable for a bow. I gave up trying to cut it down for my mast. It was taking me too long. If we can cut and carve it, it'll have to be a single-piece bow. We don't have glue to make a laminated bow or the time it would take to make one."

"That's fine. How about for arrows?"

Jay replied, "That tree lot is a tangle of all kinds of hard and soft and woody plants. There must be something that we can use in there. I didn't get a chance to explore much. I was too focused on getting my antenna up and watching for predators."

Chris poked at the fire with a stick to reposition a log and watched the sparks rise and swirl as the convection currents carried them upward. "What can we use for arrowheads?" he wondered aloud.

Jay, looking into the fire, answered, "I haven't seen any stony material around here that would work. There's some hard plastic sheeting from the rocket engine compartment that we could salvage. That's some durable stuff if we can cut it and shape it into a point with the saw edge of our knives. If we can find a rock lying around here somewhere, it'll make the job of sharpening the edges easier. We can use the same stuff for spear points too. Otherwise, we're stuck with sharpened sticks that will only poke holes in the animals, not kill them."

Chris nodded. "And a wounded animal is a very dangerous one."

Chris noted that Sandy and Dr. Rhodes hit it off well and talked most of the evening before turning in while Ron sat quietly by himself until the campfire was reduced to embers, not joining in on idle conversations with the others.

Chris and Jay sat quietly now, mesmerized by the dying fire for several minutes before Chris said, "We can take a walk to the tree lot first thing in the morning. I recommend we get a good night's sleep."

Everyone was still excited about getting together, but the new arrivals were exhausted from the long trek, so everyone entered the capsule to turn in for the night. The pod had four seats that reclined into beds.

Chris said, "Doc, you and Ron take the other two beds. I'll sleep on the floor."

"Chris, you must be exhausted," said Jay. "Why don't you take my bed? It's not the most comfortable, but it's better than the floor."

"Thanks, but I'll be okay. I have my sleeping bag."

Jay gave him a disbelieving look.

"Really," Chris said, "I'll be fine. See you in the morning."

Jay shook his head, smiled, and said, "Okay, but remember, I did offer," and climbed onto his bed.

The floor was hard and his sleeping bag thin. Chris didn't fall asleep for what seemed like hours, tossing and turning in an attempt to get comfortable. Awoken by his own body when he started to hurt, he turned over to minimize his discomfort and listened to the snoring duet of Ron and Jay. He was just starting to fall asleep again when something slammed into the pod and rocked it on its base. Chris bolted upright instantly, and the noise and sudden movement woke everyone else too.

Someone exclaimed, “What in creation’s name?” And then the pod was rammed again, rocking the capsule much harder this time. Sandy screamed. Items hanging on the bulkhead for convenience or placed on workstation tables became low-velocity missiles that either fell harmlessly to the floor or struck an unfortunate soul, adding to the frightful confusion in the darkened capsule. Chris’s tablet computer fell from a small worktable to the deck. The screen lit up from the movement, and the display showed 4:27 a.m. No one wanted to open the hatch to see what could possibly slam the capsule that hard. Low bellows could be heard through the insulated capsule bulkheads, but not much else. They all waited in the darkened capsule for the next ramming, but it never came. No one slept the rest of the night.

It was midmorning before anyone left the capsule to brave the outdoors. Jay was the first one outside, with Chris close behind, to inspect the damage caused by their unwelcome nocturnal visitors. There was a huge dent in the side of the capsule at the access cover to the rocket engine compartment. Ablative heat tiles were scattered about the ground, many of them broken and trampled into the dirt and grass.

Jay whistled and then said, “I really don’t want to run into whatever can cause this kind of damage.”

Running his hand over the side of the capsule and across a dented area, Chris said, “It’s a wonder the capsule didn’t tip over.”

The skin of the spacecraft was made of a titanium alloy four centimeters thick. A meter above the ground, there was a crushed area roughly one and a half meters in diameter and ten centimeters deep. Titanium alloy bolts two and a half centimeters thick lay broken and scattered about; the engine compartment’s access plate lay bent on the ground. Another similarly damaged area was located at a height of two meters aboveground. Chris and Jay stepped back and stared at the damage, trying to imagine the size of the beast or beasts that could cause this kind of damage. Surveying the area, they saw vast areas of grass mowed down, either eaten or trampled flat by a herd of presumably extremely large animals. Thankfully, the perpetrators of the damage to the capsule were nowhere in sight, the evidence of their visit leading off to the southeast.

Chris encouraged the others to come outside to see the damage themselves. When Sandy saw the damaged area and looked down at tracks that were two-thirds of a meter across, she looked faint. Dr. Rhodes saw her start to wobble and immediately took Sandy by the shoulders and sat her down. Jay rushed over and sat next to the love of his life, reassuring her that everything would be all right.

Ron said, "Why would they come down here? There's food for them everywhere. Why here?"

Having just come back from the edge of the depression to see whether the animals were still within sight, Chris said to Ron, "The slope of this depression is relatively shallow, so it wouldn't be hard for them to climb up the other side. But you're right—why here? I would guess it's because their food *is* everywhere. It wouldn't make any difference where they walked, so why *not* here? Here is as good a place as any other. Besides, up on the rim there, I saw how much damage was done to the grass. The path must be over a kilometer wide. The herd must have been very large, and the ones that came down here probably didn't have much choice if they were in the middle."

"But why damage the capsule?" Ron asked.

Chris replied, "It looks like it was just in their way, and they tried to move it."

Ron nodded in agreement. "Yeah, and it ticked them off when it wouldn't budge."

Chris responded, "If this wasn't so serious, your comment would be almost funny."

"Let's just make sure we don't ever get in their way," said Ron. "Being flattened by a living steamroller is not how I want to go."

"I agree," Chris replied.

Chris looked up toward the capsule just as Dr. Rhodes stepped out. "How's Sandy?" he asked.

Dr. Rhodes said, "Seeing the size of those prints really upset her. I took her into the capsule and gave her a mild sedative. She should sleep for a few hours."

"Okay," Chris said. "Ron, Jay, and I are going to head over to the trees to see what we can use for weapons. We'll be gone for a while."

"That's fine," said Dr. Rhodes. "I'll keep an eye on Sandy. Be careful."

"We will."

The men gathered the needed tools to get the wood for their weapons and hiked toward the tree lot. When they reached the edge of the trampled grass area, Chris crouched down to examine the grass and the area where there should have been a trail from the group's arrival the day before. Being the ever-mindful xenobiologist, he noticed an oddity about the grass—it had recovered within a day of being bent aside by their passage to Jay and Sandy's capsule, erasing their trails. On Earth, it could take days to weeks for tall grass to recover like that. Unless the grass here was crushed underfoot, it looked undisturbed by the next day. He noticed the grass stem near the base was relatively brittle and would break when trampled or sheared and then regrow from the stub.

Chris turned to Ron and said, "Miranda Stevens would be interested in this if she hasn't already noted it in her area. Look at the broken ends of the grass. It's like shards of glass sticking up. We wouldn't want to walk around here barefoot; it would slice our feet to ribbons."

Starting from a few centimeters above the ground, the lower two-thirds of the grass blades were tough and fibrous. Chris Elliott could see uses for this tough fiber in making rope, roofing material, fletching for arrows, and eventually clothing if necessary. The upper one-third of the grass blade was flexible and soft and, as he had discovered earlier, made a rather comfortable bed mat.

There was no sign of animal activity on their way to the tree lot. Jay, hoping for another encounter with the female pidogg, kept looking for trails in the grass, but she was nowhere to be found. Upon arriving, the three men spread out to search for the type of tree that might suit their needs. Taking out their knives, they tested to see how easily the wood cut. They rejected most of what they found because it was too soft. A few trees looked promising. One tree in particular, Ron dubbed the Goldilocks tree. It wasn't too hard, and it wasn't too soft; it was just right.

"Chris, Jay, come test this tree branch. I can't bend it with one arm very well, but it seems good and springy and may be just what we're looking for."

Chris and Jay made short work of cutting the branch, which was just about the diameter for a bow, and trimmed it to length. Chris, being heavier than Jay or Ron, stood the wood section on its end and leaned on it to see if he could break it. The piece bent well when subjected to considerable force and straightened when he let up.

After several unsuccessful attempts to break the test branch, Chris said, "Looks like we have a winner."

They now had wood for their bows. It had strong tensile strength and yet remained resilient enough for repeated flexing and extending without breaking or splintering. They could make many bows with the wood from this tree. It took the three of them a planet-side hour to cut it down.

The wood for arrows came from a woody bush that grew straight and whose stems were about the correct diameter. It took two trips from the tree lot back to the capsule to carry the material for their bows and arrows and another trip for the spear-making wood, for which they chose very hard and small-diameter trees.

Once back at the campsite, Chris and Jay began carving weapons. Ron wasn't of much use carving the bows with the use of only one arm, so instead he entered the capsule and asked Dr. Rhodes if she would change his bandages, which had become loose from his carrying wood and some of the bush stems under his arm. Half of the bandage had descended to his elbow, and the rest hung loosely about his shoulder. There was dirt and bark debris on his wound. Once the arm was cleaned and the bandages were changed, Ron went outside to scrape bark and cut the arrow shafts to the proper length—a great job for a one-armed man.

Three days after the men cut down the necessary tree and bushes, the weapons were completed. The arrow shafts had been relatively easy to make. They scraped the bark off, cut the arrow to length, and cut notches on the ends for a nock and an arrowhead. Then they rolled the cut shaft on a flat surface to ensure the shaft was straight. The fletching was made from the lower fibrous section of the wide-blade grass. The main stem that ran down the middle of the blade was relatively thick and tough, and the men were able to split the stem, cut the half-blade to length, and then separate the fibers of the grass blade to resemble feather fletching. The toughest part was attaching the grass fletching to the arrows since there was no glue or tree resin that could be used in place of glue. On each arrow, Chris and Jay carved three triangular-shaped slots, eight centimeters long, from one end of the arrow shaft, positioning the slots at one-third intervals on the circumference of the shaft. They then found split-stem, feather-fletching substitutes that matched the slot size on the shaft and slid them into place. It wasn't a perfect system, and they wasted a lot of grass fletching trying to make the fletching fit the slot, but the grass was their most abundant resource, so to them it didn't matter.

An arrowhead made from the plastic found in the rocket engine compartment fit into a slot on the other end of each shaft, tied with strands of paracord, completing the arrow. When the beasts crushed in the rocket engine access cover, they had shattered a good portion of the plastic that the men were planning to use for arrowheads and spear points. It was then a simple matter of shaping the broken pieces, sharpening them, and attaching them to the shaft of the arrow.

Chris and Jay had carved the bows with great care. However, because they didn't have sandpaper, the surfaces had a semi-rough finish. The best they could do to smooth the wood was use another piece of hardwood and rub hard enough to compress back into the wood the small fibers that had resulted from the carving with the knife. They sealed and smoothed the wood of their bows a little more with some of the fat drippings that Chris had been able to salvage from the roasted rodent he and Jay had eaten earlier. The plan was to seal all the wooden weapons with drippings as the opportunity arose, to help preserve the wood.

The paracord was too thick to be used for a bowstring if left whole. Chris cut pieces of it to length, and separated the cord into four-strand groups. After weaving the grouped strands together for increased strength and for the correct diameter for the nock on the end of the arrow shaft, he tied a small bowline knot at each end of the bowstring and attached it to the bow.

Testing the bow, Chris said, "Not bad, if I say so myself. I'd guess the pull to be about twenty-five or so kilograms. That should be enough to stop anything short of large or armored game." Handing the bow to Jay, Chris said, "Here, you try it."

After pulling the bow back several times to test the pull, Jay said, "I'd say we hit the jackpot. This is really good. Let's finish stringing the rest and then test them."

Ron nodded his head in approval but didn't say anything.

Chris and Jay practiced shooting their new armaments and throwing the spears with reasonable success. As long as they were within fifteen meters with the bow and ten meters with the spear, they were able to hit their target. They vowed to get more practice when they had more time. Ron attempted to throw a spear left-handed, but all the movement caused too much pain in his right arm and shoulder. He volunteered to carry two or three of them instead. As they watched the testing of the newly created survival gear, the women oohed and aahed at the men's accomplishment, but they did it more to satisfy manly egos than because of the aesthetics and skill with the weapons. With the completion of the weapons test, Chris felt they were ready.

All the backpacks were as full as they could make them or as heavy as they could be carried. Ron's right arm continued to give him problems in terms of pain and flexibility. He chalked this up to the extra movement he'd engaged in while helping Chris and Jay carry wood to build the weapons and his sad attempt at throwing a spear. Everyone gathered their assigned gear and donned their backpacks. Chris had determined that his tablet compass was accurate enough that they could do away with the leapfrog technique for traveling in a straight line. Jay programmed a backup compass on his tablet for collaboration during the trip. Jay climbed to the top of his antenna pole, radioed the XO, got a good DF direction for their compasses, and told her they were on the way.

10

The group had gone only a few hundred meters when Chris and Jay noticed trails forming in the grass fifty meters to their left and slightly behind them. Jay asked the group to stop for a few minutes while he walked over to the leading trail. Chris and Ron followed and waited halfway between Jay and the women just in case they were needed. Jay's suspicions were confirmed when he saw that the female pidogg was following them, with her young ones in tow. As he approached her, she sat back on her haunches and let him pet her. The pups were already a quarter of her size.

"No wonder you wanted more food!" Petting one pup after the other, he said, "You guys are getting so big!"

The pups swarmed Jay, vying for his attention, making it impossible to ignore them. He tried to give all of them some attention but couldn't be sure which one was which because they were all bouncing, jumping, and changing positions so fast he couldn't keep up with which ones had been petted and which ones hadn't. The mama pidogg interrupted their fun with a sharp bark and a low vocalization. All the pups fell into place behind her.

Language—it has to be a language. These are some really smart critters, thought Jay.

It didn't take long before the other trails began to merge at Jay's position. He counted more than a dozen pidoggs in addition to the mama pidogg and her brood. Some were obviously male with their heavily muscled, large bodies. They all had that tough-guy look that implied, "Don't mess with me."

Jay was a bit wary of them, but there was no threatening posturing, so he relaxed, a little. The mama pidogg mumble-growled something, and then all the pidoggs surrounded Jay on three sides and waited. Jay gave the mama pidogg a last good scratching behind the ear and head and then left to join his group. The pidoggs followed at a discreet distance.

Jay met Chris and Ron on the way back. Nodding his head in the direction of the pidoggs as they walked back to join Dr. Rhodes and Sandy, Jay said to the men, "I guess we have an escort." Sandy was clearly nervous, but Jay reassured her that the escort was a good thing.

Ron complained, "I don't trust them, especially the males. Look at 'em—they have a mean look about them, worse than a pit bull. When they look at me, I feel like they're mentally tasting my flesh. That female even licked her chops after sizing me up while you were scratching her head!"

Chris responded, "Oh, come now. Even pit bulls have a lovable nature and can look just as ferocious. I think you're letting your distrust of canines in general cloud your judgment."

"So far the pidoggs have done nothing to show us harm," added Jay. "Other than a few stray looks, they probably feel they have to learn to trust us too."

Chris backed him up. "So far as we know, these creatures are a top predator, at least in this area. They could be the safety net that we need. If they're as fond of us as much as it appears, then I'm sure we'll learn to become fond of them too."

As he turned to walk away to the far side of the group, Ron grumbled, "I hope they're not going to learn to be fond of our flesh!"

Sandy and Dr. Rhodes appeared a bit nervous after hearing what Ron had to say. Going into biology teacher mode, Chris continued, "They may just like us for who we are. Early people made friends with the gray wolf, and it worked out to their mutual benefit. The wolf got help from our ancestors' practice of hunting with tools, which aided in bringing down larger game and provided food more regularly for them, without the wolves having to expend calories to hunt game on their own. Humans also provided the wolves safety from their predators, and since they had better living conditions, the wolves had better survivability for their offspring. We in turn got an early warning system for predators and our enemies; great assistance with hunting of game from the wolf's sensitive sense of smell; better sanitation, with wolves cleaning up the scraps around the camp; and also important, companionship. We eventually learned how to domesticate them and bred them into all the breeds of dogs today. It was thought that because of the wolf's use of a complex body language, vocalizations, and socialization, the dog inherited the needed skills to live in a social setting with humans. Today the dog is still considered humankind's best animal friend."

Ron had his arms folded in a defiant manner. Glancing at the pidoggs before looking back at Chris, Ron said, "Okay, professor, thanks for the history lesson, but how does that help us here? I still don't trust 'em."

"These animals exhibit similar behavior. They're social, they travel and hunt in packs, they use body language, and apparently they have a highly developed vocalized language. They have to hunt for their food on a regular basis, and the young ones have a playful aspect just as Earth puppies do. It's the social cognition, with their complex forms of communication, that's important. It means they are trainable and *not* functioning on an instinctual level like, say, a lizard. That's a huge advantage, especially for us. Apparently, the interaction with Jay has shown them the benefits of teaming up with us. What's important is that they're willing. It's a win-win situation," Chris explained.

Unconvinced but overruled by the rest of the group, Ron reluctantly kept quiet.

·|l|· ·|l|· ·|l|· ·|l|·

The entourage was taking its time getting to the area where the other capsule landed. When taking the needed and frequent breaks for food, water, and rest, Jay and Chris gave attention to the pidoggs. Every time they stopped, Jay made a point of sharing some of his meal with the mother pidogg and her brood. He suggested to the others that they do the same with the rest of the pack. As expected, Ron and Sandy were reluctant but were convinced to participate. Sandy chose a small female to approach. The female pidogg was a little apprehensive at first too, but after she shyly accepted a couple of pieces of dried meat at each rest stop, they warmed to each other. Ron would toss a few scraps to a pidogg or two during the meal breaks, but he didn't get close enough to any of them to bond. His general distrust of the pidoggs prevented him from accepting them as anything but a potential threat. As the assemblage of humans and pidoggs got closer to their destination, they started seeing more animals. Never one to pass up a chance to advance his professional knowledge, Chris made detailed notes of his observations on his tablet computer.

The group was within an hour of reaching Caitlyn and Miranda when a hunting opportunity arose for the pidoggs. A large area of grass had been browsed close to the ground about two hundred meters in front of them. A cluster of three animals about the size of small sheep or goats was grazing at the edge closest to the travelers. The rest of the herd was grazing at the other edge of the clearing.

Chris noticed that the pidoggs were catching some game-animal scents from the westerly breeze. He watched as they went into a sneaking stride to close in on the animals. Chris stopped the rest of the human group so that they could watch the action. Without a sound, two large males and two females continued forward, slowly and quietly, toward the unsuspecting animals. The rest of the pidogg group had stopped and now silently waited. There was no movement or noise from the entourage now except the four pidoggs on their stalk.

Like a well-practiced team, the pidoggs split up for a frontal and flank assault. One pidogg went wide of the other three pidoggs, who continued their slow, stealthy approach until they were within five meters of their quarry. The fourth pidogg, a female, had gone about a hundred meters to the right of the targeted animals. She paused a few moments to view the animals at the edge of the clearing and then nonchalantly trotted into the open field, holding her head high. Instantly, all heads came up to look at the lone pidogg. For a moment, nothing happened. Then all at once, in an explosion of movement, the herd bolted in a safe direction away from the unwelcome and dangerous visitor; at least most of them did. The three targeted game animals ran directly at the three pidoggs lying in ambush. Each pidogg picked his or her target and charged when the game animal was within one meter. The pidoggs had extremely strong jaws and very large mouths when opened wide. They quickly lunged at the game, tearing into the necks of the targeted beasts, removing huge mouthfuls of flesh in one viscous bite. Blood spurted from the severed arteries and ran from the veins of the gaping wounds. The animals went down within a few steps.

After swallowing the ripped-out section of his targeted animal's throat, the largest male made a vocalization for the rest of the pack to join in on the feast. What Chris noticed was very unusual. The adults let the pups get their fill first; then the juveniles went. Only after that did the adults eat. Two pidoggs, a male and a female, brought the human group part of the kill.

"Share and share alike," Chris said to no one in particular, making a mental note to document the behavior on his tablet later.

Chris and Jay acknowledged the gift by nodding their heads once, a kind of bow, and vocalizing their thanks. It wasn't long before every scrap of each animal was gone—bone, skin, entrails, everything. The only evidence that any creatures had died there was blood that had seeped into the ground. The juveniles even licked the blades of grass clean of blood. Moving slowly and with their bellies full and distended, the pidoggs looked as if they needed a nap after gorging themselves.

The entire group took an extra-long break. Jay radioed the XO to let her know of the delay. Dr. Rhodes and Sandy made a small cooking fire and roasted one of the front quarters the pidoggs had given them.

While the meat was cooking, Ron stayed close to the fire. "Did you see how viciously they attacked those animals? They could do that to us while we're sleeping or could attack us from behind!"

Chris said, "Yes, they probably could, but they haven't."

"Yet!"

"If they haven't done it yet, it's unlikely they will," Chris countered. "I can understand your concerns, but we need their help, and it looks like they are willing."

Ron grumbled something inaudible and started to turn away.

Annoyed with Ron's attitude, Chris said, "You know, it would be just as easy for us to attack them and kill them all. There is a trust factor here that I think will pan out for everyone's benefit, including the pidoggs'. Yes, they are menacing to look at, and they stink too, but that's probably to their advantage—and now ours. So my suggestion to you is to chill out and make friends with them. Your life may someday depend on it."

Ron scowled at Chris and sat on the opposite side of the fire from him.

Soon, the aroma of roasted meat wafted through the air. Chris, being the more adventurous, tasted the meat first. He proclaimed it a bit "gamey" but tasty and finished his portion. Everyone except Sandy had some of the meat. She put her share in her pack, saving it to give to her new pidogg friend later. Chris looked over at Ron, who was holding his right arm, but Ron was avoiding his gaze.

Three planet-side hours passed before there was any activity from the pidoggs. When Chris thought the pidoggs were ready to travel, he assembled the humans while Jay walked around talking and getting the pidoggs excited to continue the journey.

Chris and Jay were on point together; Ron walked about five

meters behind them, putting as much distance between him and the pidoggs as he could; and the women followed five meters behind Ron. The mama pidogg and her brood followed the women. Everyone was well protected, with the pidogg clan taking up the rear and flanks to form a near-perfect semicircle around the humans leading the way.

Several hours later, the group entered a dense area of twenty-meter-tall, treelike plants and one-meter scrub bushes with tiny rust-colored leaves and branches. Chris and Jay passed through to the far side first, stopping just outside the edge. They waited until the rest of the group caught up with them.

Pointing, Chris said, "There's the capsule."

The land sloped slightly downward toward the capsule and continued onward to a large body of water a little under a kilometer away.

"Look at all the trails!" Jay exclaimed. The trails crisscrossed east and west, north and south, and every which direction.

Chris commented, "These trails had to have been made sometime today, or they would have grown closed."

"That's a lot of animal activity," Dr. Rhodes said as she took in the panoramic view.

Chris pointed off to the right and said, "And look what's still making them."

Off in the distance, a little more than a kilometer to the north and just away from the water's edge, was a very large area that at first glance appeared to be devoid of grass. It was mostly a dark brown area with a smattering of black dispersed throughout. It could have been roughened landscape with shadows, except that the brown and black coloring was on the move. There were thousands upon thousands of animals, and they were large, very large. The scene made Chris think of how it must have been in early America, watching herds of buffalo covering the plains.

"This is absolutely astounding!" Jay exclaimed, leaning on his spears as if they were tall walking sticks.

Sandy walked up next to Jay, hooked her arm into his, and nodded in agreement. "Wow!" she said as she stared in wonderment at the incredible view.

The herd, if that was the term for a collection of animals that looked to cover more than four to five square kilometers of land, was moving southwest toward the group at a slow pace and would pass the humans and pidoggs closely at a half kilometer to the north.

"Oh, my! They are huge!" Dr. Rhodes exclaimed as the herd drew near her position.

The largest of the animals were almost twice as large as the extinct African elephant, but they looked more like Asian water buffalo crossed with American buffalo. The distinctive high shoulder and massive neck supported a huge head with a thick, heavy crown of bone across the top, which formed a base for shoulder-wide horns that curled to the side and front of the giant creatures. The tail appeared to have an elongated bony end like a club. At six meters tall at the top of the shoulder and fourteen meters long, the larger of the animals appeared very formidable. The top of their back was another two meters above their shoulders.

"Let's not make enemies of them," suggested Ron, who had been quiet for most of the trip.

Chris noted that many of the larger ones walked about fifty meters outside the perimeter of the herd and several hundred meters apart, apparently acting as early warning sentries. Chris said softly to himself, "What could possibly attack something that large? What would they fear? I have to document this."

He switched programs on his tablet computer and recorded a video with narration of the animal's size, coloring, and observable behavior, adding it to the previous recordings for life forms on this planet. He was also able to record the animals' soft contented bellows and the trumpeting of some of the larger animals as the herd passed by. Seeing that he no longer needed the makeshift compass, he closed out the active programming for it, leaving it on standby.

After Chris made his video recording of the herd, he said to no one in particular, "I wish I had thought to record the pidoggs' attack strategy for taking those sheep- or goatlike animals. Eh! Oh, well. I got to watch the real thing happen live instead of through the lens of a camera."

When he thought about it further, he realized that if he had been focused on the group of three pidoggs with the camera, he would have missed the female decoy and that strategy. *Smart animals, very smart indeed!* He added the pidogg attack strategy to his log.

The herd of giant grass-eaters took more than four hours to pass the group. Afterward, Jay radioed the XO to tell her that they had the capsule in sight and would be there within fifteen minutes, barring anything unexpected.

As they continued on, they saw a few animals, some small, some large, visit the lake for water and then wander about their way. With the exception of the size of the gargantuan grass-eaters, Chris was amazed at the similarity of animal development on this planet compared to Earth. The animals all had one head, a slender neck, four long legs in relation to their body size, and a tail. The ones that resembled antelope or deer were of varying sizes, some with antlers or horns, some not. In addition, all of the grass-eaters had their eyes on the sides of their head, like most noncarnivorous mammals and birds on Earth, giving them better peripheral vision to watch for predators. None of them paid the humans any attention. With the wind coming across the lake from the west, the thirsty animals did not detect the pidoggs' presence, and with full bellies, the pidoggs paid them no heed.

When the troupe reached the capsule, the pidoggs formed a perimeter facing outward, as would sentries in a war zone. Some sat while others stood, but the one thing they all had in common was their intense demeanor. Like trained observers, the pidoggs gazed over the entire area, watching for anything that could threaten them or their newfound human friends. Their ears stood tall, listening for enemies or predators that might sneak up on them, and their nostrils constantly twitched, sampling the air currents for the scent of any unwanted visitors. Chris was duly impressed.

He hadn't noticed until now that more pidoggs had joined the group along the way. *When did they join in? Well, the more the merrier. They seem very well behaved, well organized, and exceptionally intelligent. I sure hope this isn't some subterfuge to lull us into trusting them before they spring a trap on us. I'd hate to learn that Ron was right.*

Chris rapped loudly on the capsule. The XO opened the hatch, with Miranda peering over her shoulder on tiptoes. Miranda opened her eyes wide in disbelief upon seeing all the pidoggs in formation around the capsule.

Before she even greeted Chris, the XO asked in amazed wonder, "How did you get them to do that?"

Chris smiled and responded, "I didn't. They did it all on their own. They're extremely intelligent and use both vocal and body language for communication. As you can see, they're also very protective of their own, and apparently, they've accepted us as part of their extended family. Come on out and meet them." Turning to Jay, he said, "Jay, you can do the honors."

With trepidation, the XO and then Miranda stepped out of the capsule. The mother pidogg was the only adult pidogg not on guard duty, and she stepped forward to greet her new friends. There were also the smaller juveniles within the circle of sentries and the pups, who eagerly followed their mother.

Before Jay introduced the XO and Miranda to the female pidogg, he said, "I have to give her a name." He thought for a few moments and then said, "Judy. That was my grandmother's name. I think it's simple enough that she can remember it. We can name the others as we recognize the differences in the patterns on their fur."

Jay repeated a comical "me Tarzan, you Jane" sort of monologue a few times before Judy finally caught on to her name. Judy seemed to mumble something in response, keeping her eyes glued to Jay's in understanding. Jay then introduced Judy to the XO and Miranda.

Judy stood up, walked over and sniffed their hands, legs, and feet, and then, most embarrassingly, walked around and behind them to sniff their butts. All the men turned and looked away to save some dignity for the two women.

Chris smiled and chuckled to himself. *I saw that coming!*

Recovering quickly from their embarrassment, the XO and Miranda petted and scratched Judy behind her ears and gave some attention to the puppies, who were already jumping on the women's feet and legs anyway.

Smiling, Miranda said, "These puppies are so ugly they're cute!"

The XO merely smiled at them.

"How's your water supply?" Chris asked.

Turning back to face Chris, the XO said, "We've used quite a bit, actually almost all of what we could filter. We had to give up washing our hands and face. The last time we got water, we almost ended up as dinner ourselves. I'll tell you about it later."

"Well, while we have an escort, we should probably fill your available containers," suggested Chris. "That goes for all of us."

The humans and pidoggs made their way through the tall grass to the lake. Nearing the water, several pidoggs paused and tilted their heads to listen to something inaudible to the humans. They then began another hunting stalk to the north.

Chris turned in the direction that the pidoggs were heading. He pointed toward the north where they had first spotted the herd of giant animals and said to Jay, who was standing next to him, "Look over there—about a kilometer away. One of those giant creatures looks like it's stuck in mud. Let's go. I want to see how this will play out."

Everyone moved toward the giant animal cautiously, with the hunting pidoggs taking the lead position. The area was clear of any animals that looked dangerous, and any game-type animal that became downwind of the pidoggs hastily left the area as the hunters made their way toward the trapped giant.

It took ten minutes to reach the hapless animal. Upon arriving at the trapped animal, the pidoggs surrounded the great beast in a close circle. The unfortunate creature had sunk into a soft area that apparently couldn't support its massive weight. The humans and pidoggs didn't have that problem and were able to move about freely on the somewhat springy ground.

Chris jumped up and down a couple of times. "I don't think these giants can access the lake right here because of this soft ground. Did you feel how the ground vibrated when I jumped on it? It reminds me of a bog back home, except that the upper layer is dry and stiff," he said. After pausing for a moment, as if in deep thought, Chris continued. "I wonder if because the grass has more moisture here, the animal grazed in this soft area and broke through the dry upper layer of soil and got stuck. Look at all the trails and shorter grass around it. This isn't the only animal that's been eating and drinking here."

The giant grass-eater, totally exposed above its belly, couldn't move its legs because they were held fast in the thick mud. The pidoggs moved in for the kill, but every time they got close, the trapped animal thrashed its head left and right, twisting its neck in a figure eight, tipping the massive set of horns near the ground as it tried to gore its adversaries. The club-like tail guarded the animal's rear quarters, with wide, sweeping motions that struck the flanks on each side of the animal, threatening to crush the body of any pidogg foolish enough to challenge it. The creature was successfully keeping the pidoggs at bay.

"Looks like a stalemate to me," said Jay.

Everyone watched the pidoggs' unsuccessful attempt to take the quarry for a few minutes longer.

Then, having seen enough, Chris said, "It's time for a payback for the help they've given us." Chris took the bow off his shoulder and nocked an arrow. "It's also a good time to see how well these things work."

Pulling back on the bow, Chris aimed for the center of the chest just behind the front leg, hoping to hit a vital organ or a lung. The arrow flew straight but didn't penetrate deeply enough. The animal flinched at the wound and thrashed about, possibly angry that it couldn't defend itself against this new threat.

"It figures," Chris said. "Not only are they bigger than an elephant, they have a hide thicker than one too." Chris nocked another arrow on the bowstring, this time pulling the string back as far and hard as he could. The arrow penetrated somewhat deeper, but not enough to be a killing shot.

Again, the animal thrashed about, bellowing out loudly. The women covered their ears, hoping to prevent hearing damage. They could feel the vibration from the animal's cries through their entire bodies.

"Okay, plan B," Chris said.

Asking and receiving from Ron one of the spears that he was carrying, Chris approached the giant. Standing next to the animal, Chris was in awe. *Wow, this thing is huge! It's at least twice as long and tall as the twenty-first-century military tanks that I've seen in museums. I hope it's not as tough to take out!*

Even buried up to its belly, at the shoulder the animal was still more than a meter taller than Chris. He reached down and broke off the tips from two blades of grass, rolled them into tubes, and stuffed them in his ears. Ron and Jay followed suit.

Though the animal continued to bellow loudly and thrash its head and tail about wildly, it remained solidly trapped. Looking to see where he could safely approach the giant, Chris noted that because the animal couldn't move its legs, it also didn't have the flexibility to turn its head very far left or right. He knew he had to be careful of the tail. One strike of that tail could crush his skull or permanently maim him instantly. He chose a spot closer to the head and just behind the right shoulder, near where the arrows had penetrated. All the pidoggs watched intently, some sitting, others standing. Jay was standing close to the animal's head with a spear raised, yelling and dancing about to draw the creature's attention away from Chris. Caitlyn and Dr. Rhodes watched, but Miranda and Sandy turned away, still holding their hands over their ears.

Chris sprinted forward. *I have to end this animal's suffering quickly*, he thought. He used speed and his body weight to thrust the spear into the beast. The spear penetrated deeply, but still not enough to kill the animal. In pain and anger, the animal redoubled its efforts to free itself, thrashing violently and bellowing even louder than before. Jay came around and handed Chris one of his spears. Another thrust and wound. The animal was livid and in obvious pain as blood flowed from the wounds. Ron gave him yet another of the spears he was holding. Chris removed the plastic spear tip and replaced it with his survival knife.

"Are you sure you want to do that?" asked Ron and Jay in unison.

"Yeah. This beast isn't going anywhere, and it's suffering. I need to end this now. I can get the knife out later if we lose it," he said with grim determination.

Ron had one spear left, and Jay had two more for backup weapons. Jay walked around the front of the animal and poked at it with his spears to draw attention away from Chris. Chris readied the weapon and then charged. Running at the animal and using all his body weight and strength, he rammed the spear into the beast's chest, piercing the coarse fur and skin near the other two spears and driving the knife-tipped shaft in until only a handhold section of the spear was left protruding. The giant roared and swung its massive head left and right, up and down; its tail alternated between beating the ground and its flanks. New, pulsing blood gushed freely from the latest spear wound and ran down the side of the animal along with the blood flowing from the other wounds. The animal began to moan in pain. Finally weakened from the heavy blood loss, it slowed its attempt to defend itself. Its breathing became more labored as a frothy red foam, continuously exhaled from its nostrils and mouth, collected in a pool in front of the hapless animal. The creature's neck slowly lowered. Unable to hold its head up any longer, the animal surrendered to its fate. A loud gurgling, choking sound could be heard with its final gasping breath. As the creature exhaled its last, it slowly closed its eyes and stopped moving.

From start to finish, it took thirty minutes for the animal to die. Sandy tried to wipe her tears away before anyone noticed. With sad but understanding eyes, Miranda had watched the killing from the time of the final spear thrust that eventually ended the animal's suffering until it died. Seeing how the helpless animal had struggled to stay alive greatly upset her.

Miranda thought of her husband, Ted, who had been killed while on duty in the engine room aboard *Copernicus*. She could only pray that he hadn't suffered greatly. Melancholy thoughts of his scent, his dry humor, and his gentle touch during their lovemaking crowded out the present. In her mind, she pictured his crooked smile and could hear his laughter from the time they went canoeing and their dog, Roxy, decided to go for a swim and tipped the canoe over. Tears began to well up in her eyes. She would miss him terribly. Although she didn't have many close friends aboard the spaceship, the ones she'd had also haunted her dreams. Miranda's thoughts of her deceased husband were interrupted when Dr. Rhodes walked over between her and Sandy.

Dr. Rhodes placed her hands on their shoulders and said softly, "Life cannot exist without death. Chris saved that poor creature a long, slow death by starvation and thirst. Its death is not meaningless. Its body will help feed us and many other creatures, including our pidogg friends for some time to come."

Sandy and Miranda nodded in understanding, though sad nonetheless.

The pidoggs watched and waited patiently. When the last breath escaped from the giant, the largest male pidogg approached cautiously. He sniffed and licked at the blood. Then he started to bite at the skin, but he didn't quite have the technique for ripping the thick hide on the side of the animal with his teeth.

Chris assumed that if the pidoggs had ever made a meal of such a large beast, the belly skin must be much thinner and softer. *I wonder how they take on one of these monsters when they can fight back.*

Chris and Jay approached the kill, and the pidoggs parted to let them through. It pained Chris to see how much the animal had suffered before it died. He worked in silence as he pulled the deepest spear from the beast's chest. He removed the knife, which was covered with runny and clotted blood, from the end of the spear. Chris momentarily stared at the pieces of lung tissue and fat that were caught in the blade's serrations—more evidence of the grisly death. He used blades of grass to wipe that evidence from the slippery handle and blade of the knife. He then used the weapon to slice through the tough skin, exposing the fat and muscle underneath. Knowing that any carnivore typically went for the abdomen first, partially because it was the softest part, Chris continued to slit the skin close to the ground along the length of the carcass. He then made a vertical slit on both ends of the horizontal cut to make a tall flap. After retrieving his arrows and the other two spears, he used the two arrows to pin the flap of hide high off the ground. Then he sliced deeply through the fat and muscle and stepped back as the abdominal contents spilled out onto the ground.

Though the odor wasn't horrendous, it was still unpleasant for the humans, and they covered their mouths and noses. Both Sandy and Miranda turned away again. Having gotten the hint, the pidoggs greedily went for the free meal. Wordlessly, Jay repeated the operation on the opposite side to offer more places for their friends to eat. It was a feeding frenzy. This time, the smaller pidoggs had to wait until the adults had filled themselves. There was plenty for all. After the pidoggs had gorged themselves to the point they had a hard time walking, Chris and Jay removed healthy chunks of meat for their group.

Dr. Rhodes said, "If there is anything that looks like a liver, get a piece of that too. We don't have access to a natural source of vitamins and minerals around here, so we'll need to eat organ meat."

Already upset from witnessing the killing, Miranda turned pale. "I hate liver!" she exclaimed.

This time Sandy didn't flinch. "It's not that bad," she said. "I could make a really good dinner from liver if I had access to a few herbs and maybe some dried onions. The secret is not to overcook it."

"We may have to make do with salt and pepper and maybe some hot sauce from the rations kit," Caitlyn offered. For centuries now, the military had continued to offer hot sauce with the rations kit to help cover up the taste of the food.

Feeling useful for the first time since arriving here, Sandy asked Miranda if she would help her prepare the food after the men brought back more firewood and started a cooking fire. Squeezing her eyes tightly shut and trying her best not to think of a liver dinner, Miranda nodded her head in agreement.

Still in a somber mood, Chris said, "We should get our water and vacate this area quickly. The smell of this carcass is going to attract every carnivore for tens of kilometers."

The group returned to the lake area and pumped filtered water into their containers. Standing in the shallow water, the men and women rinsed what blood they could remove from their hands, arms, and clothing. Chris was especially glad to wash because his khakis were still stained with the blood of his dead shipmates. As he removed his khaki shirt and his T-shirt to rinse the blood off, he paused for several moments as the memories came flooding back—watching Ted Stevens die, the blood, the flashing lights, the roar of escaping air, the death that surrounded him, his ordeal to get off the *Copernicus*. When Jay called to him, he had to fight hard to refocus on the job of cleaning himself before rejoining the group, which was gathering to leave.

The men and women, heavily laden with fresh meat and water, slowly made their way back to Caitlyn and Miranda's capsule with the well-fed pidoggs surrounding the humans in their now-customary perimeter guard.

11

After returning to the capsule with meat from the giant beast, the group started to organize their gear and make camp. Chris and Jay headed to the wooded area to gather firewood, with several pidoggs keeping them company, while the women tidied up the campsite. Chris had recovered from his glum mood.

Sweeping his arm outward in the direction of the pidoggs, Chris said, "This is working out greatly to our advantage."

"Sure, as long as we can keep them fed," said Jay. "How easy do you think it will be to kill one of those beasts when it can stand and fight and most likely is with a herd?"

"We'll just have to devise a different strategy, that's all," Chris said, having already thought of a method.

"How so?" asked Jay.

"The easiest way would be to dig a pit and cover it with local vegetation for a trap. It'll serve the same purpose as the mud did for our kill today. Only this time, we place long, sharp stakes in the bottom of the pit to do the killing for us. As long as they don't catch on to our traps, we could live here for a very long time, keeping ourselves and our friends fed."

"I see," said Jay. "That would be a lot easier and faster too."

"And more humane," Chris added, remembering how badly the last kill had gone.

On their way back to the campsite after collecting the wood

for a campfire, Jay remarked thoughtfully, "We'll have to teach the pidoggs that fire isn't dangerous to them as long as they don't try to get too close to it."

"That shouldn't be a problem," Chris replied. "If this planet has lightning storms, the animals most likely have already been exposed to fire. Most animals have a natural fear or respect for it, especially those with fur. We'll keep an eye on them, though, especially the pups."

Shifting the load of firewood in his arms, Jay added, "If those mama miniatures keep eating like they have been, they won't be pups for very long."

Chris paused. "Hang on a minute. The straps on this backpack are digging into my shoulders."

Jay stopped as Chris set down the wood he was carrying and repositioned his backpack of wood.

Chris bent at the knees to pick up the wood that he'd dropped before picking up the conversation. "That's true, about the pups. It'll be interesting to watch their development as they mature. I've been documenting pidogg behavior patterns since our contact with them. I'd like to document how the adults teach their young. Their social structure is one of the most complex that I've ever seen, especially the way they guard against predators."

Their loads now balanced, they continued their trek back to the campsite.

"Do you think we'll be here that long—before being rescued, I mean?" asked Jay.

Chris responded with a blank look on his face. "What do you think?"

Nodding his head, the normally cheerful Jay became somber at the thought that he and the others might be here for a very long time. They walked in silence the rest of the way back.

By the time Chris and Jay arrived with enough firewood to last through the night and into the next day, the sun had set, and darkness was approaching.

Chris said to Jay, “I think it would be wise to keep a fire going all the time as a deterrent to the predators that are sure to come because of the nearby carcass. It’s going to take several more trips to the woodlot to gather enough wood to last us several days, but we have enough to last until sometime tomorrow. Now, I don’t know about you, but I’m famished! Let’s get something to eat.”

The men started a large campfire. Sandy had cut and prepared the meat for cooking, and Miranda now helped her prop the meat-on-a-stick near the fire for roasting. Dr. Rhodes had run her evaluation on the fresh meat while Chris and Jay were collecting firewood and proclaimed it safe to eat. Smelling the savory odor of roasted meat made Chris all the hungrier after the long trek, the extra work butchering the giant grass-eater, and the wood gathering, with no breaks other than for water, after they had arrived at Caitlyn and Miranda’s capsule. Taking one of the sticks with a sizable piece of meat from the fire over to a log that served as a makeshift chair, Chris sat and observed the pidoggs’ behavior while he chewed his food. The pidoggs surrounded the perimeter of the capsule, as they had before. Chris was astounded at the cooperation of the group as a whole. Never before had he seen or read of anything like this anywhere in the animal kingdom. He’d seen animal sentries before, but never as organized as this group. As the evening went on, he watched the individuals alternate between serving as an alert watch stander and then, when relieved of duty, sleeping or tending to the young. There were no signals for the watch changes. Some pidoggs stayed on duty longer, some not as long. There seemed to be no particular order to the shift changes as to which pidogg took over as a watch-stander or which one was relieved. The animals took their responsibility seriously without argument or complaint.

After finishing his meal and documenting the recent pidogg behavior on his tablet computer, Chris took a break and concentrated on what had to be done next to ensure the crew’s survival. Sitting around the campfire, Chris and Jay discussed the need for safe and permanent living quarters. The women had the capsule for shelter until the men could build more suitable quarters for themselves. Until then, the men had to sleep outside on the ground. There wasn't enough room in the capsule for everyone.

Ron had been quiet all evening. Dr. Rhodes walked over to him, noticed his pale and damp skin, and asked, "How's the arm, Ron?"

He responded, "Honestly? Not the greatest. My arm is hurting more and more by the hour. The burning is bad enough, but now there's a deep ache too. I really abused it today, especially handling the firewood and helping to make the fire. The bandages don't want to stay in place, and I have to constantly pull them back up on my arm."

"I want to take a look. Come on in the capsule where the light is better."

Ron complied.

Once inside, Dr. Rhodes instructed Ron to sit in a launch chair and removed the bandages from his arm and shoulder. Shocked by what she saw, Dr. Rhodes did her best to keep her face from showing it. The entire lower part of the burn above the elbow was white and frothy, extending upward for ten centimeters toward the shoulder. Everything above that, including his shoulder, was extraordinarily red.

"I need to clean the wound, and it's going to hurt. Would you prefer that I put you to sleep for it?" she asked.

"No, I think I can handle it, Doc. Just go ahead and get it over with."

In the warm capsule, Ron's sweating increased, and droplets formed on his forehead and above his lip. He hadn't shaved since escaping the *Copernicus*, and the droplets above his lip made the whiskers reflect silver in the capsule lighting. Dr. Rhodes placed the back of her hand to his damp forehead.

"You're running a fever too," she said.

"I thought I was just working too hard and needed to take a break," he commented.

"It's much more than that now," she said.

The doctor moved a small table next to him and prepared his arm and shoulder as if she were doing a surgery. After using disinfectants to remove any possible contaminants on the table and surrounding surfaces, she placed a large sterile pad on the table and instructed Ron to place his outstretched arm on the pad. Ron winced with pain when she straightened his arm more than he volunteered. Dr. Rhodes began by taking a sample of both the white area and the reddened area for further microscopic study. She then put an antiseptic solution on some sterile gauze and gingerly wiped the bottom edge of the frothy infected area. Ron winced and involuntarily jerked his arm, his eyes held tightly shut.

"Are you doing okay?" she asked.

"Yeah, go ahead. Let's get this over with. I'll just grit my teeth." Although he was clearly in pain, Ron tried to keep the mood light and jokingly said, "A biting stick or leather strap might help."

Dr. Rhodes continued to clean the wound. Dirt and wood debris had become lodged deep in the infected skin and had to be removed. Even as Ron did his best to stay sitting upright, as the pain increased from the scrubbing on his arm, he began to weave. Holding his breath with his eyes tightly closed and his jaw clenched hard from the pain, he appeared as if he might break his teeth were he to bite any harder. Suddenly, he relaxed, slumped over, and fell to his left. Dr. Rhodes caught him before he fell off the chair.

As Ron started to recover from his episode of pain-induced syncope, Dr. Rhodes ordered, "You're going under now, mister. No arguments."

Still dazed and in great pain, he replied through clenched teeth, "You'll get none from me this time, Doc."

Dr. Rhodes lowered the chair to the reclining position and intravenously injected a fast-acting anesthesia into Ron's left forearm. He was asleep in less than ten seconds. Just then, Chris stuck his head in the capsule to speak for a moment with Ron. Upon seeing that the chief engineer was asleep, Chris said, "I was going to tell

Ron what Jay and I discussed about building a tree house as a permanent quarters for the men and ask him his opinion on a few things."

Dr. Rhodes glanced at Chris as he popped his head in the capsule, but didn't say anything.

"What's going on with him, Doc?" Chris asked, his voice concerned. "How's he doing?"

She continued to work as she answered him. "This man has a serious infection, and I don't know if the antimicrobial meds and antiseptic ointments I'm providing him are doing any good at all. He has some kind of microorganism growing in, and on, his skin, and I can't remove the infected tissue without the risk of making him much worse."

"Is there anything I can do to help?" asked Chris.

"If you're a religious man, pray for me to gain the knowledge to figure this out and for him to heal," she said as she continued to clean the wound.

Chris went back to the campfire.

Dr. Rhodes couldn't remove the white frothy area containing the infecting microbes from his arm without surgically removing the entire upper and middle dermal layers of skin. She cleaned the rest of the burned area, applied ointment, and re-bandaged his arm. When finished, she went outside to join the others, leaving Ron asleep on the chair in the capsule. Chris had already told the group what he knew about Ron, and the mood around the campfire was solemn.

"How is he?" asked Jay.

"Not good. He has a mild fever. I gave him enough sedative that he'll sleep until morning. I've never seen anything like this before. It's similar to a flesh-eating bacterium but acts more like a fungus. The microbe is producing a foamy froth on his skin. Antibiotics aren't touching it, and neither are the antifungal drugs I have. I don't have the proper equipment or supplies to remove the infected skin without potentially making him worse. All I can do right now is wait and watch to see if his body can fight it. I have to grow the specimens I retrieved from his skin in a medium before I can do further research to see what can kill the microbes before they kill Ron. At this point, I'm not sure if even an amputation of the arm would save him."

There was not much conversation after Dr. Rhodes informed everyone of Ron's condition. Jay was glad that Sandy had decided to sleep outside with him since Ron was occupying one of the beds, still out from the sedative. Jay was snuggling with her now, but mentally he was struggling with the pressures of losing some of his best friends on *Copernicus*, dealing with the dangerous creatures here, wondering how they were going to be rescued, and now knowing that Ron might not make it. Seeming to sense Jay's mood, Judy approached with sad eyes and sat by his side.

"Can you read minds, Judy? Are you psychic?" Jay asked her.

She just continued her sad stare. He gently stroked her head and lightly scratched behind her ears. Judy leaned against him. Sandy switched sides so that she could pet Judy too. Sandy's pidogg followed and lay at her feet. Judy closed her eyes, enjoying the attention from Jay, groaning lightly, and giving the couple a gentle pidogg purr.

Chris had made animal behavior a major part of his studies while working on his PhD. Judy might not have been able to read minds, but Chris could see that she was an expert reader of body language, even picking up on human facial expressions. He marveled at how quickly she had learned how to interpret human emotions and needs based on body language and expressions. He made a mental note to add the observation to his log.

Miranda's pidogg friend came over and lay at her feet. Chris observed as she reached over and began stroking the pidogg's head and neck. The animal closed its eyes and made the pidogg purring noise, ever so softly.

"You're a natural with these guys," Chris said.

Miranda replied, "I grew up in a home with dogs. I loved them—still do, for that matter—and I know what they like." She made a funny face and wrinkled her nose and then continued. "Other than the smell, they're not so much different than the ones I had back home." Miranda stroked down the pidogg's back and started to scratch just in front of the tail.

I wonder, Chris thought. He watched as the pidogg raised her back end to push into Miranda's hand, so that the scratching was deeper. *Aha! I thought so! Just like the dogs on Earth. More to add to the documentation.* The animal purred louder and deeper, and Miranda smiled.

"I think you have a friend for life," Chris said, enjoying the interaction. He loved dogs too.

The remaining pidoggs alternated between standing watch and sleeping the rest of the night.

Chris awoke early. He'd had a disturbing nightmare about trying to get off the doomed ship. In his dream, beach ball–size meteors were shooting through the ship, punching holes that wanted to suck him into the void of space like the crew members before him. The spacecraft stood on its aft end, falling toward the planet, and the artificial gravity shifted to the aft bulkhead. He saw the ghosts of his dead shipmates beckoning him to join them outside the ship. He hated himself for turning his back on his ghostly friends, but he wanted to live! He had to climb and claw his way forward to get to the escape pods as the ship fell toward the atmosphere. When he arrived in the Emergency Departure Compartment, all the pods were gone. He awoke just as the ghosts surrounded him, smiling, and the ship began to burn up in the atmosphere. Shaking off the bad dream, he took a moment before he stood to make his 180-centimeter frame reach 190. *It was just a dream, just a bad dream.* Stretching his arms and arching his back from side to side, he reached toward the sky to touch the clouds that weren't there, working out the kinks from sleeping on the ground. *I'm not getting any younger, and this isn't getting any easier.* It was going to be another beautiful day.

Chris looked back to the capsule in time to see the XO standing at the open hatch for a moment, watching his maneuvers, before stepping down the ladder. The XO playfully asked, "Did the princess find the pea she slept on last night? I'd offer you a cup of coffee, but the supply officer missed that line item on my requisition list for the escape capsules, and we ran out of breakfast pastries last week."

Her playfulness surprised Chris. The XO never joked. *Circumstances sure make strange bedfellows,* he almost said aloud. He smiled while shaking his head. Looking around the campsite, he saw that Miranda had fallen asleep with her arm around her pidogg friend. *Strange bedfellows indeed!*

His thoughts returned to the XO. On the *Copernicus*, she was always all business, respecting military protocol and expecting it in return. This reminded him that he needed to talk to her about the chain of command while they were stranded on this planet.

"XO, may I have a word?" Chris asked.

"Certainly," she replied. As she stepped closer to him, she asked, "What can I do for you, Chris?"

"May I speak freely, sir?" In the military, female officers were properly addressed by their rank or as sir or ma'am.

With a puzzled look on her face, she answered, "Of course."

"It's about the chain of command. As you know, I hold the rank of lieutenant commander. It's more of an honorific rank due to my PhD because I'm a scientist, not a line officer. Miranda, a lieutenant, is also a scientist. Ron holds the highest rank next to yours as a line officer and lieutenant commander, but he's on the binnacle list because he's severely ill. Jay is a line officer and lieutenant; Sandy, also a lieutenant, is a supply officer; and Dr. Rhodes holds the same rank as you, but she's a medical officer. As the highest-ranking line officer here, you're in charge of the survivors until we're rescued and you are relieved by a higher command. I sort of unofficially took charge of our group prior to our arrival here, but now that we are all together, you should be in charge."

The XO studied Chris for a few moments before speaking. She turned around and took two steps away from him and toward the capsule before turning back around to face him.

"Yes, and as you correctly pointed out, I am a line officer. As the highest-ranking line officer here, I'm officially and technically in charge and responsible for the safety and welfare of my crew. However, on this strange new planet, you as a xenobiologist have vastly more knowledge of what it may take to survive. I've had training in escaping and evading, and I've even had desert and jungle survival training—but on Earth. Those skills are of little value here. I'm out of my element. If we were under attack and needed a military strategic plan, I would lead us to victory or defeat, but our situation here fits much better into your bailiwick."

Chris listened intently as would a junior officer, but he was beginning to feel uncomfortable with what he was hearing. He broke eye contact with her for a moment and shifted his weight from one side to the other, his discomfort obvious.

The XO paused for a moment, turned her back to Chris, and took one step up to the capsule hatch before turning to face him again. With the elevated position emphasizing her command authority, she said, "Look what you've already done for us. Do you realize that if it were not for you and your knowledge, we probably would have died here when our supplies ran out? Most likely we wouldn't have been able to get together as a group either, decreasing our chances of survival even more. If we get back to civilization, it's my intention to write the highest commendation within my authority for you, Dr. Rhodes, Jay, and Ron for actions and continued service well beyond the call of duty, for saving our lives and keeping us alive for the duration of our stay here." She took one more step up toward the hatch opening. "It's also *my* prerogative, as the highest-ranking officer *and* official order, that you be placed in charge of all planet-side operations. If it makes you more comfortable to review actions that will affect the group as a whole with me prior to implementation, I will agree. However, you will have the final decision in the end. Based on your past actions, I have complete faith in your judgment regarding our safety and welfare while we're marooned here."

Chris didn't want the responsibility for everyone's life. He was doing just what had to be done. He stepped closer to the capsule, to dissuade her from this decision. "Sir, I don't think I deserve—" He didn't get the chance to finish.

Straightening her stance, the XO looked down at him from the steps and said sharply, in a commanding tone, "Stop right there, mister! I will not have you disrespect me and this uniform by disagreeing with my military judgment *or* my authority. Until such time as *I* see fit, you *will* take charge of this group and do so to the best of your ability. Do I make myself *clear … Lieutenant* Commander?"

Chris stiffened upright to immediate attention. His military indoctrination was rusty, but he knew that while being dressed down by a superior officer, you stood at attention. The rest he had mostly forgotten. Looking straight ahead and not at the XO, he offered and held a salute to her. "Yes, sir! I will do my utmost to promote and provide a safe and ongoing living environment for the surviving crew of the United Earth Space Force ship *Copernicus*, until such time as rescue has been successful or the last member of the crew has died."

The XO returned the salute and stepped back down the steps to stand in front of Chris on even ground. She placed her hand on his shoulder, softened her voice, and said, "Chris, listen. I'm depending on the skill of every one of us to keep the group going. We need everyone. I especially need you. It's been your leadership that has gotten us this far. It's been your ingenuity that has gotten us together, making it easier for everyone to survive. Yes, everyone has helped, especially Jay with his pidogg friends, but without what you have already done for the group, I feel we'd be fighting a losing battle. I need you. We all need you. For heaven's sake! At ease!"

"Yes, sir!" he replied and relaxed his stance.

Trying to lighten his sudden new burden, the XO said, "Chris, look. We're going to be here for a very long time, maybe for the rest of our lives. I'm authorizing everyone to be on a first-name basis. I just ask that we all treat each other with respect. Arguments and fighting among ourselves will get us nowhere and will do nothing except jeopardize our survival capabilities. Please … call me Caitlyn."

Chris relaxed his stance further and met her eyes. "Yes, sir … Caitlyn."

They both smiled and then laughed.

The pidoggs on sentry duty were all standing. The ones facing the northeast seemed agitated. Then Chris and Caitlyn saw the commotion—two very large carnivores were fighting over the carcass of the beast slain the day before. They weren't as large as the slain animal, but were large nonetheless.

Watching the animals fight, Chris said to Caitlyn, "They remind me of drawings of the ancient and extinct giant bear *Arctodus simus*. Hmm, I haven't thought of that name in quite a while."

Sandy walked up to join them, apparently having overheard part of the conversation as she approached. "What's an *arktis sinus*?"

Chris turned to Sandy and corrected her. "*Arctodus simus. Arctodus simus* was a bear that went extinct about twelve thousand years ago. It was as tall as a man at its shoulders when it was standing on all four legs. It could reach up almost four meters high when on two legs and weighed just shy of a metric ton. It would eat anything it could catch."

"Sounds very dangerous," Caitlyn remarked.

"It was. It was the largest carnivorous land animal in North America during its reign on Earth. I'm glad they're not around anymore." Watching the giants battle, he added, "On Earth, anyway."

Whistling to catch Jay's attention, Chris nodded his head toward the bearlike creatures. Jay immediately understood the nonverbal communication and threw more logs on the fire, stoking it to bonfire size.

"If we had to, everyone could fit into the capsule, but with standing room only," Caitlyn noted.

"Let's hope it doesn't come to that," Chris responded.

The XO called everyone to the campfire for a meeting. Ron was up and about but still in pain, despite the pain meds that Holly Rhodes had given him. Once everyone was gathered, Caitlyn raised the difficult topic of how unlikely a rescue was. It could be years before it came, she warned, or possibly rescue would not come at all. She informed the survivors that Chris was to be the de facto leader of the group based on his experience and training but acknowledged that everyone was important and that their knowledge contributed to the overall well-being of the group. In addition, given their current situation, military protocol was being relaxed, and everyone could address each other by their first names. She emphasized that cordial cooperation was imperative for the survival of all in the group. Everyone agreed to abide by her decisions.

Ron was sitting next to Miranda at the fire, supporting his right arm and not joining in the conversation with the rest of the group, when Judy walked up to him and sniffed his bad arm.

Surprised, he asked, "What are you doing, girl?" He didn't really expect an answer, but he was still wary of the pidoggs.

She stopped sniffing and started to pull at the bandages with her teeth.

Startled, Ron stood up and shouted, "Stop that!"

Judy sat back on her haunches with a puzzled expression on her face. Seeing what Judy was attempting, Holly said, "I have an idea ..."

Chris's face suddenly lit up. "Yes, animals on Earth will lick their wounds to clean them," he said. "Their saliva contains enzymes that can help control infection."

"Exactly!" exclaimed Holly. "I've been culturing the microbes from Ron's arm and would like to try a test. Jay, do you think Judy will let me collect a sample of her saliva?"

"I don't know why not. She seems to like and trust us enough," he replied.

Holly disappeared inside the capsule and returned with a few swabs. She approached Judy, who indeed just sat there and let the doctor collect her samples.

"Ron, I want to take some of the gauze that has Judy's saliva on it too. It will have additional microbes on it that I may be able to culture and test. We may have to use good microbes, if we can find them, to fight the bad microbes."

"Sure, Doc, take as much as you want," he said somewhat sarcastically, resigned to his fate and not expecting a miracle. He gave Judy a distrustful glance.

Dr. Rhodes went back into the capsule and retrieved the growing samples of the infectious microbes from a makeshift shelf where they stayed warm and could grow. Placing them on a small workstation desk, she took a sterile swab and carefully smeared the saliva in different quantities in separate areas. She then took a section of the bandage with Judy's saliva on it and laid it across another area in the dish, saving some for later microscopic study. She labeled each container and then, content with her work, rejoined the others outside.

Looking up at Dr. Rhodes as she approached, Ron asked, "Doc, what do you really expect to happen?"

"Under these circumstances it's difficult to predict. The biology on this planet has evolved under similar yet different enough circumstances than on Earth that I need to test my theories on how to defeat the survival mechanisms of the microbes infecting your arm. Microbes are the most abundant life form and the most versatile at adapting to environmental changes on any planet. Some can adapt to challenges within minutes to hours, others from days to weeks, whereas larger life forms may take centuries to change, if they can adapt at all. All non-microbial life forms, both plant and animal, have to adapt to keep up with the microbes' ability to quickly change.

Only the life forms that are able to adapt their immune responses quickly will survive. It's a constant battle—microbes are trying to survive by feeding on what's available to them, and the higher forms of life have to create immunity against the microbes. Without the ability to adapt, any species will go extinct. With her innate ability to adapt to disease-causing entities on this planet, Judy's body may have, must have, formed a way to beat this type of microbe. We'll know in a day or so when I check the samples." Holly turned and walked back toward the capsule.

As Holly passed Ron, he looked away and faced the ground. "If I last that long, Doc," he said softly but seriously.

She stopped and turned back to face him. Softening her demeanor, she approached his left side and placed her hand on his good shoulder. "I'm doing everything I can, Ron. The one thing I have no control over is time. I need time to determine the best course of action to help you." Concerned with the way Ron was holding his right arm, Dr. Rhodes asked, "You still appear to be in pain. Do you want more pain meds?"

Without looking up, he shook his head and replied, "No, not yet. I'll put up with as much as I can for now. I don't want to become a burden by being dopey on drugs. I also don't want to put anyone else at risk because I don't have my head on straight."

Giving him a light pat on his good shoulder, she said, "Okay, but for now you'll spend your nights in the capsule, not on the ground outside."

Turning his head and glancing up only enough to catch her eyes before looking back to the ground, Ron said softly, "Thanks, Doc."

12

The pidoggs standing perimeter duty became agitated again, sounding off with low growling and huffing noises. The ones resting stood and watched intensely in the same direction as the sentries. Chris noticed their concentrated demeanor and scanned in the direction the pidoggs were staring. A battle of the giant carnivores over the carcass had ended. The loser, bloodied but not seriously injured, was hastily vacating the immediate area and moving in the direction of the group's campsite. The giant bear was about halfway to the campsite when six male and four female pidoggs made off in its direction to intercept the animal before it got much closer. The pidoggs that were supposed to be resting automatically filled in the ranks for the pidoggs that had left to defend the group. Chris shouted to everyone outside to be prepared to cram into the capsule. Holly was already inside. Ron herded Miranda and Sandy to the hatch and waited outside to watch the action. Chris threw a couple of logs on the fire while Jay stirred the fire to get it going better.

Chris turned to Caitlyn and pointed in the direction of the oncoming danger. "You'd better get into the capsule. It may get dicey out here."

She agreed and made a hasty retreat to the capsule.

"I want to see this," said Jay.

"I do too, but before that animal gets within a couple hundred meters of us, we bail to safety."

"Roger that," Jay said.

When the pidoggs got within two hundred meters of the creature, they started barking, growling, huffing, and snapping their teeth while charging the animal head-on. The bear slowed its headlong retreat from its defeat, trying to take in the new threat. Seeing that it was hopelessly outnumbered, it skidded to an abrupt halt and turned east at high speed, retreating now toward the edge of the wooded area, with the pidoggs in hot pursuit. The men watched as the sentries chased the giant carnivore out of sight around the corner of the woodlot.

As they walked back to the capsule to let the women know it was safe to come out, Jay smiled and said to Chris, "That was amazing! I wonder if its ego got bruised by being bested twice in row!"

"I hope it learned the lesson that being around here is dangerous. I'm not crazy about having something that large and hungry anywhere near us," Chris said emphatically.

"Amen to that!" responded Jay.

"We'll still have the winner in the area for a while. Until that carcass is consumed, it'll keep close by," commented Chris.

As the two men approached his position outside the hatch, Ron added, "Hmm. Maybe we should keep more than one fire going."

"I think that's a good idea," Chris said. "How about three in a triangular pattern around the campsite?"

"More might be better, but it would take a lot of wood, not to mention all the work, to keep them all going," Jay added.

Noticing Ron supporting his arm at the elbow again, Chris asked, "How's the arm?"

"Not so good. Any movement at all sends lightning blasts of pain up through the shoulder and into my neck."

"I'm sure that Doc will come through with something," Jay said confidently.

"I hope so. My mood is worsening, and the pain is getting so that I'll need to take her stronger pain meds more often. I'm worried that I'm going to cause a problem for the group or become some critter's lunch because I can't move fast enough while in a drug-induced stupor."

"That's not going to happen," Chris assured him. "We'll take good care of you. After all, who else here has the skill to engineer the men's tree house that we still need to discuss building?" Chris smiled, trying to lighten Ron's mood.

"You do," Ron said dejectedly. "It seems that you're the jack-of-all-trades around here."

Chris shook his head. "Not as much as you think. I still need verification that anything I design will stand the rigors of a UESF engineering inspection, and that's you, my friend."

The corners of Ron's mouth turned up a bit. "Thanks, Chris. I hope I'll be well enough to help build it too."

The carcass-winning bear had finally eaten its fill and wandered away from the kill. Sensing an opportunity to eat, the pidoggs took advantage of the abandoned food source. The group that had chased off the challenger went first. After eating their fill, they returned to their duty stations and relieved the on-duty sentries so that they too could feast on the leftover meal. The rotation continued until all the pidoggs had eaten. Not forgetting the humans or the juveniles, three pidoggs brought back three large pieces of meat, dropping two between Jay and Chris and another off to the side for the youngsters. The young pidoggs attacked the meat, and in short order it was gone.

"I wish my résumé included linguistics skills," Chris said. "I'd love to get into their heads to find out how they think. It's not unusual for an animal to adopt another animal of a different species. I've seen ducks and chickens adopted by dogs and cats. Once a crow took care of a kitten and helped raise it to adulthood, and they were lifelong best friends. However, our situation is even more incredible. It's like a pack of hyenas adopting a pride of lions, both predators in their own right, but supporting each other in times of need."

"Not only supporting, but protecting too," Jay said.

Chris nodded in agreement. "Exactly. It must be their natural instinct for survival. They're obviously not the largest predator here. Although they're formidable, one or two against the likes of that giant bear wouldn't stand a chance. However, as a group … let me rephrase that … as a highly trained, coordinated group, they do very well indeed. It's almost like watching military maneuvers, except they don't have to be trained how to do it. They have a natural hunting and protective instinct as a group."

Later in the day, Chris and Jay left with an escort of pidoggs to gather more wood to feed the three hungry fires they had burning. One of the younger male pidoggs parted company with the group for less than a minute to chase down a rodent that it then brought to Jay and laid at his feet. Jay nodded his head and said thank you. The young pidogg, clearly feeling proud of his accomplishment and holding his head high, rejoined the escort pack. It was apparent, though, by the way one of the older pidoggs dressed him down that it was not all right for him to have left the group while on duty. Chris smiled sympathetically, totally understanding how the young male felt. It took most of the day and many trips, but by evening they had collected enough firewood to keep the three fires going for several days. It was dark by the time Chris and Jay finished stacking the firewood and were able to sit, rest, and get something to eat.

The stars seemed exceptionally bright in the clear evening sky. Everyone gathered around the campfires, trying to stay warm in the cool night air. Every so often, a pidogg would rise and relieve an on-duty sentry. Dr. Rhodes, Ron, and Miranda were huddled around one campfire, while Jay and Sandy snuggled together at another. Chris saw that Caitlyn was sitting alone at the third campfire. He walked over and poked at the fire with a stick to reposition some of the logs, to get them burning better, and sat down next to her. Chris quietly finished logging his daily pidogg observations and those of the bearlike animal on his tablet computer and then shut down his computer for the evening and tucked it away in his backpack. Enjoying the peaceful evening, Chris watched heat from the fire carry spiraling sparks upward into the night air. The only sounds were the crackle of the burning logs and the low tones of Jay and Sandy talking quietly.

As they warmed themselves alone by the campfire, Chris noticed that Caitlyn seemed lost in thought and leaned a little closer to her. Wanting to take up her offer of being less military and more friendly toward each other, he asked, "How did you come about joining the UESF?"

"It's a long story," she replied.

Holding up an imaginary electronic calendar, he said, "Just a minute, let me check my schedule … Hmm, I seem to have the time if you do."

Returning his smile but still gazing into the fire, Caitlyn leaned toward Chris close enough to touch shoulders. She spoke in a quiet voice. "When I was a child growing up in a small town near Indianapolis, Indiana, I dreamed of becoming an astronaut, taking part in important missions that would help replenish raw materials that our burgeoning population was exhausting. I wanted to become a pilot for an asteroid mining ship or do some other job that would get me off our overcrowded planet. It might have been selfish of me, but that's what I wanted at the time. As I grew into adolescence, I began to understand more about the complexities and difficulties of living on an overcrowded planet. I wanted to do something that was bigger than I was and still be able to contribute to our society. I thought of becoming a doctor, but I didn't have the passion that doctors need to treat people on an individual basis. I needed a different challenge, one that would stress me physically as well as mentally. As a preteen, I joined a Civil Air Patrol composite squadron as an airman basic. As I progressed through the cadet program, I had numerous senior-member mentors, many of whom were former or retired military personnel. I also had help from the squadron's senior cadets with the protocols I needed to learn. Are you familiar with the Civil Air Patrol and what they do?"

"Not really," Chris said.

"It's an all-volunteer organization, and it's the civilian auxiliary of the United States Air Force. The organization began seven days before Pearl Harbor was bombed in 1941. Pilots and observers would fly single-engine aircraft to patrol for enemy submarines that might attack merchant shipping along the coasts of the continental United States. If they spotted an intruder, they would notify the US Naval forces to the whereabouts of the sub. Many times the Navy was too far away to help, so the government authorized the CAP aircraft to carry bombs. They got credit for sinking or damaging two submarines, but just as important, they chased many of them away."

Chris bent forward and poked at the burning logs with a stick. The flames blazed a little brighter.

Feeling the cold air where Chris had been in body contact with her, Caitlyn leaned closer to the fire to remain shoulder-to-shoulder with him as she continued. "The CAP operates in a military manner, with rules and regulations for guidelines, and is very similar to the way the United States Air Force is organized and operated. CAP has three main branches, emergency services, aerospace education, and a cadet program. The emergency services branch conducts search and rescue operations for missing aircraft and people, as well as disaster relief services, which include assisting federal, state, and local government agencies by performing aerial photography, sandbagging rivers or creeks to help prevent flooding, delivering food and water to people in need, and other similar duties. It also has an elaborate nationwide radio communications network and is prepared to be used as an emergency backup for the nation's communications if there is a widespread telecommunication network failure. Aerospace education has to do with flying, model rocketry, and anything that has to do with outer space activities." Caitlyn hesitated for a moment. "Am I boring you with all this?"

Chris shook his head. "Not at all. I find it interesting how certain events early in someone's life can make such an impression that they lay the foundation for how the person lives the rest of her life. I can see how the Civil Air Patrol gave you a great start to your military career. Please, continue."

"You're exactly right. It had a tremendous influence. For me it was the cadet program. It trains young adults in aerospace education, which includes five separate hours of introduction to flying where they actually get to fly an airplane. That's where I fell in love with flying. The cadets learn United States Air Force military customs and courtesies and proper protocols with an emphasis on physical fitness, character development, discipline, and leadership. The cadets can also participate in emergency services activities if they take the training."

Caitlyn noticed that Chris seemed to be more relaxed and to be enjoying their time together. She didn't mind that he snuggled a little closer, and she wondered if it was just to share warmth.

She paused for a moment, slightly distracted but enjoying his closeness, before she continued. "In order to make rank, a cadet is expected to not just learn the information and be able to regurgitate it for a test; the cadet has to demonstrate and put his or her knowledge into practice by becoming a mentor and leader him or herself. As a CAP cadet, I was fortunate enough to participate in the emergency services program and participated in many search and rescue and disaster relief operations. I also took advantage of the aerospace education program and received my private pilot's license just after I turned sixteen. Once I started flying, I was hooked for life. I was able to complete my pilot training with instrument and commercial ratings while still a cadet. I also excelled in the cadet program. I received the Spaatz Award, the highest obtainable as a cadet, and was one of the youngest cadets to make rank as a cadet colonel in the Indiana Wing, but I wanted more."

Caitlyn shivered a little from the cold as a light breeze blew through. Chris put his arm across her shoulders and pulled her a little closer. She didn't object.

Chris asked, "If you already had the highest awards, what else was there?"

"Nothing more from the CAP, so I entered the Air Force Reserve

Officers Training Corp at Purdue University in West Lafayette, Indiana, as a non-scholarship student and became the cadet commander within a year. After two years in the Air Force ROTC, I switched programs to the Navy ROTC at the University of South Florida in Tampa, Florida. I switched because I wanted a chance of becoming an officer on a spaceship. I joined the UESF when I was twenty-three years old, six months after graduating at the top of my class in college. Although I was fully qualified for a commission as an officer, I was sent to Great Lakes for boot camp in Lake County, Illinois, north of Chicago. At first, I thought it was because I'd completed my degree as a non-scholarship student and completed only two years in the naval program. I brought this to the attention of my boot camp company commander but was ignored. With the military training I had as a CAP cadet, I didn't argue with my superiors, even though I disagreed with their decision and inaction."

Chris used the stick in his free hand to shift a burning log to get a better blaze going and asked, "What did you do?"

Watching the sparks dancing upward on the heated air currents, she said, "Obviously, I was disappointed, but once you are in the military, they own you, and as you know, you can't disobey orders without suffering dire consequences. After boot camp, I was sent to train as a hospital corpsman, and I graduated at the top of my class in field medicine. I soon made rate as a third-class hospital corpsman. When the chief yeoman at my first duty station was making the rate increase in my service record, he noted a serious discrepancy, a wrong entry, which for some unknown reason had not been caught by the system computers. Someone else's grades, including their name and service number, were mixed in with my records, and my ROTC training records were missing. When my ROTC records were restored, and the proper test scores were entered into my record, I immediately applied and was accepted to the U.S. Navy Officer Candidate School, where I graduated at the top of my class. Since I had been accepted as enlisted personnel when first joining, I was required to attend Officer Candidate School prior to becoming a commissioned officer. I accepted the mistakes as an extension of my CAP character-development training with no misgivings. I actually got to experience, on a small scale, what it would have been like to become a doctor and was glad to have had the experience."

After stifling a yawn—he was tired but not at all bored, he assured her—Chris remarked, "That's a fascinating story. As I said before, I find it interesting how early events can shape one's life. I can see how your Civil Air Patrol experience influenced your career decisions." Chris knew that he was tired, that he was repeating himself, but he didn't want to end the night just yet. "By the way, you never told me how you got off the ship."

Snuggling a little closer in Chris's embrace, using the chill in the air as an excuse, she said, "I was a couple of decks below the bridge and on my way to engineering to confer with Ted Stevens about an engineering drill that was to happen on his watch when the meteors struck. When the debris and escaping air started flying past me, I lost my balance and began tumbling down the passageway. I managed to stop my own headlong tumble by grabbing hold of an open doorway, and I managed to stay upright while I got an oxygen mask from one of the nearby emergency cabinets. I tried to communicate with the bridge and the captain, but all comms were out. I eventually made my way to the EDC when the abandon-ship sirens went off, but with all the debris flying about and clogging the passageway, it took me longer than I thought it would. I waited in the EDC until the loss of air pressure felt like it was going to cause my eyeballs to burst before I decided to abandon ship, and that's when Miranda came stumbling in, badly injured. I helped her into a pod, and we made our escape together."

Chris turned, looked into her eyes, and said sincerely, "Well, I for one am very glad you made it off the ship." Chris tried to stifle another yawn.

Caitlyn imagined that fatigue from the many trips carrying firewood finally was getting the better of him. "We should get some rest," she said, seeing how hard he was trying to stay awake.

Chris insisted that he walk Caitlyn to her capsule before leaving her for the evening. Only partially able to suppress the next yawn, he said, "I'm sorry. I just can't stop yawning. I still want to hear how you were almost dinner."

"You will, later. Right now, you need to get some sleep. I'll see you in the morning. Good night." Caitlyn couldn't help but smile.

Yawning again and turning away, he said, "You're right. In the morning then. Good night."

Caitlyn stood at the hatch and watched him walk away for a long moment before closing the hatch.

Dr. Holly Rhodes, Ron, and Miranda had turned in for the night about an hour earlier. Covered with only a survival blanket, Jay and Sandy lay curled up near the fire, warmed a bit more by their lean-to shelter that Jay had rigged using two silver survival blankets suspended between sticks to reflect the heat of the fire back on them. They had fallen asleep in each other's arms. Judy, ever protective of her own, was lying awake next to them, her pups sound asleep nearby.

For several weeks, it was relatively peaceful for the group. The pidoggs were ever vigilant when on duty. They were extremely efficient in their organization for sharing workload, food, and rest breaks. There was even some time for playful activities with the juveniles. Sticks of wood and pieces of vines that would have become kindling became great tug-of-war items but usually didn't last too long in their sharp teeth. Chris had to remind everyone that anything left on the ground became a plaything for the young animals and to keep the camp neat. Small hunting parties of six to eight pidoggs would come and go. Mostly, they were successful with small game and even some of the larger animals, which they gladly shared with their human friends. Chris and Jay successfully honed their bow and arrow skills and became proficient in hunting the plentiful game in the area. While hunting for food, they learned more about the layout of the land and kept their eye out for building material and an area more suitable for a permanent shelter.

Chris awoke to a cool but sunny morning, peeled back his sleeping bag, and then stretched and yawned before climbing out. He walked over to the fire and stirred it to life before throwing on a couple of new logs. Miranda joined him at the fire.

"Morning, Chris," she said.

"Good morning, Miranda," he responded.

"It looks like it's going to be another beautiful day," she said, gazing skyward.

"Yes, it does," he said while rearranging the smoldering logs.

As Chris repositioned the burning wood, some ashes became airborne in the fire's convection currents. Caught in the light breeze blowing from the west, the ashes drifted across the fire. Miranda suddenly grabbed at her left eye.

"What's wrong?" Chris asked.

"Something flew into my eye. I think it was a cinder from the fire."

"Let me take a look," he said.

"That's okay. Okay … I think I got it," she said as she turned away from him and started toward the capsule, wiping away the tears from under her eye.

"Let me take a look anyway," Chris insisted.

She hesitated and then reluctantly stopped and turned around to face him.

"Ah. Now I know why you didn't want me to look," he said as her eye continued to water and began to redden.

"It's pretty obvious, isn't it?" she said reluctantly.

"Having one blue eye and one brown eye isn't a crime, you know," Chris said.

Holding a brown contact lens in her hand, she turned away

slightly and glanced at the ground to break eye contact. Miranda responded, "Maybe not, but when you're a female, any physical detractors are usually hidden or camouflaged somehow. And you have to admit, with my dark hair and complexion, my blue eye stands out like a clown at a funeral."

"Oh, come now. It's not that bad," Chris said.

"You have no idea what it's like to be different. When I was a young girl, I used to get people staring at me all the time. I was teased unmercifully by other kids until I started wearing a brown contact lens to make my eyes look the same. Finally, the teasing stopped, and life went on normally for me." Sighing deeply and wiping away the tears that were still forming from the irritation, she said, "I suppose it's just as well. I'm almost out of lenses anyway."

"I take it Doc knows?"

"Sure. She's been supplying the contacts for me since I reported aboard *Copernicus*. The condition is called Waardenburg's syndrome, a nonthreatening genetic flaw. Apparently, it wasn't something that the UESF thought was disqualifying enough to keep me from serving," she said as she turned and tipped her head down to look away from Chris.

"Well, I think you still look beautiful, and so will everyone else. Don't give it another thought," Chris said, trying to console her.

Still somewhat embarrassed and covering her blue eye while pretending to wipe away more tears, she cocked her partially raised head to look up at him and with a small smile said, "Thanks, Chris."

Stepping out of the capsule, Dr. Rhodes spied Ron sitting near one of the fires. "How's your arm today?" she asked.

"About one point higher on the Richter pain scale," he responded, looking up at her from the portable folding chair to see if she caught the joke.

She either didn't get it or was ignoring it. "I got the final results from the samples I took and tested, and the results are promising."

"You don't sound too enthusiastic, Doc. What's the bad news?"

Trying to look cheerful about the good news, she said, "The saliva we collected from Judy proved very effective for the infection that you have in the reddened area near and on your shoulder, but"—she hesitated for a moment—"minimally effective for the white area just above your elbow."

"What does that mean?"

"It means that we can treat the shoulder and several centimeters below it on your arm successfully." She broke eye contact and paused for another moment before she continued. "It also means that if we can't find a natural cure here for the rest of the infection, you may lose your arm." Dr. Rhodes made eye contact again.

Ron turned pale and turned away to look at the ground. There was an uncomfortable pause before he said, "Terrific."

Dr. Rhodes dropped in front of Ron so that they were face to face. Taking a serious but gentle tone, she said, "Ron, look at me."

He raised his chin a little to turn and look up at her, but mostly with his eyes.

"If we have to take the arm, it will only be to save your life. When we're rescued and back to Earth, tissue banks can use stem cells harvested from your blood to grow you a new arm. It takes only a few months to grow with the new accelerated growth hormones, and then surgeons can attach it. Within a year and with some therapy, you'll have the full use of your arm back."

"Like I said … terrific. You know as well as I do that it's unlikely we'll be rescued. That means that I'll be dragging everyone down as a handicapper around here. I'm already unable to do much work with my left arm *and* with the limited use I have of my right hand. With only one arm and hand, I'm sure I'll be even less useful, even if the pain does go away."

Using a gentle tone but assuming the command authority of a military doctor, Dr. Rhodes stood and said, "I'm not going to say it will be easy, but we'll still have you, and everything that you can contribute will still be of benefit to the group. You haven't lost the arm yet, and I'm doing everything in my power to see that you don't.

So don't give up on me yet, mister. Now, let's find Judy and get that upper arm treated."

Dr. Rhodes was able to collect enough saliva from Judy to treat Ron's arm several times. It wasn't very hard. Even though Judy was a stern mother when it came to her offspring, she was actually quite playful with the humans. Holly was able to tease her with a piece of meat, getting her to salivate freely before giving the treat to her. Once the collection was made, Judy got her treat, and everyone was happy, except Ron.

"Ron, you're acting like a juvenile."

Looking at the doctor but not catching her eye, he said, "Maybe, Doc, but you're not the one having dog spit spread all over your arm and shoulder."

Continuing to stir the saliva in a cup, she asked, "Have you ever eaten honey?"

"Sure."

"That's bee spit mixed with pollen. It's more the thought of it than the process. This doesn't even have an odor."

"No, but it's slimy."

Dr. Rhodes looked squarely into Ron's eyes and responded sternly. "So was the dead and infected tissue I scraped off your arm, but you don't hear me complaining. And it was smelly too."

Embarrassed, Ron looked down and away. "I'm sorry, Doc. Really, I am. I just feel so useless, and the pain is unrelenting. It's getting to me."

With understanding but not sympathy, she said, "I know. Can we get started?"

Facing to his left so that he didn't have to watch, Ron said, "Okay, but let's get this over with quickly before I gag and puke."

Dr. Rhodes smiled as she poured the saliva over Ron's shoulder. As it made its way slowly down his arm, she thoroughly enjoyed the look on Ron's face. She continued to spread the saliva over the white area of infection using a tongue depressor with the hope that it would slow the growth of the unknown microorganism.

"How does that feel?" she asked, still smiling.

With his face scrunched in unpleasant disgust, Ron replied, "When you were pouring that stuff on my shoulder, I was reminded of a video I once saw of a gazelle on an extremely hot day in Africa salivating excessively while its fawn lapped it up before it could hit the ground. It made me gag then, and the thought of you pouring that stuff on my shoulder is bringing back all those memories. Yuck and double yuck!"

Dr. Rhodes couldn't help but chuckle as she finished the treatment and re-bandaged his arm and shoulder.

13

The air was getting cooler by day, and it was downright cold at night. Dr. Rhodes and Ron stayed at the campsite during the day while the rest of their party headed to the wooded area where Chris had found a place to build a suitable dwelling for the men. Ron wanted to help, but at the insistence of Dr. Rhodes, who was worried about reinfection, he stayed back at the campsite, being as useful as she allowed. As long as the wood was cut so that he could pick it up with one hand, he could keep the campfires burning. However, maintaining the campfires only *seemed* to be effective at keeping the campsite safe. The pidoggs always had the first opportunity at chasing away any would-be opportunistic carnivores before they came anywhere near them.

The pidogg family seemed to be growing, but not because they were reproducing. It seemed that word had gotten around that living with the humans was a good thing and made life easier, and to a certain extent that was true. There were close to eighty of them now. The pidoggs that stood guard duty had fewer hours to stand watch because there were more watch standers. When the men and women would head to the wooded area to work on the men's quarters or to gather more firewood, there were more pidogg escorts available, making the work party feel safer. The problem was that their hunting parties were coming back with fewer and fewer game animals, causing tension within the pidogg group as a whole. The giant beast in the mud that had provided food for a while was long gone.

Chris and Jay were the first to notice the tension. Sitting around one of the campfires, Chris said to Jay, "I think it's time to dig a pit and see if we can trap one of those giant beasts."

"I agree," said Jay, "but they're several kilometers to the northeast. Do you think we can dig a pit, line it with stakes, and cover it without becoming a food source ourselves? There are still several of those giant bears traversing through this area every few days, and who knows what other carnivores are lurking about that we haven't seen yet?"

"Yes, it'll be a challenge. I think if we have the pidoggs with us, they'll provide protection from any carnivore. It's the pit that will be the hard part. Digging the pit will be backbreaking enough, but getting rid of the excess soil will be just as bad. We'll have to make sure we spread the excavated dirt over a large area so that it doesn't raise the ground level and discourage an animal from walking into the trap."

"How are we going to get them to step into the trap? What are we going to use for bait? Their food is everywhere, and we certainly can't dig a pit where they're at now. Somehow, we have to hide our efforts and lure them in. And we still don't know if they're aggressive and will attack if they see us, or if they'll run from us," said Jay, thinking aloud.

"Based on my observations, I think they'll run," speculated Chris. "We have two options. The first is that we observe them to see if we can discern a pattern of movement and then dig our trap where we think they will go. This could take several weeks to months. I should have been doing this the entire time we've been here, but that wasn't high on the priority list. The other option is to dig our trap and stampede them in that direction. We have the pidogg allies. I think they're smart enough to figure out what we're doing and go along with it. However, stampeding the herd has dangers in and of itself. We could get seriously injured or killed while preparing the pit;

we, or the pidoggs, could get crushed by one of their sentries or the herd when we entice the herd to stampede; or the stampede could take a new vector, destroying the camp and the capsule in their effort to escape. At least those are the major dangers that I can think of for the moment. I'm sure there are more."

"You're right. The pidoggs are always with us when we leave camp, so that minimizes the danger of other predators attacking us. I think if we dig a pit far enough away from their current grazing area and in an area that points away from the campsite, we should be okay," said Jay.

"I know it sounds simplistic, but then maybe it will be simple," replied Chris. "Okay, let's go talk to the XO and the group. I want everyone's input on this because it'll be dangerous."

That evening at the campfire, everyone ate stored rations and saved some of the scraps for the juvenile pidoggs. Chris discussed the proposed plan with the group and the options for the hunt.

"Right now the animals are approximately five kilometers away. If we dig the pit about two kilometers downwind from them, they shouldn't spook. We'll need the pidoggs' help, though, with driving the beasts toward the pit once it's complete. I don't know how many of them will travel with us when we go to dig the pit or when we're ready to drive the animals. My hope is that they'll understand what we're doing and that most of them will participate, especially when we make the drive. The giant sentries are what make me nervous. They look aggressive and might attack anything that gets near them or the herd. Does everyone understand the need for this venture and the dangers involved?"

Both Sandy and Miranda wore expressions of fearful apprehension, but they didn't object.

"Okay then. We start tomorrow morning."

The morning air was brisk, and the blue sky was partly cloudy. A light westerly breeze made the air feel cooler than it actually was. During breakfast, Chris saw that Miranda was exceptionally subdued, avoiding conversation and even eye contact with anyone. As everyone got busy cleaning up the campsite and getting ready for the big workday, Chris made like he was busy, but he wanted to find out what was troubling her, so he walked over to her.

"You seem a bit quiet this morning. Are you okay?" he asked.

Still avoiding eye contact, Miranda sighed and said, "I'm fine, I guess."

Chris pressed for more information. "You seem troubled. What's really going on?"

Miranda looked up at him. A tear was forming in her blue eye. "I had a dream about Ted last night. I mean, it started out as a dream, but it ended up being a nightmare. I really don't want to talk about it right now." She turned away, wiped at her eye, and joined the other women. Chris stood there for a moment, wanting to console her, but not sure how. Looking downward for a moment, he shook his head, understanding her sorrow. He too had lost close friends on *Copernicus*, and their ghosts also haunted his dreams.

Chris and Jay organized all the tools they needed while the women prepared food for the day. Everyone packed their own backpacks. Dr. Rhodes and Ron were to stay behind while everyone else joined as part of the work party. The pidoggs that weren't on guard duty were awaking, yawning, and stretching long, slow stretches to bring on the new day. It still amazed Chris to see how wide the pidoggs' mouths were when they yawned. When the work party departed the campsite, more than half of the pidoggs left with them, and the rest stood guard duty or went hunting. The group continued northeast for five kilometers before stopping to survey the area around them.

Taking a water break and seeing that Miranda seemed to be doing better, Chris started another conversation with her. "This place must be pretty boring for you professionally, with no flowers or fungi to investigate and study. Just a few woody plants, grass, and more grass."

Nodding, she replied, "You're right. I've documented about as complete a record as I can. Dr. Rhodes did let me borrow her microscope so I could do some cell structure studies, and I found pretty much the same type of cells as we have on Earth, with the usual crew of organelles like Golgi apparatus, mitochondria, vacuoles, chloroplast, nucleus, and such. I did get to do a more thorough study of this grass, though. It seems to grow from rhizomes and not from seeds. With seeds, using them like a grain, we could have made flour for bread of some kind or even eaten it like rice, but only if we had found seeds."

Chris scratched at his growing beard and nodded thoughtfully at the suggestion of using seeds for food. He hadn't seen any in his travels, so it had never come to mind. For that matter, he hadn't seen any nuts or fruit on trees or berries on bushes either.

Miranda continued, "They also have a very deep, thick, and interconnected root system that probably requires only one or two good rains a year to sustain the plant's entire ecosystem."

Glad for the insight into the grass physiology but mildly disappointed with his own professional progress, Chris said, "Well, about the only thing I've been able to document is animal behavior, not that their behavior isn't important, but there just hasn't been the time for me to study even one creature in-depth, let alone the diversity of animal life out here." Chris saw movement to his right and said, "Ah, here comes Jay. Back to the business at hand."

Relieved that Miranda had managed to come out of her funk, Chris cut their conversation short as Jay approached. He finished his water, pointed to the north, and said to Jay, "We're right on the southern edge of the herd. I recommend we head due north for one more kilometer and dig our hole. We can use that small grove of trees that's a little further to the northeast as a source of stakes for the pit and as a barrier for the herd. That way, when we stampede them, hopefully they'll funnel between that northeast grove and the woodlot we passed to the southeast of us. That herd is large enough to fill the entire area. We should get at least one animal in the trap."

"Sounds like a good plan to me," Jay said.

When they arrived at the chosen site, the XO approached Chris. Gesturing toward the other women, she asked, "What would you have us do?"

After thinking it over for a moment, Chris said, "This is a large undertaking. I'll mark the perimeter of the pit. You, Miranda, and Sandy will start by shaving off strips of the top layer of dirt with grass attached to make the equivalent of sod, which we'll use to camouflage the hole once we're finished. Jay and I will walk to the trees over there and start cutting and shaping our stakes. After you strip off the sod layer, start digging. I think a two-and-a-half-meter pit will be enough. We need enough depth so that even if the creature lands on its feet, the stakes will be long enough to puncture well into the abdomen and chest to kill it quickly and humanely. I don't want to go through what we had to the last time."

The look on Sandy and Miranda's faces confirmed that they agreed with Chris.

The men and fifteen pidoggs headed to the wooded area while the women started removing the grass in strips. The remaining pidoggs spread out in their familiar circle around the working women. Upon arriving at the edge of the tree line, Chris and Jay wasted no time in locating suitable trees to make the killing stakes. Needing at least nine three-meter stakes to plant in the pit, Chris and Jay worked quickly and had the trees on the ground in less than an hour. Trimming the roots and branches and cutting the stakes to length took another hour. Food was available for the pidoggs, but not in the quantity that they were accustomed to since their ranks had swelled to the eighty animals now concentrated at the campsite. The pidoggs took turns taking advantage of the small rodents that seemed to be plentiful in the area, filling their bellies for the first time in several days while the men worked cutting and shaping the stakes. Finished with their project, and surrounded by the now contented pidoggs, the men wrapped the stakes together with vines and dragged them back to the pit the women were digging.

Jay said, "I'm glad this wood is dry and light. I can't imagine dragging all these stakes if they were wet." Even in the cool air, both men had worked up a good sweat.

Chris smiled and kept the pace steady while the pidoggs maintained their vigilant semicircle around the men.

Arriving at their destination, Chris saw that the women were busily digging in the pit. He said admiringly, "Nice job, ladies."

The women had the grass cut into sod-like strips that were laid in even rows at the side of the pit, which was already a meter deep.

Caitlyn glanced up without stopping and said, "Hi, Chris. Did you get everything you need?"

"No. Jay and I have to make a trip back to the wooded area to get some small stuff to use as roofing for the trap." Chris looked over to where the women were dumping the dirt from the hole and said, "I know it's a pain in the neck, but you'll have to start carrying the dirt much farther out. Try to work the dirt between the blades of grass as best you can, without matting the grass down too. It has to look normal."

The XO stopped digging for a moment and wiped her right forearm across her forehead, smearing a wide streak of soil and sweat across her skin. Sweat was dripping in rivulets from her face, shoulders, and arms. She was wearing a sleeveless tank top, and sweat washed irregular channels through the accumulated dirt on her exposed skin. Glancing up at Chris with a look of annoyance, she mouthed something that he couldn't quite make out and then went back to work. Chris figured that whatever she'd said, it wasn't worth asking her to repeat it.

On the return trip to the woodlot, Chris said to Jay, "I have a thought. Do you think we could train the pidoggs to drag some of the branches, kind of like a sled dog dragging a sled?"

"I don't know. They've been extremely helpful and have been intuitively anticipating our needs. I suppose we could try."

Once back in the wooded area, the men downed several small-diameter trees and enough vines to make the false roof for the trap. Working on the idea of making some of the pidoggs working animals, Chris fashioned two dual harnesses for the pidoggs, plus two single-person harnesses for himself and Jay from additional vines. He tied large bundles of branches, more vines, and the small trees to the ends of all the harnesses. The pidoggs watched with curiosity. Chris motioned for Jay to place half of a dual pidogg harness over his shoulder. Chris put the other half over his. Using body language, he motioned Jay forward. They dragged their package about twenty meters and stopped. Jay took his harness off and motioned to the nearest pidogg to come to him. The pidogg complied. Jay offered his half of the dual harness to the pidogg. At first, the pidogg cocked his head and looked at Jay and then the harness with a quizzical expression. Jay offered it again. This time the pidogg let him place the harness over his head. At Jay's urging, the pidogg took tension on the line and looked at Chris. Chris nodded his head and gave a "forward" command with his free arm. The pidogg started pulling. The large male started to out-pull Chris to the point that Chris was at a trot trying to keep up. Chris had to call a halt to the uneven contest, and he promptly rewarded the animal with verbal accolades and a good head and back scratching. Two other males approached Chris. He offered his harness to the largest pidogg, who immediately slipped his head into the loop.

While Chris was working with the pidoggs, attaching his half of the double harness to the large male and hooking up the other dual harness to two more eager volunteers, Jay ran back to where the two single harnesses were already attached to more trap door material. He placed a harness loop over each shoulder and started to drag them to where Chris was waiting. When one of his pidogg escorts nudged him on the side of his left leg, he stopped. The pidogg looked up at him, then at the harness, and then back at Jay. Seeing movement on his right, he turned and saw another pidogg standing there, anxiously stepping from one front foot to the other like an excited racehorse chomping at the bit, waiting for the starting gate to open.

Jay grinned and said softly, "Oh, this is gonna to be good!"

Walking between the pidoggs that were dragging the trap door material, Jay met up with Chris, whose pidoggs were already excited and ready to work. They all headed back to the trap. While trying to keep up with the pace, the men discussed their good luck with the pidoggs.

Chris said, "This is hard to believe. They not only caught on right away, but they're eager to do it!"

"I wish we'd thought of this before we dragged those stakes all the way back," said Jay, already starting to breathe hard from the light jog back to the worksite.

"No kidding. But I want to make sure that we're not working them to the point they feel they're being abused," Chris said.

"I think they're having fun. Look at 'em. They're like teenagers trying to prove who's the strongest or the fastest. To them it's a game. They love it!"

"You're right, but let's see if we can convince our new working animals to share the *fun* with their buddies."

Chris and Jay stopped the procession and traded animals at the harness. Chris didn't want the pidoggs to deplete their strength in case they were needed to defend the group in the face of an attack. It worked. All of the pidoggs wanted a turn at the harness.

Miranda was on her way back into the pit after taking a bucket load of dirt to spread out on the grass when she spied the men. Seeing that they were jogging without strain and then realizing that the pidoggs were doing the work, she shouted down to the other women, "Caitlyn, Sandy, come on up here and look at this!"

Caitlyn and Sandy exited the pit. All with crossed arms or hands on hips, the women waited for the men to approach.

"Did you plan this all along?" the XO asked, looking directly at Chris.

"Ah, no," Chris said sheepishly. "Actually, I thought of it on our way back to the woodlot for the second trip."

"Sure you did," Miranda said sarcastically, giving them a nasty scowl.

Sandy wasn't looking too happy either.

Jay stepped forward and said, "It's true—really, it is."

Chris looked at all three women and seemed to be choosing his next words carefully. "Uh, it appears you could use a break. How about Jay and I take over for a while? Go get some water and get a little rest. We'll dig for a while." As they entered the pit, Chris and Jay smiled an innocent smile at the women.

As they walked over to their backpacks to get some water, the women passed stern looks back. Caitlyn said in a low voice that the men couldn't hear, "Dig a while—ha! They can dig their way to the other side of the planet after that trick!"

The other two smiled.

The women had the pit completed to two meters deep. The men finished the last half-meter and leveled the bottom. They arranged and dug the postholes and planted the stakes to offer the best chance for a quick kill no matter which way the animal fell on them. The women, still grumbling among themselves, finished their break and helped the men from the pit.

Chris showed everyone how to weave the sticks and branches together to form a stable trap roof for the pit, securely tying all the joints with multiple wraps of thin vines. After they'd finished with the roof, they placed the sod on the lid of the trap and tried to drag it into place.

"It's too heavy! How are we going to do this?" complained the XO.

"We make it a game of tug-of-war and enlist the pidoggs to help," suggested Miranda. Miranda had spent many hours playing with her dogs back home in the winter, and she figured the pidoggs would enjoy a good challenge too.

After securely tying vines to the trap door to act as tug-of-war ropes, Chris and Jay mimicked the tug-of-war motion and then offered the vines to the nearest pidoggs. They were eager to help, a little too eager in fact. The pidoggs pulled the trap door two meters too far before Jay could stop them, and then he had to convince them to let go and pull it back from the other side. They were having fun.

"It's getting late in the day, and I think we're done here," Chris said. Dirt had collected and muddied on his sweaty shirt and exposed skin. "Let's mark the pit with sticks at the corners and sides of the trap so we don't accidentally fall in ourselves. I'm sure that the trap would support all our collective weight, plus a few pidoggs, but I don't want to take any chances."

The walk back to the campsite was considerably slower and quieter than the trip out that morning.

The next morning Chris outlined the plan. "We have to sneak behind them and spread out in a long line before we attempt to start the stampede. When everyone is in place, call me on your handheld radio to let me know. I'll coordinate the start of our attack after everyone is set. We have to be careful. One miscue and someone could die. Jay, I want you to start out early and get to the other side by going around the long way. If you go out as far as the pit and head north before you angle back toward the herd, you probably won't be noticed. Do you think you can get about ten pidoggs to go with you?"

"I should be able to. When anyone leaves the camp even for a short jaunt, anywhere from ten to twelve of them usually go."

"Good. Stay on the north side of the herd. When the stampede starts, that should keep them from turning the wrong way. Let me know when you get in a good spot to start, but stay hidden."

Next, Chris turned to the XO. "Caitlyn, you and Sandy will follow after Miranda and me; stay low in the grass, and you should be okay. At a distance you'll probably pass as smaller grass-eaters."

"Got it."

"Miranda, you and I will head out about an hour after Jay leaves. We'll follow along the lake's edge as close as we can, staying low and hidden in the grass. I'll drop you off and continue on a bit further. XO, you and Sandy follow us twenty minutes later. XO, stay on the end of the herd, and Sandy, you continue for another half-kilometer. Again, everyone be careful that you're not seen. When I give the signal, everyone jump up and down, wave your arms, shoot the rifles into the ground, and make as much noise as you can. Stay away from the sentries, and don't charge them! Pick a spot between them. I don't know how they'll react, and we can't risk them charging us. I'm hoping that once the herd startles, they'll just run along with them. The idea is to funnel them toward the trap. Encourage the pidoggs to charge the herd. They'll most likely join in on the fun anyway once we get going. Is everyone clear on the plan?"

Everyone nodded.

"Good. Everyone take a rifle and two spears for personal protection in case we run into other predators that the pidoggs can't manage. It's unlikely to happen, but just in case … Jay, head out and call me when you make your turn toward the lake. That should give us enough time to get into place."

"Yes, sir!" Jay responded.

Jay headed northeast. His plan was going to take him past the trap, and then once he was around the end of the herd, he would eventually angle back toward the lake to get behind the animals and wait for Chris's call. Fifteen pidoggs joined him.

Seeing how excited the pidoggs were, Jay said softly to the nearest ones, "You guys know something big is going to happen, don't you? I hope you're right."

Fifty minutes later, Jay made a call to Chris. "We're headed northwest toward the lake. I can see the edge of the herd, but it may take a little longer to get into position. They're spread out a little more today, and the wind will carry our scent if I get too close before I'm set up. Over."

"Roger. Call when you're ready. Chris out." Chris put down his handheld and looked around. "Okay, Miranda, you're with me. Let's go."

Chris and Miranda grabbed their spears and headed northwest toward the lake. Twelve pidoggs left with them. The sentry pidoggs watched them go.

Twenty minutes later, the XO and Sandy were on their way with ten pidoggs as their escort.

The chilly breeze was almost nonexistent, but what was blowing came from the northeast, keeping the hunting party's scent from reaching the herd. Jay had to travel further to the north than anticipated to keep the herd from catching his and the pidoggs' scent. He called when he was finally in position. Then Caitlyn and Sandy called to say they were in position. Chris dropped off Miranda and was a half-kilometer from his intended position.

The pidoggs were anxious, eagerly waiting to see what the humans had planned. They knew it was a hunt, and for big game, but the strategy was unknown to them. They were all crouched, ready to spring into action. A young male juvenile in Jay's group couldn't contain his nervous energy any longer and let out a quiet excited yip. Always on the alert, one of the giant sentries heard the sound and bellowed a warning. The nearby members of the herd immediately started moving away from the alert. Although the herd was extremely large, and the alert could not be heard for more than a couple hundred meters—the crunching of the brittle lower stems of grass while the herd moved around, the munching sounds, and low contented bellows of the animals muted the warning—the giant beasts that heard the initial sentry's warning took off, and the others were startled into running with them. Great hooves beating on the ground, the herd headed southwest away from Jay's location.

Seeing movement and dust in the air, Chris suspected that something had gone wrong from Jay's location and called on his handheld. "Jay, what's going on?"

"One of the pidoggs got excited and barked. A sentry heard it and let out a warning. They're headed toward the campsite!" Jay shouted anxiously.

Near Chris's position, the herd continued to graze peacefully, not yet aware of the danger to the north. Chris wasted no time. "XO, Sandy, Miranda," he shouted into the radio, "the herd is on the move toward the campsite. Fire the rifles into the ground! Make as much noise as you can, *now*! Doc! Are you listening in?"

"I heard you. Ron and I will take refuge in the capsule. Be careful out there."

"Roger, Doc. Chris out."

The animals at the north side of the herd that had started moving first gradually recruited more as the panic spread. The sentries to the southwest were scattered up to four kilometers away, but the sound of beating hooves carried well ahead of the moving herd from the north. As the noise carried further south, more animals were recruited into running from the sound. Not yet alerted to the danger, however, the central and southern section of the herd continued to graze lazily. Chris, Miranda, the XO, and Sandy leaped from their hidden positions and started yelling at the top of their lungs, jumping up and down, and waving their spears high with one hand and shooting the rifles with the other. The pidoggs, eager and ready to go, started running at the herd, barking, growling, and snapping their teeth menacingly. The nearby giant sentries sounded their alarm, and the rest of the herd started running to the east away from the new danger.

Chris saw it coming. The animals stampeding southwest, in their mad rush away from the danger Jay and his pidoggs posed, started merging with others headed east. The frightened giants already on the run were weaving and turning through the congested throng. With ever-decreasing space between them, the animals began to collide. As the collisions became more violent, animals started falling to the ground, unable to get up. The fleeing animals crowded together, tighter and tighter, blocking the view forward. The unfortunate creatures that had fallen were crushed by the onrush of animals that were unable to stop as the herd continued running forward, unaware of the plight of the fallen that lay in front of them. More of the giant creatures joined in the mass of fallen flesh. Similar to freeway automobiles driving too fast to avoid a pileup ahead, the great creatures, confused as to which way to run, ran in any direction that offered escape. Some had no clear area to run and died in the mass of bodies that continued to accumulate. The pidoggs charging into the melee added additional fear and confusion to the already chaotic scene.

The ground underfoot vibrated with the weight of millions of metric tons of living flesh on the run. It felt like a mild earthquake. Unable to predict where the giant beasts would head next, Chris yelled over the thundering hooves into his radio for everyone to head for the lakeshore. The herd didn't have far to run before the ground would become spongy but would still support the weight of the humans and pidoggs. He figured that the soft ground, which would gradually turn to mud at the water's edge, could offer his group a modicum of safety because it would eventually slow and trap the charging animals. His quick thinking saved the life of everyone in his group.

A wall of animals, in their attempt to escape the mass chaos, charged westward toward the lake. Seeing the lake directly ahead, the lead animals started to turn south again. Only a few that were on the outside edge of the turn became trapped in the soft ground, successfully blocking the rest of the terrified creatures' path toward a slow but certain death. More and more animals joined the stampede, fleeing southwestward until the bulk of the herd was running in the same direction. The capsule and sentry pidoggs were directly in line with the onrush of tens of thousands of panic-stricken giants.

Ron was lingering at the hatch to the capsule, watching what action he could see in the distance. The dust cloud obscured his vision of the bulk of the herd coming his way, but he didn't waste time before taking action. He knew they were too far from the lake to take refuge there. Warning Holly of what was about to happen, he told her to strap into a seat. With a vivid recollection of his launch from the *Copernicus* and his reentry experience, he wasn't looking forward to strapping himself in again. Sensing Ron's hesitation, Dr. Rhodes had him sit first and then put as much padding under the strap for his right arm and shoulder as she could quickly muster. She made sure his straps were cinched tightly, despite the pain they caused. Dr. Rhodes did the same for her own straps. The capsule began to vibrate as the running creatures approached. The items on the table and workstations vibrated off and crashed to the floor. It wasn't long before the wall of living steamrollers reached them.

The leading edge of the stampede went around the capsule because those animals had a clear view ahead. But rising dust and animals to the front obscured the view of the capsule for the approaching creatures until they were nearly upon it. At first, they only lightly brushed the sides of the capsule, rocking it gently. As the bulk of the stampeding animals approached, however, the brushing became bumping, which quickly became slamming, and then with no room left to maneuver, animals crashed into it. The noise in the capsule was deafening.

The giant animals slammed into the capsule hard. The capsule was slammed again and again, harder with each new collision. Holly gasped from the force of the jolting from one side to the other as the frequency and intensity increased. Holly saw that Ron had his eyes closed and teeth clenched. She could only imagine the pain that must be rocketing through his arm and shoulder. The capsule teetered, tipped, and eventually crashed onto its side. She heard Ron cry out in agonizing pain, and as the capsule tipped over, she screamed, unable to contain her rising fear. The escape pod started to roll. With every collision, the capsule jolted harder, rolling faster and faster as the stampeding animals rammed and slammed the sides of it. There was no space between the panicked animals to allow them to avoid crashing into the capsule. The capsule began to spin from end to end from the uneven collisions, like a spin-the-bottle game, and the rolling continued. Everything that was not in a locker or secured became a deadly missile flying about the capsule's cabin. Like clothes in a dryer, loose items tumbled repeatedly, breaking against hard and soft surfaces alike. The noise was deafening. Minutes seemed like hours. Holly watched Ron vomit, and the ensuing spray stuck to the debris in the tumbling compartment. The violent ride and the smell from Ron's vomit finally tipped Holly's normally strong constitution, causing her to follow Ron's lead. She spewed even more than Ron. The putrid odor permeated the air, and fluid and semisolid chunks of partially digested food adhered to everything they touched. The odor, concentrated in the capsule, made her and Ron retch even harder. As something hard struck Holly's head, a light flashed briefly but brightly in her eyes, followed by darkness.

Vomit covered the bulkhead, the deck, the overhead, the equipment, and the two sick, severely injured, and now unconscious passengers. The tremendous noise and vibration eventually softened to a low rumble, fading to an eerie silence as the herd passed the capsule and thundered off in the distance. The rolling and spinning capsule eventually slowed, finally coming to rest with Ron lying in his seat on his back, his neck bent unnaturally off to one side, and Holly hanging from her straps near the new overhead.

After the stampede began, it became obvious that the sentry pidoggs' barking and aggressive charging wasn't going to stop the oncoming storm of hoofed death. The pidoggs bolted for the safety of the lakeshore. Once the stampede had passed, they followed the retreating animals and soon found the capsule. The pidoggs set up their perimeter guard, nervously shifting from foot to foot while on the lookout for danger and whimpering with obvious worry because they could do nothing more for their human friends trapped inside, except wait for the other humans to arrive.

14

From their separate locations, Chris, Jay, and the three women surveyed the carnage before them. Many hundreds of animals lay on the ground dead or dying. The few that were still moving had major injuries. They would be easy prey for the large carnivores that were sure to come. Most of the pidoggs were already ripping at the bellies of the dead animals or feasting on the exposed contents of animals whose bodies had burst apart from being crushed. Some pidoggs stayed with the humans, standing guard and waiting for their turn at the feasting table.

"My Lord! What have I done?" Chris whispered in anguish. Seeing so many dead or dying creatures caused him great mental pain. "This wasn't supposed to happen. I only wanted one animal—"

Jay ran up, out of breath, and interrupted his dazed thoughts. "Chris, I can't reach Doc or Ron on the radio." He had run the kilometer along the lakeshore to get to Chris's location.

Snapping out of his melancholy state, Chris called Caitlyn. "XO, can you see the capsule from your position?"

"Negative. I can't see it from here; there's too much dust in the air. Do you want me to head back?"

"Affirmative. Make sure they're okay and give me a call."

"Wilco. XO out."

Now that his thoughts were more focused, Chris turned back

to Jay. "Let's make sure they're okay first; then I want to get as much meat as we can carry and harvest some of the skins too. We can build a smokehouse to preserve the meat. A wooden frame and some of these skins should work well. I'm sure food will be in short supply with winter coming. The smoke will help tan the hides for use as warm clothing and blankets too. We don't know how bad or how long winter will be, and I don't like the prospect of a slow, cold, starving death."

Chris and Jay were examining one of the dead animals when the XO's radio call came through.

"Chris, this is Caitlyn. The capsule is gone! The stampede came through here and somehow took the pod with it!"

Chris's heart sank. "What? Are you sure you're at the correct location?"

"Affirmative. Remnants of the fires are scattered all through here."

"Great! What next?" he muttered under his breath. Exasperated and worried, he responded, "XO, this is Chris. We're on our way. Break. Everyone head back to the campsite. We'll regroup to locate Doc and Ron and the capsule. Chris out." Turning to Jay, he said, "Time to move!"

Chris and Jay jogged the entire way back to the former campsite. Arriving out of breath, the men scanned the area. Here and there were the burnt remnants of the fires that had been intended to keep predators away, but which were obviously totally ineffective against the out-of-control herd giants. The somber faces of the women greeted the men. Sandy had tears of worry running down her cheeks as she greeted Jay with a full-body hug. Holding him tightly, she gently sobbed on his shoulder.

After a hasty assessment, Chris addressed the group. "We need to find them before nightfall. If they're alive, I'm sure they'll need our help. Let's head out."

Silently, with the pidoggs in their traveling guard formation, they followed the flattened grass to the south.

⁂ ⁂ ⁂ ⁂

Miranda was about 150 meters ahead of the rest of the group with her pidogg escort when she saw sunlight glint off the pod's dirty and dented skin. Pointing off to the southeast, she shouted, "There it is!"

Everyone took off at a fast jog. Several minutes later, they arrived. The capsule was badly beaten up, but there were no holes in it that Chris or Jay could discern. The capsule was lying on its side. The hatch was a little over a meter from the ground.

Miranda asked in wonderment, "How could it have rolled so far?"

Chris looked over the capsule before he responded. "There were at least five square kilometers of animals trying to run by it, kicking and shoving it ahead of them. I don't think there is more than a few centimeters anywhere without some kind of dent or damage."

Jay and the XO were pounding on the hatch, trying to get some kind of a response from inside. They both looked at Chris, shaking their heads. Nothing.

"They must be unconscious or … dead," Chris said solemnly.

Thinking aloud, the XO said, "If we can get into the rocket engine compartment, there should be a tool of some sort to open this hatch." Not waiting for an answer, she walked around the capsule, located the engine compartment's service hatch near the top, and said to the men, "If I can get a boost up there, I should be able to gain access and get that tool."

"How tall are you?" asked Chris.

"One hundred seventy-six centimeters," she responded.

"Jay is a little taller than you and can reach the hatch if he stands on my shoulders. It'll be easier if you let him open it first," Chris said.

Chris squatted down, and Jay climbed on his shoulders. Jay located the recessed thumbscrews and attempted to open the hatch.

"They're stuck!" he shouted.

"Here, try this," Chris said as he tossed his survival knife to Jay, so that he could pry up the thumbscrews' folded-down top..

A few seconds later, Jay shouted, "Got it open! It's pretty dark in there, but it's all yours." He jumped to the ground.

After boosting the XO onto his shoulders, Chris hoisted her to the opening.

Peering in, she looked at the three-meter drop to the other side. "I can get in here, but I won't be able to get out. It's going to take two of us to do this," she said.

"I'll help her. Give me a boost up again," Jay said to Chris.

Chris boosted Jay to the opening as Caitlyn dropped to the new deck on the other side of the hatch.

"Found it!" shouted the XO. Caitlyn tossed the wrench to Jay, who passed it down to Chris.

Jay asked Miranda for a spear and then lowered the handle of the spear for Caitlyn to hang on to while he pulled her out of the capsule. Chris was already working on the hatch. Three minutes later, the hatch was open.

The horrendous smell of fresh vomit assaulted the group before they even entered the damaged capsule. When Chris stepped in, what he saw was almost beyond description. The spectrometer was smashed beyond repair. Supplies that had been stored in the loose backpacks were scattered on any surface that was horizontal to the ground. Broken slides and Petri dishes littered the escape pod's bulkheads, which now were in the position of the deck. The microscope frame was bent, and the lenses no longer pointed to the slide holder. The autoclave, mounted to a counter surface, was badly dented and scratched. Medical quick-reference material that the doctor had been reviewing lay cluttered in small jumbled piles. Holding his shirt over his nose in an almost useless attempt to filter the stench, Chris spotted Ron lying with his upper body half out of, but still strapped into, his chair, his head lolled to one side. Small cuts and large bruises covered his exposed skin. His uniform was covered in vomit, and the padding and uniform under the strap of his right shoulder and arm were soaked in blood.

Checking Ron's pulse, Chris let his makeshift nose filter drop. He gagged once and then shouted to those outside, "He's still alive!"

A drop of blood fell on his left cheek. He looked up and saw Dr. Rhodes hanging from her seat straps, face swollen, bruised, and bleeding. She wasn't moving.

"Let's get them out of here, now!" Chris shouted.

Gagging and choking on the smell inside the capsule, Caitlyn and Jay unstrapped Ron and gently carried him outside. Miranda and the XO started cleaning the blood and vomit from his face, neck, and arms. The outer layer of skin on his right arm, where the white infection had set up, had bunched down by his elbow, completely detached from his arm. The smell from the infected arm was worse than the vomit odor. Holding her breath, Sandy went back into the capsule to retrieve a bottle of antiseptic, scissors, and gauze from a locker, but she couldn't hold her breath long enough and emptied her stomach contents onto the chair that Ron had been occupying. Fortunately, the locker doors all remained shut. Everything in the storage spaces had tumbled, but the supplies weren't damaged or broken. Ron remained unconscious while they did what they could to clean and bandage his wounds with what they had at hand.

Jay went back in the capsule to help Chris. "How can we get her down without hurting her more?" he asked, getting somewhat used to the smell but holding his hand over his nose just the same. "It would take a couple of hours to make a ladder, and I don't think we have that kind of time."

"I agree," said Chris. "We could try to roll the capsule until she's on the bottom, but then the hatch would be above our heads, and we'd have to lift her to the hatch too."

"Well, then after we get her down and unstrapped, someone holds onto her and we roll it some more until the hatch is accessible," offered Jay.

"Given the circumstances, I think that's the best we can do. Okay. Let's do it."

Chris and Jay climbed out of the pod and discussed with the women how they planned to get the doctor out without causing more injury.

"If only Ron was able to help us," Jay lamented. "He's the mechanical engineer. I'd be willing to bet he could figure out the length of the lever and the forces needed to roll this monstrosity."

Chris said, "I'm sure he could, but we're going to do it the old-fashioned way … by trial and error. XO, you and Miranda grab your spears and help us try to roll the capsule."

Sandy stood off to the side and watched the rest position their spears slightly under the massive capsule.

"When I say heave, everyone lift together," Chris called out. "Try not to break your spear; it's at least two kilometers to that woodlot to the southeast to get another stick. Ready! Three, two, one, *heave*!"

The capsule rolled thirty centimeters on the first try.

"Again! Three, two, one, *heave*! Again! *Heave*!"

Five minutes later, the capsule had rolled to a position where it was safe to unstrap the doctor. Sandy took Jay's place on the spear, and Chris boosted Jay to the hatch, where he dropped inside. Jay checked the doctor's pulse. "She's alive, but her pulse is weak."

"Okay. Can you hold her and walk around the bulkhead as we roll the capsule again?" Chris asked.

"Yeah, she's pretty light. I can do it," Jay said.

Taking care not to slip on the slimy surface or trip on the debris, Jay carefully removed Holly from her seat while Chris readied the crew outside to roll the capsule.

"I'm ready! Go!" shouted Jay.

Hearing Jay, Chris shouted, "Standby! Ready? Three, two, one, *heave*!"

Four minutes later, Holly Rhodes was lying next to Ron on the ground. The XO and Miranda had retrieved blankets from a locker in the capsule and had placed some under them to keep their body heat from being siphoned off into the ground. While Holly was being tended to, Chris and Jay made a quick trip to the nearest woodlot with several pidoggs to gather firewood. Soon, several fires were blazing while the XO and Miranda constructed a silver-sided emergency blanket lean-to to reflect heat from the fire to keep Ron and Holly warm. The XO retrieved a first aid kit from the capsule, and with assistance from Miranda, she cleaned and bandaged Holly's wounds. The pidoggs not on sentry duty looked and acted worried. They walked around restlessly, quietly whimpering, glancing in the direction of the severely injured pair whenever they passed close by.

Recovering from her nausea, Sandy asked, "Is there anything else we can do for them?"

Glancing over at Holly, Chris answered, "The only person here who could answer that … can't. We just have to wait this out."

Sandy hugged Jay and cried.

Taking turns maintaining the fires and watching over Holly and Ron, no one slept much that night. The weather was turning colder, and the capsule was not functional lying on its side and as beaten up as badly as it was. Everyone spent the night outside. Chris was the only one with a sleeping bag; the rest had to make do with blankets from the capsule that had been stored in lockers. Morning arrived with no change from the unconscious crew members. Their breathing and pulse rates were steady, and they were kept as warm as the group could make them. The healing had to come from inside them. Other than the first aid already given to them, there was nothing more anyone could do.

Chris stretched and yawned, still in his sleeping bag. Miranda was on watch. Climbing out, he asked her, "Any change?"

"No. Not even a twitch. They're just breathing steadily."

"Okay. Let's get the others up. We have to make plans for getting us a better shelter."

With that, Miranda and Chris gently roused the others from their restless dreams. The pidoggs were moving around the makeshift camp, with several wearing worried expressions and stopping by to sniff the unconscious pair.

Chris called a meeting while everyone ate a meager breakfast. “We have to build another shelter that will carry us through the winter and keep us warm too. We’re going to have to abandon the shelter that we were building back at the now-destroyed campsite. It’s too far from here, and with Doc and Ron injured, I want us to stay nearby. We don’t know how long they will stay unconscious or what other injuries they may have that may prevent them from traveling when and if they do wake up.” Pointing to the southwest, Chris said, “My thoughts are to head to the woodlot over there to see if there is a way to construct a tree house of some kind. I think that will offer the best protection from any nocturnal predators and further experiences like we had with the giant grass-eaters at Jay’s capsule. First, though, I want to get some wood and vines to make a sled of sorts to collect meat and especially furs from the dead giants. We can make weatherproof shelters, blankets, and clothing as the Plains Indians did in early America. The pidoggs seemed eager to pull branches and such before; I think we can get them to pull small sleds.”

Jay said, “We should get started now, before the predators start coming around en masse.”

“I agree,” said Chris. “Any questions? None? Good. Ladies … stay here and keep the home fires burning; Jay and I will head out. It shouldn’t take us too long to make the sleds. Let us know via radio if there are any changes in Ron or Holly.” Looking over at Jay, he said, “Let’s go.”

As they left the campsite and walked toward the woodlot, Chris ran the fingers of both hands through his hair and interlocked his fingers behind his head. He looked skyward while holding the back of his head and exclaimed, “What a disaster! Winter is coming, we have to start from scratch for shelter, our provisions are running low, and Doc and Ron may not live; it's not looking good for the good guys."

Jay stared vacantly at the ground. "I don't know what to say other than that I'm really sorry. I feel that this was all my fault. It was one of my pidoggs that started this whole mess."

Dropping his hands to his sides and turning to look at Jay, Chris said, "How could you have prevented it? You couldn't. The pidoggs are still wild animals. There was no way you could control them. It's not your fault, so stop beating yourself up over it."

Still staring at the ground with his shoulders slumped, Jay put his hands in his pockets and walked the rest of the way to the woodlot in silence.

Their immediate tasks took their minds off Dr. Rhodes and Ron. After looking around the woodlot, Chris and Jay collected enough wood and vines to make six sleds large enough to carry a couple of hides or a hundred kilos of meat each and then started building. The sleds were simple affairs, two skis with several cut branches tied across the tops for a platform. The hardest part was drilling holes through the sides of the skis with their survival knives to pass vines through so that the vines wouldn't have to be tied under the runners of the skis. They were crude implements, but sturdy. Once the harnesses were made and attached, the pidoggs were eager to help. Chris and Jay decided to test the sleds with dried wood that they could use for firewood; they could stop by the new campsite to drop off the wood and check on Holly and Ron before going on to collect the meat and furs.

"How are they doing?" Chris asked as they arrived.

"Holly has stirred now and then, as if she was having a nightmare or something, but Ron hasn't moved," Sandy said.

The XO stood and said, "There's nothing more I can do here. Sandy and Miranda have everything under control. Want some help?"

"Sure," Chris replied. "I want to be back here well before dark, and with you along it'll go a lot faster."

It was a six-kilometer hike to where the giant animals were lying. There were still a few severely injured ones roaming around in circles or meandering about their dead comrades as if looking for a dead mate. The live ones didn't seem to be aware of any of the activity around them. Except for the pidoggs that were with Chris, Jay, and Caitlyn and the ones on sentry duty at the campsite, the rest were feeding on whatever animals they could open up.

Walking up to one of the dead animals, Chris said, "These animals are unbelievably large. It's going to take two of us to skin this thing. Jay, you and I skin it, and Caitlyn, you start carving off the front and hindquarters. Leave the skin on and don't worry about being neat about it."

"Okay," Caitlyn said. "If you can open up the abdomen, I'll try to get the liver too. Doc said we needed to eat organ meat for the vitamin content."

"You got it."

Chris started by making a slit along the bottom of the belly skin as close to the ground as he could. Working to the rear of the animal, he then sliced around the hindquarter, leaving the skin on the leg, before cutting vertically over the top and to the ground on the other side. Jay continued the long slit close to the ground and forward toward the neck, over the top to the front quarter, and inside the leg to the belly slit, again leaving the skin on the front quarter. Pulling the skin back from the neck toward the rump, the men removed the bulk of the skin while the XO removed the front and rear quarters and placed them on the sleds.

"I'm not looking forward to this part," Chris said as he sliced through the belly muscle to expose the abdominal contents. He scrunched his face into a disgusted scowl and gagged. "Eww! That smell is awful! The stomach and intestines must have ruptured when another giant fell on this one, killing it. That is the grossest odor I've ever smelled!" He gagged again.

Chris and Jay began pulling out the contents of the abdomen, periodically ducking away to catch some fresh air, and finally pulled out enough to expose the liver.

Holding back a gag, Chris said to Caitlyn, "There you go … I don't know how butchers can stand to do that."

As Jay repeatedly inhaled deeply from his mouth and exhaled through his nose to clear the odor from his nose and sinuses, he wiped the blood and stomach contents from his arms and hands on the soft grass tops. Jay replied, "The biggest thing they deal with is a cow, not an elephant, but I would imagine that you could get used to doing just about anything." Catching a whiff of the abdominal odor again and holding back a gag, he said, "Well, almost anything."

"I will tell you one thing for sure—their job is safe from me!" replied Chris.

When she climbed out of the abdominal cavity, Caitlyn had blood in her hair, on her face, and on her arms. Her clothing was soaked with it. She was carrying a piece of the liver the size of a juvenile pidogg, holding it close to her body to keep from dropping the slippery organ meat. She set the liver on a sled and turned toward the men, looking visibly annoyed.

"I don't want to hear complaints from either of you!" she said as she took turns gagging and inhaling deep breaths of clean, fresh air. Then she lost it and vomited.

Both men stayed quiet until arriving at the next animal.

It took ten hours of work to skin four animals and salvage eight front and hindquarters. They figured even one liver would last them long enough that it would go bad before they consumed it all and so didn't retrieve another. Caitlyn didn't complain. Chris encouraged the pidoggs that were with them to get their fill before heading back to the group.

The trip back was slow going. With full bellies, the pidoggs didn't pull as vigorously. Chris and Jay rotated them frequently, being careful not to overwork them. Their four-legged friends still seemed to enjoy the challenge as if it were a game of strength.

Arriving back at the new campsite, Chris, Jay, and Caitlyn cleaned up the best they could with the limited water left in the capsule. Chris saw that Holly was sitting up and drinking something hot. "Doc, it's good to see you awake! How do you feel?"

"As if I spent the night in a clothes dryer. I thought I had broken my neck just before I passed out. I felt the vertebrae in my neck crunch when something hit my head, forcing my neck hard to the side. My head is pounding, and my neck is sore. My shoulders feel as if someone pulled my arms from their sockets and put them back in. And my hips, along with everywhere the seat belt harnesses rubbed, are chafed and bruised. Every time the capsule was slammed, it would jerk our heads left and right. I honestly thought we were going to die. I don't know how long I lasted before I passed out. It seemed like hours." Taking another sip from her cup, Holly asked, "How far did we roll?"

"Three and a half, maybe four, kilometers."

"What happened?" she asked.

Chris explained to her how the stampede had started and how, with roughly four to five square kilometers of giant beasts on the run, the capsule had ended up being like a soccer ball, kicked and shoved through the herd, eventually falling back until they ended up here.

Holly's head hurt, and she was having a difficult time concentrating, she explained. But she listened to everything intently while carefully sipping her drink, doing her best to avoid the cuts on her lips.

When Chris finished, Holly said, "I should look at Ron. He got banged up pretty good too. I saw the spectrograph swipe against his bad arm at least once."

"Are you sure you're up to it?" Chris asked.

"Yes, I'll get by. Help me up and get my medical kit; it's in one of the lockers. Thank God I put it in one; with that thing tumbling about, we'd most likely be dead."

Opening her kit, Dr. Rhodes retrieved a pair of scissors and cut the bandage from Ron's arm. "Whoever cleaned this up did a good job." Looking around at those standing behind her, she said with a small smile forming, "Where's my new assistant?"

Caitlyn was standing nearby at one of the fires, roasting a piece of meat. She handed her meal-on-a-stick to Miranda to finish cooking it and approached the doctor. "I guess that's me," she said.

"This looks professional. Where did you get your training?"

"I was a battlefield-trained hospital corpsman, third class, before attending Officer Candidate School," Caitlyn said.

Dr. Rhodes said, "You don't look old enough to have gone that far in the enlisted ranks before making the rank of commander. How do you stay so young-looking?"

Caitlyn smiled and half-kiddingly said, "Vitamins. Thanks for the compliment." She turned away as she started to lightly blush.

"Well, you did a nice job. Here, take this flashlight and check his pupil reflexes. I'll check the rest."

The doctor and XO did a brief field examination of Ron and cleaned and re-bandaged his arm.

"His arm doesn't look as bad as it did before. Maybe that infected skin sloughing off will help," Caitlyn suggested.

"You're right. The accident, as bad as it was, may have just saved his arm. It did what I was afraid to do. Let's plan on checking his arm at least twice a day."

Caitlyn nodded.

It was early the next morning when Ron began to moan. Sandy, who was standing the fire watch, woke Holly and Caitlyn. "Ron's starting to come around. I think he's in pain."

"I'd be more worried if he wasn't," Holly said as she threw off her blanket and made her way to Ron. Sitting cross-legged on the ground at his side, Holly put her hand on Ron's forehead, checking for fever. He had none.

Opening his eyes and trying to focus through the blur, he said, "If I'm dead, this must be hell, and I'm paying for all my past transgressions."

Holly and Caitlyn looked at each other and smiled.

"He's going to be all right," Holly said.

With his eyes closed tightly again, Ron said, "If this isn't hell, it sure isn't heaven. I must be alive; I feel every nerve in my body telling me so."

Smoothing the hair on his head, Holly said softly, "Ron, I'm going to give you something to ease your pain, but not enough to get rid of all of it. I need you to be able to tell me where you hurt when I examine you."

Through his gritted teeth, Ron said, "You'll get no argument from me this time, angel lady."

15

Everyone celebrated Ron's awakening from his mild coma with a hearty breakfast of giant-beast liver and meat, even Miranda, washing it down with hot smoke-flavored water. Even the pidoggs seemed eager to say hello to Ron, nosing up to him and accepting a good head scratching from his left hand. He was finally convinced they wouldn't eat him. The mood in the camp was good.

Chris was eager to get started on building the new shelter. Although not a prude, Chris wanted a two-room shelter built, one for the men and the other for the women, in deference to the XO as the commanding officer and for Miranda, who had lost her husband. While collecting wood for the sleds, he and Jay had located an ideal place to build a more permanent abode. He sketched out his plan in the dirt with a stick. Chris, Jay, Sandy, and Miranda headed to the woodlot to get wood for drying and stretching the skins and more wood for smoking the meat. The usual escort of pidoggs accompanied them.

Holly and Caitlyn walked down to the lake with their escort of pidoggs. Caitlyn washed the rest of the previous day's blood from her body and clothing the best she could without soap, and Holly filled a container with filtered water. By the time they returned to the campsite, Chris, Jay, Sandy, and Miranda had returned.

Holly and Caitlyn joined Chris and Miranda, who were scraping the skins for hanging near a fire to dry, while Sandy and Jay shaped and cut branches to form the framework for drying the skins and smoking the meat.

With the housing plans in mind, Sandy asked Jay, "Why don't we build a large single-room shelter instead of two smaller rooms?"

"A smaller room is easier to heat in the winter. You'll be glad the rooms are small if it gets really cold," Jay explained.

"Sharing body heat is a good way to stay warm too, you know," she said coyly.

Jay gave her a quick glance, smiled, and continued to work.

It took four days to cut enough logs for a framework and tie them together in the trees. They made a simple ladder that permanently attached to the bottom of the tree, and from the top of it, a retractable rope ladder made from heavy vines continued upward to the two-room tree house. The vine ladder could be pulled up to keep smaller climbing predators from having easy access to their rooms.

That evening everyone wore their warmest attire and sat closer to the campfire because of the chill in the air. Discussion of the housing project continued.

"We're going to need more skins for the sides and to make blankets and cloaks or coats. I suggest that we leave the fur on the skins too," Chris said.

"I hope they haven't gone bad, being on the dead animals for all this time," Jay replied.

"We might be able to find one of the badly wounded ones and finish it off, or one that recently died. We'll go and look first thing in the morning," Chris said.

With a good chill to the air, everyone slept close to the campfire that night.

Early the next morning, there was enough of a chill in the air to frost their breath. The men and women all wore blankets wrapped around them to ward off the cold while everyone except Holly and

Ron made their way back to the dead giants. Arriving at the site that would in time be a boneyard, they discovered that the cold air had helped to preserve the meat and skins of most of the dead animals.

Studying the scene, Chris said, "You know, in a million or so years, future archeologists are going to dig up these bones and think this must be a place where these animals went to die. I wonder how many times our archeologists examined a dig and made wrong assumptions based on the leftover evidence."

"We could leave them a note," joked Jay.

That got a chuckle from the group. Everyone was in good spirits.

They were on their sixth animal when the pidoggs went on alert. One of the giant bears had approached a nearby, previously skinned, and partially eaten animal. It didn't seem to want to tangle with the pidoggs. Paying them no attention, it dove headfirst into the abdominal cavity searching for delicacies left behind by the humans and other carnivores.

"When we finish skinning this animal, we need to leave," said Chris. "It's going to be close to dark by the time we get back, and I don't want to run into anything that's hungry when we can't see well enough to defend ourselves. These full sleds would make us tempting targets."

"I agree," said Jay. "If we make a wide enough detour around our hungry friend out there, we should be okay. I hope the pidoggs' presence will be enough to discourage any others."

Finished packing up the fruits of their labor, they headed back to the camp with the pidoggs doubled up on each sled. "I'm so glad these guys enjoy this stuff," Jay said to Sandy. "It would take weeks for us to do this, not to mention the danger of becoming some creature's dinner ourselves."

With compressed lips and knitted eyebrows, Sandy frowned at Jay, disliking the comment about becoming dinner.

Once back at the campsite, Jay said to Sandy, "Did you notice that hungry bear-creature didn't even take his head out of the carcass as we passed by?"

Sandy ignored him. She was still upset, thinking of the comment about becoming dinner.

"How are you doing?" Chris asked Ron as he stretched out a skin on a crudely made stick rack to dry by the fire.

"Pretty good, I guess. The pain isn't as intense as it was before. Doc said that flesh-eating fungus infection seems to be gone, and once my skin heals, I should be as good as I was before the burn."

"That's great to hear! Caitlyn mentioned that when she and Doc went down to the lake the other day, they saw fish for the first time. If Doc says it's okay, do you want to go for a walk?"

Smiling, Ron replied, "I may look brain-damaged, but I can assure you, I'm not. Don't even ask. Let's just go!"

Chris grabbed a few empty water containers and a backpack with a water filter, and they set off for the lake. A dozen of the resting pidoggs got up and joined them.

At the lake, in the dimming light, Chris and Ron scanned the water for fish. Ron pointed out a couple large ones about a half meter in length. They darted out of the way when another fish a meter long approached.

"Eat or be eaten," Ron mused.

"That's the way of the wild," Chris responded as they watched the larger fish swim away. He noticed some fist-size rocks and small boulders in the water. "Those rocks will make a great fireplace if we can get enough of them. Let's get wet and toss some on the shore."

Stripping down to his underwear, but keeping on his belt with his sheathed knife, Chris entered the cold water to mid-thigh and shivered. Ron removed his boots, rolled up his pant legs, and entered the lake but stayed in shallower water. Chris started tossing rocks to Ron, who in turn tossed them in a pile on shore.

After they had collected quite a mound of rocks, Chris felt a bump on the back of his legs. Alarm bells started going off in his head, instinctively freezing him in place. All he could think was *Shark!* Being a biologist, and knowing that some Earth sharks inhabited freshwater rivers that could lead to lakes, he was cautious. Slowly turning his neck and upper body, he saw part of a log floating on the water half a meter away. He gave the log a shove and watched it float away. His racing heart slowed. Turning back and reaching into the water for another rock, he felt the bump again. Reaching for the knife in his belt, with a reflex-like action, Chris slashed elbow-deep into the water. Feeling resistance against his knife, he started for shore as a blue cloud began to billow behind his legs. The cloud trailing him swirled in uneven streaks. Suddenly, the water erupted where Chris had slashed at his would-be attacker. Several of the nearby fish, taking advantage of the free food, viciously ripped apart the hapless victim. At one point, a large fish lifted the prey out of the water, its head supporting a mouthful of razor-sharp teeth. The victim, which looked like a bottom-feeder, was devoured in less than a minute. The pidoggs watched the action from the safety of the shore as the men made a hasty retreat from the water.

Reaching the shoreline and putting on his boots, Ron asked, "Did you notice that the pidoggs didn't go in the water?"

"Not until I was almost to shore. They must know something we don't—like *it's dangerous in there!*" Chris remarked as he dressed.

"Well, now we know. But why did the water turn blue? I'm assuming that was fish blood, but I thought blood was always red," Ron said.

"Only if the blood is iron-based. That fish probably uses copper-based hemocyanin in its blood plasma like we use iron in our red blood cells for our hemoglobin to transport oxygen."

"Basic biology—it's been a very long time ago for me."

"Yes, but it grows on you," Chris said.

"Yeah, I agree about the *growing on you* part," Ron said, with a look to his arm.

Laughing at the unexpected humor, Chris said, "I'm really glad to have you back, my friend." He gave Ron an affable slap on the back and squeezed him across the shoulders in a manly, one-armed hug, and they walked back to the campsite smiling.

⁂ ⁂ ⁂ ⁂

"Do you think the tree huts will take the weight of the rocks plus us and our supplies?" Sandy asked Jay as they loaded the rocks into backpacks. Chris had asked her and Jay to help retrieve the rocks from the shoreline.

"Yeah, I'm pretty sure. Those vines are some tough stuff. They were actually harder to cut than the branches, but still flexible enough to tie in a knot. Besides, Ron approved of the construction material and the way we built the shelter," Jay answered.

"I hope that stuff doesn't rot over the winter," she added.

"You and me both, babe. You and me both."

Finished with the rocks, Jay and Sandy filled the water containers left by Chris and Ron. It took four trips to carry everything back to the campsite.

The work crew hung the skins up for the walls and roofs for the two-room shelter in a day. They also built an outhouse near the shelter. They considered this a luxury item since until then they had just traveled a short distance from the campsite to use the tall grass, always going in pairs for protection.

Ron's arm was not yet ready to use, especially for climbing a ladder, but he took his time and was able to make it into the shelter for an inspection. "You guys did well! Under the circumstances, overbuilding is okay. You have my seal of approval."

Smiling, Chris said, "Thanks!"

"We aim to please," Jay added.

In the construction of their new two-room tree-hut home, the men made a flexible but strong covered bridge connecting the women's hut to theirs since each hut was in its own tree. Ron had helped design the bridge so that the trees could sway with the wind without destroying the bridge. Both shelters had the rope ladder/wood ladder combination. Chris had picked trees that were relatively close to each other to facilitate structural integrity of the finished product.

Climbing down to the ground, everyone gathered at the base of the trees that supported the new shelter and admired their hard work. Sandy gave Jay's hand a gentle, loving double squeeze and looked somewhat sad; they wouldn't be able to cuddle and sleep together once everyone moved into their new home. Jay returned the squeeze with an understanding look in his eyes.

Noticing the sad expressions on Jay and Sandy's faces, Chris decided to get their minds off their dilemma by getting everyone back to work. "Let's get some supplies up there. This is our new home now. Jay, you and Sandy get some vines rigged with a platform for hauling our gear and supplies up there. Ron, kick back and enjoy watching everyone work while you can. Your arm will be better before you know it. XO, Miranda, let's go back to the campsite and pack up our stuff for transport. Doc, you get to pick a corner in the men's quarters to be sickbay after you get your medical supplies up there. We have an extra corner."

Miranda, feeling delighted about her new, roomier apartment, snapped Chris a crisp salute and said, "Aye-aye, sir!" She turned and headed to the campsite with an extra bounce in her step.

Chris and Caitlyn smiled at each other, holding eye contact for a little longer than necessary, with Chris looking deeply into her brown eyes, before joining everyone as they got busy.

Back at the campsite, Miranda asked Chris, "What about the pidoggs?"

"What about them?"

"Aren't we going to build them shelters too? Winter's coming, you know."

"You mean a dog house? In order to shelter all of them, we'd have to build a dog hotel!"

"Well, yeah, sort of," she responded.

Caitlyn, who was stacking supplies from the capsule for transport to their new home, looked over at Chris with an expectant smile. "Well?"

"They're wild animals; they don't live in shelters," he said, looking back and forth between the two women.

Wearing a mock sad face, Miranda replied, "They're more like pets now, almost dependent on us."

"Don't mistake their friendliness for their being like lovable pets. Those *pets*, as you call them, could bite off your leg with one swift snap of those jaws if they had a mind to. I think it's more the other way around. They adopted us. They've been protecting and providing for us since they escorted us here. We've become dependent on them."

Miranda sulked.

Chris, feeling bad that he might have hurt her feelings, relented. "Okay. If it makes you feel any better, once we get settled, and I mean really settled and have nothing to do, I'll talk to Jay about building some simple lean-to shelters for them."

Miranda perked up. "Thanks, Chris. You're the greatest!" she exclaimed with a smile. She gave him a bear hug and a kiss on the cheek that made him unexpectedly, lightly blush with embarrassment.

Seeing him redden, Caitlyn chuckled. "I didn't know you were so sensitive."

Realizing that Caitlyn had noticed him blush made him flush an even deeper shade of red as he turned away from her and toward the work at hand.

16

"It's getting colder by the day, Chris," Jay complained.

Chris nodded. "And it's only going to get colder."

The last few days had been gloomy and overcast. Everyone was busy cutting and fitting the fur skins into blankets, cloaks, and warm boots.

"How did the American Indians or the Eskimos do this?" asked Miranda wearily.

Jay answered, "The Indian women would chew on the leather until it was soft enough to make moccasins and clothing. Want to try it?"

Sandy made a disgusted face, as if he had asked her to eat a worm.

Caitlyn added, "Yes, but that was deer skin, and it wasn't anywhere near as thick as this."

"True for some Indian tribes, but the Plains Indians had buffalo hides to contend with, which would have been about half as thick as this," said Chris.

"Too bad the capsule computers didn't have any data on the Amish culture. Didn't the Amish do everything by hand?" asked Miranda.

"Not exactly," said Chris. "They just didn't use modern conveniences that required electricity or fossil-fueled equipment like automobiles and chainsaws. They did have metal hand tools as such, many of which they made themselves. They essentially lived in a time capsule that kept them in the 1800s. We don't have the metal or a way to forge tools as they did, but we can build some useful items with what we have available. For example, we could make a spinning wheel to form thread and create a board for weaving it into cloth for clothing with the natural material we have here, like plant fiber and pidogg fur. That's a start. It's going to take time to get where we really need to be to feel comfortable, but time is something we apparently have a lot of."

"You don't really expect a rescue, do you?" Sandy asked pointedly.

Everyone's eyes turned down or looked away. Sandy's sad but expectant eyes stared right at Chris.

He said softly, "I don't have an answer for you, Sandy. There's still a chance that some Earth station will pick our signal out of the ether and find us, but it would take many years after that to effect a rescue. I don't want to crush your hope and say no, there's not a chance, but we have to prepare for a long-term stay here. I want to be rescued as badly as you do, but I'm a realist. I live in the here and now, and right now, I'm preparing us for the worst. I know that as long as we all work together, we *will* persevere. It's not going to be easy, but it's far from impossible."

Sandy looked down at the floor, nodded her head in acknowledgment, and leaned a little harder on Jay.

The next morning, the wind picked up speed, with strong gusts from the east-northeast. The hides on the tree hut walls and roof were buckling noisily in and out, and the temperature dropped to around three degrees Celsius. An intermittent pitter-patter began lightly on the walls and roof.

Looking out the door of the men's hut, Ron said, "Looks like we might have a storm brewing us up some trouble."

"I was wondering when this place got rain," Chris replied.

The trees were starting to move the hut in an uneven rhythm. Soon, the women joined the men in their hut.

Standing in the open doorway, Chris said, "I don't know, but I don't like the looks of the sky; look how dark it's getting. The temperature has dropped quite a bit too. Notice that we can see our breath?"

A stronger gust rocked the trees and hut.

"Do we have any rations from the capsule left?" Chris asked the XO.

"Yes. We have enough to last about two weeks. We've been good at getting local food and haven't had to use any rations except a little salt and pepper to flavor the meat and a few vegetable packs."

Chris turned his head and listened. "The wind is coming more from the east now. That's unusual. I wonder if it portends bad things to come."

An hour later, the rain began to intensify. Within another fifteen minutes, the rain was a steady downpour with occasional wind gusts that rocked the trees. Braving the weather for a moment, Chris peered out the door, looking for the pidoggs.

"The pidoggs are hunkered down. We still have sentries around our trees, but the rest are lying in small circles, as if guarding a central figure."

Satisfied that the animals were doing what they were used to doing in bad weather, Chris popped back inside. "I think we should plan for a long stay in our huts. We need to make sure the huts don't leak and get our blankets and furs wet. We can stay warm by sharing body heat if necessary." Thinking of Sandy, Chris said, "If you ladies would be more comfortable staying with us in here, you're welcome to bring your warmest nighttime attire and bedding and camp out with us."

Not one to waste an opportunity to stay with Jay, Sandy said, "I want to stay here."

No one objected. The women left to get their belongings and brought them back to the men's hut. Since the women preferred to sleep with the men, the second tree hut would be used as a sick bay and for food storage, eating, and storing the equipment they'd salvaged from the capsule.

The rain continued, and the air turned colder to just above freezing. Sandy was happy as a bug in a rug, warm and snug with Jay under the same fur blanket. Holly and Ron snuggled close for warmth in their shared fur blanket. Chris was a little uncomfortable having two women in bed with him, but with Miranda and Caitlyn nestled on either side of him, at least everyone was warm. Chris had shown everyone how to weave their own grass mattresses earlier, and it had taken only a few strips of leather to tie them together, so everyone was comfortably warm and cozy on the shared padded beds covered with thick animal-fur blankets.

The rain hadn't slowed or stopped. The men had been able to create a small fireplace of sorts for heat and cooking in the second hut with the rocks collected from the lake, but two weeks of sleeping, eating, and more sleeping and eating in the small rooms was starting to get on everyone's nerves. The small talk and anecdotes that kept boredom at bay had waned. True to their original promise to the XO, no one lost their temper or became unruly with each other, but the mood wasn't good.

"When is this rain going to stop?" complained Sandy.

"It'll stop when it stops," Miranda answered curtly.

"Let's keep it civil, please," Caitlyn said.

"I'm sorry. I must be getting cabin fever. I'm really sorry, Sandy," Miranda said apologetically.

Sandy ignored the apology.

"I'm going to go down and visit with the pidoggs. Want to come?" Jay asked Sandy.

"No thanks. I hate being wet. Being wet *and* cold tops being just wet every time."

"I'll go with you," said Chris.

The men donned their fur capes and climbed down the ladder to the ground. Judy approached Jay and leaned on his leg for a good wet head scratching. Chris paid attention to a couple others that came by to say hello. The rain wasn't as driving inside the tree lot, but just outside in the clearing, it was coming down in waving sheets, driven by gusts of wind.

"The lake level is rising more and more each day. It must be already past the escape capsule," Jay said.

"I hope the seals on the hatches will hold. There are still salvageable goods in there," Chris replied. "If this rain keeps up, it won't be long before the water reaches here."

"Maybe in a day or two by the looks of it."

"We're also running low on food supplies. How about you and me taking a walk over to the creature graveyard to see if we can find some meat that's still palatable?" Chris asked.

"Why not? We're already wet. Unlike Sandy, I'd rather be wet than bored to death, even if it is cold," Jay replied.

"Great! Let's let the women and Ron know what we're up to," Chris said.

Climbing the ladder into the shelter, Chris and Jay collected their weapons and the fur head coverings they'd made. Chris gave Ron a radio to monitor while they were gone.

"We're going to keep our radios off until we need to make a call, but you keep yours on. The solar charger isn't working as well as it could be in this low light," Chris said to Ron. The tree canopy, the heavy overcast sky, and the rain prevented much light from reaching the tree shelter. The ambient light was the equivalent of what they would normally see thirty minutes after sunset. That didn't allow for much charging of radio batteries or the one emergency light that Ron had been able to procure from the escape pod, but it was enough to travel safely.

Twenty pidoggs went with the men as they left the safety of the tree shelter. Four pidoggs pulled two sleds with tie-down material for the meat. "These guys must be bored stiff to want to go out in this stuff," Jay commented.

"You're right, and their enthusiasm level isn't what it usually is either, but apparently, duty calls, and they are not ones to shrug off their duty." Chris paused for a moment and then asked, "What do you say we stop by the capsule on our way?"

"Why? That's at least a kilometer out of our way."

Smiling, Chris asked, "Have you anything better to do?"

"Good point. Sure, let's go."

The men headed a little more to the west. As they neared the capsule, they could see that the water had already reached it.

Jay said, "Look, it's rocking in the wind. It's already starting to float. I guess that answers the question about the seals. We'd better tether it to the ground so it doesn't blow into the lake."

Chris and Jay took a few of their cargo tie-down vines and sticks and secured the capsule in place.

"If the water gets any higher, maybe we could float it to the tree lot near the shelter," Jay said. "What do you think?"

"It's possible. This thing must weigh tons, though. If the wind pushing on it doesn't pull out our stakes, we should try soon. My guess is that tomorrow the water may be high enough to float it completely off the ground as long as the seals hold."

"Sounds like a plan," said Jay.

On their way to the dead giant beasts after securing the capsule, Chris asked, "How serious are you about Sandy?"

"Very. I've never married—or had a serious relationship, for that matter. I've had my flings, but nothing that grabbed me deeply."

"Are you sure the feelings you have for her aren't just because she's available and we're all stuck here?"

"Yeah, I'm sure. I see in her something that the other women I've been with didn't have. Sandy is confident in her own abilities, but very willing to admit that she has weaknesses. I find that honesty quite appealing. The other women I dated had ambition and an almost testosterone type of drive. Frankly, I have enough testosterone of my own. I don't need a mate who will try to outperform me every time a challenging situation comes up. I'm a team player, but I don't want to always be challenged on my decisions or ability either."

"True, but there are many women who can handle the same challenges as a man, and in some cases, even better."

"I understand that, but I'm not into competing with my mate. I want a mate that's comfortable making decisions in her field of expertise and willing to accept decisions that are in mine. If we share a common attribute, then I'm willing to discuss it with her and reach a mutual decision without arguing over who's right. I don't want to be in competition with a woman because she has something to prove to herself or to anyone else. Just to prove that she can be better than a man? No thanks! Sandy is not like that at all. She has a gentle and sensitive feminine side, and that's very, very attractive to me."

"I can't argue with that. She seems to get upset easily, though," Chris said.

"She's been hurt before. Not physically. She was mentally abused by her former husband. But yeah, you're right. When circumstances are beyond her ability to resolve or understand, she does tend to get upset."

"You know you're rescuing her from those episodes, don't you? That can lead to a dependency issue that may not make for a healthy relationship."

"I'll take my chances. I do love her, and she says she loves me. I believe her, and that's good enough for me. Her actions back up her words."

"Then why not make it permanent and marry her?"

"If she would have me, I would."

"Then do it."

"How? We don't have anyone here that can perform a legal ceremony."

"Sure we do. The mayor of a town can perform a wedding. So can a ship's captain when out to sea."

"Okay. We don't have a town with a mayor or a ship with a captain. Who would perform the ceremony?"

"Well, Caitlyn was the executive officer on *Copernicus*, and since the captain was killed, she is technically the captain of the ship. She could do it."

"No ship, no captain," Jay responded.

"Not exactly. Technically, we're still considered in the military and under military guidelines since we're survivors of a shipwreck, so she's still in charge."

"Hmm, you may have a point. I'll broach the subject with Caitlyn before I ask Sandy."

"Good man. I wish you luck."

There were several giant carnivores working away at some of the carcasses, including an adult bear with two juveniles tearing away at one of the smaller beasts, but none of them challenged the men or pidoggs when they passed. Chris and Jay watched as the smaller of the two juveniles crawled into the abdominal cavity of the dead animal, feasted for a short while, and then wiggled out, its previously dark tan coat now a deep crimson red.

"I have to give it to the pidoggs. They never, never let their guard down. Did you see how they shared responsibility in watching the carnivores?" Chris asked.

"No, sorry. I guess I was lost in thought about marrying Sandy. I'll make sure that from now on I keep my head in the game."

They finally found two carcasses that seemed to be okay for harvesting meat and fur. The first two they sliced into had almost knocked them over with a rotten meat smell. Interestingly, the pidoggs, sniffing the air and licking their chops, seemed to be enjoying the stench the way humans would savor the smell of baking bread.

On the way back to the tree huts, the rain picked up in intensity.

"Monsoon season," complained Jay. "Weeks of rain with little or no letup. I wonder how long this will last."

"Do you want me to guess?"

"No, you'll probably say something like two to three months, and that won't improve my already miserable mood any."

Chris smiled. *That's exactly what I was going to say.*

❖ ❖ ❖ ❖

Back at the tree shelter, standing inside the women's hut with heat, Chris and Jay explained that the meat from the giant grass-eaters was not going to last. The cold weather had helped to keep it fresh, but it wouldn't last much longer.

"What we need is a good freeze," Miranda suggested.

"Oh, bite that foul tongue, woman!" Caitlyn said somewhat jokingly, but with serious intent. "It's plenty cold enough out there!"

"True," said Chris, "but what's of more importance right now is getting the capsule over here before it blows out over the lake. We need to do that first thing in the morning."

"How?" asked Caitlyn.

"It's already floating on the lighter end. By morning the water should be deep enough to drag it here and attach it to some trees," Chris answered. Chris and Jay both stripped to the waist and stood next to the fireplace where it was warmer.

"What good is it to us now? We stripped it bare when we moved in here," said Miranda.

While drying his face and hair with a dry shirt, Chris said, "There are plenty of salvageable items on board. We may end up using parts of the hull for something in the future. I just don't want to close the door on the possible uses we may still get out of it."

"It's impossible. We can't possibly use the hull for anything other than a shell," argued Miranda, "and it's all beat up to boot."

Chris said, "My father used to tell me, 'Long live your imagination. Dare to dream the impossible, for someday the impossible will become the new reality.' That was when everyone thought that faster-than-light travel was impossible."

"Touché." Miranda surrendered.

Rain continued to pound the animal skin walls and roof throughout the night. It sounded like kettledrums beating to several conductors working different scores at the same time, including thunderous accents from the occasional flash of lightning. Drumming mezzo piano was followed by a flourishing crescendo to fortissimo and a decrescendo back to mezzo piano, without regard for meter or the ears of the occupants. Sleep came hard for everyone. Dawn brought fresh winds to buffet the skin walls with ever-increasing waves of an almost waterfall of rain.

Jay looked outside the door of the living quarters to see that the water was already over a meter deep at the base of the tree. "We can't go out there today. It's too dangerous in that deeper water. We're probably going to lose the capsule."

Chris partially opened a tied-down window flap to take a quick peek outside. Immediately, the flap of skin he had loosened and pulled aside was ripped from his hand by the wind, and the tie-downs came back to slap his cheek. "Ow!" he cried out. They'd hit hard enough to leave a red mark. Rubbing the stinging area, he grumbled, "You're right. Besides, we would need the pidoggs to tow the capsule back, and the water looks too deep for them to touch bottom well enough to pull. I don't think the paddle-like tails of theirs would produce enough power to do it against this wind either."

Sandy asked, "Are they still out there?"

Not wanting to be slapped again, Chris hesitated before peeking out. Gripping the edge of the flap and the leather tie-down stings, he peeked out. After looking all around, he said, "I don't see them."

"Where would they go? Are they dead? Did they drown or get blown away by the storm?" Sandy asked. Worry lines now creased her forehead. She had become quite attached to the pidoggs, especially Judy and her pups and the small female that had befriended her.

"I don't know," Chris said. "They must have some survival tricks. This weather has to be seasonal, like the monsoons on Earth. When the rains stop and the waters subside, the animals recover and life goes on."

In the storage hut, Dr. Rhodes removed the bandage on Ron's arm. "I don't know how you did it, but you beat that red infection *and* the white one. There's an old health care saying, 'the power of the body can heal the body,' and you certainly proved that point."

"Thanks, Holly. That infection would have killed me for sure. I think you're minimizing your part in this."

"No, not really. I tried all the medicines I had. They didn't work. I was afraid to remove the infected skin from your arm because we didn't have a sterile environment for the surgery, and I could have made the infection much worse. Apparently, it didn't matter. Once that skin was removed—the hard way, I might add—the saliva trick worked."

Ron quivered. "I still get queasy thinking about that stuff. Yuck!"

Holly smiled a genuine, caring smile. "Your arm is almost completely healed. There will be some scarring where the infection went deep, but you have full function back already. You won't be needing bandages anymore. All that pink skin will be back to normal in a few months."

Ron hugged her in appreciation—and then spontaneously kissed her. She let him. They held each other's gaze for a moment and then kissed again, this time a long, deep, passionate kiss. They were still embracing when Caitlyn walked in to get a canteen to catch water from a leak in a corner.

"Oops! Sorry!" she exclaimed upon seeing them. With an ear-to-ear grin, she grabbed the canteen, made an abrupt about-face, and said over her shoulder, "Carry on!" She left them looking like two young teenagers caught necking by the girl's mother.

Recovering from their surprise, they laughed a good, soul-deep, hearty laugh, something that no one there had heard in quite a while.

17

The rain slowed but continued for another two weeks. The water continued to rise to the tops of the roots of the trees even after the rain stopped. The overcast thinned, and the days began to get longer, warmer, and brighter. The pidoggs returned to the area, which comforted the group, and watching the pidoggs swim and play gave them some entertainment.

"We're almost out of food," Sandy said as she came from the supply hut. "How are we going to get more food when the water is so high?"

"I saw the pidoggs swimming and diving for fish the other day. What we need to do is learn to fish," Chris said. "There's plenty of water out there now and no predators to worry about. The fish probably follow the high water to new feeding grounds, but heaven only knows what they eat. If there weren't so many predators near the lake's edge, we could have tried to catch fish then, but there's nothing to stop us from trying to catch them from here now. What do we have that we can make a hook from?"

"We might be able to make a fishing spear by modifying a spear point," Ron offered, eying one of the spears in a corner. "We could also modify an arrowhead and tie the arrow with a length of string to a makeshift spool on the front of a bow."

"Good ideas! But I'd still like to try a hook and line too, just to increase our chances," Chris said.

Jay, who had been taking a nap in the corner, had been awake for some time, just listening to the conversation. With his eyes still closed and his hands folded across his chest, he interjected, "Take an arrowhead and reshape it. That plastic is some tough stuff. It should make a great hook."

"We could, but from what I remember of the fish we saw, they have big sharp teeth that could slice through any line that's not made of metal," said Ron.

Chris responded, "You're right … I do remember."

"How about using a fishing net? Couldn't we fashion one from some thin vines?" Caitlyn asked.

"Sure," Chris said. "I like that idea. It's a lot of work to make one, but if you want to take on that project, that would be great. For now, I think our best bet is to chum the water with some scraps and either spear the fish or shoot them with bow and arrow. I still have a good amount of paracord that we can strip to make a retrieval line for the spears and arrows. Let's do it."

The women got together to plan how to make the net. All the talk about fishing brought back fond memories for Miranda. Her father used to take her fishing on a pond on their property. *The property—only twelve light-years away. How I miss the times we shared there,* she thought. The memories brought tears to her eyes. *Will I ever see it again?* Quickly wiping away the tears before anyone else noticed them, Miranda made some suggestions on how to tie the knots. Having something constructive to do helped lift everyone's mood and relieved some of the building tension between them.

Chris took one of the spears and fashioned the spear-tip end so that it would accommodate a barb that would keep the fish from sliding off. He also drilled a hole in the other end of the shaft for the retrieval rope.

Ron focused on making leather string, cutting a fifteen-centimeter circle of leather and splitting it several times to make thinner circles. Now he had four fifteen-centimeter circles of leather. Using the thinnest piece and starting at the outside of the leather circle, he used his knife to cut a thin continuous strip in a spiral pattern toward the center. To expedite the softening of the leather string and to make it stretchable, he put it in his mouth and chewed it while Chris and Jay worked on their part of the spear.

Jay made the barb that was to attach to the spear. He had to reach outside the door for a branch and became soaked in the process.

Chris used the wet leather string that Ron had made to tie the barb securely to the shaft. He knew that as the leather string dried, it would tighten. Chris tied a length of paracord through the hole in the end of the spear so that after being thrown, the spear could be retrieved.

The men had created a near-perfect double-barbed fishing spear. Being busy gave the men and women a purposeful feeling again. The men continued to make two more fishing spears. Ron, finally feeling useful again, whistled a tuneless song when he wasn't chewing on the leather string. He didn't have an ear for music, but no one complained. He was finally back to his old self.

The water was receding slowly, with the top half-meter of roots now showing at the base of the trees. Chris and Jay climbed down the ladder of the living quarters, while Ron descended the ladder of the cooking hut. Sitting on the root tops of nearby trees, the pidoggs watched the men. Chris and Jay, each with a spear in hand, balanced themselves on the root tops on opposite sides of the tree. Ron stayed high on his ladder to act as a spotter. An hour passed before Ron saw and pointed to a good-size fish swimming near the surface.

"Chris! To your right and behind you, about a meter from the tree!"

Turning, Chris saw the fat fish, more than a meter long, swimming slowly near the base of the tree. As he patiently waited for it to come into range, he carefully raised his spear. The back of the spear hit the tree trunk before he could get it into a high enough position for the throw. Repositioning his feet on the root tops, he again raised the spear and waited. With a quick, short throw, Chris sent the spear point through both sides of the fish, the barbs keeping the fish from slipping off the end.

"Got it! I got it!" he yelled.

The fish fought viciously despite being pierced all the way through. Chris hauled in the line on the spear and repositioned his left foot so that he could reach down and grab the spear to pull the fish from the water, but his foot slipped off the root top. He quickly replanted his foot on the next lower root, but the struggling fish pulled him off-balance. He belly-flopped into the water, but when his head popped to the surface, he was still hanging onto his spear with the attached fish. Gasping from the shock of the cold water, Chris started to laugh at his own expense. Jay and Ron laughed along with him.

Ron suddenly stopped laughing, however, and shouted, "Chris! Get out of the water! *Now!*"

A six-meter fish was swimming with purpose directly toward Chris. Once Chris got the cape he was wearing out of the way, it took him two strokes to swim to the ladder where he could pull himself up to safety. Chris still had the spear with the fish in his hand as he climbed the ladder, the spear hanging behind and a meter below his feet. Not wanting to go away hungry, the great fish that had been heading for Chris cleared its upper body from the water with a flip of its tail. It displayed row after row of razor-sharp teeth as it cleaved the front one-third of the fish cleanly from the spear before splashing down and disappearing into the dark flood waters.

Shaken from his close encounter, Chris clung to the ladder, catching his breath. More movement in the water caught the men's eye. A ten-meter fish had one of the giant bear-creatures in its great maw. The men watched with trepidation as that denizen of the deep swam slowly out to deeper water with its prize. Chris continued his climb to the hut. Ron and Jay joined him.

"That was razor-close," Ron said when he reached the top. "If you had been just a second slower …"

"Big splashes attract big fish," Jay commented.

Caitlyn and Miranda helped a shivering Chris Elliott remove his wet fur cape and shirt.

Pointing at the dripping wet cape, Chris said, "If that was any larger, I wouldn't have made it to the ladder. It got in my way swimming, and the increased weight from being wet didn't help." Through chattering teeth he said, "Thanks, Ron. You saved my life."

"Don't mention it, big guy. I only played a small part in it. I still owe you plenty for saving mine."

The men described the incident to the women, including the monster fish with the giant bear in its mouth. Sandy had such a look of despair on her face that Miranda sat next to her and hugged her. Tears began to flow down Sandy's cheeks. She was crying openly now.

Between sobs, she said, "We're never going to make it. It's just too hard. It's too dangerous! We can't even take a walk outside without something wanting to eat us. I … I can't take it anymore!"

Jay sat down on Sandy's other side. Putting his arm around her too, he did his best to comfort her. "We have each other. All of us together can make it. Okay, yeah, it's hard. So what! We've done all right so far. Each time we go out, we learn more about what's good and what to stay away from. Don't forget, we have Judy and her friends looking out for us too."

The thought of Judy and her pups helped to calm Sandy's sobbing. Jay continued to hold and reassure her.

"Doc, how do we know this fish is safe to eat?" Ron asked, changing the subject. "This fish has blue blood."

"With absolute certainty?" Holly responded. "We don't. Without my spectrograph, it's almost a guessing game. The pidoggs are eating the fish without ill effect, so by mimicking what they eat, we may be okay. The octopuses and squids on Earth have blue blood, and they are safe to eat, but there's only one way to find out, and that's to try it. I suspect the fish use copper instead of iron for oxygen transport. That's why their blood is blue. Oxidized copper in blood turns blue. There are copper-toxicity symptoms that we can watch for just in case: gastrointestinal distress, vomiting—especially if we vomit blood—black tar-like stools, jaundice, and at worst coma that can lead to death. Our bodies normally regulate the amount of copper we store, so any excess is supposed to be excreted. Long-term effects of copper poisoning would include liver and kidney damage and then eventual death. So my suggestion is that we limit our intake at first and see if it makes any of us sick. Drinking plenty of water will help too. In the short run, since we will not be consuming the blood itself, we should be okay. Let's take this fish to the other hut and cook it. If it smells good, we give it a try. If it tastes good, we eat it."

Forty-five minutes later, the air was filled with the aroma of roasting fish.

"This is really good," Chris mumbled with his mouth full.

"I think we have a winner here," said Ron, also chewing on his portion.

"Remember," Holly said, "let's not eat too much until we find out how well we can tolerate it."

Jay said, "There's not that much here; the fish that almost got Chris took his share first."

That got a nervous chuckle from everyone except Sandy. She was still recovering from her crying episode.

The sun had set, and all was calm. The wind died down, and a gentle, quiet peace came over the area. The group was settling in for the night when they heard splashing in the water not far away, similar to the sound of children playing in a pool. There were no other sounds for about a minute. Then a high-pitched yelp sounded, followed by more frantic splashing and another yelp. A lone pidogg made a barking-growling sound for several seconds and then began a wailing howl. Another and then another pidogg added to the wailing. Still more pidoggs joined the chorus. The cacophony was almost deafening.

Covering his ears with his hand, Chris shouted, "There must be fifty of them howling out there!"

Everyone covered their ears.

"That's the same kind of howl that Judy made when she lost her mate," Jay shouted back.

"I bet they lost a member or two to the fish," Ron added.

With Ron's comment, the mood in the hut went as dark as the night was black outside. No one spoke, but everyone hoped that the lost pidoggs weren't their close friends, not that it mattered that much; they loved them all. Sandy started to cry softly again.

The next morning was bright and sunny. The air temperature was warmer with the promise of a pleasant, though cool, day. The water continued to recede and now was only chest-high. From the hut smaller fish could be seen swimming near the base of the tree.

"Caitlyn, why don't you try your net out on those fish at the base of the tree?" suggested Chris.

"That's a great idea! Miranda, want to help me catch some fish?"

"Sure, why not?" she replied.

Caitlyn and Miranda climbed down the ladder and stood on the root tops.

"Have you ever thrown a fishing net before?" Caitlyn asked.

"No, have you?"

"No. Tell you what, I'll throw the net, and you hold the rope," Caitlyn said.

"Okay," Miranda said, climbing a few steps up the ladder. "I can see the fish better from up here, so I'll tell you when to throw."

"Wilco." After all their time on the planet, Caitlyn and the others were still using some of the radio communications shorthand, including the one for "will comply." Old habits were hard to break.

"Here comes a small school now … wait … wait … now!" Miranda shouted.

Caitlyn gave the net a circular heave, and the net separated in a wide circle from the rocks that were tied to the edges as it hit the water and sank toward the bottom.

Surprised at the near-perfect throw, Miranda exclaimed, "I thought you said you couldn't throw a net!"

"I didn't say that I couldn't throw a net; I said that I'd never thrown a net before."

"Well, you did pretty darn good for a first try."

"Beginner's luck. I used to watch nature shows now and then when I was a kid, and I just mimicked the motion."

Miranda began pulling up the net. Empty. They both laughed. But several tries later, there were two half-meter-long fish tangled in the net.

"Yes! Yes!" Miranda shouted. They were both excited. Smiling with excitement while climbing the ladder, Miranda said, "I can't wait to show the guys that women can help catch food too!"

"What have we here?" Jay asked approvingly as Miranda and Caitlyn entered the shelter with the fish in hand and smug looks on their faces.

Holding up their trophies, the two women looked at each other and announced in unison, "Lunch." They looked at each other once again and laughed.

"Well, what about dinner?" Ron asked with a phony disappointed look on his face.

"You'll just have to wait until after lunch to have dinner," Caitlyn said, using her best mom voice.

The mood in the hut was definitely picking up.

Between bow shooting, spearing, and casting the net for fish, the group ate well. Everyone had lost weight from eating the high-protein diet. Both the men and the women were slim and trim at 10 percent or less body fat. The water level at the base of their trees continued to drop. When the water receded to less than a meter, the fishing became poor. Fortunately, while the fishing was good, they had caught enough both to eat and to dry some for later consumption.

"We need to find another source of food,"Chris said. "Sandy, how much fish do we have left?"

"About three days' worth," she replied.

Sandy's mood had improved somewhat. She wasn't going through the deep bouts of depression that she'd experienced before, but neither was she showing feelings of happiness. Dr. Rhodes diagnosed her condition as clinical depression. The med kit didn't include antidepressants, though, because all applicants to the United Earth Space Force were heavily screened for mental disorders and specific personality traits. Being away for months to years at a time from civilization and having to live within the confines of a space station or spacecraft required a special breed of personality. The world's submarine forces used similar tests on Earth because of the almost claustrophobic conditions aboard the boats. People who couldn't make the grade were not accepted into the program. Dr. Rhodes was going to recommend adding an additional consideration to the already exhaustive testing: long-term despair. Jay did what he could to make sure that Sandy wasn't stressed, but it was an uphill battle.

Miranda kept Sandy busy while everyone else conferred about the food situation.

"The water level is only knee-deep right now and continues to drain away. I haven't seen any of the large predatory fish since the water was waist-high. Has anyone else?" asked Chris.

Everyone shook his or her head, some murmuring, "No."

"I think that it's probably safe to start walking around as long as the ground will support us. We'll have to be careful how and where we step and keep an eye on each other. Opinions?" Chris asked.

"I think we should go back to the area where those giant grass-eaters got stuck in the mud during the stampede. If they weren't attacked and eaten before the floods came, they may still be alive. Thinner, but alive. We could use the meat," Jay suggested.

"I suppose it's possible," said Chris. "Considering how well the animal that we killed was able to fend off the pidoggs, if the trapped grass-eaters weren't too weak from hunger or thirst before the flood came, it wouldn't surprise me if they were able to ward off the bear-creatures too."

"I agree," said Ron. "The floodwaters didn't get high enough to drown them. I suppose those sharklike fish may have had their chance at them, but we won't know until we take a look."

Dr. Rhodes commented, "I could use a break from fish too. I'm worried about protein poisoning, though. We need to find a source of carbohydrates and better fats. Our bodies can only handle a certain amount of lean protein before it becomes toxic to the liver and kidneys. Our bodies are already showing the signs of no carbohydrates in our diets. The fats that we've been able to get from the meat and raw fatty fish have done an okay job of sustaining us, but we need a more complete food source. What I recommend is that if we can get a grass-eating animal of any type, we also harvest the stomach contents to supplement our diet."

Caitlyn was quick to question the doctor's wisdom on this. "Eww! How gross, Doc! What can that possibly do for us?"

"For one, it can keep us alive. We can't digest grass, which seems to be the most plentiful resource here. It's mostly cellulose, and our bodies don't contain the enzyme that can break it down to sugars. Grass-eaters and certain insects have microbes that live in their stomachs or intestinal tracts that do break it down. From what I've seen, and maybe Chris can back me up on this, animal life on this planet also uses a form of sugar for energy. The contents of the stomach and intestinal tract should have the enzymes already working at digesting the cellulose to a simple form of sugar. Sugar is a carbohydrate, the same thing we use in our bodies for energy; we just convert it to glucose, another form of sugar. We can't live on protein alone. We have to have a more balanced diet, or we will slowly die, regardless of how many calories we consume."

"Yeah, but what's it going to taste like?" Jay asked.

"Probably bad," replied Chris. "We might be able to wash some of the acids away and make a tea of sorts with what's left. That wouldn't be as bad."

"Tea?" Sandy asked.

"Yes, tea," said Chris. With a look of mild disgust on his face, just thinking about what he was going to say, he continued. "We could also treat it like a mushy seaweed salad and eat it plain. Why do you think carnivores go for the intestines first? Not necessarily because it tastes good to them. It's where they get carbohydrates, vitamins, and minerals too."

Chris continued, "Let me tell you a short anecdote about hidden nutrition. Several hundred years ago, when zookeepers started keeping lions, they couldn't figure out why the caged animals were slowly getting sick and dying. They were feeding them raw meat and plenty of calories and supplementing their diet with additional vitamins and minerals, but it wasn't enough; something was missing. They eventually figured it out. The nutrient the lions needed was in the hair and skin of their natural food source. Once they started adding that nutrient to the lions' food, the lions stopped dying from malnutrition. We need to find a reliable source of carbohydrates, vitamins, and minerals also, or we'll start showing signs of malnutrition, with its inevitable progression to disease and death."

Holly added, "The other option is to make a meal of sorts from the giant grass-eater's feces. Large animals like that have incomplete absorption of nutrients in their digestion process, so some of the nutrition remains in the feces. Not as much as intestinal contents, but survivalists do it as a means of staying alive. Which would you prefer?"

A loud chorus of "yuck," "ick," and "eww" proceeded. Holly smiled a gotcha smile.

"We need to find a cow for milk," suggested Ron.

"That would be very helpful, but I don't know if any of these animals are mammals, do you, Chris?" asked Holly.

"Not that I've seen so far," Chris answered. "If they had nipples,

I would have seen them while butchering the animals. I don't even know if the animals we've seen so far lay eggs or bear their young live." Shrugging his shoulders, he said, "Sorry."

Holly added, "Well, we need to start looking for more food variety if we plan on staying healthy. We need a source of vitamins, including vitamin C. I've noticed that our gums are becoming red instead of the pink color they should be, and that's the beginning of scurvy. If we want to keep our teeth and our immune systems up, we need to do better on the vitamin front."

Chris started to put on his fur hat and cloak. "Okay! Who wants to brave the elements and potentially dangerous flora and fauna to find more food?"

"Count me in," said Jay.

"Me too," said Ron.

"I'll go," offered Caitlyn.

"I'll keep the home fires burning for you," Miranda said.

"I'd better stay here with Miranda and Sandy," said Holly. She didn't want to say it aloud, but she wanted to stay to keep an eye on Sandy.

"Good," Chris said. "Everyone who's going will need a cape and hat too. It may be warmer outside, but the water will suck the heat from us pretty quickly. Don't forget your weapons."

Holly joined Miranda and Sandy in the other tree hut while preparations were made for the hunt.

Wearing their fur accessories and carrying their spears, bows, arrows, and survival firearms, the group descended the ladder to the watery ground below.

"The ground's a bit spongy, but we're not sinking, so I guess we're good to go." No sooner had Chris spoken than loud splashing noises got their attention. Something was running through the water directly toward them, many somethings. With no time to ascend back up the ladder, they faced the oncoming attack shoulder-to-shoulder, with spears raised and bows drawn.

Judy made her appearance first, followed by six of her pups that were no longer pups, but good-size juveniles. With a great sigh of relief, everyone lowered their weapons. Many more pidoggs joined in the joyful occasion.

"Judy! Come! Good girl!" Jay called. Fortunately for him, Judy didn't jump on him as an excited dog would its owner in a cheerful greeting, but leaned against his leg instead. She weighed nearly eighty kilograms and probably would have broken bones had she done so. Unfortunately, she had not yet passed her good manners to her offspring; they were splashing water over everyone as they gleefully jumped up and down on the hunting group, competing for attention. The offspring, weighing thirty-five kilograms, nearly knocked the XO into the water in their excitement. A sharp retort from Judy brought the juveniles back under control. A good head and back scratching for every approaching pidogg reinforced the relationship between human and pidogg as they celebrated their seemingly long-anticipated reunion.

"Well, the rains did one thing good for us," stated Caitlyn.

Puzzled, Chris asked, "What's that?"

"The pidoggs actually smell okay for a change!"

Everyone got a good laugh.

With the pidoggs rejoining the humans, Chris suggested using them to pull sleds for carrying the food back to the huts. The welcoming committee satisfied, the hunting party started off, with the pidoggs forming their usual protective semicircle around the humans and with four willing pidoggs eagerly pulling two sleds in the middle behind the humans. The sleds floated on the water, making the pulling easy—too easy, in fact. The sleds kept gliding forward and bumping into the towing pidoggs until they learned to pull with a steady pace.

"It looks like that ruckus we heard the other night was Judy losing two of her pups. She had eight before, and now only six," commented Jay as the group headed northward.

"They're so intelligent, and their grieving is so real, even to us," Ron said. "I wish there were a way we could offer our condolences to her."

"I think they know. Maybe someday we'll learn to communicate verbally. There's so much we could learn from them, and they from us," commented Chris.

Suddenly, six pidogg guards on the right charged through the water at an unseen foe. It was over in a matter of seconds. The pidoggs had spotted a fin that had broken the surface for just a moment and attacked the would-be assassin. It took two pidoggs to heft their trophy back to the startled humans. The pidoggs dropped it in the water in front of them, minus the head.

"I see they haven't lost their touch," said Ron.

"It's a good thing too," added Caitlyn. "Look at the size of that thing. It could have taken off your foot in one bite."

Chris took out his knife, evenly divided the fish, and had the group feed it to all the pidoggs.

"They never cease to amaze me," commented Chris as the last of the fish disappeared down the gullet of a large juvenile. "Let's keep moving. I think we're in good hands, or paws, or jaws," he said, chuckling.

The hunting party made good time getting to the area where the giant beasts were trapped, even though the grass looked more like seaweed lying flat on the surface of the water, pointing in the direction of the flow toward the lake. On the way past the area where the capsule had rested after the stampede, they noticed that it had indeed floated away and was nowhere to be seen.

"Will you look at that?" asked Jay.

Three of the nearby animals had been reduced to tattered skin that was floating on the surface, still attached to the bones.

"Let's collect that skin," said Chris, pointing off to the right, "and then take a look at those animals over there. They're still upright and whole."

Arriving at the animals, they saw that the first one was obviously dead, but the other two were very much alive. Chris noted that the grass had been cleared in front of and to the side of the animals as far as they could reach.

"It's time for payback again," Chris said to his group. "Give me a hand cutting this dead one open to let the pidoggs eat. Then we'll take on the next one."

It didn't take the pidoggs long to catch on that the first animal was theirs. The monsoon season had been hard on the ones left alive. Their bodies were lean, bordering on skinny, with ribs poking through their skin. The food was welcomed with grunts, murmured growls, and groans of delight as they wasted no time filling their bellies.

The men made short work of dispatching the first live animal, ending its suffering quickly while Caitlyn helped keep watch with the pidogg sentries for both waterborne and land threats.

Making the incision in the abdomen above the waterline and cutting open the top of the stomach, Chris discovered that it was empty. "No sense taking this. There's nothing in it. Caitlyn, I'd like your help to get the liver and what fat stores we can find. Ron, you and Jay start skinning this animal. When you get to the top, get the back straps. That will be the easiest to remove and carry."

Being hungry and having done this before, the group didn't take long to finish and start back. Stopping to look back at the still-alive trapped animal and feeling sorry for it, the XO convinced the men to pause long enough to harvest grass for the starving creature. It took everyone an hour to collect enough grass to feed the unfortunate animal for several days. They cautiously pushed the grass with their spears to a spot the creature could reach. At first, the animal bellowed and weakly thrashed its head and tail about in fear, but soon the smell of fresh grass calmed it as hunger trumped its fright. Smiling, Caitlyn watched the animal eagerly eating as they departed the area.

The way back was slower. The weight of their haul caused the sleds to sink in the water. They didn't lower completely to the bottom, but the grass lying flat on the surface resisted their progress.

Caitlyn asked, "Do you think it would be possible to domesticate those giants?"

"It's unlikely," responded Chris. "It would be worse than trying to domesticate African wild water buffalo. If we tried to fence them in, they'd just walk through the fence. We don't have anything to offer them that would make them want to stay. Now if we had corn or another grain that would taste better than the grass, maybe, but we don't."

"Well, it was a thought," she said.

When they were within sight of their hut's tree lot, Caitlyn pointed to the east side of it and asked, "What's that over there?"

"Where?" asked Chris.

"Over there just to the left and on the edge of those trees. I saw something shiny flash, like a reflection or something," she said, continuing to point in the direction of the object.

"There it is. I see it," said Jay.

"Okay, I see it too, but what is it?" asked Chris. When the reflection could be seen, the glare off the object was too bright to identify it, and it was too far away to see clearly. "Ron, you and Caitlyn take the sleds back to the tree shelter and unload our cargo."

"Sure thing," replied Ron.

Chris said, "Jay, you're with me. Let's go check it out."

Chris and Jay headed southeast with fifteen pidoggs to investigate the shiny object while Ron and the XO continued southbound, with the remaining pidoggs forming a new protective semicircle around them.

Half an hour later, Chris and Jay recognized the object as one of the single-person escape capsules.

"I don't believe it! When the floods came, it must have floated, and the wind blew it all the way over here," said Jay.

The two men quickened the pace as much as the water and grass would let them. As they got closer to the capsule, Chris said excitedly, "Look! Another one!"

Jay, hardly able to contain his excitement, said, "You're not going to believe this, but there's the third! Look over there; it's wedged in those trees."

For the second time in his recent adult life, Chris offered a silent prayer of thanks. "We're going to have to hurry to make up some harnesses so the pidoggs can help pull them back to the tree huts before it gets dark."

With a bit of sadness in his voice, Jay said, "I bet my capsule stayed in that low spot and filled with water. With the rocket engine hatch cover off, the water would have flooded the compartment, making it too heavy to float."

"If we find it again, the living area should be dry unless the seal on the hatch was disturbed from that slamming the capsule took," Chris said.

Jay nodded his head in agreement and then shook off the willies from remembering that night.

Arriving at the first two capsules, the men started hacking at vines in the nearby trees to make three crude, three-pidogg harnesses. After attaching vines to the two capsules and to the pidoggs, Chris instructed Jay to head back.

"I want to get that third capsule. You go on ahead. I'll be back as soon as I can," said Chris.

"You're going to be cutting it kind of close, to get back by dark or just after, aren't you?" Jay asked.

"We don't have much choice. At the rate the water is receding, it'll probably be too low by tomorrow for us to pull it around the woodlot."

"Okay. Just be careful."

"I will."

Jay headed off with six pidoggs pulling hard and only two

sentries. Chris headed to the last capsule with seven eager-to-serve pidoggs.

It took an additional half hour for Chris to slog his way through the water and long grass to the third capsule. Wasting no time, he hooked the harness to three pidoggs and the capsule. It took twenty minutes to free the escape pod from the trees, but they were then immediately on their way. With four sentry pidoggs watching over the group, he felt relatively safe and began leading his group back to the shelter. While they were hauling the capsule around the north end of the tree line, halfway to the west end, two giant bears popped out of the woodlot two hundred meters from Chris and his crew of pidoggs. The creatures, hungry and seeing Chris as an easy meal, didn't waste time either, and they splashed through the water at a dead run. Chris quickly slipped the harnesses off the tethered animals and entered the capsule, slamming the hatch shut, dogging it tight, and cutting himself off from a view of the events outside. He wasn't a moment too soon.

The bears, ignoring the threatening pidoggs, covered the two hundred meters in less than ten seconds and went after the larger, easier, and slower game—the human. They slammed into the capsule, threatening to rock it over onto its side, clawing at the hatch.

Barking, growling, and making enough noise to raise the dead, the pidoggs attacked and retreated repeatedly, finally gaining the full attention of the giant creatures. Since the giant carnivores couldn't get to Chris, the bears gave up on the capsule and charged the attacking pidoggs. The pidoggs were fast. With their paddle-like tails and their muscular legs, they could plow and turn through the water as if they were on dry land. They split into two groups and were around and behind the attackers before the giants could turn to face them.

One pidogg got a solid bite and tore the Achilles tendon of the largest and slowest of the two creatures, hobbling it. The smell of blood and the fight encouraged the pidoggs even more. Again, the pidoggs charged, and the giants bellowed and met the charge head-on. The hobbled creature was not as fast as its partner and fell back. Seeing an opportunity, two pidoggs split around to the back of the hobbled animal. One of them had to duck under the vicious swing of a heavily clawed paw. Cutting back to the great animal's hindquarters, both pidoggs were able to hit the Achilles tendon area again on the remaining good leg. One pidogg neatly cut the tendon, and the other removed a chunk of flesh, totally hobbling the unfortunate creature. The other giant returned to protect her mate. The two bearlike creatures were now back-to-back, trying to protect each other against the savage attack of the pidoggs.

Chris could faintly hear the battle going on outside the well-insulated capsule, but he didn't dare crack the hatch to take a look. With paws larger than his head, one of those creatures could rip the hatch right off its hinges, reach in, and spear him with those twenty-centimeter talons like a fork stabbing an olive from a jar. *My kingdom for a porthole! I have to see what's going on!*

The sound of teeth snapping, reminiscent of gunshots where the weapon never ran out of ammunition, permeated the air, punctuated by the barking and growling of the pidoggs and the roaring of the larger animals. Chris noticed that the sound was concentrated in just one place. *The pidoggs must have wounded them. Do I dare chance it?*

Chris waited five more minutes. Then, noting that the volume and direction of the sound had stayed the same, he cracked the hatch to peek through the sliver of the opening. What he saw totally amazed him. The two giants were back-to-back with, apparently, several deep gashes; blood was flowing profusely down their fur. He opened the hatch a little wider to get a better view. One pidogg lay floating on its side, bleeding from a long, deep gash that extended from the middle of its side to the front shoulder. Still breathing, it was having a hard time holding its head out of the water. The remaining six pidoggs were unrelenting. The female giant noticed the hatch open with Chris standing there, taking her focus off the pidoggs for a few seconds. That's all it took for one of the pidoggs to rush in and clip an Achilles tendon on her with a viscous bite and then retreat to safety. Bellowing out in anger and pain, she turned toward that retreating pidogg. As a trained team of fighters, two pidoggs distracted the larger male bear toward the same side as the retreating pidogg. That left the other Achilles tendon on the female exposed and unprotected. A large male pidogg made the run and the bite. The female giant was quick, but not quick enough to prevent the debilitating injury. As the attacking pidogg retreated toward safety, a sweeping paw caught up with him. The giant bear lifted the 120-kilogram male in the air and heaved him easily thirty meters. Landing with a heavy splash, the pidogg didn't move, not even to lift his head from the water to breathe.

Seeing their pack mate killed enraged and energized the remaining five pidoggs. With both giants now severely hobbled, the pidoggs' strategy changed. They worked as two separate pairs and a lone pidogg, and each pair chose one bear-creature to target. The separate pairs charged the giants from the same side, drawing attention away from the lone, large male pidogg that was left on the opposite side of the large animals. When the bear-creatures' heads were turned toward the attacking pairs, the large male made his move. He dashed forward and then leaped into the air and onto the back of the female giant. He immediately began taking huge bites of fur and flesh from the back of her neck. Finally reaching the spine, he severed the cord in one vicious bite. She slumped helplessly into the water, still alive but unable to move and soon to drown as her nose and mouth disappeared under the surface of the knee-deep water.

The male giant turned to see his mate collapse. One of the pairs of pidoggs saw their chance and repeated the same maneuver on him. As the pidoggs jumped on the back of the giant, he rolled over and trapped one underwater, partially underneath him. The other pidogg, a large female, stayed on top of the rolling animal and finished the kill by ripping a section of his spine from the side of his neck. Frothy blood covered her face, snout, shoulders, and chest as she jumped to the ground with the prize still clenched in her teeth, while the creature's head and snout disappeared below the surface. The fight with the giant bearlike creatures was over. The pidoggs gathered around the submerged and drowning pidogg that remained trapped beneath the giant animal, helpless and unable to save her.

Chris watched the fight in fascinated horror. He exited the capsule and raced to see if he could save the trapped female pidogg. The male bear was still snapping his teeth while drowning but otherwise couldn't move. Chris reached underwater and raised the head of the pidogg above the surface. The female coughed out water and gasped for air. Chris got the attention of one of the victorious pidoggs and motioned for him to approach. Chris positioned the pidogg against the upraised head of the trapped animal and ran to the woodlot to get a branch that he could use as a lever. Returning, he positioned the branch close to the trapped female and shoved it under the giant. Placing the lever on his shoulder and grunting loudly, he lifted. The great bear was too heavy. He couldn't get enough advantage with the lever to move the creature enough before the branch broke. He ran back to the woodlot again, looking for anything he could use for a better lever and a fulcrum. He found a two-meter section of a fat log leaning against a tree and a thicker branch next to it. Chris was barely able to drag them, but adrenaline was a powerful ally. Placing the log close to the giant and placing the lever over the log and under the creature, he heaved with all his weight. The giant moved. Chris jammed the branch further under the creature, moved the fulcrum closer, and heaved on the lever again. A large pidogg male watched what Chris was attempting to do and added his weight to the lever by jumping up and hanging from the end by his teeth. The giant animal rolled enough to allow the trapped female to wiggle free. Relatively unharmed thanks to the spongy ground, she waded over and licked at Chris's hand while leaning heavily on his leg, in appreciation for saving her life, he suspected.

Chris ran to the wounded pidogg, who was still struggling to hold her head above water, gently lifted her, and placed her carefully in the capsule. He did the same for the dead male. After he had hooked three of the remaining pidoggs to the harnesses, they continued their trek, unchallenged, to the tree shelter.

When Chris arrived at the tree houses two hours after dark, Ron and Jay helped him position the capsule near the other two escape pods and securely tied it to a tree. The bottom of the capsule was already bumping the ground when they finished as the water continued to recede. Opening the hatch, Chris looked in to find that the female pidogg who had been injured first, and who had struggled so long to hold her head above water, had died. Tears flowed freely down his cheeks and onto his bloodied shirt. The pidogg family watched as he set both dead animals near the base of a tree, just out of the water. The pidoggs began their sad ceremony of death.

Watching through tears of sorrow, Chris called up and asked the others to come down to commiserate with their pidogg friends. As Judy had done before, each pidogg approached the bodies, placed their right foot on the heads of the deceased animals, and howled. When all of the pidoggs had finished their private grieving ceremonies for each dead pack mate, they all bowed together. They then raised their heads and began howling their death song in unison.

It was a sad yet beautiful moment, witnessing these intelligent beings saying good-bye to their loved ones. Chris was certain of one thing: these were sentient beings, not unthinking animals. They might not utilize tools, but they were definitely self-aware.

He made a silent pledge to himself: *If I ever get off this planet and back home, I will do everything in my power to come back to study them and bring experts to learn their language. This I promise.*

18

By the next morning, the water had all but receded. The ground was wet and spongy, but the sun was out, and the day ahead was looking good. Sandy and Dr. Rhodes finished performing an inventory in the supply hut and made their way down the ladder. Miranda, Ron, and Jay were already inspecting the capsules and giving the pidoggs some attention.

Chris and Caitlyn were still in the hut, finishing their after-breakfast chores.

"Yesterday was very scary," commented Chris.

"I bet it was. You could have been killed!" exclaimed Caitlyn.

Chris stopped and looked at her. "I'm not talking about me; I'm talking about how the pidoggs were willing to defend me to the death." He paused for a moment to calm his rising emotions. "They were literally fearless. As a military commander, you would give your eyeteeth and your first three children to have troops that would fight like they did. Watching the coordination of their attacks, the viciousness of the fight against two animals that were at least ten times their size, would have made any commander proud. The selflessness and the sacrifice of the individual for the benefit of the group …" He paused for a few moments, unable to finish the sentence as he began to relive the emotional trauma. Gathering his composure, he continued. "The miracle of it all is that they won. But there was no victory dance, no celebration. To them it was just another day on the job. When it was over, they wanted to harness up and help me get the capsule back here. They could have just run away when the creatures attacked—I was safe in the capsule—but that's not their way. I feel that it was my fault that two of them lost their lives. If I hadn't wanted to get that third capsule so badly, they would be alive today."

Caitlyn walked over to stand by Chris and put her hand on his shoulder. "As a biologist you already know the answer to that. You just told me. It's their way," she reminded him.

"Knowing it and feeling it are two different things. I know that I should be objective about this, but they were my friends too. That's what makes this so difficult. Objectively, I know that those animals are two top predators that compete for the same food source in the same area. Even if I hadn't been there, they most likely would have fought at some point. But I *was* there, and I *did* bring them to the spot that brought them together where they may have felt they had no other option except to fight."

"You don't know that for sure."

Chris turned away from Caitlyn, took a few short steps to the open window, and stood there, looking out. "That's what makes me feel so bad about this. I *don't* know. I would have been fine where I was. They should have run away."

Caitlyn walked over and put her hand in his. "Well, today is another day, and they have mourned their lost pack mates. They've moved on, and I think you should too."

Chris turned to face her and then looked at the floor. "I know that intellectually, but my heart says differently. I guess I haven't finished my grieving process yet."

With a consoling smile, Caitlyn said, "I'm going to tell you this as a friend, not as your commander, but treat it as if I am ordering you. Go spend some time with the pidoggs. I'm sure they have their ways to help you feel better."

His head still down and his eyes closed, Chris nodded and then left to take her advice.

As soon as Chris stepped off the ladder, six pidoggs were there to greet him—the female that he had saved, the large male that had assisted him with her rescue, and four juveniles that apparently belonged to them.

She has a family! he thought. The female approached and sat right in front of him. The male and the juveniles respectfully sat just behind and to the side of her.

Kneeling down in front of her and giving her a good head and neck scratching, Chris said, "Hello, girl! I'm so glad to see you! I hope you're feeling better today." With a tight-lipped smile, Chris turned and took a long moment to look at each of the pidoggs sitting at her side and then looked back to her. Her eyes communicated the gratefulness and respect she had for him. She looked deeply into his eyes, and he into hers, for several long moments.

Maintaining their deep eye-to-eye contact, he said, "I see you've brought your fami—" The word caught in his throat. The emotions he had been holding back suddenly broke through. Tears started flowing freely down his face again. The female stood slowly and gently placed her head and neck on his shoulder, giving Chris a badly needed hug. The rest of her family crowded around and pressed their bodies against his, their way of showing support and appreciation, he was certain. Chris put his arms around the male and female, hugging them tightly, and openly wept.

Several long minutes passed before Chris regained his composure. Releasing his hug and wiping away the tears, Chris smiled as if a heavy burden had been lifted from his shoulders. He gave the male and female a good head and back scratching and paid special attention to the juveniles, with the approving parents standing by. Standing up to his full 180 centimeters, he took a deep breath, glad to be alive and with his friends.

The next morning, the sun shone brightly through the few clouds that floated high in the sky, and the water continued to recede toward the lake. Chris walked over the still-wet ground to one of the capsules and poked his head inside to see Jay going through the lockers and Sandy itemizing everything on a tablet computer.

"Hi Jay, Sandy," Chris said.

"Oh, good morning, Chris," Jay responded, not turning around.

Sandy acknowledged Chris with a nod.

Looking at Jay, curious, Chris asked, "What are you doing?"

"I've been going through the capsules to see what usable items we might have, and I've found quite a bit. Most important, at least to Holly, is that we have more rations and vitamin packs. You hadn't used any that were in your capsule, so the entire two-week ration kit is intact."

"What we really need is a refrigerator to store any fresh food we collect. It's going to get warm, and I'm not fond of spoiled meat," Chris said.

"Fat chance of that," Jay replied.

Sandy, without looking up from her tablet computer as she continued to type away, asked, "Why?"

"What do you mean, why?" Jay countered.

Seemingly irritated that Jay couldn't comprehend a simple question, she responded, "What I mean is, why is there only a fat chance of getting a refrigerator?"

To Jay, the answer was as obvious as the day was long. He answered, somewhat sarcastically, "The capsules are supplied with dried food, canned food, and military rations that don't need refrigeration, so they don't equip the pods with one—that's why."

Sandy stopped what she was doing and looked at the men with an incredulous expression. "Then why not make one?" she asked.

"Because we don't have a refrigerant, for one, or a cabinet for another," Jay said, becoming a bit annoyed with Sandy challenging him.

Letting the tablet computer drop to her side, Sandy pointed to one of the lockers. "We can make a cabinet by recycling some of the lockers. I don't understand why you scientifically minded men can't figure out how to use the capsule's air-conditioning units to build a simple refrigerator. Make a box from the lockers, salvage some insulation from the capsule, cut a hole in the back of the locker, and place it over the air-conditioner vent."

Chris and Jay looked at each other and then at Sandy.

Giving in and sighing, Jay said, "I knew there was a reason I love you." Over his annoyance, he gave her a quick hug and peck on the cheek.

Chris said, "We may have to connect the batteries from the other capsules together for backup power when the sun sets, but it sounds very doable."

"Since I've become more of a pessimist anyway," said Sandy, "if we never get rescued and the equipment eventually breaks down, we could make a functional refrigerant using our urine to make ammonia. Urine contains urea, which has carbon, four atoms of hydrogen, two atoms of nitrogen, and oxygen. If we let the urine sit for a while, bacterial action will break down the chemicals to make ammonia, which is one atom of nitrogen and three of hydrogen. As long as we have power to run a compressor and can salvage an evaporator, we should be able to collect the ammonia gas and have cold storage during the warm weather. My chemistry degree has to do me good at some time. It might as well be now." Sandy made this contribution without any excitement or enthusiasm in her voice.

"If we need to, we could make that work," said Jay. "Sandy, you're a genius!"

Upon discussing the refrigerator design with Ron, the men decided that it would be better to have smaller refrigerators in all three capsules and not make one large one for exactly the reason Sandy had given—it could break down.

It took several days for each capsule modification, but they now had enough storage space for almost a week's worth of meat in each capsule. The water had receded back to the lake during the capsule refit, and the ground was drying well. The weather was warming into the high teens Celsius, and the grass was now standing tall, lush, and green.

Climbing down the ladder from the tree hut, Chris spotted one of the male juvenile pidoggs in a hunting creep. He froze on the ladder and watched. He couldn't see what the pidogg was after, but he never tired of watching them in action. After continuing his creep for about twenty meters, the juvenile paused and then lunged in the grass. The pidogg lifted his head high with the captured creature in his mouth, as if showing off his catch. None of the other pidoggs gave him as much as a glance. The catch looked like a large Earth bat with leathery wings. With one wing protruding out the front of his mouth, the young male had to open his mouth to reposition the bat-creature for eating, but he opened it a little too wide. The creature was still very much alive and was determined not to be eaten. Flapping its wings furiously, the winged animal startled the juvenile pidogg into opening his mouth just enough to make good its escape. The look of bewilderment on the juvenile's face was priceless.

Chris chuckled to himself. *Maybe it is a good thing none of his buddies saw this. If the pidoggs are into teasing their own kind, he's just been spared a moment of humility.*

Undeterred, the young male set off on another hunt, sniffing and following the trail of unknown game. *Ah, yes. The determination of youth; it's wonderful to see it in action.*

As he approached one of the escape pods, Chris met Jay sharpening his knife on a stone at an outdoor workbench that they had constructed for modifying the air-conditioning units to refrigerators. "It appears this planet has winged creatures," said Chris. "I just saw a juvenile's attempt at catching one."

Not looking up, Jay said, "That's good, I guess. What did it look like?"

"Mostly like those fruit-eating bats of South America—leathery wings, patchy brown fur, large body, and a more than two-meter wingspan."

“Thank you, professor, for sparing me the minute details,” Jay said with a smile, poking fun at Chris’s normally exhaustive descriptions.

Chris smiled in return. “Force of habit is hard to break.”

“So where’s the fruit? I could stand a nice juicy peach or a crisp apple about now.”

“I don’t know. The bat-creature was on the ground before making its getaway, and I haven’t seen any others yet,” said Chris.

Thinking aloud, Jay said, “I wonder if they’re edible.”

“If you can get over the ugliness of a gargoyle face, we could try it. That one pidogg seemed to want to eat it, but when he opened his mouth a bit too wide, the thing escaped.” Chris chuckled as he remembered the scene. “The look on his face when the bat started flapping his wings like mad was … sorry, you had to be there to appreciate it.”

“If we see more, I’d like to try to take one with the .22 rifle,” Jay said.

“Sure, just make sure there aren’t any pidoggs about to pounce on it.” Looking around, Chris asked, “Do you know where Caitlyn and Miranda are?”

“They left about three hours ago to see if that giant grass-eater was still alive. Miranda told me they were going to feed it if it was still there. I think she feels sorry for it.”

“How many pidoggs went with them?”

“I didn’t count them, but maybe fifteen or so. Caitlyn told me they would be back in about five or six hours. They took a couple of spears and a rifle with them.”

Chris said, “Okay. I just hope they don’t run into trouble.”

The radio in the nearby capsule came to life. “Base camp, this is Caitlyn. Over.”

Chris jogged over to the capsule and climbed in. “This is base camp. Over.”

Recognizing Chris’s voice, Caitlyn said, “Chris, we are seeing thousands of flying animals over here. There are different kinds and sizes. Should I gather some if I can? Over.”

"Yes, by all means. I saw one of the pidoggs catch one earlier today, but it got away. Just be careful. Over."

"Wilco. We should be back within a couple of hours. Caitlyn out."

Chris stepped back outside to join Jay. "Well, it appears we're going to get to sample some different cuisine tonight after all, but only if the pidoggs determine it's edible."

"I'll look forward to it," Jay said, continuing his work.

Caitlyn and Miranda returned with six flyers representing four distinct species. They were all bat-like with fur-covered bodies, leathery wings, and ugly faces featuring a mouthful of vicious-looking teeth.

Placing their catch on the bench, Caitlyn said, "Here you go. The rifle was spot-on, accurate. Hideous-looking buggers, aren't they?"

"I'd swear these were Earth bats except they don't have much in the way of ears," Chris remarked.

Four juveniles wandered over to the bench to sniff the bat-like flyers.

"My guess is that they don't have echolocation capabilities," Chris said as he continued to examine the heads.

"If they don't have bat sonar, what do they eat? How do they find their food?" Miranda wondered aloud.

"The teeth say they're carnivores, so to answer your first question, probably insects. You don't have to have echolocation to catch them. Birds back home do it all the time, but in daylight only."

"Then they must be pretty hungry; there aren't any insects here," Caitlyn said as she turned one of the bats over to examine the teeth.

"We will know in a minute or two," Chris said as he removed his knife from the sheath on his belt.

Opening up the abdomen on one of the bats, Chris looked for a stomach. The abdominal contents looked similar to that of Earth animals, with a stomach and intestines, but without a proper dissection and study, he didn't want to conclude the purpose of the rest of the organs. The first bat had nothing in its stomach or intestinal tract. Opening up two more revealed the same results. However, the fourth bat had partially digested contents in the stomach.

Caitlyn, Ron, and Miranda had crowded around to watch the dissection. "What is that?" asked Miranda.

"It resembles chitin, the exoskeleton of an insect. See this? It's the joint of a leg, and this must be half of a set of pincers." Chris was in his element. Strange new biology. He loved it. When he opened the abdomen of the last two bats, he found remnants of insects in their stomachs too.

With concern, Chris asked, "Where were these animals when you harvested them?"

"They were all on top of dead giant grass-eaters," said Miranda.

"Were there any on the ground?

"Yes, by the thousands. They had to land somewhere. Some landed on the animal carcasses, where they were easier to shoot. Why?" asked Caitlyn.

"It means that we may be in for some trouble. I want everyone in the hut in fifteen minutes. We need to talk," Chris ordered.

Sitting on small benches and stools made from pieces of firewood, the group gathered to hear what Chris had to say.

"I fear that we're going to be facing a major assault by insects in the very near future," Chris said.

"Bugs?" asked Ron.

"Yes. I can't tell you what kind, but the arrival of that many bats portends bad things to come."

"How do you know that for sure?" asked Sandy.

Chris answered, "These bats are most likely migratory animals. They aren't restricted to an area by geographical boundaries like lakes, rivers, or even oceans. They go where there is food. If they exhaust a food source in one area, they just move on to the next. We haven't seen any insect life since we arrived here, with the exception of the few that Ron saw on our first day."

"But why now?" asked Sandy.

"This is springtime on this planet," answered Chris. "On Earth, springtime is usually the time of renewal. Animals that have been hibernating awaken, mate, and soon have their young. Insect larvae that have been dormant during the cold winter months awaken and, if ready, make their transition to adulthood. Eggs will hatch when environmental conditions are right. I don't know what we're up against, but with the arrival of this many insect-eaters, I would bet my PhD there *will* be a hatch sometime soon. If we're lucky, the swarms may only last a few days and not weeks."

"What can we do?" asked Caitlyn.

Chris said, "For one, we need to make some kind of netting that can go over our faces. Many flying insects are attracted to our eyes, nose, and mouth because of the moisture or because of the carbon dioxide we exhale. Being warm-blooded and moving can attract them too. We need to have every square centimeter of skin covered. I don't know if the insects will be like mosquitoes or beetles, but I for one don't want to be a test subject."

"Insects can also be a host to a variety of diseases," said Holly, "especially the type that live off our blood, as do mosquitoes, ticks, and fleas. With the type of infection that Ron had on his arm, the medicine I have didn't do him any good at all. We need to be extra careful to not get bitten."

"We don't have anything like mosquito netting, unless someone added it to their survival kit and left it in their capsule," Ron said.

"We may have to make do with a thin shirt or something over our face, something that we can see partially through," said Jay.

Chris nodded. "Whatever we have, we'll need to use. Let's scrounge around the capsules and see what we can come up with."

Everyone headed down the ladders and to the capsules except Sandy, who stayed behind to investigate the inventory on her tablet computer instead.

Walking toward one of the capsules, Ron and Jay disturbed a few flying insects that were poised at the grass tops. The pidoggs that were accompanying the men jumped and snapped at the insects, which then flew chest-high to the men.

"It appears that it's already started," Ron said to Jay.

"Where are they coming from?" Jay asked.

Parting the long blades of grass to expose the dirt, they saw several five-centimeter-long insects that had just worked their way to the surface from under the dirt. A small rodent ran in front of Jay, caught an insect in its mouth, and scurried away before the pidoggs saw it.

"I think we're in trouble. If the bugs are that big now, how large will they get later?" asked Ron.

"You know, now that I think of it, soon after we got here, when I went back to investigate a dead pidogg that turned out to be Judy's mate, it was covered with insect-like creatures that came out of the ground. They had the body devoured in just a few hours," said Jay.

Ron gave Jay a look of dread. "Flesh-eating bugs. Terrific. Wait'll Chris and the rest find out about this."

Chris, Holly, Miranda, and Caitlyn had the same experience as they headed toward the other two capsules. Bugs were crawling from their underground homes, with some readying to take flight.

After checking the capsules, everyone gathered back outside. "I didn't find anything that could be used for netting," said Chris to the group. "How about you guys?"

Everyone shook his or her head.

As they hustled back to their home in the trees, Chris said, "We need to make our shelter as bug-proof as we can, and we don't have much time."

When they climbed the ladders to the huts, the first person up each one had to brush crawling insects from the rungs. These were non-flying insects. A few bats were in the air searching and snatching the few insects that made it airborne, as well as some of the crawlers that were swept off the rungs, before they could hit the ground. When a bat buzzed the grass tops, a juvenile pidogg lying in wait made his leap and almost made the catch. In avoiding the young male, the bat flew directly into the waiting jaws of the juvenile's female companion. Two chomps and a swallow made short work of the bat. Not deterred by his failed attempt, the male pidogg took his position again. Ever alert, the two pidoggs lay in wait for their next victim. The expectant looks on their faces made it obvious they were enjoying the challenge.

Inside the tree shelter, everyone took a corner to look for gaps that bugs might use as an entrance. The wind whipping through the trees during the rainy season had stretched the hide walls somewhat, leaving long, narrow gaps between the individual pieces of hide.

"We have to tighten these up," Ron said, pointing to the leather stitching.

"I hope this works. I'm not looking forward to sharing my bed with any of those creepy crawlers," commented Caitlyn, with a slight shudder.

Chris reminded them, "Soak the stitching with water to make it stretch first. As it dries, it'll make a tighter seam. Don't forget to check the floor-to-wall and wall-to-roof edging too."

Everyone took a wall, tightening the leather stitches until their hands hurt. Whenever someone finished a wall, he or she would then inspect someone else's work to be doubly sure that all the walls were sealed tight. Chris looked outside and noted that some of the pidoggs were digging for insects and making a good meal from them.

"It appears our friends down there are enjoying the new arrivals," Chris said.

"Good. I hope they eat them all! I hate bugs. That's why I'm a botanist, not an entomologist," said Miranda.

"How about spiders? Do you like them?" asked Chris.

“No! They’re the worst kind!” she exclaimed.

“Spiders eat bugs. They’re our friends … unless, of course, they bite you,” Chris teased.

That got a chuckle from the other men. Caitlyn frowned at Chris to show her disapproval of his morbid sense of humor.

Holly added, “On Earth, most insects are edible by people too, but it’s the thought of eating them that’s not too appealing.”

“You got that right!” exclaimed Miranda with an apprehensive look, worried that Holly might add them to their meager menu.

Sandy quietly worked her wall. She was devoid of emotions and not participating in the lighthearted banter. Dr. Rhodes tried engaging her but was given simple one- or two-word replies—mostly “yes,” “no,” or “don’t know.”

Pulling Jay to the side when Sandy went into the supply hut to inspect the seams there, Holly quietly said, “I’m worried about Sandy. She’s not participating in any conversation unless asked a direct question. She doesn’t show her emotions one way or the other. She’s going through the motions of existing, and that’s about it.”

“What can we do about it?” Jay asked.

“Clinical depression is usually treated with medications that let people feel better about themselves. Meds are usually used concurrently with counseling to help. The meds gently lift people out of the hole of depression and let them participate in society without being a danger to themselves or anyone else until the counseling roots out the cause.”

“You mean she could be dangerous?”

“Probably not to anyone else, but to herself, yes, it’s possible.”

“What can I do?”

“Spend time with her.”

“That’s it?”

“There’s not much else any of us can do. Hopefully, she’ll work out of it. If not …” Dr. Rhodes shrugged her shoulders.

“Okay, I’ll do what I can.”

"Thanks. That's all anyone can ask. You're a good man, Jay. She's lucky to have you."

Chris, Jay, Ron, and Caitlyn left the confines of the hut to bring up food from the refrigerators and to see how the insect hatch was progressing. Ten pidoggs accompanied them.

"I'm seeing more crawlers on the ground than flying insects in the air. Maybe this won't be as bad as you thought," Jay said to Chris.

"The calm before the storm," replied Chris.

"Most of the pidoggs are gone," remarked Caitlyn. "I wonder where they went."

Ron said quietly to Chris, "Remember the episode with the fish?"

Chris nodded. "They know more than we do. Most likely they're preparing for the worst."

Stepping into the clearing and approaching the capsules, Chris looked to the north where Caitlyn and Miranda had first spotted the bat-like flyers. The bats were in the air by the thousands now. *Are they in the air feeding or because some predator spooked them? Maybe they just like flying?*

"I want to take a look at the area over there to the north where the bats are gathering. Ron, are you up for a little hike?" asked Chris.

"Sure, let's go," he said.

"May I come along?" asked Caitlyn.

"Sure. Jay?" asked Chris.

"No, I'd better stay and keep an eye on Sandy. Doc thinks my presence will help her."

"I understand." Glancing at Caitlyn and Ron, Chris said, "You know, we're taking a chance of getting bitten. Do you still want to go?"

Ron and Caitlyn nodded in agreement.

"Okay. Let's get our weapons and head out."

Gathering a spear and firearm each from the capsules, Chris, Ron, and Caitlyn headed north. Twelve pidoggs joined the group and surrounded the men and woman in the ever-familiar semicircle of protection.

"The pidoggs are acting nervous," said Caitlyn. "Look at them. Their ears are pricked up as if they're listening for something, and they're constantly glancing around. What does that mean?"

"They're on alert for something. Just keep looking for anything out of the ordinary," Chris answered.

"Everything here is out of the ordinary," Ron stated.

"Only when compared to Earth," Chris responded while continuing his scan.

Many flying insects had climbed to the tops of the grass blades and took flight when the group brushed by. The pidoggs paid them no attention. Chris brushed off a crawler from his right shirt sleeve but picked up the one from his left sleeve for a closer examination. The bug had heavy pincers on its head and a two-section body. The legs had three sections and were thick, hairy, and strong. It was almost black in color. The outer shell was hard, and the edges of the top shell were scalloped like a serrated knife, sharp enough to cut skin if you were to slide hard enough against it.

"Look at this. This is similar to what I saw when I opened the stomach of that bat. The bats must be on the ground feeding on these critters. Let's get a little closer. I want to get some video recordings," Chris said.

"Do you think they pose a danger?" asked Caitlyn.

"Not that I can tell yet," Chris replied. "It appears they have a readily available food source, so we should be okay. Just be careful and don't get cut brushing these bugs off of you. I don't want Doc mad at me for dragging you out here."

The group was at the halfway point, three kilometers from the main collection of bats, when the pidoggs started to whimper. Chris called a halt to their trek. The pidoggs were anxiously looking about in all directions with nervous anticipation.

When Chris bent down to pet one of the pidoggs, the animal barely acknowledged him. The large male was obviously agitated. As he continued to stroke the head of the male pidogg, Chris scanned the area for trouble and said, "Something's not right."

Then everyone could hear it.

19

The buzzing started softly at first. A low dark cloud began rising from the grass all around them, and the noise crescendoed as more of the insects took to the sky. Flying carnivorous insects began diving into the cloud and swooping back into the air, repeating the process again and again. Spreading out over the expanding cloud, the bats continued their feeding frenzy too. Millions upon millions of flying insects were on the move, darkening the sky as they rose higher and higher, spreading out over the land.

Shouting to be heard as the noise level rose, Chris exclaimed, "Let's get out of here! *Run!*"

Guarding their eyes and faces with their arms and hands, everyone turned and ran. The pidoggs, still in their semicircle formation, raced along with them. No one spoke. They couldn't. If they opened their mouth, a bug would fly in it. Swatting them away was almost a waste of energy because the insects were concentrated all around them. The group could see only a few meters in front of them as they ran. The only way they could tell the direction back to the tree house was by following the trail of trampled grass they had created on their way out.

The flying insects were relatively large—between four and six centimeters long. Ron noted that the larger of them were the same type of bug that had landed on his rifle his first day here. One snatched a smaller flying insect half a meter in front of Ron, biting off the smaller insect's head before flying off with its trophy.

Out of breath, the group reached the woodlot where the tree shelter was located. The flying insects were not as numerous inside the tree line, so the visibility was better.

Reaching the shelter, Chris shouted, "Caitlyn, up the ladder, go, go, go!" When she reached the vine ladder, he shouted to Ron, "You're next!"

As Ron climbed his ladder, Chris ran to the other hut's ladder. As he was climbing, he saw the pidoggs digging furiously. By the time Chris finished ascending the ladder, the pidoggs were already half a body into their work. Entering the hut, just before he closed the door, Chris looked to see how the pidoggs were doing. All he could see was dirt being thrown from holes. The pidoggs were in the holes, digging them deeper and blocking the entrances with the excavated dirt.

The noise level was not as loud in the hut. Most of the insects were still in the field, with only half the density venturing into the wooded area, but the surrounding area was still thick with them.

Ron raised his voice over the buzz outside and said, "I don't think these bugs are dangerous. A good share of them are the same kind that I encountered earlier."

Chris turned to Caitlyn. "Did you get bit at all?"

"No, but I bit one of *them* when I opened my mouth to take a breath. It flew about halfway in before I spit it out."

"How did it taste?" Miranda asked, chuckling. She shared Caitlyn's dislike for bugs.

That drew a nasty look from Caitlyn but no verbal response.

"If these bugs are all we have to contend with," said Chris, "it won't be so bad; at least they don't bite. Hopefully, they're like mayflies that hatch, mate, and then die within a day or so."

"What are mayflies?" asked Sandy.

"A mayfly is an insect that lives most of its life as a nymph in clean fresh water—usually a stream, but some live in lakes too," explained Chris. "The adult mayfly will live from minutes to days depending on the species. The male has to find a mate, and then the female has to lay her fertilized eggs before she dies. Swarms of mayflies have been dense enough for Doppler weather radar to follow them. They're a great food source for fish and birds. In the mornings and evenings, automobiles, buildings, poles—virtually all surfaces—are coated with a living carpet of them. The ground and waterways get littered with their dead bodies for as long as the hatch continues, making walkways and roads very slippery."

Smirking, Jay said, "Thank you, professor."

Smiling back, Chris said, "Sorry ... She did ask, you know. There's more if you want."

Without emotion, Sandy said, "No, that's quite enough. Thank you."

"How much food do we have up here?" Chris asked Sandy.

"Enough to last about three days. It's mostly dried fish, but we do have some smoked meat. I also dug up some grass roots to try to make a tea. Being from a green plant, it may be a source of vitamin C. Besides, it's really not bad-tasting if you can stand tea that tastes like grass." Sandy gave a slight smile.

Dr. Rhodes immediately noted the dry humor, the change in Sandy's demeanor. *Maybe she's coming out of her depression. We need to keep her busy and useful.* "Well, there's not much more we can do today with that horde out there. Sandy, how about some of your soon-to-become-famous Tau Ceti g green grass-root tea?" asked the doctor.

After the sun set, the buzzing noise from the flying insects quieted down considerably.

"At least they're not nocturnal," Ron commented.

Two hours after the noise stopped, their ears were still hearing the buzz that was not there. Miranda complained about the annoyance.

"Tinnitus is what it's called. Commonly known as 'ringing

in the ears,'" Dr. Rhodes explained. "We were exposed to a very loud noise level for an extended time. It's hard to say if it will be permanent; that happens only when there is damage to the hairlike projections in the inner ear. We should make some earplugs from the scrap hide. Leather plugs won't be a perfect solution, but they will help lower the decibel level and protect our hearing." She paused for a moment and then chided herself. "I should have thought of that sooner." Dr. Rhodes then retrieved some scrap leather to make earplugs for everyone and asked Sandy to assist.

After the group had turned in for the night, every so often they would hear a *thwack!* on the leather sides of the hut—pilot error on the part of flying insects trying their skills at nighttime navigation.

"Until they've had instruction on how to fly under instrument conditions, they should stay on the ground," grumbled pilot Caitlyn. "How can we get any sleep with them smacking the walls every few minutes?"

"Oh, cry me a river! We could do better if someone didn't wake us up every few minutes complaining," griped Miranda.

Chris, trying to cut short an argument, said, "Ladies, please! Keep it civil. Try counting them instead. If that doesn't bore you to sleep, nothing will."

Everyone was exhausted from lack of sleep and worry about how long the bugs would be massed out there. Just before dawn, the buzzing noise began anew.

Groaning, Ron said, "Another day, another dollar. I could use some change instead."

The intentional pun got a few additional groans.

Continuing in the same vein, Jay said, "If you want change, you could change underwear with Chris."

That even got a groaning chuckle from Dr. Rhodes and Caitlyn—guy humor.

Getting up and handing out the new pieces of leather for earplugs, Holly reminded them, "Don't stuff them in too far, just far enough to dampen the noise level."

The leather was thick enough that when it was cut into a strip two centimeters long, with the width the same as the depth, the earplugs worked better than expected. The noise was loud but bearable and not damaging to hearing.

Peeking out the door, Chris said, "The pidoggs have buried themselves in a hole to get away from the swarming bugs. It looks like they blocked the entrance hole with dirt to keep the bugs out too. They must have dug a hole deep enough to insulate them from the noise. My guess is that they go into a form of hibernation. That would allow them to conserve body fluids and energy, thus greatly lowering their need for food, water, and oxygen for as long as the insect hordes are on the surface."

"Makes sense to me," Jay commented. Walking over to the door and peeking for himself, he said, "I wish we'd built a screened-in porch. It's gonna get hot in here, all buttoned up like this."

"While we're at it, building the porch, that is," Ron said, somewhat sarcastically, "we should consider rocking chairs and homemade beer too."

"I don't know about the beer part, but we should consider expanding our home here," Chris said. "Rocking chairs are a possibility, as is a porch. If all the bugs here are large like the ones out there, we could fashion a screen of sorts by weaving grass, like an open-weave basket, only with a tighter weave."

"Always thinking," said Miranda, shaking her head.

"That's why you guys pay me that big fat bonus at the end of the year," Chris said in jest.

Holly asked, "How bad did it look outside?"

"I'd say at least as bad as if not worse than yesterday," Jay said. He removed his earplugs for a moment. "Yup, worse. The rest of the pidoggs are still hiding somewhere."

Sandy prepared everyone something to eat and served her hot grass-root tea.

"This tea is really good," Jay praised. "What gave you the idea?"

"When Chris mentioned making 'tea' from the stomach contents of the grass-eaters, I remembered that in culinary school we had to learn the history of some foods, and tea was one of them. It was discovered when some Chinese emperor and his army stopped to rest. This emperor liked to have his water boiled before he drank it, but the servant doing the emperor's bidding didn't notice a leaf falling into the hot water and served it with the leaf. The emperor tried it and liked it, so tea became a regular menu item. At least that's one of the stories. Anyway, primitive cultures used roots, leaves, stems, berries, and heaven knows what else in their herbal drinks and remedies. I thought that I'd try it, and it worked, but only the root part tasted okay. We might not be able to digest the plant material itself, but digestion turns all the nutrient parts of food into a liquid-like slurry anyway, so that vitamins, minerals, sugars, and amino acids can be easily absorbed by our intestines."

"You really do know your field well," Holly said complimentarily. "Let's talk later about how herbs and medicines were made and used, okay? I'd like to learn more."

Nodding her head and with a slight upturn of her mouth into a smile, Sandy agreed. "Sure, Doc."

Sleep came hard again that night. The buzzing noise had increased to near daytime levels and continued through the night, and the stiff leather earplugs were making everyone's ear canals sore.

Finally giving up on the attempt to sleep, Chris got up. His movement disturbed Ron, who—also unable to sleep—joined Chris. Trying not to disturb anyone else, the men moved to the supply hut.

Pulling out one earplug at a time and sticking a finger in each ear to massage his ear canals, Ron raised his voice above the buzzing outside. "Join the service and see the universe. Visit exciting and exotic places. Isn't that why you joined?"

Chris smiled. "No. Actually, I was forced to join or go to jail for having an inappropriate relationship with the president's underage daughter."

Ron grinned. "The president doesn't have a daughter."

"Right about now, I'm wishing he had."

Both men laughed.

Overhearing the men as she walked in, Caitlyn asked, "Does he have a young son? I could use some jail time myself. At least it would be quieter than here!" Caitlyn started to laugh.

Exhausted and mentally fuzzy, it took the men a second to get the joke and join with her in laughter.

Caitlyn raised her voice to be heard. "This volume is hard to take. When I was growing up, my family lived a few kilometers outside a small city in a rural area. In summertime, I would sit on our porch listening to the cicadas buzzing in and out of the trees, and I actually looked forward to it. At night, the sound of crickets chirping and frogs croaking used to put me to sleep. I think I've used up a couple of lifetimes' worth of those summers in one day here."

"At least they're out there and not in here," Chris said.

Suddenly, a scream came from the other half of the shelter. Jumping up, the threesome hurried to the room, with Chris leading the way. Miranda was standing against a wall screaming and almost running in place as she frantically brushed at her clothing. Remembering Miranda's fear of bugs and thinking she was having a bad dream, Ron reached over and turned on the emergency light he'd salvaged from the capsule. But Miranda wasn't running; she was stomping.

Bugs were crawling on the floor, on the walls, and over the blankets that she had thrown off in her panic. Holly, Jay, and Sandy were now up and brushing bugs off their blankets too and joining in with the furious stomping. Sandy was screaming, and Jay was shouting. In three areas of the fur that served as the rug floor, there were holes; bugs had chewed through the hide and were crawling through the holes into the hut. Like ants on a foraging run, these insects were in a hurry. Chewing on the edges of the holes, the insects were making short work of the leather, exposing the branches that served as floor slats and looking for more to eat. Meanwhile, new holes were appearing in the floor, walls, and ceiling, with more bugs pouring through. As the holes in the walls enlarged, flying insects entered, buzzing through the empty space.

"Ow!" cried Miranda. Hiking up her pant leg, she pulled a four-centimeter beetle-like insect from her leg. The insect had a section of her skin in its half-centimeter-long thick, black pincers. Jay and Sandy cried out in pain as they too pulled skin off while removing the bugs that had managed to crawl up and inside their pant legs. One of the flying bugs landed on Ron's exposed hand and started to make a meal of him. Ron swatted it flat before it could bite him. The insect had a soft body and smeared a pinkish fluid where he squished it.

"We can't stay here!" Swatting at the bugs in the air, Chris shouted, "Everybody! To the capsules! *Now!*"

Chris held open the door to the outside to help with the evacuation, while hundreds of bugs took advantage of the open door to get acquainted with the inside of the shelter. Urging his friends on, Chris shouted, "Let's go, people! Hustle!"

The noise level outside was as loud as jet engines at full throttle. Predawn was breaking on the horizon, offering enough light to see about fifty meters, and the insects were making the most of it. The view outside was frightfully chaotic. Flying insects of all kinds now filled the air and eagerly entered the hut, looking for a meal or a clear area to mate. Swatting at the bugs around his head and face and brushing insects off the top of the ladder, Chris helped Jay start down so that he could clear the rungs of bugs for those following him. Ron was already doing the same at the ladder from the storage half of the shelter and soon was halfway to the ground, with Holly and Miranda following close behind. Sandy, Caitlyn, and then Chris followed Jay, all windmilling their arms at the swarm as they descended the ladder. The ground was a living carpet of insects.

There was no grass as far as Chris could see; it had been eaten level with the land by the hungry mass.

As everyone immediately ran toward the capsules, Miranda lost her footing and slipped, falling to the alive, insect-slick, moving ground. Both the flying and the crawling insects were on her before she could get to her knees. Screaming in pain as they pinched and pulled the skin and flesh from her body, she rolled over and over, trying to get them off her but collecting more instead. She pulled at the living, biting blanket enveloping her, their clawlike feet clinging stubbornly to her skin, her clothing, and the hair on her head. She rose to a sitting position and continued the frantic brushing and pulling at the beetle-like carnivores, putting long, deep gashes in her hands. Some of the insects stopped to drink from the pools of blood that collected where she sat before climbing her ravished body to partake in a fresher feast. Carnivorous flyers swooped down, picking their choice of delicacies from Miranda, mindless of the pain and agony caused when her flesh, gripped by the insects' pincers, pulled away with them.

Ron had followed Holly toward the closest capsule from the abandoned shelter and was just ahead of the others. Jay, Sandy, and Miranda were headed toward the next-in-line capsule, and Chris and Caitlyn were trailing the others, overseeing the exodus to the capsules. Jay stopped when he saw that Miranda had fallen and started to turn back.

"Get Sandy into the capsule! I'll get Miranda!" Chris yelled at the top of his voice, hoping to be heard and motioning with his hands in case he wasn't. Chris urged Caitlyn to hurry to the safety of the farthest capsule.

Jay turned back toward the next-in-line capsule again, almost sorry for stopping because pausing for that moment had allowed the crawlers to climb his legs up to his knees. Half-running and half-stomping, Ron, Jay, and the other women made it to the safety of the capsules.

Meanwhile, Chris hooked an arm under Miranda's and pulled

her to her feet without stopping. He stumbled and slipped as he tried to stay upright while pulling and brushing the feeding insects from her bleeding body the best he could while on the move. Chris reached the nearest capsule just before Ron shut the hatch behind him and Holly—Miranda needed to be with the doctor. Ron helped lift Miranda inside and then closed the hatch. Doing his best to sweep away the bugs that were landing and climbing on him, Chris ran to the capsule that Caitlyn had entered and banged on the hatch. She opened it quickly, and Chris climbed in, slamming it shut behind him before too many insects entered.

Brushing, swatting, and stomping the insects wherever they landed or crawled, Chris and Caitlyn finally cleared the capsule of live bugs. Their carcasses littered the floor. The capsule had been designed as a survival refuge and living quarters for one person, so inside there wasn't much floor space for two people to maneuver. Still breathing hard from the exertion, Chris lowered the back of the chair to make it a bed and allow them both a place to sit.

"Man! That was close!" Chris exclaimed.

The noise that had been deafening outside was audible but bearable inside the insulated capsule, and they could talk in only slightly raised, if not normal, voices.

"Miranda is in a bad way," Chris said.

"What happened?"

Chris slowly shook his head and bowed it toward the deck of the capsule with his eyes closed, unable to stop replaying the images in his mind. "She slipped on the insects and fell onto that crawling horde. They had her completely covered in seconds. I did what I could to remove them when I got to her, but they had already done so much damage, and they were tearing hunks out of her as I pulled them off. It was horrible!"

"Is she going to be okay?"

"I have no idea. I saw Ron and Doc as they were just getting into their pod, so I ran there with her, thinking that Doc may be able to help her. Ron helped me get her in, but she was still covered with hundreds of bugs. I'm sure Doc will do everything she can, but all she has with her is the first aid kit that's stored in the pod. There was no time to get her med kit."

"I can't imagine this happening every year. How can any animal survive on this planet with this kind of assault by these insects?" asked Caitlyn.

"I saw the pidoggs digging holes. They know how to survive. I guess the giant grass-eaters have that especially thick skin and coarse fur for a reason. I think even those beetle-type bugs would have a hard time getting through their hair, as coarse and stiff as it is."

"Do you think those bugs were able to chew their way through the walls and floor because we had the fur on the inside?" asked Caitlyn.

"I'm not sure. The fur might slow them down, but probably not stop them. My guess is that we weakened the skins by stretching them too much, or maybe by getting them too close to the fire when we dried them."

"If the fur only slows the insects from getting to the skin, how do those grass-eaters survive?" Caitlyn asked. "They can't dig holes like the pidoggs—or hide in the lake without getting stuck in the mud."

"Those flying bats probably help them. You said the ones you shot were on the tops of the grass-eaters, didn't you?" Chris asked.

"Yes, even the live one that was stuck in mud had several on him, now that I think of it."

"They may have some kind of symbiotic relationship. I didn't see many bats flying around here at all. Mostly the carnivorous flying insects."

"What do we do now?"

"We wait," said Chris, but he'd barely gotten out the words before changing his mind. "No. No, let's give Ron a call on the radio to see how Miranda is doing."

Chris lifted the radio microphone from its holder and called. "Ron, this is Chris. Over."

"Go ahead, Chris."

"How's Miranda?"

"Not good. Not good at all. She's unconscious, most likely from the pain and shock. Doc is doing her best to clean her up and keep her alive, but she is missing a lot of skin, with big chunks of muscle missing too. She's lost a lot of blood, and the bleeding hasn't stopped yet. It took us a while to just clear the bugs from her body and kill them. They were making fast food out of her. If you hadn't gotten to her when you did, I'm sure she would have died within another minute or so."

"Roger. Thanks. Keep us informed of her condition. Chris out."

Mulling over in his mind what had transpired in the last two days, Chris returned to the radio. "Jay, this is Chris. Over."

"This is Jay. Over."

"How's Sandy holding up? Were you listening in to Ron and me?"

"We heard. She's taking all of this kind of hard but otherwise doing okay."

"Good. We're going to be stuck … let me rephrase that … safely tucked away in these capsules until the insect threat has diminished."

"Roger. Sandy just asked what we're going to do about living quarters since those bugs destroyed the huts. Any thoughts?"

Chris addressed her directly. "Sandy, we don't have to start over completely. The framework is still there. We'll just fill in the frame with wood this time instead of animal hides. We have the entire warm season to rebuild. This bug situation won't last forever. It will pass. Be patient, and we will get through this. I promise. Over."

"Thanks, Chris. Jay out."

"You're welcome. Chris out."

"It's going to be cozy in here with two of us," said Chris. "It won't be as comfortable come nighttime, though. You can have the chair. Once we sweep up these bugs, I'll curl up on the floor around the base." With an "oh well" expression on his face, Chris continued, "I'm kind of used to it."

With their immediate situation under control, Caitlyn smiled. Her voice and demeanor softened. "Thanks, Chris. You're a good man and, I might add, an excellent leader. You show all the qualities and capabilities that leadership requires. Now you know why I put you in charge here. I couldn't have done this. As bad as it is now, it would have been much worse had I been running the show. You figured out what had to be done, organized us, kept us together, and accomplished everything that we needed to survive."

"Except for Miranda. She might not make it," Chris said, slightly turning away and looking down at the deck.

Caitlyn grabbed his arm and turned him to face her. With a hand on each of his arms now, she said, "Oh, stop it! You're not God. You can't be responsible for accidents. Miranda fell. If it had been ice, and she'd cracked her head open, that wouldn't be your fault either. You are doing everything the way it's supposed to be done, so quit beating yourself up over it."

"I suppose you're right," he said, looking back up at her.

Looking him straight in the eyes, she said, "You're darn right I am."

Still thinking of Miranda, Chris turned and nodded his head in the direction of the doctor and Ron's pod. "With three in their pod, I wonder how Doc and Ron are going to manage."

Caitlyn smiled, let go of Chris, and sat on the bed. She said, "Oh, I wouldn't worry about them," and then told him about what she'd encountered in the supply hut upon retrieving a canteen. That brought a small smile to Chris's face.

The next morning, Chris called Ron on the radio. "How's Miranda?"

"The bleeding has stopped, but she's only semiconscious and in serious pain. Holly needs to get the pain meds in her kit to help her. She's already used up all the supplies in the first aid kit and needs more bandages and antiseptic ointments too. There wasn't enough in the first aid kit to cover all the wounds."

"Roger. Understood. Stay put. Chris out." Chris turned to Caitlyn. "I have to get that med kit for Holly."

With a frightened, concerned look and a raised voice, Caitlyn said, "You can't go out there! You'll end up like Miranda!"

Chris blurted, his voice raised in frustration, "I can't just sit here knowing that Miranda is suffering and might die!"

"As a military leader, sometimes you have to make difficult decisions," Caitlyn countered, "and in the making of those decisions, sometimes people die. Making that kind of determination is difficult, and it's something that you have to learn to live with."

Standing at the hatch with his hands on the dogs, Chris remained silent for a moment. Turning and looking over his shoulder, he said, "I'm a scientist, not a military leader. Maybe I don't want to live with the results of that kind of decision, especially if there is a chance that I can help."

"Chris, please don't go out there. We need you … I need you." Caitlyn stepped over, put her hand on his shoulder, and turned him around to face her. Looking at Chris with pleading eyes, Caitlyn said softly, "Please … don't do this."

She drew closer to him, wrapped her arms around him, and placed her head on his chest, closing her eyes as tears started to form.

Chris put his hands on her shoulders and held her for a moment. Speaking softly, Chris said, "This is something that I have to do. This is the kind of person I am. If it's humanly possible, I do what I set out to do. I promised you that I would look after this group until we were rescued or the last person died. I intend to keep that promise. Miranda is not dead yet, and if I can help keep her alive, I intend to do that. I *will* be back. I promise."

Caitlyn pulled away but didn't let go of him. She reached up and kissed him gently on the cheek. Holding his gaze, she replied, "You better, mister. I'm counting on you."

With that, Chris opened the hatch and stepped outside, closing it quickly behind him.

The swarm was not as bad as it had been the day before, and

he could see small, occasional gaps of brownish-black dirt between the ground crawlers. Dead and dying insects littered the ground, with live ones feeding on both live and dead ones, and others were in their mating embrace. Swatting at the insects that were attacking him, Chris saw movement to his left. It was Jay, running with a first aid kit.

Not stopping, he shouted to Chris on his way by, "I'm giving this to Doc to help out Miranda. Sandy and I are patched up good enough for now." Jay swatted at several flying insects that were trying to get at his face and exposed skin as he ran.

Chris shouted after him, "I'm heading back to the hut to retrieve Doc's med kit. Tell her that I'll be there as quickly as I can."

Jay acknowledged him with a wave and continued on his errand of mercy while Chris ran into the woodlot toward the hut, jumping from one clear patch of ground to the next or quickly high-stepping on the insects to keep the crawlers from climbing on him and to keep himself from slipping on them.

Reaching the tree that held the shelter, Chris brushed both flying and crawling insects from the ladder rungs and climbed to the top. What he found at the top wasn't the inside of the hut anymore. All that was left was the framework and leftover hair from fur lying on the floor slats. Chris quickly found and retrieved the med kit.

Briefly pausing to look through the wooden framework, Chris noticed the green on the trees. *Strange—the vines we used to tie the wood together and the leaves on the trees are untouched.*

With the med kit in one hand, Chris reached out with his free hand and broke off one of the leaves from a tree. He set the kit on the floor slats and removed his knife from its sheath. He sliced open the thick waxy leaf and rubbed the thin sap on the back of his hand. The sap didn't burn or make his skin itch or tingle. He rolled up his sleeve and smeared more of the sap on his arm. He extended his bare arm as an invitation for a bug lunch, but none of the insects that approached ever landed. Chris cut a dozen whole leaves and stuck them inside his shirt for transport. After smearing more sap from the cut leaf on his face, neck, and other exposed areas of skin, he grabbed the med kit and headed down the ladder. Upon reaching the bottom, he smeared some of the sap on the top of his boots and the cuffs of his pants. Purposely, Chris shuffled his way into a pile of crawlers that were feeding on some of their dead comrades, heaping them on top of his boots. They couldn't get off his boots fast enough. He picked up one of the dead beetle-like bugs, smeared the plant sap on its body, and set it back on the ground. None of the other beetles touched it. He then picked up a live one and dropped it on his exposed arm. The bug quickly crawled to the edge of his arm and leaped toward the ground. A flying insect-eater caught it midair and flew off. Choosing a live beetle, he smeared it with sap and tossed it into the air. Three flying insect-eaters approached it but then backed off at the last instant.

Finished experimenting with his newfound bug repellant, Chris ran to deliver the med kit and leaves. When he banged on the hatch, Ron opened it just enough to collect the kit and the leaves.

"What are the leaves for?"

"Bug repellant. It works like a miracle. I'm hoping it doesn't cause a skin rash—I have it all over me. Don't use it until I let you know how I fare later."

Now he took his time walking over to Jay and Sandy's capsule. There he explained his discovery to them and handed over a few of the leaves, cautioning them not to use the leaves until he found out whether the sap was toxic to his skin.

Finally, Chris banged on the hatch of his own refuge. Caitlyn opened it a crack and then stepped back from the opening, letting in only a few flying insects with Chris. Chris entered all smiles and quickly closed the hatch behind him. Caitlyn rushed to hug him, but before she could, Chris stepped back, holding up the remaining leaves in his left hand as a barrier between them.

"Keep that thought, though. I found a bug repellent that I used on my face and exposed areas. If you hug me, and we both get a rash, everyone will start wondering ..."

With a karate-like sweeping block, Caitlyn brought her right hand up and moved the hand holding the leaves out of her way and hugged him tightly anyway. "I don't care what people think."

Dropping the leaves, Chris returned the full-body hug, holding her close and gently but firmly in his arms.

The next morning, Chris notified the others via radio that he'd developed no side effects from the leaves and that they were most likely safe to use.

The plague of insects was almost over. When Chris surveyed the area, he found that the waxy green leaves on the trees in their woodlot and the vines covering the trees were the only green vegetation left anywhere that he could see.

Chris walked over to Holly's capsule to see how Miranda was faring and banged on the hatch.

Holly opened it a crack.

"How is she, Doc?"

Looking around to see if it was safe before stepping outside, Holly said, "I have her pain under control, and she's actually doing much better."

Greatly relieved, Chris said, "I'm so glad to hear that."

"Against my better judgment," she said quietly, "Ron insisted on trying some of the bug repellant on himself last night so he could get more fresh water from the lake—we used all the water we had cleaning up Miranda's wounds and depleted our supply. Anyway, it's really tight with the three of us in the capsule, and as he was squeezing the sap from the leaves to rub on his skin, some of it dripped on Miranda's face and arm. Since we didn't have any water to wash it off or any clean cloth to dab it up, I had to let it dry. I figured it couldn't make her much worse. Chris, it's not only a bug repellant; it has better healing ability than my meds! The leaves are like a super aloe plant!"

"That's great! I bet that's how primitive humankind discovered the healing effects of herbs," he said.

"If weeds and seeds can do the job, I'm all for it," said Holly. "Come on in and see the person whose life you saved."

Upon entering the capsule, Chris saw Miranda sitting up and drinking some hot broth that Ron had made for her from the meat stored in the modified refrigerator. She was wearing enough bandages to qualify as an Egyptian museum exhibit.

When Miranda saw Chris, what he could see of her face brightened. Her eyes, brown and blue both, had some sparkle as she smiled through the bandages.

"How are you feeling?" Chris asked her.

"Much better. Most of the pain is under control, and that sap is working really well. It helps take the pain away too. Doc said the scarring should be minimal. I can't thank you enough, Chris. You risked your life to save mine." With tears brimming, she said, "Risking sounding corny, you are a true hero; you are *my* hero, and I can't thank you enough."

By the next evening, all the bugs were either gone or dead, their carcasses piled everywhere. The following morning, Chris stepped out of the capsule to stretch his frame. Sleeping on the floor of the capsule he had been sharing with Caitlyn was still uncomfortable. Jay and Sandy walked over to say good morning as he stretched. Even Sandy had a smile on her face this morning, and an amused Chris silently speculated as to why.

"Why don't we get that bench back at the tree shelter and carry it to Doc and Ron's capsule? We can make a fire and have breakfast together," Chris suggested.

"Sure. Sandy, honey, why don't you keep Caitlyn company for a little while? We'll be right back."

Caitlyn, who had come to the hatch just in time to hear Jay, looked at the three of them in turn and smiled. "Come on in, Sandy. Let's talk," she said.

An hour after eating breakfast, everyone was enjoying the beautiful day and good company. Even Miranda had improved enough to join the conversation.

"How are you feeling, Miranda?" asked Sandy.

"Well, thanks to Chris, I survived a very close call." Miranda looked down at her bandages, smiled, and added, "Other than being dressed up for a horror film, I'm feeling much better. Thank you for asking."

Chuckles came from around the table, even from Miranda.

Chris turned to Caitlyn and said, "Speaking of close calls, are you ever going to tell me how you escaped being some critter's lunch?"

Caitlyn laughed. "Sure …" She told everyone the story up to the point when Miranda closed the hatch. "I was certain I was about to die. Miranda was closing the hatch. I could see her sobbing, but I knew I was too far away to make it with the monster just a few meters behind me. I didn't blame her for shutting the hatch. The animal could have knocked me down, gone for her, and come back later for me. I could feel the beast's breath on my neck. Miranda had closed the hatch, and I knew I was a dead woman, so I was just praying that the pain wouldn't last too long. Then—"

"Hey, look, here come the pidoggs!" Jay said excitedly, cutting Caitlyn off.

Judy came right up to Jay, nuzzled his leg, and gave his hand a good lick.

Scratching her head and shoulder area, Jay said, "How are you, girl? Did I ever miss you! Did you miss me?"

Sandy joined in on the other side, giving Judy a good scratching behind the ears, but not before giving Jay a playful jealous pinch on his arm as she passed him.

The female pidogg that Chris had saved and her family stopped by to give their greetings too before heading off on a hunt back in the wooded area. By Chris's count, more than forty pidoggs came by.

Some then left for hunting, and the rest assumed their sentry posts as if nothing had happened.

"I hope that the others moved on to better feeding grounds and didn't become insect food themselves," Chris said.

"Me too," said Jay.

Caitlyn smiled and said, "You know, these guys are really handy to have around."

Glad to see the pidoggs but also somewhat annoyed that Caitlyn's story had been interrupted, Chris said, "You're right, but … how did you escape being eaten?"

Caitlyn smiled but stayed silent for a moment, apparently enjoying keeping everyone in suspense. Finally, she said, "It was the pidoggs. Remember when I said that the two pidoggs had made their kill and that the bearlike creatures were going to steal it before they saw us? The rest of the pack was apparently nearby and saw the one chasing me. They attacked it just before it was set to catch me. I'm not exaggerating when I say I could feel that animal's breath on my neck. It was that close. There must have been ten pidoggs that tackled that beast like a pro football offensive line hitting a quarterback. I heard and felt the rush through the grass, and then came the growling, barking, snarling, snapping of teeth, the angry roar of the giant …" Caitlyn paused for a moment as the emotion felt during the near-death experience caught up with her again. She looked down and wiped at her eyes.

Everyone remained quiet and waited. They were captivated by her story, especially Chris, who'd had his own personal experience with the same giants.

Composing herself, Caitlyn continued. "It was … surreal. The pidoggs attacked their natural enemy and left me alone. The bear was so close to me that one of the pidoggs brushed me as it made its attack and knocked me off-balance. Trying to regain my footing, I couldn't stop myself from running until I ran into the side of the capsule. It was then that I turned around to see the pidoggs chasing after the creature, with one still on top of its back, hanging onto the creature's neck with its teeth. I stood there for what must have been ten minutes, catching my breath and trying to make sense of what had just happened." Now more composed, she chuckled a little and said, "Now that I think of it, that must have been one heck of a ride for that pidogg. It was being tossed about like a cowboy doing a bad ride on a Brahma bull!" Caitlyn paused and was only partially able to hold back a silly laugh when she chanced a glance at Miranda. "You should've seen the look on Miranda's face when she finally opened the hatch to my insistent knocking! She thought she was seeing a ghost!"

Seeing that Miranda and Caitlyn were enjoying the story too, everyone laughed. When the laughter finally died down, Chris took Caitlyn's hand in his and said, "The pidoggs *are* an amazing animal, and I'm very grateful that you were saved."

Caitlyn, still smiling, looked deeply into Chris's eyes. "Yes, they certainly are."

The mood in the camp was good. They knew they were beating the odds. They knew they could survive here on this almost inhospitable planet, just as surely as they knew that help was not going to come.

Chris took a sip from a container of hot, smoky broth. He got a far-off look in his eyes and said, "You know, I've studied a lot of animals on different planets, including those on Earth, but learning about them is not the same as having to live like them and, in our case, live with them. What I mean is … you can only learn so much about them when after a day in the field you get to go back to your comfortable climate-controlled room, shower whenever you feel like it, eat a nice hot meal several times a day, and have time for recreation and fun. When you actually live and have to survive in the same environment as they do, you don't just learn about them; you begin to understand and *really* know them. You get a much deeper appreciation for how difficult life truly is, especially for the individual being. 'Eat or be eaten' is not just a phrase; it's truly life-or-death out here."

As Chris set his cup down, Dr. Rhodes said, "You're right. It's hard to conceptualize the hardships that creatures in the wild have to face on an everyday basis when we have all the conveniences of modern society. Our technology has brought many, many benefits to us as humans, making our lives safe and comfortable. However, as much as we already know about technology, biology, and life in general and how to affect the outcome of disease and infirmity, we still have a lot to learn. I've learned so much already while on this planet. Sometimes hardship brings knowledge, sometimes death. We've been extremely fortunate here."

A bright light, low on the eastern horizon, caught Chris and Ron's attention. Noticing their long gaze to the sky, everyone turned to look at what had captured the two men's interest.

"That's got to be one very large meteor," Chris said.

The object, trailing a long line of fire, streaked across the sky, a black, smoky path following in its wake.

As the object passed overhead, perhaps three kilometers from the ground, Ron shouted, "That's the *Copernicus*!" The dead ship was making a last appearance before crashing on the surface.

Everyone watched the sky spectacle in awe.

"There was no sonic boom," Ron said.

"What does that mean?" asked Sandy.

"It means that friction in the atmosphere has slowed the ship—or what's left of it—below the speed of sound and that it will be crashing soon," Ron replied.

"It's going to impact somewhere over the water," said Chris.

"I've heard of large meteors hitting the ocean and causing great tsunami-type waves on shore," said Miranda with serious concern in her voice.

Ron shook his head and clarified for her. "That's unlikely in this case. The *Copernicus* is not traveling fast enough, nor does it have enough mass to do that. From what I could see, she's still pretty much intact as far as size, but without the speed, the energy released when the ship hits the water won't be nearly enough to make that kind of wave. We'll be lucky to see a ripple on the shoreline."

"That's good to know. We've had enough trouble with floods," said Jay, to the nods of everyone else.

The radios in all the capsules suddenly crackled to life. "United Earth Space Force ship *Copernicus* survivors, this is United Earth Space Force ship *Josephine Brookfield*. Over."

20

Jay moved as if he'd been practicing for this moment all his life and was the first to get to a radio. "*Brookfield*, this is *Copernicus* survivors! Over!" he excitedly answered.

Stunned and shocked and in disbelief, the group rushed to gather around the hatch to hear the radio conversation. When the realization that they were going to be rescued began to sink in, tears of relief streamed down Sandy and Miranda's cheeks as all the pent-up emotional tension released, melting away like darkness leaving a room when a door slowly opens to the bright light of a sunny day. As Holly leaned in to hear better, she put her arm around Ron's waist, and they smiled at each other.

"*Copernicus* survivors, this is *Brookfield*. How many survivors are there? And state your current situation. Over."

"They're all business, aren't they?" Chris said to Caitlyn as he hugged her from behind.

Jay responded, "*Brookfield*, this is *Copernicus* survivors. There are seven of us with one needing immediate medical attention. Over."

"Roger. Seven survivors with one needing medical attention. Who's in charge? Over."

"That would be you, Caitlyn," Chris said. "I formally relinquish my command, sir!" He smiled and gave her a casual salute.

Caitlyn looked deeply into Chris's eyes and hesitated for a moment before she turned and stepped into the capsule. She took the offered microphone from Jay. "*Brookfield*, this is Commander Caitlyn Clayton Carver, executive officer of the *Copernicus*. It's good to hear another friendly voice. How did you know to rescue us? The radio signals shouldn't have reached Earth for at least twelve more years. Over."

A different voice answered, "Commander Carver, this is Captain Joseph Penningway, commanding officer of the *Brookfield*. It's a long story, one that we can discuss later on board over a good hot meal, but the short answer is that we have improved FTL technology that allows us much greater jump distance than ever before, shortening the time it takes to travel. It took us only one month to reach you from Earth. We have pinpointed your location and will have a shuttle there within an hour or so. Welcome home!"

Everyone had tears of joy in their eyes. Holly and Ron were hugging. Jay and Sandy hugged and kissed and then began to jump up and down in their excitement, still holding hands. Caitlyn stepped out of the capsule and hugged Chris, burying her head in his chest to keep him from seeing her tears. They held their embrace for a long moment. Not forgetting Miranda, who still had bandages covering a good share of her body, everyone gathered around and placed their hands on her shoulders or somewhere it was safe to touch without causing her pain to include her in the joyful occasion.

Wiping away her tears, Caitlyn composed herself, once again the executive officer. Stepping up to the highest step of the capsule, she said, "It's been four months, and our time here is almost over. It's certainly been a grueling challenge here, one that I'm not eager to repeat. Before all this happened, we were shipmates, working in close quarters and in harmony with the ship's routine. In spite of the difficulties here, we came together and used the same teamwork that a ship-borne crew requires, met the challenges to the best of our abilities, and formed a cohesive and workable team to beat the odds … and we survived! I can tell you that I, for one, am greatly relieved that the trials on this planet are almost over."

She stepped down, stood on the bottom step, and reached for

Chris's hand, which he freely offered. Holding hands with Chris, she took a moment to look into the eyes of each crew member, taking in their smiles and tears, deeply feeling their emotions, experiencing them herself. She smiled and paused for a moment longer when she took in Chris's smiling gaze. Giving his hand a double squeeze, she continued. "I can't thank you all enough for your contributions that made this supreme test of survival a successful one. I can, and will, say that from the bottom of my heart, I am proud to call each of you my friend." She wiped away a rogue tear with her free hand before going on. "I am almost embarrassed but especially sad to have to tell you that when we board the shuttle, regular military protocols will be back in force and observed, but when in private, I'm still Caitlyn to you … thank you." She stepped to the ground and slowly walked away hand in hand with Chris toward their shared capsule.

"We're going home! I can't believe it! The first thing I want to do is take a long, hot shower!" exclaimed a very excited Sandy.

"And shave and change into clean clothes," added Jay.

Holly said, "What I'm going to do, after I take the longest, hottest shower the captain will allow, is sleep until my eyelids fail to stay shut."

As Chris and Caitlyn walked slowly to their shared capsule, the excited chatter of their friends faded into the background. Still holding Chris's hand, Caitlyn said, "You know that when we get back, I won't be able to be with you, don't you?"

Chris looked at their clasped hands, sighed a deep sigh, and said, "Unfortunately, yes … I understand. You're my commanding officer, and military regs say that you can't have a personal relationship with your subordinates."

Caitlyn stopped and turned to face him as they reached the capsule. "I may never have the chance to tell you this again. I want you to know that I care deeply about you and that if fate, and you, will have it that we can be together after this, I'll welcome it."

Chris smiled and squeezed her hand tightly. Caitlyn turned and led him into the capsule.

Chris said, "I'm due for a promotion to commander soon. If I'm not in your chain of command—"

She turned around, put her fingers to his lips, and shut the hatch.

Two hours later, everyone was gathered near a clear area where the shuttle from the *Brookfield* would touch down.

"In some ways I'm going to miss this place," Jay said. "I'm glad they're late."

"It's the pidoggs, isn't it?" asked Chris.

"Yeah, that's a good part of it. I love the way Judy looks up at me when I give her a good head and ear scratching and licks her mouth, but there's more to it than that. We were … we *are* a good team. We gave it our all. It was hard …" Jay paused. "No, it was more than hard. It was like Caitlyn said—'grueling'—but it brought out the best in each of us."

Chris responded, "With Judy, that's most likely a reflex. The head scratching stimulates the same pleasure centers in the brain as eating a tasty snack."

Jay closed his eyes, shook his head, and chuckled. Still smiling, he said, "Thank you, professor."

Chris smiled, having done that on purpose. "It's part of human nature," he said. "In truly troubled times, good people get together to make the best of a bad situation. We did that and more. We built friendships with each other here that will last our entire lives and, as a bonus, intelligent alien friends also. I hope that someday we can come back and study them more closely. We can learn so much from them about this place. I hope that Judy and her friends are still alive to remember us and welcome us back into their clan." Looking over Jay's shoulder, Chris said, "Speaking of Judy, here she comes now … and with presents!"

Judy and two of her juvenile brood dropped three large rodents at Jay's feet.

With an ear-to-ear grin, Chris asked, "You want that fried or fricasseed?"

Both men laughed.

21

"*Copernicus* survivors, this is *Brookfield* Shuttle Rescue One. Over."

Jay answered the radio call. "*Brookfield* Shuttle Rescue One, this is *Copernicus* survivors. Over."

"We're approaching your location, ETA ten minutes. Over."

"ETA ten minutes. Roger. We are standing by. *Copernicus* survivors out."

Chris's thoughts reflected a melancholy mood. *Ten minutes. Ten minutes of waiting can seem like an eternity.* As he remembered some of the harrowing events that had occurred during their time on this planet, that train of thought continued. *Birth, life, death—for some ten minutes is an entire lifetime; for others ten minutes can determine their fate for the rest of their lives … ten minutes.*

A deep sigh escaped him as he looked at his surroundings, the memory of the moment searing permanently into his mind.

All the pidoggs that remained after the insect invasion were assembled, not knowing exactly what was to take place, but apparently sensing that something big was about to happen.

"How do you know, girl?" Jay asked while giving Judy a good head and back scratching. Judy licked her chops but gave Jay a look that could only be interpreted as sad.

"They just do," Chris said, giving the female he had saved and her mate a good going-over. "I never gave you a name, did I, girl?

Maybe I should name you after one of my grandmothers. How do you like the name Gladys? Bridget? No? Well, they probably wouldn't approve of it either." He sat there for several minutes petting his newly acquired, lifelong friend while giving her a sad smile.

Although Miranda's hands were in bandages, she still managed a gentle petting of the pidogg that had befriended her with the tips of her fingers. Sandy, Holly, Ron, and Caitlyn all had their good pidogg friends there too and paid special attention to their offspring.

"I think they're empathic or telepathic or something," Jay said. "They just know how you feel or what's going to happen and then do the right thing for you."

"I suppose it's possible, but I can tell you that they are at least excellent readers of body language," Chris replied.

"Always the scientist," Jay said, smiling and shaking his head while smoothing Judy's fur.

A few minutes after the shuttle landed, technicians from the *Brookfield* swarmed the capsules to gather as much information from the pod's computers as was available. All the gear that was still usable was loaded aboard the shuttle. Samples of the meat and fish were taken, as were the waxy leaves from the trees and pidogg saliva for medical testing and reproduction. The ship's photographers took photos and videos of the area, including the trapped grass-eater and the pit that was to be a trap, for the ship's historian. The historian wanted to document how a determined crew could beat the odds when seemingly everything was stacked against them and then write a survival manual for future UESF reference. Commander Carver talked some of the shuttle crew members into digging around the trapped giant grass-eater enough that it could eventually escape on its own, and others rendered safe the pit the survivors had dug by filling it with dirt.

The good-byes brought mixed emotions. The pidoggs' expressions were sad and knowing as the humans boarded the shuttle. The shuttle crew was gracious, kind, and thrilled to have been part of this great adventure, albeit a small part. The survivors, relieved to be aboard and on their way home, busied themselves with small talk among themselves and the shuttle crew as they strapped in for launch, trying not to think of the friends they were leaving behind. Chris and Jay, the last to board, turned around to wave good-bye to the group assembled around the shuttle. As the large hatch was slowing closing, they saw Judy lift her paw high into the air as if to say farewell. Then as she lowered her paw to the ground, she bowed, followed by the rest of the farewell entourage.

Fighting back his tears but failing, Chris thought as loudly and forcefully as he could, *Judy, if you can read my mind, I will be back. I promise.*

With that, the hatch shut.

Captain Penningway, a rather short, somewhat paunchy, dark-haired man, impeccably dressed in his formal uniform, the four bands of gold gleaming on his sleeves, greeted the survivors as they exited the shuttle bay.

"Welcome to the *Brookfield*!" he said, greeting each of the survivors with a hearty handshake, except of course, Miranda, who was sitting in a wheelchair. "Corpsman! Get this crewman to sickbay, on the double!" Turning to the rest of the group as the first-class corpsman wheeled Miranda down the passageway, the captain said, "I'm delighted that I could be of assistance in your rescue. The ship's supply officer, Lieutenant Junior Grade Ryan Grimm, will get everyone new uniforms, and the logistics officer, Lieutenant Eric McAllister, will get you berthing in officers' country. I'm sure that what you want right now is a hot shower, clean uniforms, some chow, and rest, and you can have them in any order you prefer. Chow is set for the wardroom in one hour. I'd like to hear your story, Commander."

"Yes, sir! In one hour."

"See you then," he replied. The captain turned and walked away down the corridor.

As they followed the logistics officer to their new quarters, Chris wanted to say something to Caitlyn, but she was back in her military mindset, observing strict military protocol. *Oh, well. It's probably better this way,* he thought.

Lieutenant McAllister showed them their respective quarters, which happened to be across the passageway from each other. Both Lieutenant Commander Elliott and Commander Carver thanked the young officer for his assistance. As he departed, they opened their respective doors. They stepped in, turned around, and looked into each other's eyes, a lingering look of understanding and caring. A gentle but sad smile arose from both of them as they faced each other across the passageway. The doors slowly closed.

Showered, shaved, and smelling good for the first time in months, the survivors gathered at the captain's table in the wardroom, occupying seats normally used by the junior officers. Dr. Rhodes cautioned them to go easy on the carbohydrates and rich food because their systems might revolt rather suddenly to their reintroduction.

The captain entered the wardroom.

"Attention on deck!" the chief steward announced.

All at the table stood, snapping to rigid attention until the captain was seated.

"Seats," ordered the captain.

While dinner was being served, Captain Penningway asked, "Commander, please tell me how it came about that the *Copernicus* was destroyed and how you managed to escape and survive."

"Briefly, sir …"

Four hours later, she finished.

"A complete narrative report will be available for your pleasure by tomorrow evening, sir. We have detailed notes of the flora and fauna, weather data, and more that will also be added to the ship's record of this planet by this time tomorrow, sir."

"That's quite the adventure. I'm sure there will be awards given to each of you for your bravery and perseverance in the face of such adversity."

"Yes, sir. Thank you, sir … Captain, may I ask a question?"

"Why, of course."

"How did you know to rescue us? The emergency radio beacon signals should have taken at least twelve years to arrive at Earth. Even given the fact that a 'missing ship' alert would have been sent out when we didn't arrive at our scheduled time, UESF Command wasn't expecting us for another twenty months. We were to have been here studying this planet for at least another two months before *Copernicus* was to depart. You arrived here roughly four months after we arrived and made our escape to the planet's surface. The distress signals were active for only four months."

The captain smiled. "You are correct. You were on a five-year mission and totally out of rapid communication range for the entire period. Until our scientists can figure out a way to communicate over the distances at which we are now required to operate, you and anyone else outside our solar system are effectively on your own." The captain shifted in his seat and slowly sipped at his coffee. "I think the chief steward outdid himself with this coffee and meal. What do you think?" There were nods and murmurs of approval. "The *Brookfield* was in the final stages of construction when you left. She was launched and commissioned two years after your departure. We had the usual underway trials that took another year. What you couldn't have known is that several months later, scientists working for the UESF finished greatly refining their calculations for the FTL engines, allowing for much longer jumps between waypoints. Our computers were upgraded with much faster quantum processors and the new software installed. We are no longer restricted to a speed of C times nine. The new equivalent limit is 144 times C."

That garnered a few low whistles and murmurs from the survivors.

"Yes, sir, that's fantastic," said Caitlyn, "but that still doesn't explain how you received our distress signal that *is* restricted to C."

Smiling, he said, "The simple answer is … we didn't, exactly. We didn't know about your distress signal until we arrived here."

That brought puzzled looks from all the survivors.

After a bit of dramatic pause and with a politician's flare, the captain continued. "We were sent here to upgrade the computers on *Copernicus* with the new faster processors and improved calculations so you wouldn't have to take a year and a half to arrive back at Earth. We received your distress signals as we returned to normal space in this solar system. We knew that you were supposed to be in this area, but we didn't know this planet existed until we heard the distress signals broadcasting from your escape pods. A quick calculation and another jump, and we arrived in time to see and track the *Copernicus* to her final resting place. She's lying in shallow water about two hundred kilometers west of where we rescued you. Most of her structure is still above water, so I'm sure there will be a salvage operation in the near future, whether by us, the Galileo, or the new ship that is being built as we speak."

"A new ship? Does it have a name yet?" asked Caitlyn with increased interest.

"Not as yet, but soon. It should be ready for underway trials in about six to eight months. With the new faster-than-light speeds now obtainable, the UESF has plans to use the new ship for further exploration of our galaxy. Does seeking out new life forms and making first contact with intelligent beings sound like an exciting mission to you? They're also still looking for a captain for her. If you're interested, I'll put in a good word for you. You are vastly more experienced than anyone else that's up for the new billet."

"Yes, sir! I certainly am interested! Thank you, sir!" Caitlyn replied with her award-winning smile.

Captain Penningway continued, "The new ship will have capabilities that even the *Brookfield* doesn't have. She'll have a larger crew, and since the time away from home will be about the same, at five years, the shipbuilders made her large enough to accommodate many of the crew's families. That's a departure from normal regulations; however, we're entering into a new paradigm with space travel. Five-year missions are a long time to be away from home and family. The only way the UESF can keep talented people interested in serving in the space fleet for these long missions is to allow immediate families aboard."

That brought looks of surprise from all at the table.

Clearly pleased with the response from the survivors, the captain smiled and said, "We'll be home in a month. All of you will get your accumulated leave of thirty days per year, plus an additional sixty days of survivor's leave. That should put you back on active duty status just in time to become acquainted with the new ship, before the shakedown cruise, should you be fortunate enough to receive a billet aboard her. The UESF is going to need experienced hands on board, so all of you stand a very good chance of getting the new assignment. In the meantime, you are all our honored guests. Please feel free to wander about the ship as you choose. You will have no duties aboard the *Brookfield*, so get comfortable. I run a relaxed military ship; it's much better for morale and *especially* for our guests."

Captain Penningway looked at the survivors at his table and rose to leave the wardroom. All those in the room rose with the captain and stood at attention.

"As you were," he said to the room generally before turning back to the survivors. "You are all off duty until we arrive back at Earth Station II. *Enjoy* your time off," he said, giving a subtle wink. With that, the captain left the room.

"What do you think the captain meant by the wink?" asked Sandy as they all headed back to their cabins.

"What wink?" asked Caitlyn, smiling.

As they continued down the passageway to their cabins, Dr. Rhodes said she had to do a more thorough physical exam on Ron to make sure he was going to be fit for duty when called back, and when they arrived at his cabin, she entered with him. Jay said he had to explain some communication theory to Sandy, who was very curious about RF energy and how it worked, and entered her cabin. That left Caitlyn and Chris walking in the passageway to their cabins.

"You really want that captain's job badly, don't you?" asked Chris.

"Yes, I do."

"What does that mean for us?"

"Mmm … I think it will work out just fine," she said with a coy smile. "We'll cross that bridge when we get to it. Right now, we have a whole month to *not* think about it."

Standing in the passageway outside their cabins, hands at their sides, they gazed into one another's eyes for several long moments. Caitlyn was the first to speak.

"You know, military rules strictly prohibit any *public* displays of affection."

"Yes, Commander, I am fully aware of the implications of PDA aboard a military vessel."

As she invited Chris into her *private* cabin, she commented, "It's going to be a long month back to Earth."

Smiling as he entered her room, Chris said, "I certainly hope so."

CPSIA information can be obtained at www.ICGtesting.com
Printed in the USA
BVOW08s2154081215

429800BV00001B/9/P